# SEARCHING FOR SOFIA

## BOOK THREE IN THE PORTRAITS IN BLUE SERIES

## PENNY FIELDS-SCHNEIDER

**PFS**

# COPYRIGHT

First published 2021

Copyright © Penny Fields-Schneider

Publishers Note: *Searching for Sofia* is a work of fiction. It includes a number of fictitious scenes which include people who lived in the time period covered by the writing. All attempts have been made to recreate conversations that are based on true events in the public record or in keeping with the publicly perceived nature of the character. Every effort has been made to treat the memory of all real people with respect.

Cover design by Stuart Bache

ASIN B085XTBM99.

ISBN 978064848 0532

200000521

**Have you read books One and Two?**

Searching for Sofia is the third book in the Portraits in Blue Series. Whilst not essential, you may like to consider reading books one and two in the series before continuing.

**Book One: The Sun Rose in Paris (E-book, Paperback and Audio)**

**Book Two: Searching for Sofia (E-book and Paperback; Audio 2021)**

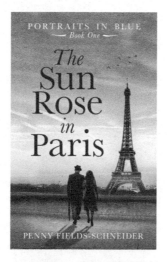

# SEARCHING FOR SOFIA

# PART I

*MELBOURNE*

# CHAPTER 1

'*A*re you awake, love? I have a cup of tea here for you.'

Jack stirred. He lifted the blanket to see his mother's face peering down at him, a frown crossing her brow. He looked at the clock on the dresser—eleven.

His head thumped with the same dull ache that he had been living with for days, and he winced at the light streaming into the room. His parents' house? Pulling himself up, he watched his mother settle the saucer on his bedside table before sitting next to him and reaching for his hand.

The sadness in her eyes was fathomless, and unable to bear it, Jack closed his own. He sank back into the pillows, hoping sleep might shield him against the visions relentlessly assaulting him.

The roaring fire; Scotty gone. A steady pounding filled his chest and a lump formed within it, growing and solidifying into an enormous stone so large that it was hard to breathe. Gasping for air, Jack tried to control his sobbing breaths. They were part of his life now. Every morning, on waking and remembering. At unexpected moments through the day, when the magnitude of their loss caused him to double over, as though someone had hit him in the solar plexus. Haunting him in the cruel night hours when darkness obliterated distractions. Then, he would succumb to the depths of his pain. Strangled wrenching sobs that released a torrent of tears, until his aching head lay against a soggy pillow.

His baby with the raggedy mop of black hair and laughing, mischievous eyes–gone. And in her pain, Sofia too had withdrawn from him, and now she was missing.

In barely a month, Jack's life had been totally shattered. His little family destroyed. The two people he loved most now lost to him. He berated himself for letting his grief engulf him so severely that he'd allowed Sofia to slip away.

The preceding week at Montsalvat was a blur, Jack's memories veiled in guilt, the pain fuelled by Sofia's heartbreak and, even worse, by the accusations that lurked in the dark eyes which refused to meet his.

Images of the fateful day were like a cinema newsreel that constantly replayed in his mind; Matcham racing up the stairs yelling "Fire!"; he and Justus rushing outside to help douse the flames; the realisation it was his and Sofia's own cabin alight, yet relief that most of their possessions were safely packed, ready to be loaded on Mervyn's truck and transported to their new home.

If only he'd been in the cabin with Scotty rather than spending that last hour with Justus, appeasing the Master, reassuring him that there were no hard feelings, that he and Sofia would to return to Montsalvat for visits, often.

Jack's breath caught as he recalled how he and Justus had looked over the balcony where Sofia had been leaning against her bicycle calling up to him. She'd been about to pedal into town to buy cleaning products–determined to leave their cabin spotless. Nobody would ever accuse her of being a dirty Spanish peasant, she'd told him that morning, and Jack had known that she was still piqued by her memory of the cruel comment Justus had made years earlier.

Sofia had waved to them, and they'd waved back, but her words, 'I've just put Scotty to bed. He's asleep,' had been lost to the breeze. The message that, had he heard it, may have averted the tragedy.

But Jack hadn't heard it. It had never occurred to him that Sofia was uttering more than a simple farewell–letting him know she was leaving for town. He'd assumed Scotty was with Sonia, having a final walk around the grounds of Montsalvat, looking at the bird's nest by the dam and chasing lizards in the undergrowth. A walk he would have loved, no doubt picking a bunch of wildflowers for Sofia, and on receiving them, she would have clasped them to her face, inhaled their perfume, and thanked him for being the sweetest, most wonderful boy in the world. Scotty would have beamed his broad, toothy grin in pleasure.

Again, sobs rose in Jack's throat, and with a groan he pushed the unbearable images aside. However, more thoughts of Sofia filled the space, offering no release from the torment.

Sofia riding towards them as they'd attempted to douse the fire, calling out even as she pedalled furiously. Her tormented words becoming clearer as she'd approached and finally abandoned the bike to stumble the last few yards towards the cabin, where the fire was almost under control. 'Scotty's in the bedroom!'

Jack would never forget her crazed expression as she'd glanced at the boxes of clothing and pots and kitchen items set on the gravel alongside her tea chest from Spain, her eyes searching the gathered crowd for her baby. And never would Jack forget that moment when he had realised the enormity of the tragedy that had befallen them.

# CHAPTER 2

'Okay, Jack. Up you get. We have work to do.'

Margaret's voice broke through the fog of Jack's half sleep. He rolled over and saw the tray his mother had left by his bed hours earlier, and his eyes landed on the clock: two thirty PM. Was it the same day? Jack did not know, nor did he care.

'Jack! Up! At least sit out of bed so we can talk.'

He felt the bedspread being pulled back and rolled over, looking at her. Like his mother's, Margaret's eyes were shadowed with grief, but her expression was resolute; she wasn't going to let sorrow get in the way of action.

'Come on. Here is a chair. You don't have to get dressed. Just sit up so we can talk… make a plan.'

Resigned to her demands, Jack climbed out of bed. He felt so tired, he could barely hold his head up. Illness combined with the emotional toll of the past few weeks had taxed his body. He'd barely eaten since Scotty's death and Sofia's rejection, and living in the cold, derelict caravan those first few days, he'd succumbed to the clutches of a nasty chest infection. At that time, not caring if he lived or died, Jack had neither the energy nor will to fight it.

He knew that it had been Margaret's determination to get him away from Montsalvat that had saved him. However, while his fever and

8

hacking cough had settled, the total exhaustion seemed impossible to shake.

Always pragmatic, today Margaret forged beyond her usual words of sympathy.

'We need to find Sofia, Jack. I thought she'd be home by now... I've asked around, to no avail. And I am pretty sure that she hasn't returned to Eltham. Do you know where she could be?'

Jack shook his head. He had no idea. When he and Sofia had first arrived in Australia, they had lived here in his parent's home, and Sofia had spent her days with his mother while he'd gone to work. And then, when they'd met Justus and the Meldrumites, together they had joined the artists and lived at Montsalvat; the retreat had been their whole world for the past five years. Jack couldn't imagine anyone outside of that world to whom Sofia might have turned.

'Maybe Sonia knows something,' he suggested.

'Sonia? The Skipper girl?'

Margaret had never been overly involved with the Montsalvat artists. Indeed, when she returned to Australia shortly before the birth of Scott, she'd been horrified to find Jack and Sofia living out at Eltham.

'Justus is just using you, Jack,' she'd complained. 'He is holding you back. You are barely painting, anymore! Montsalvat may be an artist's retreat, but from what I can see, Justus is simply indoctrinating you all with his philosophical mumbo jumbo and using your labour to bring his fantasy to life. For God's sake! What sort of artist opposes exhibitions?'

At that time, Margaret's criticisms had fallen on deaf ears, for Jack and Sofia had loved their life at Montsalvat. They'd immersed themselves in its building projects and were filled with excitement as finally the baby they'd both longed for was coming. The retreat's lifestyle, full of healthy physical activity and rich with the company of patrons and students devoted to art, held a magic for them that not even Margaret could deflate.

'Yes, Sonia Skipper and Sofia were always close. Really close–like sisters. And Helen might know something, too. She and Sofia worked

9

in the garden most days. Perhaps she'll remember something that Sofia said.'

'Okay. I'm going to take a few days off work. See if we can find her. How about we head out to Montsalvat tomorrow? We need some leads. You make sure you are up early. I'll pick you up at nine.'

~

The next morning, whilst washing and dressing, Jack pondered Sofia's whereabouts. Like Margaret, he'd thought that she would have returned to Montsalvat, or arrived on his parent's doorstep when she was ready. However, Sofia had done neither. Where could she be?

Had she, like himself, fallen ill? Certainly, Jack understood the savage toll grief took on one's health. Not only physically, but on one's mind and spirit. The wild desperation. The refusal to accept reality. The heart-wrenching pain caused by memories of a little boy's voice calling out for his mummy and daddy.

How he wished that he had kept Sofia close to him in the days following Scotty's funeral, rather than accepting her decision to stay with the Skipper girls. At the time he'd given her the space she seemed to need, expecting it would only be for a few days. He'd never doubted that eventually they would move beyond the heartbreak of losing Scotty together.

What Jack had not anticipated was that he would be overcome with illness. That he'd lose perspective and track of time and be oblivious to Sofia's absence.

As they walked to Margaret's car—a 'New Beauty', the model similar to his own father's T Ford, if not somewhat worse for wear—Jack felt Margaret's eyes upon him. He knew that with his recent weight loss, his usual lean figure now looked haggard in the baggy trousers and checkered shirt he'd put on that morning.

Climbing into the front seat, he gave her the barest shadow of a smile. 'Okay, detective, let's go. I also thought… perhaps Sofia might have gone to the house… you know, the one that we were about to move into.'

The thought had just come to him, and he wondered why he hadn't considered it before.

'Maybe she has, Jack. Good thinking. We'll check there first.'

Arriving at Eltham, they found the cottage, but even as they parked out the front, it looked bereft of life, and Jack's sharp knock was greeted with a hollow echo. Nobody was here. Next, they travelled to Country Realty, who'd handled their rental application. The agent, Mr Johnson, greeted Jack soberly.

'I'm sorry, Jack. Really, really sorry. The missus cried for a week. A terrible thing for you and your wife–dreadful!'

Jack nodded, struggling for a response, and Margaret intervened.

'We are looking for Sofia,' she said. 'Jack's wife. We haven't seen… she has gone away for a few days. You know. Just wanted some time alone. We want to make sure she is okay.'

'You don't know where she is?' Mr Johnson asked, clearly surprised.

'No, not really,' Jack replied, feeling irresponsible. Negligent, even. What sort of man loses his wife? A voice within him echoed, *What sort of a man loses his child?*

'I am sorry, mate. I haven't seen or heard from her. Perhaps the missus has. I'll ask, but I don't think so. She would have mentioned it if she had, I'm sure. I am glad you called in because… well, I didn't know if you'd still be wanting the house. You don't have to decide now. Take your time. Next week will be fine.'

While Mr Johnson's news was disappointing, it wasn't surprising. The notion of Sofia living at the cottage had been a long shot. There was nothing for it but to drive to Montsalvat. As they motored by the familiar eucalyptus trees that he'd passed a hundred times before, Jack gazed at them as if they might hide the key to the mystery of Sofia's whereabouts. Turning into Mount Pleasant Road toward Montsalvat, his chest tightened and his heartbeat raced as a sense of dread washed over him. How could it be that this place, constructed with so much joy and optimism, was now so steeped in tragedy?

The first person they encountered was Matcham, who was stacking up a pile of logs near the carpark. Preparing for a fire, Jack supposed, and his hands trembled uncontrollably.

Seeing them, Matcham walked over, and wordlessly he reached out and embraced Jack. It wasn't entirely clear who was comforting whom. They patted each others' backs before separating, tears in their eyes.

'How are you going, mate?' Matcham asked. 'Sorry. It was a silly question, I know. I just don't really know what to say.'

'It's okay Match. There is nothing to say. But thanks.'

Steering away from the usual path to avoid the cabins, where a faint smell of charred wood lingered in the breeze, they walked towards the Great Hall. Justus and Lil were sitting outdoors, Max next to them. Jack's heart wrenched at the lonely sight Max's little figure presented, as he hummed to himself while he pushed his small wooden tractor along the gravel.

'Jack,' Lil cried, attempting to stand. However, today was one where her legs were refusing to move. Significantly, it had been this condition of Lil's—when one night, unable to walk, she'd collapsed to the floor of the dining room and crawled to the table—that had been the impetus for his and Sofia's decision to leave Montsalvat. On that occasion Sofia had risen to assist, as Lil clambered to her seat, but Justus had ordered her to sit down, insisting that they should not submit to the demand for attention that was clearly springing from Lil's subconscious. That night, Sofia had sobbed in Jack's arms, insisting that they leave Montsalvat and find their own place to live; she refused to bring up Scotty in such a heartless environment.

'Jack! Good to see you. How are you doing, son?' Justus shook hands with him and greeted Margaret wearily. Over a decade earlier, she, Justus and Lil had been fellow students at Max Meldrum's art school. However, where Justus had been the prize pupil, Margaret had found their teacher insufferably patronizing to his female students, and Justus, a bore. Her scorn for the Meldrumite's methods had never been shielded well.

Today, Justus looked a little stooped. The Master was a stubborn man, a man who hated anything that he could not control. For him, problems were addressed, ignored or disdained. Rarely did they play on his emotions. Furthermore, everyone knew that Justus hated illness and death—he usually avoided funerals—but he did attend Scotty's. As the master of Montsalvat, Jack knew Justus would have felt the tragedy on the grounds of Montsalvat was deeply personal.

Jack stepped forwards to hug Lil and was surprised at how fragile she felt in his arms. 'Good to see you, Jack. I'm glad you've come back.'

'It's good to see you, Lil. Are you well?'

'Yes, I'm fine. Just the usual nonsense. But you… you look awful, which I know is to be expected, after all that's happened. Are you sleeping? I can prescribe you something if you like.'

'I'm okay, Lil. It's not easy, but I'd rather just work through it.'

'Sure, Jack. But remember, sorrow can do terrible things to a person's mind and body. You and Sofia might like to meet with me… talk through your grief. You might even find it helpful to come back here …'

Lil's transformation, seamlessly slipping into her professional mode, felt strange. Her training as a doctor, anaesthetist and counsellor may well have funded much of Montsalvat's building program over the years, but this was the first time that Jack had ever been a recipient of her professional skills.

'We are actually looking for Sofia,' Margaret interjected, her words barely disguising her impatience with the Jorgensens and their attempts to draw Jack back into their world.

A frown creased Lil's forehead. 'Sofia? She's not with you–not at your parents' home?'

'No, Lil. We don't know where she is. We thought perhaps Helen and Sonia might know something.'

'Certainly. No doubt you will find them up at the cottage. They don't travel far these days.'

'Let us know if we can do anything, Jack. And don't forget, Montsalvat's your home, at any time you wish. Living here could even help the grieving process.' Justus nodded his agreement with Lil, and despite Margaret's impatient grimace, the Jorgensens' kindness drew tears to Jack's eyes.

'Thanks, Justus, Lil. I appreciate that. We'll head up to the cottage now and see if the girls know anything.'

A few minutes later, arriving at the cottage on the hill, Jack and Margaret were greeted by the Skipper sisters, whose rounded faces matched their bellies, the swelling revealing that they were both in the final weeks of pregnancy.

'Don't ask,' Jack muttered, anticipating the question on Margaret's mind. *How could these two young women, sisters—unmarried sisters—dressed in billowing smocks and looking every bit like enormous beach balls, simultaneously be pregnant?*

'Jack, how are you?' they each cried, hugging him in turn, tears threatening all around.

Ignoring the question, he said, 'You might remember Margaret—Helen and Sonia Skipper.'

'My, oh my!' exclaimed Margaret. 'Have we got time to talk or should we be rushing you both off to the maternity ward before you each pop like corks?'

The girls laughed. 'No, we still have a few weeks to go, but thank goodness it will all be over soon,' Sonia replied.

'And the fathers? I hope they are not some local scoundrels who've left you high and dry. Too much of that goes on, and it's always believed to be the girls' faults.' Margaret looked sympathetic.

'No, no. Arthur Munday is the father of my baby, he lives here—the pathetic creature that he is. He didn't know what he wanted to do about the pregnancy, so I saved him from overtaxing his brain and told him exactly what I planned to do. Keep the baby and get rid of him! I think he's still in shock.' Sonia had lost none of the feisty bravado that she'd shown at the dinner table seven months earlier, when Justus all but expelled her from Montsalvat when she'd declared to one and all that yes, she was pregnant, and no, she had no intention of marrying the older, dour, indecisive father.

'Good for you,' said Margaret. 'You shouldn't be forced to do anything against your wishes. I don't expect it will be easy, though. You know what people can be like!' She turned to Helen, a question in her eyes.

The other Skipper sister's voice was quiet as she said, 'My baby is Justus'.'

'But isn't Justus married to Lil...? The same Lil who's living down in that cottage we've just left, with Justus' son, Max?' exclaimed Margaret, who was never scared of stating the facts.

'Oh yes, he certainly is.' Sonia's twinkling eyes communicated the amusement with which she viewed the plight Justus had created for himself. 'That's what makes it all so entertaining. One minute, he's about to throw me out as a disgraced harlot. The next minute, on discovering that he's gotten Helen pregnant, he's gone and declared that our community will be a model of social progression! A place where a wife loves her husband so much, and is so understanding of his needs, that she permits him to have his floozy *and* her baby live with him! And, of course, once Helen was pregnant with his child, he could hardly kick me out, could he?'

'Enough, Sonia!' Jack wondered whether Helen's ire was directed at Sonia for highlighting Justus' absurd inconsistencies, or in fact because she lacked enthusiasm for Justus' notion that Montsalvat was the setting of an advanced social structure. Turning from them, she muttered that she would put the kettle on and retreated indoors.

Despite having grown up with cousins who were members of the Bloomsbury set, whose very lives epitomized an extraordinary frankness towards matters of a sexual nature, Margaret made it no secret that she found Helen's position untenable.

'Trust Justus Jorgensen,' she said with barely disguised scorn. 'That is exactly what I would expect from him. He was always one to justify his own appalling behaviour. I suppose he started by painting nudes of Helen, and then lured her into his bed.' Sonia nodded. 'And now, somehow, he's managed to assuage Lil by complimenting her for being so understanding of his needs. Give me strength!'

Sonia laughed. 'That's the way it happened! Never mind. We cobble along okay. Operate in our own little bubble. It's not as bad as you might think.'

'I better slip in and see if Helen needs a hand, the poor thing!' Margaret replied.

Minutes later, Margaret and Helen reappeared with a tray of mugs and a plate of Anzac biscuits, and Jack rose to fetch the heavy teapot. After their cuppas were poured, he decided it was time to address the real purpose of their visit.

'I was wondering if you know where Sofia might be.' As he spoke, it occurred to him that perhaps Sonia and Helen were actually participants in Sofia's disappearance—supporting her decision to be alone. He hoped they'd be honest enough to tell him what they knew.

'She's missing?' Sonia asked. 'No, Jack, surely not!' The worry in her voice was sincere, assuring him that she knew nothing of Sofia's whereabouts. 'We thought she was with you. That she had gone down to your parents' place, the poor thing.'

'It's so awful, Jack, we feel terrible for you both,' Helen added. 'Dear little Scotty. A few hours pass and I forget about the accident, and then it all comes back at the most unexpected of moments and I almost collapse with sorrow. I can't begin to imagine what it must be like for you and Sofia.' Jack jolted. Ignoring the pain that Helen's words had unintentionally caused, he quizzed the girls.

'Did Sofia ever mention anyone she might have met… say, in town here, or perhaps in the city—you know, after her trips into Melbourne?'

'No, I can't say she did,' said Sonia. 'Sure, she knew some of the villagers, the shopkeepers and so on. I don't recall anyone that she was particularly close to, though. She occasionally used to speak of the mothers… you know, those that had babies around the same time that Scotty was born, but she hadn't mentioned anyone in particular, lately.'

'What about any of Justus' students, perhaps one of the women?' Jack was appalled to find himself asking others about his own wife's friendships. Shouldn't he know these things? Didn't Sofia used to tell him everything that was important to her each afternoon on his return from work?

It was clear that neither Sonia or Helen had any information that would help them to find Sofia, and quickly finishing their tea, Jack and Margaret bid them farewell.

～

16

Jack tried to fight off the desolation rising within him as they left Montsalvat. That morning, on waking, he had been sure that today he'd find Sofia. His heart ached from wanting to see her, to know that she was alright, and, in his helplessness, a heaving sob rose from within.

Margaret pulled over and reached for his hand.

'Jack, we are going to find Sofia. Don't you worry. She's got to be somewhere. Let's just think about this.' Grasping his hand, she squeezed it tightly, and his sobs slowly settled.

'I'm sorry,' he said, 'I'm sorry!' Margaret shook her head.

'No! Don't apologize. I can't begin to imagine how you must be feeling. I've been thinking, Jack, do you think that Sofia has turned to the Spanish community for comfort?

Jack nodded. He should have thought of it himself. There had been an elderly Spanish couple who had a restaurant! Sofia was so excited when she'd met them. She'd insisted that he come with her to meet them also. He remembered how he'd watched them speaking together, the way they'd unconsciously launched into Spanish, their words flowing so fast that he could barely follow as they'd reminisced about the country and the friends they'd each left behind. Eventually they had recalled his presence and apologised for excluding him. The couple had loved Scotty, patting his head and tickling his chin, and then the lady had vanished for a few minutes, returning with a biscuit for him. Later, when the Tomlinsons had farewelled these new friends of Sofia's, Jack had thought of their neighbours in Malaga, their warmth and support for Sofia, and he'd considered the sacrifice she'd made crossing the world with him to live in Australia. He'd asked Sofia if she missed Spain.

'It's okay, Jack,' she'd replied. 'I won't say that I don't miss the finca and the gallery, Aunt Jovita, Stephan and my friends. But that's in the past. I am happy here. I have you and Scotty. I love our life amongst the gum trees. Montsalvat is a wonderful place to raise a child. Here, we have family. Scotty has grandparents. We have the community. They are our family now.'

'There was a place, Margaret,' he said. 'A Spanish restaurant over near Russell Street. Sofia loved visiting the couple who ran it. Perhaps they might know something?'

An hour later, walking up and down the streets and laneways around Russell Street, Jack stalled for the third time, peering through the window of a Chinese restaurant. Could this be the same building that had housed the Spanish restaurant Sofia had brought him to, over a year earlier?

Cautiously, they entered, and were greeted by a Chinese gentleman who smiled broadly and waved them towards his tables. They shook their heads at his offer, and a lengthy discussion ensued. His English was only marginally better than their Chinese, however Jack and Margaret established that he'd opened his restaurant the previous September, and that the restaurant had once been leased by a Spanish man and his wife. That was the extent of the facts that he could share, and given their difficulty communicating, Margaret was not convinced.

'Bloody hell, Jack. How do they expect to fit in if they can't even speak English?' she exclaimed in frustration.

Jack looked at her, aghast, at once reminded of Sofia's experiences when she'd first arrived to Australia and had experienced rudeness just because of her dark complexion and Spanish accent. Realising her error, Margaret tried to make amends. 'No, no, I wasn't thinking of Sofia. She was easy to understand,' she backtracked, before changing the subject. 'Let's visit a few of the surrounding shops. Perhaps someone might shed some light on the whereabouts of this Spanish couple.'

After fruitless visits to first a jewellery shop and then a shoe store, they entered a butchery, and the man at the counter confirmed that the Chinese restaurant had once been owned by a Spanish couple, but he knew nothing more. Finally, they entered a paper shop, its shelves overflowing with newspapers, magazines and stationery. A man, so small that he barely reached Margaret's shoulder, appeared from behind the counter.

'Yes, I knew Mr and Mrs Santos. They were lovely! They'd come up every morning to buy *The Sun*, wanting news about the war in Spain. They had family there, and naturally they were terribly worried for them. Such kind people. Mrs Santos used to give me a jar of biscuits from time to time. I think she felt sorry for me, not having my own missus to bake for me and all.'

'Do you know what happened to them?' Jack asked.

'Not really. When Mr Santos died, the restaurant had to be closed. There was no way that Mrs Santos could have managed it alone, but I know that leaving wasn't easy for her.'

'Yes, but where did Mrs Santos go after she closed the restaurant?' Margaret broke in.

'I couldn't say, but I do know that they often used to catch the train down south… Geelong, I think it was, on Sundays. They had some family there or friends, at least. Someone they used to visit, that's for certain. Of course, Mrs Santos might have gone back to Spain. I have often wondered how she is. If you see her, please send her my best wishes. Tell her that I miss her biscuits. I have never tasted anything so wonderful!'

Thanking him, they left.

'Looks like we're off to Geelong,' Margaret said as they returned through the city streets. 'How about tomorrow? How about I pick you up at eight thirty?'

'Thank you, Margaret. I do appreciate your help with this.'

'Of course, Jack! I'm worried about Sofia too, you know.'

Jack did know. Margaret had been with him and Sofia through their best and worst times, from the heights of Jack and Andrés' exhibitions in Paris, to the night that Andrés had collapsed and been taken to hospital. And she had been with Jack and Sofia in Spain for the last weeks of Andrés' life. Margaret was more than a friend to them both— she was the sister that neither he nor Sofia had ever had.

# CHAPTER 3

*A*t eight-thirty the following morning, Margaret arrived at Copelen Street. Walking from his bedroom to the hallway, Jack could hear his mother speaking with her, her voice quavering with emotion.

'Thank you for all of this, Margaret. You are a wonder. William and I, we simply wouldn't know where to start looking… Do you really think that Sofia might be in Geelong? It seems such a long way from here. I did think that we might have heard from her by now. Time is passing though, isn't it? I hope that she is okay, poor thing. I can barely sleep for worrying about her. Oh, here is Jack now. How are you, love?'

Jack mustered a smile by way of reply and kissed his mother reassuringly. It was dreadful for her and his dad to have lost not only Scotty, but now Sofia, whom he knew they'd loved like their own daughter.

Travelling across the city, Jack studied Margaret's *Collin's Road Guide* and realized that Geelong was a lot farther away than he'd thought, way out southwest of Melbourne, near the entrance of Port Phillip Bay.

He considered her vehicle dubiously. Purchased only a few months earlier, it had managed the short drives they'd taken yesterday without any problems. However, the New Beauty—her 'little beauty' as Margaret called it—was ten years old. He hoped it was up to the long trip ahead of them and that they wouldn't find themselves stranded on the roadside halfway to Geelong.

Shaking aside his concerns, Jack determined that whatever the day brought, he would cling to the optimism that he'd woken with.

As the morning sun had filtered through his curtains, he'd pictured the moment when he would finally lay eyes on Sofia. How she would sink into the warmth of his arms and he'd hold her tight to him, as if never to let her go. The perfume of her freshly washed hair, the sweet, intoxicating aroma that had become part of Jack since he'd known her, had filled him even as he'd lain alone in his bed, and it was as though she were right beside him.

'It will be okay,' he'd imagined whispering to her, kissing her eyes, her forehead, her lips, and her reply had come as clear as if she'd been right there beside him.

'Yes, Jack, it must surely get better. It is good to be home. I have missed you so much.'

The image of their reunion seemed so real it was like it had actually happened.

And when he arose, he'd felt sure that today they would find her. However, for that to happen, he needed to be sharp—his mind alert to all possibilities, not weighed down by disappointment and grief.

'Perhaps the post office will know who's who in the village,' he suggested, and Margaret responded to his upbeat tone with a smile.

'Good idea,' she said. 'Surely they know everybody in Geelong. And anyone Spanish, or who receives mail from Spain must surely stand out.'

Jack's mind now streamed with possibilities. 'We could also try the dairy—if Mrs Santos is in Geelong, she is bound to have a milk delivery.'

His confidence that Sofia would have connected with people in the Spanish community increased with every mile. It made sense that when times were tough, people gravitated to their roots. He was positive that they were on the right track.

At ten thirty, arriving in Geelong, Jack was amazed to see brightly lit shops, modern buildings, and even the presence of trams in the main street. The pealing of bells startled him, and looking upwards, he saw two bronze figures—first a man and then a boy—emerging from a bell tower high above them. Suddenly pangs of doubt enveloped him; he'd expected Geelong to be a small rural village, much like Eltham, not this bustling city.

The post office was a formidable bluestone building—its gleaming counter manned by a large lady who proved both willing and able to share a wealth of encouraging information about the Spanish families who had settled in Geelong.

'Oh, yes, we have lots of Spaniards here… quite the little Madrid we are. I don't know what has brought them all to our town, but really, I am glad that they are here, for the Spanish surely are the loveliest of people.'

'We are looking for a Mrs Sofia Tomlinson; she may have arrived quite recently.' Margaret cut to the chase.

'No, I haven't heard of that name…' The woman's forehead crumpled into lines of concentration.

'What about a Mrs Santos?'

'Oh, no… I don't think so… Here, look at this. I shouldn't be giving out personal information, but this page here might be helpful.'

With a wink, Mavis Jones, according to the engraved badge riding up and down her broad bosom, slid an open page of the *Sands and McDougall Directory* across the desk and tapped alongside a surname —Valverde. 'And if you were to drive out along the Great Ocean Road for fifteen minutes or so, you will see a farm, Velverde's Market Gardens. You might like to buy some nice fresh tomatoes! I hear that they employ quite a few Spanish workers. The Valverdes are one of the leading Spanish families in Geelong. If the lady you are looking for is here, they'll know!'

~

Wasting no time, they returned to the car and Jack felt jittery with nervous tension, sure they were mere minutes away from finding Sofia.

'It's just the sort of place Sofia would go. You know, working in a market garden. She loves growing things almost as much as she loves art.'

Margaret agreed, and as she drove, they chatted excitedly, easily imagining that Sofia would be out in the fields, working the rows of tomatoes, her mind seeking healing and peace amid the plants.

An icy wind buffeted the vehicle as they approached a tiny village called Anglesea, and seeing a sign labeled The Great Ocean Road, they turned right. The road was newly formed, barely a ribbon of gravel, and a second sign warned drivers to proceed with caution, that the next eighty miles was subjected to roadwork and they could expect long stretches allowing one-way traffic only. Gazing to his left, Jack studied the deep blue of the sea, seething with white caps stirred up by the wind. It was the Bass Strait, he knew, renowned for its treacherous coastline, where over the centuries numerous ships had been flung against its rocky cliff faces.

'Watch out!' Jack exclaimed as Margaret maintained a continuous commentary on the geographic marvel of the road they were traveling upon—how it had only recently been built, and that, should they continue driving, they would encounter blow holes, sea caves and even a dozen sea stacks standing together, collectively titled 'the Twelve Apostles'. 'Stop talking and concentrate! We'll be over the edge before you know it and you'll be able to greet the Twelve Apostles personally!'

'None of your cheek, or I'll be pushing you into the blow-hole!'

As they meandered west, a large, colourful sign appeared.

'Velverde's Market Gardens,' Jack read, impressed by the image of smiling bright red tomatoes, wearing top hats and checked suits and carrying walking sticks. Created by a sign-writer with a sense of humour, he thought.

Driving towards the house, he looked at the broad, neatly tended fields on each side of the roadway, where dozens of labourers—mostly woman—moved among the furrows, with large baskets strapped onto their waists. 'Sprouts,' announced Margaret confidently as she parked the car against the fence.

'Sprouts!' repeated Jack. 'Brussel sprouts? How on earth do you know that they are picking sprouts?'

'I wouldn't have a bloody clue, Jack. What do I know about growing vegetables? Mine come from the greengrocer in a nice brown paper bag. I'm just imagining that they are sprouts. Let's go.'

Together they ascended the stairs leading onto the home's shady verandah, its entry protected by a wide roof. After rapping on the door, they were greeted by a lady whose handsome, sun-weathered face was framed by a mass of black curls.

'*Hola*! Ana Valverde. Can I help you?' Her greeting was warm, and her marked Spanish accent instantly transported Jack back to the time when he'd lived in Malaga.

Introducing himself and Margaret, he explained their mission, describing how his wife had suffered a recent shock, and in her distress had... vanished. Once again, the spoken word sounded so bizarre that Jack could scarcely believe he was saying it. He continued, 'The lady in the post office, well, she suggested that there were Spanish people living out here, along the Great Ocean Road, who may be able to help us, so we came for a drive.'

Ana listened carefully. While Jack did not provide details, her matronly disposition and warm, caring eyes reflected a woman who understood the nature of a shock that could make a wife disappear and likewise, the worry that this would arouse in a loving husband.

'And you think that your missing wife, your Sofia, she would come here? To Geelong?' Her frown was thoughtful.

'Yes, it's possible. Sofia is Spanish.' Jack explained how he and Sofia had been married in Malaga and lived there with Sofia's brother, Andrés, for three years. How it had been Andrés dying wish that Jack should take Sofia away from Spain—away from the troubles that were brewing—and bring her to Australia.

'That is a sad story, but it was good advice. He was a wise man,' Ana said. 'It is terrible what Franco is doing to Spain.'

'Two years ago, Sofia met an elderly couple in Melbourne, a Spanish couple. They had a restaurant there. Sofia used to take our little boy to see them. I even met them myself, once. The restaurant is closed now, but the man who owns the news agency nearby seems to have known them well. He told us how Mr Santos had passed away, and that he thought Mrs Santos may have come to Geelong. He believed they had friends or family here.'

'It seemed possible that Sofia would be drawn to her Spanish roots after all that she has been through,' Margaret added.

Ana's eyes lit up. 'Of course. Yes! It is Aunty Lavita, you are seeking. Not really my aunt, but a group of us travelled to Australia together, back in 1913. Ever since then, we have all remained close. Over twenty years now! We migrants must stick together, you know. I am not saying that Australia hasn't been good to us! But here, we are like a big Spanish family. Together, we remind our children of the old country. We share celebrations—births, deaths and marriages. Harvests and plantings. We dance the flamenco and crush the olives. Geronimo and Lavita have been as grandparents to all the little ones who have been born here in Australia. We were very sad when Geronimo passed away, bless his soul.'

'So, Mrs Valverde, Mrs Santos... Aunt Lavita, she is here in Geelong?' Margaret was always quick to cut through to the task at hand.

'Yes! Aunt Lavita has finally joined us. There was nothing for her in Melbourne after Geronimo was gone. She now lives with her niece, Rosa Castillo, not so far away. I will write the address for you.'

Ana returned with a folded slip of paper, and after handing it to Jack, she accompanied them to the car in the driveway. Just as Margaret started the engine, she reached out, placing her hand upon the door, and added a final thought, her words sombre.

'I feel I should warn you—I have not heard anything about your Sofia. If she were here, I am sure that I would have been told. You mustn't get your hopes up. But you never know. Perhaps Aunt Lavita will know something. May God bless your search. I will pray for you and for your Sofia, pray that she is returned to you safe and sound.'

Refusing to allow his optimism to be crushed, Jack decided that just because Ana hadn't heard of Sofia, it didn't mean that she hadn't made contact with someone in the Spanish community. Perhaps Mrs

Santos had other acquaintances in Melbourne that Sofia had met. Surely not all the Spanish in Victoria lived here in Geelong.

Twenty minutes later, after navigating the winding road, this time with their backs to the sun, again they entered the streets of Geelong, guided by the lines drawn by Mrs Valverde on the page accompanying the address.

They turned right onto a broad tree-lined avenue—Claremont Street—and Margaret idled past the houses, all near-identical neat weatherboard homes, then paused in front of one that stood out from the rest. Most of the houses were shades of pale pink, yellow and blue, but this house was brilliant white. And, while neatly mowed lawns bordered with pansies and lilacs adorned most yards, this house held a celebration of terracotta pots, each one bursting with cascades of pink and red flowers. A set of enormous concrete vessels lined its driveway, their bushes forming a miniature avenue, and still more pots formed a cluster on the broad front porch. But the absolute giveaway that this was the home of a Spanish resident was the concrete statue, colourfully painted, of a man with a broad moustache perched on the back of a donkey his hand aloft, situated beside the entry, as if to greet visitors. Jack was sure this was the house they were seeking before he even noticed the swirling iron numerals attached to the front wall.

The door opened before they'd even stepped onto the porch, and the warm welcome they received from the young woman was a sure indication that Ana Valverde had phoned ahead, giving notice of Jack and Margaret's pending visit.

'*Hola*—come in,' she said, wiping floury hands onto her apron. 'Jack and Margaret, *Oui*? Rosa Castillo. Welcome. Aunt Lavita is sitting outside, shelling peas for our dinner. She is expecting you. Please, follow me.' Weaving through the house, they came to a back porch where a lady sat in a wicker chair, a large bowl resting on her lap full of freshly shelled peas. Jack immediately recognised her. This dear old lady, somewhat reminiscent of Sofia's Aunt Jovita, had been connected to his wife; hopefully she held the key to finding her!

'Good morning to you both.' She peered at them from under heavy wrinkled eyelids. 'Oh, now I remember you,' she said, looking at Jack. Despite her advanced years, her English was clearer than the heavy accents of either Rosa or Ana Valverde. No doubt a result of years of work at her city restaurant, where she would have been forced to speak English not only to her customers, but also to the merchants who serviced the restaurant, Jack thought.

'Hello, Mrs Santos. Thank you for seeing us.'

'You are very welcome. It is lovely to have some visitors. Nobody ever comes to see me!' she said. 'I was most surprised when I heard a young couple were in town seeking my whereabouts! Your dear wife is missing? Sofia? Heaven forbid!'

'Yes, we have been searching all over. I can't imagine where she's gone. I was hoping you may have some ideas… Perhaps there are some connections in the Spanish community that Sofia has made?'

'But why would Sofia leave her home? She was always so happy— so full of joy.'

Jack found himself explaining the details of the fire that had taken Scotty's life, and the overwhelming grief that followed. Sadly, he admitted how he was sure Sofia blamed him for the loss of their son.

'I am so, so very sorry.' Mrs Santos dabbed a snowy white handkerchief to her eyes. 'This is truly terrible, just awful! I am sure you will find her. You say you think that she blames you? No, Jack. She loves you. I know this by the way she spoke about you. Her withdrawal, this is her sorrow speaking. She is sad, and grief has affected her reason. When Sofia thinks clearly, then she will come home, of this I am certain.'

Jack hoped Mrs Santos' insight was correct, but wasn't so sure, as memories of Sofia's accusing, pain-filled eyes rose before him, accompanied by echoes of her anguished cry. *You saved my paintings, but you didn't get Scotty!* A stabbing pain filled his chest.

Margaret looked across at him, an expression of concern on her face, and took over the conversation. 'So, you haven't heard from

Sofia then, Mrs Santos? Can you think of anyone else Sofia might have turned to? Perhaps someone else in the Spanish community?'

Mrs Santos shook her head as she pondered the question. 'I just don't know… We used to talk about babies. Your dear little boy. We loved him, Geronimo and I. She only came in every month or so, but we looked forward to her visits. We are also from Malaga, you see. It's a big city, but still, we knew the same people. Talking to Sofia was like stepping back in time. Sofia insisted that we speak in Spanish; she didn't want her mother tongue to get rusty! Could she, perhaps, have returned to Malaga?'

No! Sofia wouldn't have left Australia! She loves it here.' Jack's reply was curt. The idea that Sofia would leave not only him, but Australia, was unthinkable.

He remembered how she'd woken with a song in her voice every morning. A kiss for him, a joke for Scotty. How she'd pull their squealing toddler into their bed, and nuzzling him, declare that she was the luckiest woman alive to have the two most handsome men in the world to care for. Scotty would giggle and wriggle out of her arms, scampering over the bed, climbing over Jack, who'd respond with exaggerated cries caused by being poked and prodded by Scotty's sharp fingers and knees jabbing into his eyes, ears and mouth.

'Ouch, you little rascal… you wait until I get you…'

Now, without the joy of Scotty to delight her each morning, could Sofia have left Australia?

He knew that Sofia had often searched the newspapers for information about the Spanish war, and she was deeply saddened by the bloodshed and destruction caused by Franco and his troops. But he'd never sensed she would want to return there. Perhaps she'd missed her home much more than he'd known!

'Have you asked at the churches, Jack?' asked Mrs Santos. 'Sofia mentioned visiting St Patrick's from time to time. You know, the new cathedral in East Melbourne.'

Jack didn't know, and again he tried to look unfazed as he absorbed still more information about his wife. He wondered if he'd known Sofia at all. Without doubt, her and Andrés' lives were entwined with the Catholic church in Malaga. If they'd been in Spain,

Sofia would have turned to Father Sebastian immediately. The man had been far more than a priest to her. But not once, ever, did Jack imagine Sofia turning to a priest, or even attending church, since they'd been here in Australia. With a stab of guilt, he recalled how Scotty's funeral, organised by Lena and Lil, in consultation with himself, had been held at the small Presbyterian church in Eltham. At the time, Sofia had been in shock and was under heavy sedation. The idea that she might have preferred a Catholic mass for their son had never entered his mind.

Sensing his bewilderment at the talk of churches, Mrs Santos continued, 'Oh, we Catholics are funny, Jack. We may not talk about our beliefs much. However, as soon as there is a birth or death or a spot of illness about, we run to God and our saints for comfort!'

She was quiet for a moment, then added, 'There's another thing that worries me. Have you thought to look for Sofia at the hospitals? Sometimes if people have a shock, they are not themselves. Confused, even. Someone may have taken Sofia to a doctor or even to the hospital. Please, I think you must check that she is not at Kew!'

'Kew?'

'Jack, I am sorry! I don't mean to alarm you, but Sofia is grieving badly. She is not herself. You said that she barely spoke after Scotty died, that she had reverted to speaking Spanish? If she is very low, someone might decide that she needs care. Psychiatric care. I think that perhaps you should check Kew, as well.'

Jack felt his shoulders slump, and suddenly, he wanted to leave. Sofia was not here in Geelong, and he was no closer to her than he'd been yesterday morning. Sure, they had some more leads, but they were options that he could barely contemplate. His wife in a hospital! An asylum! Surely not!

He reached down and hugged the old woman farewell, avoiding the dark sorrow-filled eyes gazing back at him.

'I am sorry, Jack. I, too, will start asking around. There are not many Spanish people in Victoria, especially now that the government has tightened its rules as to who is allowed to come to Australia. White-skinned English-speaking people! Pah! Such nonsense. Anyway, it should make it easier to find one young Spanish woman.

Perhaps if you leave me your contact details, I can let you know if I hear anything.'

Jack wrote his parents' phone number in the notebook Mrs Santos offered to him, hardly daring to believe that anything good would come of it, and in turn, promised that he would let her know as soon as Sofia was found.

The return journey to Melbourne seemed endless. Exhausted, Jack lay back in the seat with his eyes closed. He tried to free his mind of emotion in an attempt to find clarity and hope. For the last hour of the journey, he drifted to sleep, and he was surprised when he awoke to the familiar sight of his mother's rose bushes outside the car window.

Blearily, he looked at Margaret and shrugged. He was out of ideas. Hospitals! St Patrick's Cathedral! It all seemed so unlikely.

'Jack, we will find her. We are not going to lose faith,' Margaret said, but he noticed that her sassy confidence was absent. 'Tomorrow morning, same time, same place. Let's see if the Catholics have any leads for us!'

The next morning, Jack and Margaret resumed their search, driving over the Church Street Bridge and through the streets to the north of the city. The beautiful gardens surrounding Parliament House caught Jack's attention. It was just the sort of place that Sofia would have enjoyed strolling through, with Scotty perched in his pram. From here she'd possibly glimpsed the spire he could see in the distance, majestically extending hundreds of feet into the sky. The church was massive, its bluestone walls trimmed with sandstone, dozens of arches framing doorways and windows, the whole construction embellished with carvings and iron. Only just completed, the building was an impressive tribute to the Gothic architecture of bygone centuries. With the proficiency of a tour guide, Margaret explained how St Patrick's Cathedral had taken not years, but decades to build, and it was only due to the determination of Archbishop Mannix, the current head of the Catholic Church in Australia, that the project had been finished at all. Apparently the archbishop was a fiery Irishman with a penchant for action and a reputation as a trouble maker that extended across the globe. Frequently, he'd challenged Irish political leaders, and then in Australia he'd continued to influence political debate, demanding the establishment of an education system for the children of Catholics, and vehemently opposing a referendum to allow conscription, during the Great War. The Cathedral before them had been wallowing in a half-built state since its inception in 1848, until Mannix had taken up the cause to see it completed. Now the all-but-completed building was both the tallest and largest church ever to be constructed in Australia. Leaving the vehicle, they walked around to the side, where Margaret added explanations of naves, transepts, sanctuaries, chapels and sacristies that left Jack's head spinning.

'How on earth do you know all of this?' he asked, wondering whether Margaret was, in fact, Catholic and he'd never known.

'I have contacts, Jack,' she teased, her tone light, maintaining the optimistic manner with which they'd started the morning. 'You know my neighbour, Alan.' Jack didn't, and in fact had never once been to Margaret's apartment, but he nodded anyway. 'Alan is an artist. These days he works in glass... He's mad about medieval stained glass. A few weeks ago, he told me how he'd landed a position with Yencken & Co, a company that restores stained glass in churches. When I got home yesterday, he was in the carpark, and it occurred to me to ask him about the cathedrals in Melbourne, just in case... well, in case St Patrick's turns out to be a dead lead. So, I asked a few questions. You know, how many? Where they are? In case there's a dozen of them. For all I knew, there could be one on every corner, just like the pubs. Instead, I got a lecture on St Patrick's. He is mad about the place. Told me all about its architecture, which then evolved into a lesson on stained glass. He adores these windows... has come to study them himself, loads of times, apparently.'

Following the direction of Margaret's hand, Jack turned and looked at the dozens of windows set within the building's ornate arches.

'These are not just the decorative religious images that I had always thought them to be. There is far more to them, so he told me. Just like paintings, they are full of symbols and stories, clever combinations of colour placed in accordance to how sunlight falls across them and through to the interior. It was all rather fascinating!'

∼

As they entered the cathedral, Jack was immediately awed by its interior, which was possibly even more impressive than the outside of the building. From the gleaming, intricate patterns of the mosaic flooring to the soaring vaulted wooden ceilings, attention to detail was evident on every surface. A morning Mass was in progress, so he and Margaret slid into a pew at the back and quietly listened, waiting for the priest to be free to speak with them.

∼

Though Sofia was Catholic and they'd been married in a Catholic church, Catholicism remained a mystery to Jack. Throughout his school years, boys and girls in Catholic-school uniforms shared the same trains and trams as he and his schoolmates, but they seemed to belong to another species. Their religion was full of mysteries, traditions and rules; the Pope in Rome, the status of Mary as the Mother of the Church; the rituals of the confessional, and the long strands of rosary beads that were used to accompany prayer. Most of the Catholics in Australia stemmed from the Irish, unlike the Protestants with their British heritage. The religious divide was accompanied by a social divide; Catholic people mixed with other Catholics, attended the same churches and schools, and ultimately, they married Catholics, as likewise, Protestants clung to their kind. Additionally, the Catholics tended to align with the politics of the Labor Party. While for some people the religious divide was reinforced by deeply held prejudices, Jack's parents had always taught him to be respectful of other people's beliefs. William's work at Goldsbrough, Mort & Co meant he dealt with people of various nationalities and religious persuasions, and often William had heard him say good and bad could be found in all people, if one was to go searching.

The voice of the priest echoed throughout the chamber. Listening to the rise and fall of his words as they fell in a smooth, melodic cadence, Jack was surprised. He concluded that the gentle rhythm of the sermon's delivery compensated for the parishioners' lack of understanding, for if he wasn't mistaken, the sermon was being delivered in Latin, and hence utterly incomprehensible.

While Jack was eager for the service to finish so he could enquire if there'd been any visits from a young Spanish woman in recent weeks, he relaxed into the peaceful atmosphere enveloping him. Without thinking, words like "trust" and "faith" swirled forth, resurrected from his past experiences of sitting in pews beside his mother in the Church of England, even as the Latin words of the priest washed over him. It was as if this building were a sanctuary from the storms of life and if one sat very still, strife could be eradicated. Order could be restored. Even, perhaps, a lost wife might return to her husband's side. All Jack needed to do was pray, trust and wait.

He looked up as the words of the priest fell away, replaced by the harmonious voices of a choir accompanied by the swelling chords of a pipe organ, whose dozen or more impressive brass pipes rose to the ceiling.

Unconsciously, he sank to his knees, buried his head in his arms and sought the ear of God—begging for forgiveness for losing Scotty, that his boy be granted eternal peace and joy and protection, seeking His intervention in the search for Sofia, requesting a sign that would show that she was safe and well. His reflections evolved into an appeal: please let no harm come to Sofia, please let Jack find her today! And then his appeal further evolved into a promise: if Sofia were found, Jack would repay God. He would attend church services weekly; he would join with the thousands of faithful devotees across the world who rose on Sunday mornings to attend Mass; he would forever be thankful, if only God would deliver to him this desire of his heart.

Tears forced their way through Jack's tightly clenched lids as he gave himself over to the power of the swelling chords. He was lifted in their exaltation, carried by them, as they rippled over the floors and climbed the walls, rising ever upwards, until they reached the lofty heights of the ceiling, sure and deep, confident of their destination to heavenly places. Jack submitted himself to their power—captivated, cocooned in a rapturous ecstasy that was surely from the harmonies of angels as the notes cascaded like a waterfall, washing him with their truth and hope and surety. So deeply transported into this spiritual realm, Jack lost all perspective of his physical presence, and it was only when he felt the firm touch of a hand upon his shoulder that he opened his eyes. Looking around, he felt disorientated by the reality of his surroundings. Exquisite as they were, they offered no match to the transcendent experience he'd been awoken from. With reluctance, he wiped his face with the back of his hand and returned to a world that now seemed diminutive.

The church was all but empty. Margaret, standing to his right, had a stricken look on her face, while to his left, an ancient priest looked upon him with calm benevolence. His kindly expression reminded Jack of Father Sebastian, and again, he wondered why he had not thought to look for Sofia in a church before now. Of course this is where she would come! This is surely where anyone who was suffering would seek solace.

'I don't wish to impose, sir, but if you would like to talk, I am an excellent listener. Perhaps not as good as He.' The priest chuckled, in the gentle lilting tones of the Irish, before glancing skyward. 'But I do my best. Or maybe it is the confessional that you would prefer?'

Jack shook his head. 'No, sir, I mean Father. I am not a Catholic. We just came because my wife is missing. I thought you could help us find her.'

'Now, I can't make any promises. That sounds more like a job for God than me.'

'We thought that Jack's wife, Sofia, may have come here,' Margaret interrupted, as though she thought the task Jack had described sounded a little daunting—as if they expected him to be a prognosticator or soothsayer, conjuring missing women from nowhere.

'You see, Jack's wife is Catholic,' Margaret continued. 'She, they, have had a terrible tragedy with the loss of their little boy, and, well....

34

it has been hell. I mean. Sorry. Just terrible. Heartbreaking. We knew that Sofia was struggling, as you would expect. But we did not expect that she would vanish. We have been searching for here everywhere.'

'Does she usually attend Mass here? Where do you live?' the priest asked quietly.

Jack took over the story, describing how he and Sofia had been living in Eltham for the last five years. Telling the priest about the birth of their little boy, who had given them such happiness. He explained how Sofia had borne many losses in her life.

Again, the priest's eyebrows rose, causing Jack to add further details.

'We met in Paris,' he said. 'I met her brother, Andrés, first. We were students at art school together and we clicked from the very first day. He was a... a real artist. Very talented. He had a lifetime of painting. Their father was an artist too, with a studio and gallery.'

'Their mother died at birth,' Margaret added. 'So it was just Sofia, Andrés and their father. And then, when the twins were twenty, their father died too. They nursed him together, but he had cancer or something. After that, Sofia and Andrés were left with each other.'

'And,' continued Jack, 'in Paris, after winning the Académie Julian's prize, Andrés collapsed. He was in hospital for weeks. I was supposed to come home, here to Melbourne. But I couldn't have left Sofia to manage alone, could I? So, I stayed with her until Andrés was ready to leave the hospital, and then I went with them to Malaga to see him home safely. Sofia and I were married after the first year. By Father Sebastian. A Catholic Priest.' Now that he had started, Jack found he could not stop speaking. 'It was wonderful, our life in Malaga. However, Andrés' illness returned, and he just got worse. He knew he was dying, and told me to bring Sofia here to Australia after he went. He knew, even then, that Spain was heading for trouble, but Sofia would not hear of it. Then eventually people began losing their jobs. They stopped travelling. And with no money, they stopped coming to the gallery. So, as Andrés requested, I brought Sofia here, to Australia. She seemed happy enough...?' Even Jack could hear the question in his words, and was encouraged by Margaret's nod of agreement.

'She was happy, Jack. Sofia was very happy!'

Jack continued, 'Sofia loved art. It was her life. We both wanted to go to Montsalvat. We were happy there. However, she had enough of... living on the retreat.' Jack skipped the conflict with Justus. 'We had just found a nice little house in Eltham... and then...' He could not complete the sentence.

Margaret put her arm around him. 'They lost their little boy,' she finished. 'There was a terrible accident. A fire. Scotty died.'

A silence enveloped them for a moment, and then the priest spoke.

'And this was very recent, this terrible tragedy?'

'Yes. Five weeks ago. It's now almost three weeks since we've seen Sofia. We have no idea where she is.'

The priest nodded, thoughtfully. 'Jack, I am so sorry to hear of your loss. This is a very fresh wound and it is very painful. You will always have a scar, a reminder of these terrible events. There will always be haunting memories. But in time, there will be good ones too. As for your Sofia... She might have been here. We have so many visitors, I couldn't be sure. I feel like there was a young woman with dark hair who used to come here. I haven't seen her for many months, now. We never spoke, but I recall that she used to light candles, and then she'd pray. Perhaps these candles, they were for her brother and parents?'

Jack agreed. Perhaps the woman had been Sofia, but where was she now?

'You are not Catholic?'

Guilt flooded Jack, as though perhaps he'd committed some sort of sin for praying to the God of Catholics.

Father Simon shook his head, realising he had been misunderstood. 'I was just going to ask, would you like me to pray? This is a problem for God. Perhaps we could even light a candle for Scotty. I suspect that is what Sofia would do.'

Jack nodded in agreement, and the priest handed him a tall taper, gesturing to where several small tea lights had already been lit. Margaret's hand squeezed his as the priest intoned a prayer for Scotty's soul and for Sofia's safety, health and speedy return to her husband.

Stepping out into the sunshine, Jack felt bereft. Any comfort derived from the priest evaporated amid the streaming sunshine and bustling city traffic, which seemed overwhelmingly ordinary in a world that was anything but normal.

'Are you alright?' Margaret asked when he stumbled on the cobblestone gutter, and Jack shook his head.

He did not know what he was. They were no closer to Sofia than a week ago, when they'd started their search.

'What would you like to do?' Margaret asked. 'Shall we try the hospitals? Do you think we should check Kew like Mrs Santos suggested?'

The anger that erupted from within him surprised Jack. 'No! Sofia's not in a hospital. She is not at Kew! She's strong. She is just angry with me. She will be somewhere safe. I know she's alright. She has to be!'

'Okay, Jack. Okay. A pub, then? How about a pint?'

Jack nodded. 'That is exactly what I would like.'

'I know where we'll go.' Weaving through the streets to the north of Melbourne, they motored towards Carlton, eventually arriving at a large red brick building with a sign out the front: *J.C. Watson Wine Merchants: fine table wines to accompany your meal.*

Jack had no appetite, but the thought of drinking wine, lots of wine, sounded good.

'You've been here before?' he asked, noticing the familiar manner with which Margaret was greeted when she ordered two glasses of sherry.

'Here is one place where a woman can come and not be leered at. Besides, lots of artists come here. You can always find someone who's ready for a good argument!'

Slumping into his seat, Jack felt immensely tired. For the last five weeks his life had been hell, and today, with his hopes of finding Sofia dashed yet again, he was utterly drained. He just wanted her and Scotty back with him, his life to return to how it was before the fire. Resisting the tears that again threatened, he looked around at the lunchtime crowd.

As Margaret had said, all types of people were gathered there.

Women with greying hair hanging loose, and men bearing the small goatee beards common to artists. A young man in a well-worn tweed coat sat with his pen out, writing in a thick notebook. An author, Jack wondered. Two men with thick European accents sat nearby, speaking a language that Jack did not recognise. Jack was surprised to see them looking at ease as they spoke the foreign language in this public place. Very often migrants were frowned upon when they spoke their native tongue in public; their status as New Australians came with an expectation that they would forsake their mother tongues and their national traditions. In all regards, they were expected to look like and act like the white Australian population of their new country.

He found it hard to focus on Margaret's words, her analysis of their search, her suggestions of where they could look next. Instead, he focused on the glass in his hand, downing it and replacing it with a second and then a third.

A man with dark skin, standing just outside the entrance, caught his eye. It was a rare sight to see an Aboriginal person in the pubs of Melbourne. Rare to see dark-skinned people in any places frequented by white Australians. No one at his school had dark skin. There were, of course, the housemaids like Nina, who used to help his mother out and the occasional railways employee to be seen. Many of the farmers who sold their wool through Goldsbrough, Mort & Co had Aboriginal workers of course. The man looked about thirty-five and was dressed in neat grey trousers and a snowy white shirt. It was obvious that he was a workman, calling in for a lunchtime pint with his two friends—the two whitefellas standing at the bar.

'Three pints,' asked the taller of the two.

The bartender frowned, glancing at the entrance. 'You're not buying for that fellow?' He nodded towards the man on the step.

'Three pints,' repeated the man, ignoring the question.

'I'm sorry. I can't serve him. It's illegal.'

Jack looked at the face of the man standing quietly at the door, his hat in his hand, now shaking his head at his workmates, discouraging them from reacting to a ruling that he was obviously familiar with.

Without thought, Jack strode to the bar and stood alongside the two men.

'Three pints,' he said, banging his hand on the bar. 'In fact, make it four.' Jack's voice held a growl that was foreign to him. His hands were balled into fists.

Margaret's voice sounded in the background, calling for him to return to the table, but Jack ignored her. His mind was ablaze, inflamed by factors beyond the laws which made it illegal for pubs to serve alcohol to Aborigines.

'Bastards. Bastards, every one of you,' he called, remembering the slights that Sofia had received during her time in Australia. Shopkeepers who'd ignored her when she stood with her beans and carrots in her cane basket, waiting to be served. The dress-shop assistants who'd told her that their change rooms were unavailable. The hair-dresser who'd directed Sofia to a place where 'she would be more comfortable'. While he had known that these events had hurt Sofia, she'd always accepted the rudeness as inevitable, and he, in turn, had accepted her quiet reasoning. At times he had felt anger on her behalf, but never, not once, had he stood up for her. Not until this moment, when every ounce of his rage erupted, belatedly, in Sofia's defence.

'How dare you?' he demanded, his words cracking. 'I insist this man be served immediately.' Jack's fist slammed onto the bar, causing a tray of glasses to rattle threateningly. 'He's done a hard morning's work and has earned the right to a beer, just like everyone else here.'

'It's not that I don't want to serve him,' the barman muttered nervously. 'It's just that I would lose my job. My boss, he could lose his license.'

The two workmen beside him, who'd been keen to make a stand for their Aboriginal friend five minutes earlier, look at Jack with apprehension before muttering that they would find somewhere else to drink, and with a dubious nod of thanks towards him, they left.

'Now see what you've done! You've embarrassed that man. Made him feel ashamed. What on earth did he ever do wrong?' Jack ranted at the injustice he'd just witnessed.

'Call the police, he needs to be locked up.'

Jack reeled to where he heard the voice, ready to continue the tirade with anyone who wanted to argue with him.

'Jack, it's time we left,' Margaret rose from the table and walked to the door. 'Come on. Now!'

Looking at her, his anger spent, Jack followed her to the car.

They drove in silence, each lost in their own thoughts until Margaret pulled over outside his parents' home. Overcome by despair, Jack clenched his fists and beat upon the dashboard.

'Where is she, Margaret? Where can she possibly be?'

'Oh, love, come here,' she said, reaching out to him, and he fell against her shoulder, dissolving in drunken, hacking sobs.

'We won't give up, Jack. We just have to keep looking. One thing's certain—Sofia must be somewhere, and we will find her!'

Jack tried to believe her. He had to feel hopeful—he'd lost Scotty, forever. How could he live without Sofia?

As he clung to Margaret, trying to control the ragged sobs, neither Jack nor Margaret noticed the taxicab glide past them, its left indicator flashing as it pulled into the curb, nor did they see the expression of shock followed by despair on its passenger's face as the vehicle paused for a brief second before accelerating into the distance.

# CHAPTER 4

*T*he following week, Jack rarely left the house. Margaret had returned to work, although she promised him that the following weekend, they would continue their search. In the meantime, she said that she would make some phone calls and hoped that perhaps he might remember something that could help their search.

On Wednesday, Marian surprised Jack by bringing a letter to him that had been delivered with the morning mail.

Jack turned it over, mystified, then carefully slit it open. The message typed on the single page was brief.

*Dear Mr Tomlinson,*

*Could you please make an appointment with Mr Stevens at the Melbourne Branch of the Commonwealth Bank at your earliest convenience? There is a matter that he would like to discuss with you.*

*Yours faithfully,*

*J Simpson.*

*Branch Secretary*

. . .

Jack was startled. Why on earth would the bank manager be contacting him?

Rather than speculate on the purpose of the request, Jack decided that he would visit the branch immediately and thankfully, was shown into the bank manager's office, immediately.

'Mr Tomlinson, thank you for coming in. How are you?' The manager's eyes searched his face.

Jack was slowly becoming used to this, the way people looked at him differently. His parents' friends, the workmates who'd visited to see how he was going. It was as though their eyes pierced into him, searching beyond his skin, with its grey tinge and heavy lines, in an attempt to see into his mind; to try and fathom the thoughts that must accompany one whose life had been so beset with tragedy.

Did the manager know about the death of Scotty? Surely he couldn't have heard that Sofia was missing?

'Thank you for coming in today. I just wanted to have a chat. Something has been on my mind and I preferred to speak with you face-to-face. It may be nothing—I may well be barking up the wrong tree—but I knew that I couldn't let it rest until I spoke with you.'

Jack was mystified.

'You see, your wife, Sofia, you know that she came in last week. She withdrew a large sum of money. Not that that's a worry. It's hers to withdraw. It was how she looked that concerned me.'

What! Sofia was here? Last week?

'How was she...? Where is she?' Jack asked, tripping over his words, his mind racing.

'I couldn't say. So, you are telling me you have not seen Sofia? Not that it is any of my business, of course.'

Jack returned the man's gaze and shook his head.

'Okay...' The manager looked thoughtful. 'Let me tell you what happened. It would have been about Wednesday, and she arrived quite early in the day. She looked unwell, tired. No, more than that. Beyond tired—exhausted. Upset. My teller thought that perhaps she must have been ill. She asked to withdraw one hundred pounds, an enormous sum of money—which, again, is of no consequence. But it seemed unusual.'

Again, Jack nodded.

'She just seemed so… distressed. I have not stopped thinking about her and I wanted to check with you, in case something is amiss.'

'Did she tell you where she was living?' Jack asked, ignoring the flicker of surprise across the bank manager's face.

'No, Jack. Where she was living did not come up, but I did ask her for a contact phone number. Would you like it?'

The manager passed a slip of paper to him with the digits *8-4-2-8* written on it. 'All the best, Jack,' he said as he shook Jack's hand and patted his shoulder. 'I am sure whatever the problem is will sort itself out. Life usually does.'

Stepping through the glass plate doors and onto the street, clutching the tiny slip of paper with four numbers, Jack did not know whether to laugh or cry. At last, he had a contact for Sofia!

~

Dazed, Jack walked to the post office and stood in line outside the row of phone booths, nervously jingling two ha'pennies in his hand. Every booth was taken, and it was hard to resist the urge to tap on their windows, ask them to hurry. Didn't they realise he had an urgent call to make?

He re-read the number on the slip of paper for the umpteenth time. It meant nothing to him.

Finally, it was his turn. With fingers trembling, Jack juggled the handset, placed the coins in the slot and dialled.

'Good morning, sir. How can I help you?' The voice was curt and sounded loud, as if the woman speaking was very close.

'Hello. Hello—I am looking for my wife. For Sofia. Can I speak with her?' Jack tried to control the quaver in his voice.

'Sorry, sir. There is no one by that name here.'

'What do you mean? Sofia gave this number to our bank manager. She is there!' Jack heard a shrillness enter his voice that sounded like it was coming from someone else.

'Sir, just hold the line, please.' The line went quiet.

Within minutes, a second voice came to the phone. 'Hello. Can I help you?' Not Sofia's. This was an older voice. Friendly, but firm.

'I am trying to find my wife. I think she may be staying with you.'

'Can you tell me her name, please?'

'Sofia. Sofia Tomlinson. She is Spanish. She gave our bank manager your telephone number.'

'And who are you?'

The question seemed meaningless. What business was it to this lady who he was?

'Jack! I am Jack Tomlinson. Her husband. I need to see her!'

'Jack, I am sorry. That won't be possible. Sofia is no longer with us.'

'But where is she? Are you saying that she was there?'

'I am sorry, sir. That is all that I can say. I am sure that she will contact you when she is ready. Good day, sir.'

Before Jack could speak, the steady hum of a dial tone droned in his ear. No! In disbelief, Jack rattled on the handset, hoping to retrieve the connection.

'No. No… no… no….' With each word, he pounded the handset against the bench top, oblivious to its splintering case and the shocked expressions of the onlookers waiting in line to use the telephone.

'Sir, please step out.'

It was a policeman, one of the many who walked, baton in hand, attempting to maintain peace on the city's streets.

Trembling, Jack opened the door.

'You realise that you have just damaged public property—so now, you need to come with me, and we will have a little chat. Are you going to walk with me sensibly, or do I need to use these here handcuffs?'

Jack stared at the metal loops in the man's hand, at the blue uniform adorned with brass buttons and badges. He could barely comprehend what was happening.

'Come on, man. Make up your mind. Here.' Jack felt the vice-like grip of a hand on his shoulder, propelling him around before thrusting him along the street. There was nothing for him to do but walk, and he matched the steady stride of the policeman, whose blank face gave nothing away.

Minutes later, they arrived at the Bourke Street Police Station, and following a murmured conversation, Jack was sat before a sergeant, a man built like a bull: his head huge, his cheeks heavy with reddened jowls, his nose bulbous, the whole arrangement perched on shoulders that looked to be a yard wide and utterly devoid of a neck.

'So, sir. We might begin with you telling me your name.'

'Jack… Jack Tomlinson.'

'You look like you are in a bit of a state, Jack. What's going on?'

'I'm looking for my wife. Sofia.'

'So, she's missing, is she? And how long has she been gone?'

'I don't know. Weeks. We've looked everywhere.'

'Have you reported her absence to the police?'

'No!'

'No… why on earth not? Had you been arguing?'

'No—not at all.'

'Was there a bit of rough stuff?'

Jack just looked at him, blankly. Surely the sergeant was joking.

'You know. A slap here and there. Sometimes it happens.'

'No… no, certainly not. I love my wife. She loves me.'

'Well, Jack. Wives don't just vanish for no reason.'

'We had an accident. There was a fire. Our son….'

Tears flowed as Jack again tried to make sense of events and put his thoughts into words.

'I am sorry, son. Sometimes life deals a rotten hand. Just catch your breath for a minute. I will make us a cup of tea. White? Sugar?'

Jack was thankful for the sergeant's tact in leaving him alone to collect himself. In minutes he was back, a cup of tea in each hand, the yellowed mugs tilting precariously as he placed them on the desk. The sergeant's keen eyes upon him were now softened with concern.

'How about you tell me all about it? Let's start at the beginning'

For what seemed like the dozenth time, Jack relayed the events of the past weeks, finding that although the story had gotten longer as the details of his and Margaret's search the previous week were added, it had become no easier. He finished by describing today's visit to the bank manager and the frustrating consequences of the phone call that he'd made.

'You've got that phone number there?'

Jack gripped the slip of paper, now crumpled from where he'd been holding it in his fist. It was his only link to Sofia, and he was reluctant to let it go.

'Come on. Let's see what I can find out. I'll give it back to you when we've finished.' Lifting the handset on his desk, the sergeant reached to take the paper from Jack. He smoothed out its wrinkles before dialling the numbers before him.

Jack held his breath. He heard the ringing tone and the voice of a female answering the call.

'Hello. This is Sergeant O'Neil from Bourke Street Station. Can you please tell me who I am speaking with?' The barking tones of the sergeant foretold that he was someone used to getting the information he needed, without fuss. 'Mary. Yes, well, good afternoon to you, Mary. Can you please tell me the name of the organisation with whom I am speaking?'

There was a pause, followed by murmuring from the other end of the line.

'Mary, I know that you might not give that information out to anyone, but at this minute you are speaking to the police, and this is important. I don't need to get a court order to get a few simple answers to a few simple questions, do I?

'Okay… You do that.'

The sergeant rolled his eyes, and Jack suspected that Mary had passed the call on to her supervisor.

'Hello, Mrs Blake—is that correct? I am Sergeant O'Neil, from Bourke Street Station. I am dealing with a missing person concern and I understand that you have had contact with the said missing person.

'Okay. So, you are a women's refuge. I guessed as much. And which one would that be?

'Yes, I understand the importance of confidentiality. I know that you do a wonderful job caring for women in need. A very important job. Yes, it certainly is. However…'

'Mrs Blake, I can assure you I am not acting on behalf on an abusive husband.

'Sofia Tomlinson. Her husband is Jack Tomlinson. From the story he has just told me, I suspect that his wife could be ill.'

Jack watched the sergeant, trying to read his expressions as he spoke, raising his inky pen to jot down a note from time to time.

'So, she just left, you say? And when would that have been? Five days ago… hmm… did she tell anyone where she was going?'

'Spanish…? Okay…. Trauma? Yes, that would be right. The poor woman has suffered a great deal. Recently lost a young child. Well, if I need any more information, I will call you back on this number. And Mrs Blake…' The sergeant's voice adopted a commanding tone. 'If you see Sofia Tomlinson again, I want you to phone Bourke Street Station pronto, and ask for Sergeant O'Neil. I need to know that she is safe and well. Do you understand? And you may like to encourage her to contact her husband. He is missing her terribly. The chap's in a right mess. There is a lot more to this story than you might imagine.

'Thank you and good day to you, too.'

Returning the handset, the sergeant looked at Jack, sympathy in his warm brown eyes.

'Where is she?' Jack asked.

'Unfortunately, I still don't have the answer to that question. It appears that Sofia stayed at one of the women's refuges here in Melbourne. She was found in a bit of a state a couple of weeks ago and was picked up by a concerned citizen, who took her there.'

'A woman's refuge! Where?'

'I don't think that's important at this minute, Jack. They like to keep that information to themselves, and by law, that is their right. Mind you, if I need to, I will have that answer in an hour. There are not too many refuges in Melbourne. But they are not breaking any laws, and they offer a much-needed service. Some women have dreadful lives. They need to escape their husbands. The sad thing is that most can't, the poor things—so good on the ones that do! However, the refuges can't have abusive husbands hollering on their doorstep, making threats and creating a ruckus at all hours of the day and night, can they now?'

'I wouldn't do that!'

'From where I'm sitting, I've learned that none of us really knows what we'd do when things fall apart. Look at you, for instance. Did you imagine that you would bash a telephone to pieces and be arrested for damaging public property when you got out of bed this morning?'

'Am I being arrested?'

'No, Jack. I think we can dispense with that particular concern at present. Seems like you have enough problems without adding any more. Mind you, if you go around vandalising the city again, I will be forced to lock you up, so you better think carefully about how you handle this.'

Jack nodded dubiously. Looking at the sergeant, who had discovered more about Sofia in five minutes than he had in days of searching, it was as though he was looking at the world through a grey mist; and very little of it made sense.

'So, what did she say?' he asked.

The sergeant referred to the notes before him. 'Apparently Sofia was found sitting on the stairs of the Melbourne Town Hall in the wee hours of the morning a couple of weeks ago. A Friday night, or I should say Saturday morning, it was.'

He leaned back in his chair to check the calendar hanging on the wall beside his desk. 'Possibly the fourteenth of May. Apparently, she was huddled on the stairs—frozen, and muttering in Spanish... Is Sofia Spanish?'

Jack nodded, not wishing to interrupt the story.

'Whoever found her took her to the refuge, which is a good thing. She would have been safe there. They look after each other, that's for sure. Much safer than if she were wandering the city streets. Anything could have happened to her... doesn't bear thinking about. The thing is, the whole time Sofia was at the refuge, she barely spoke. Some women do not speak of their problems for weeks;

others, it all comes out in the first five minutes. But when Sofia arrived, she didn't even answer the most basic of questions, and then when she did start speaking, they couldn't understand her for she was speaking in a foreign tongue. They were sure that something terrible had happened, but couldn't make sense of it. And for all of their support, the women who run the refuges don't pry. They just offer warmth and safety. They understand that the women who come to them need rest—not just physically, but mentally, too. Women who escape their husbands have usually been through a lot. That's not to say it's always the husband's fault, mind you. Marriage can be complicated.'

'So, what happened?'

'They felt that she was getting better. She started to help around the place, talk a little. She began speaking some English words. They say it's a good sign when the women show some interest in life. You know, get out of bed, get dressed. Sofia even went out a couple of times. To the bank, I'm guessing, from what you've just told me. And then last week, she just vanished, and they haven't seen her since. She left a ten-pound note on her bed—they were stunned. Didn't think she had any money at all, and they found that! She didn't say where she was going… didn't even say that she was going at all, for that matter, but they seemed to think she might have been planning to return to Spain. They found a couple of flyers in the bin. You know the sort of thing—shipping timetables, etc.'

Jack felt the colour drain from his face. Surely not!

'Mate, are you alright? I know this is all a shock, and after all you've been through, it must be terrible. I'm thinking… how about you file Sofia as a missing person? Then I can make a few things happen behind the scenes.'

'I don't know… She doesn't seem to want to see me.'

'Look. You've both been to hell and back in these last couple of months. Neither of you is thinking straight. You've disconnected from each other. Sometimes tragedies will have that effect on a marriage. But for now, we just want to know where Sofia is and to be sure she is safe. You'd like to know that, wouldn't you?'

Jack nodded. Of course he wanted to know that Sofia was safe. His dear wife, lost somewhere out on the streets of Melbourne—staying at a refuge! Heavens, how had their lives come to this?

Jack stopped the thought there. He knew how it had come to this. Visions of flames licking up the walls of the cabin, the smell of smoke and the flash of incredulous, dark, accusing eyes seared his conscience.

Woodenly, Jack answered the sergeant's questions, watching the movement of the older man's hands wielding his nib as he scratched the details of Jack's sentences onto an official looking form. Jack was reminded of a similar experience, when he'd answered the probing questions of police officers following Scotty's death, and it took all his self-control to respond. Just like then, the information that Jack had to offer was scant. It seemed unbelievable that the narrative of the disintegration of his life with Sofia could be reduced to a few paragraphs on a Missing Person's Report

'Okay, Jack. That will do me for now. How about I run you home? You don't look in any state to be riding the trains today.'

'I'll be alright,' Jack said.

'No, Jack. It's on my way home. I insist. Come along, or I might decide to arrest you after all.'

Jack's brush with the law shook him up. Never had he imagined sitting opposite a policeman explaining why he'd vandalised a phone or being driven home in a police vehicle.

In the days that followed, Jack was determined to remain calm. Surely the sergeant, with the investigative skills of the Victorian Police Force at his fingertips, would locate Sofia for him. Each morning he rose early, washing and eating breakfast with his parents; and when William left for work, he went out into the garden, weeding, digging and mowing. At ten thirty AM each morning, Marian carried a tray to the back patio and they drank tea and ate biscuits together. After their morning tea, Jack accompanied his mother to the shops, pulling her wicker basket on wheels for her; and on their return, he finished another hour outdoors before eating lunch and then lying down on his bed for an hour. He'd try to read and then sleep, but mostly he just stared at the ceiling, and from time to time he'd retrieve the crumpled notepaper and look at the phone number. The slip of paper with four digits neatly written in the bank manager's handwriting was the nearest thing to physical contact that he'd had with Sofia, and yet even that had proved fruitless.

The sergeant was right. If Jack knew the address to where this phone number led, he couldn't have resisted arriving on its doorstep. Pounding the door. Calling for Sofia. Begging to be let in. Even now, having been told that Sofia was no longer there, he wasn't satisfied. He wanted to go there—hunt through each room. Open every cupboard, check every nook and cranny, just in case she was lost somewhere within the walls of the refuge and they couldn't find her—as irrational as that sounded. What he would give just to see the bed that she'd lain in. To lie on it, as if by absorbing her lingering presence, he might capture her thoughts and guess her movements.

And six days later, the news that he'd been waiting for arrived—in person, for he heard the knock on the door and Marian's call, 'Jack, you need to come down. A policeman is here to speak with you.'

Jack knew it was Sergeant O'Neil. He must have found out something. Rising, he was not sure if he wanted to leap for joy and run towards the news, or if he should drag his feet, slow everything down and delay having to hear words that were beyond anything he could bear.

'There you are, Jack.' Sergeant O'Neil stood from where he'd been sitting in the lounge-room and shook his hand, then followed with a pat on his back. 'How are you doing? It's all very difficult, I know.'

Did he really? Jack wondered, staring back. 'Have you heard something?'

'Well, I guess you could say it's both good news and bad news. Sofia appears to be safe and well. That's good news, isn't it?'

Jack nodded. Of course it was.

'However, her name was on the passenger list for the *Strathnaver*, which left for London last Thursday. It took a while, but we've contacted the ship and corroborated that Sofia is on board, and she appears to be well. It's a little awkward. We don't want to make things too difficult for her, you know, have the entire ship gossiping about her, but I requested via the captain that she be asked to return a message to you, you being her husband and all. I have it here.'

Jack's hands trembled as he accepted the telegram the sergeant offered him.


DEAR JACK STOP GOING TO AUSTRALIA WAS A TERRIBLE MISTAKE I KNOW THAT NOW STOP YOU BELONG THERE AND I BELONG IN SPAIN STOP I WISH YOU TO PLEASE FIND HAPPINESS AGAIN


Jack shook his head incredulously even as he read the words. No... no... What was she thinking? Did she think so little of him that she'd leave? Despise him so much that she'd cross the world to get away from him? It could not be any more clear—she did not wish to see him again. Blood pounded in his ears with a swishing sensation and he slumped onto the table, his head in his hands.

First Scotty, now Sofia—gone from him forever!

'Jack, what's happened?' He barely comprehended Marian's presence as she stared at him, tears streaming down her cheeks.

'Mum, she's gone.' And for the first time in two decades, he leaned against his mother's breast and cried as though his heart would break.

'There, there... It will be alright; you wait and see... shh...'

Over his mother's shoulder, through blurred eyes, Jack saw the sergeant pick up his hat and find his way to the front door, pausing on the threshold, and looking toward him with a look of sorrow before he departed, quietly closing the front door behind him.

# CHAPTER 5

'What do you mean, you want to go to Montsalvat? Why?' Margaret's voice was sharp.

'I need to get some things.'

'Do you want me to drive you there? Are you sure this is a good idea?'

'Margaret, I am going out there today whether you want to come or not. I don't care either way.' Jack felt a tiny stab of guilt when he saw Margaret wince at the sharpness of his words.

'Okay, then. Let's go.'

He followed her down the hall. He'd been surprised when she'd arrived this morning and assumed that his mother had called her. Today he felt disconnected from them both. He could see them and hear them, but their presence felt dreamlike.

He'd watched her hug first his mother, then his father when they met at the front doorstep. He'd heard his mother's words. 'We are so glad that you could come! He's been on about it all morning, Margaret. Perhaps he'll talk to you. He's barely spoken a word since the sergeant left, and now he's insisting that he's going to Montsalvat. He's barely eaten for two days, and I am sure that he hasn't slept. He looks awful. I don't know what's possessed him.'

'Never mind, Marian. I will see if I can make sense of it. I'll take care of him, I promise.'

Jack could have asked, 'Why are you talking about me as though I'm not here?' but to ask required energy, and he didn't care to exert himself. He didn't know why he wanted to go to Montsalvat himself. He just knew that he needed to get away from Copelen St. This wasn't where he and Sofia belonged. What he really needed was a driver's license. He'd buy himself a car. He wanted to go wherever he liked, whenever he wanted. The railway system had always served his and Sofia's needs, but in the last few weeks of driving around with Margaret, he'd fully appreciated the freedom a motor vehicle could provide. And today, he felt restless. He wanted to just go, and it annoyed him to feel beholden to Margaret.

On the drive, he sat silently, ignoring Margaret's questions, wishing he'd stayed with his original plan and caught the train.

'How did you sleep, Jack? Are you hungry…? We could get something at the bakery.'

The very thought of eating made him nauseous.

Worse were Margaret's comments regarding Sofia. 'Jack, she is just upset. She's not thinking straight. Perhaps you should go to Spain, look for her there. Talk to her. It's not safe at present, though. I can't even imagine how she would get to Malaga, what with the war and all.'

Jack's hands clenched in his lap.

A few minutes later, Margaret, evidently still not comfortable with his silence, tried a different tack. 'I had a letter from Ginny last week. Quite a surprise. Wonderful writer that she is, I hardly ever hear from her. Just Christmas cards, really. Her and Leonard are thinking of moving to Sussex to be closer to Ness. She is very worried about Ness. Ness has never recovered since Julian died… '

A silence filled the car and Jack guessed that Margaret's words had stalled when she'd realised that her news from England was far from uplifting. He recalled the awful tale of how Ness's son, a quiet young man he'd met in Sussex when he'd visited Charleston all those years earlier, had defied Ness and Clive's wishes and enlisted as an ambulance driver in the war against Franco, barely a year earlier. Seven weeks later, the ambulance he was driving had taken a hit and

Julian had been killed outright. The memories of the awful story aroused an overwhelming sense of bitterness in Jack. A sense of hopelessness in a world where terrible things happened for no reason. Where despite a person's best efforts to do the right thing, and be happy, fate could snatch it all away in a moment of time.

'Life is awful, Margaret. People die. Terrible things happen.' The words were out of Jack's mouth before he had time to think, and they chilled the air. He and Margaret completed the journey in silence.

# CHAPTER 6

The first sound to greet them as they stepped from the car was the wailing of babies, their shrill tones piercing the air, as if each was trying to outdo the other in volume.

Jack ignored the startled glance Margaret cast towards him. *She's worried that I will be upset,* he thought. But he wasn't. In fact, the cry of the newborns was one of the nicest sounds that he'd heard in weeks. Innocent, with no association to the terrible event that had occurred. He was just sad that Sofia and Scotty were not here to see them.

Walking towards the Great Hall, they could see Helen and Sonia sitting on the veranda, each bouncing a baby on her lap.

'Jack! Good to see you,' Sonia said, her face lighting with pleasure. 'How did you go finding Sofia? Is she okay?'

'No, Sonia. Sofia's gone back to Spain. I'd really prefer not to discuss it.'

'What! Is she—'

He cut Sonia's shocked response short. 'Oh, my, who have we here? You'd swear that they were twins.' Jack's delight at the tiny bundles, now hiccupping and shuddering their way into silence, surprised even him.

'They almost are, that is for sure! You wouldn't believe it. I went into labour at midday and then Sonia followed at three. There's only two hours between them!' said Helen, laughing at the astonishing coincidence.

'So, a boy and a girl?' Jack felt confident that the little blue and pink bonnets were a fair indication of each baby's gender.

'That's right—Saskia, she's mine and Sebastian, he's Helen's. Cute as buttons, aren't they? Especially when they are asleep!' Sonia was beaming, and her clear eyes and healthy glow reflected the extent to which motherhood suited her. Even Helen, although very thin, looked better than when Jack had seen her last, and he hoped the baby might bring her the fulfillment that her relationship with Justus had always seemed to lack.

'Hi, Margaret. Good to see you again. Grab a chair and you can have Seb.'

'What about you, Jack? Saskia would love to be held by her Uncle Jack!'

'So, when were they born? Tell me all about it.'

They chatted for a few minutes about the excitement of the consecutive deliveries, and how the whole atmosphere at Montsalvat had transformed since the arrival of the babies.

'It's quiet here today,' Jack said, looking around. 'Where is everybody?'

'Oh, most of them have gone down to San Remo. A painting weekend. Mum and Dad stayed back, but they've gone shopping. They'll be home soon. I think everyone is just trying to escape these two little screamers.' On cue, Sebastian squirmed in Margaret's arms and let out a roar.

Helen stood holding out her arms to take him from Margaret. 'Time to put this one to bed...'

'We might leave you to it,' Jack said. 'I'd like to look at the van.'

'Great to see you, Jack. You too, Margaret. Hopefully we'll catch up soon!' Sonia said, hugging Jack as he left.

'Don't worry, you will,' he replied.

~

The lightness of mood that he'd felt in the presence of little Saskia and Sebastian receded within the short distance of the walk to the van.

In a poor state when he'd last lived here, the van was now utterly derelict. Its screen door swung in the breeze, the catch broken; and when Jack tried to close it, he discovered the hinge had pulled from the frame. At once he was struck by the contrast to the past, when he and Sofia had first lived here; and he fought the lump in his chest that was expanding, threatening to obstruct his breathing. He needed to pull himself together. Sofia was gone. Just thinking about it pained him, and in a bid to control his emotions, he cast his mind to the practicalities before him.

An almighty mess greeted them as he opened the van's door. A tangle of sheets, towels and clothing was strewn across the floor. Cups, some bearing the dregs of half-drunk coffee or sour milk, and a long-rotted bowl of bananas contributed to an overwhelming stench that filled the air.

Wordlessly, Jack began throwing things outside, one by one.

'What are you doing?' Margaret asked.

'Cleaning.'

'Okay. Good idea. So, what are you thinking?'

'I'm moving back here.'

'No… Surely not!'

'Sure I am, Margaret. This is where I belong. I can't keep living at Mum and Dad's house, staring at the ceiling.'

'I just don't think it's healthy for you to be living here, Jack.'

'Well, where is healthy for me, Margaret? What would you have me do? Because I'm damned if I know!' Jack's mood transformed into bitter anger, and the snarl in his voice surprised even himself. 'I haven't read the guide that tells me what I am supposed to do when my son dies and my wife leaves me!'

'Jack, calm down. I didn't mean to upset you! I'm just worried, that's all.'

'Stop worrying. It's not helping anything. All I know is that we have spent weeks trying to find Sofia, to mend things with her, and now she's gone. I am out of answers… I am out of everything… but I know that I need to be here.'

For half an hour, he and Margaret worked in silence, emptying the van of every removable object, the vast majority of which was fit only for the rubbish dump. Margaret then headed for the kitchen, hoping that she might find some cleaning products, while Jack dragged the mattress into the sunshine, then crossed to the tank to fill a bucket with water. Already, he was feeling better. At least he'd found a purpose— to create a home for himself.

On his way back to the van, he heard the sound of a vehicle arriving on the gravelly surface of the carpark, followed by voices. They belonged to Lena, Mervyn, and Matcham.

'Jack, good to see you. How are you doing…?'

'Yes, well. You know.' The question was always impossible to answer, and Jack changed the subject. 'Congratulations to you both… the babies are lovely. Well done. And I suppose you are the uncle of the year, Matcham.'

Mervyn beamed, and Jack was pleased for him. The old rogue Justus may have taken control of Mervyn's family, but he could not take over his role as grandfather. Well, at least he couldn't take over Sonia's baby. With Justus the father of Helen's little Sebastian, Mervyn might find his role as grandfather challenging!

'Are you moving back?' Matcham asked, spying the bucket at Jack's feet. 'Is Sofia here? I have missed her…'

'No. Sofia is not here. She has returned to Spain.' He'd better get used to saying it, he thought, even though the words stuck in his throat.

'Spain?' Matcham replied, incredulous.

'Leave it, Matcham. That's Jack's private business,' Lena said.

'Yes, but…'

'Matcham, see if your sisters need some help. In fact, you can carry these down to them.' Lena loaded his arms with two bags of groceries.

'Jack, your belongings… you know, the boxes and bits and pieces you had packed from the cabin. They're stored on our back porch. No need to rush, they're not in the way, but there might be something amongst them that you need.'

'Thanks, Lena. I'll pop over in a while and have a look.'

'It's good to have you back, Jack,' Mervyn said. 'Let us know if there is anything we can do.'

'Yeah, mate. Thanks. I'd better get back to the van. The place is in a mess, but it shouldn't take long to sort out. I'll see you up at the house when I have finished.'

~

An hour later Margaret stood back and assessed their morning's work.

'It's looking good, Jack. Almost fit for human occupation now that the rats' nests and cobwebs are gone.'

'Yes… and thanks, Margaret. Thanks for helping me today.' He hoped his show of appreciation would compensate for this morning's unkind behaviour.

The van was undeniably shabby, barely resembling the cosy home that he and Sofia had shared here when they'd first moved out to Montsalvat. There were splits in the bench-seat cushions and the linoleum floor had lifted in several places. Yet overall, it looked clean and smelled fresh, thanks to the last hour, when every surface had been scrubbed with first bleach and then Bon Ami.

'So, you are staying here tonight? You are not coming back to Copelen Street with me?'

'No, Margaret. I need to be here…' Jack knew that she doubted his choice, but appreciated that she didn't argue with him. 'Would you mind letting Mum and Dad know for me? They'll be upset, but I can't help that. Tell them I will call on them later this week.'

'No worries, Jack. Your mum will probably murder me, but that's okay. I will deal with it. I'll pop in on my way through and let them know. How about we head over to the Skippers' before I leave? You can get some clean blankets and things for tonight. We can load the car with anything you might need.'

Lena must have heard them coming, for she had cups out and a pot of tea brewing by the time he and Margaret stepped onto the porch.

'Margaret, good to see you,' she said. Jack left them in the kitchen, for he could see Mervyn on the veranda, cooing to the chortling baby on his lap, while Sonia sat beside him, watching.

'He's a natural.' Sonia rolled her eyes at Jack, although the affectionate twinkle in her smile revealed her pleasure in seeing

Mervyn enjoy his granddaughter. Jack fought down the memories of how proud his own father had been when he'd first held Scotty in his arms.

'Saskia here, she is just like her grandma—loves to be up and chatting with visitors at every opportunity. Sebastian, he'd sleep all day if he could. Lucky Helen. She'll get two hours' rest now. I'm lucky to get a five-minute lie down before this little one is squawking and demanding to be up and about.'

Jack smiled, suddenly feeling calmer than he had in weeks. Yes, moving back to Montsalvat, living amongst his friends was definitely the best thing for him.

Lena and Margaret joined them, settling the tray of cups, the teapot and a plate of oatmeal biscuits on the table; and for the next half hour they chattered about Montsalvat's vegetable garden, the completion of the Great Hall's kitchen, and the latest group of students that Justus had enticed from his city lessons to join them on weekends.

'Okay,' Jack said, emptying his teacup and rising. 'I suppose we'd better clear your house of my rubbish. You'll need every bit of space you can get, now that you've got the grandchildren.'

'No hurry, Jack. Just grab what you need for now. The babies won't be running too far for a while yet,' Lena said as she led the way through to the back porch, where a dozen boxes and assorted suitcases were stacked—the goods and chattels of his, Sofia's and Scotty's life together. The large box held Scotty's toys—he'd packed it himself. And the red suitcase—it held Sofia's belongings, her face cleansers and the special soap she loved, the gaberdine trousers and flannel shirts she'd worn in the garden and the soft blue polka-dotted dress that she liked to wear on her trips into Melbourne. Her shoes... oh, those remarkable embroidered slippers that they had finally managed to laugh about; they would be tucked away in there, too, he knew.

'This looks like a box of kitchen items, Jack. I'll take them to the car?'

Jack nodded. 'These are my clothes.' He grasped the handle of a large brown suitcase, and as he lifted it clear, a tea chest was exposed. The chest that held all of Sofia's treasures from her life in Malaga: paintings created by her father and brother, along with her father's collection of Sorollas, Picassos and Matisses. Jack had been so pleased when he'd saved it from the fire, imagining her devastation had it been destroyed.

Again, the vision of Sofia pounding on the chest's frame, her blows so hard that the plywood had almost split, erupted before him. Her accusing eyes … as she'd shrieked at him. *'What, Jack? You saved the paintings, but not Scotty!'*

'Margaret—take it… get it away from here…' Jack held his arms up before him, as though shielding himself from the chest. His voice cracked as he backed away; then turning, he ran through the house and across the driveway to the safety of the van.

By the time Margaret left him, it was five o'clock and Jack was glad for the silence inside the van. Lying on the bed, he looked at the discoloured patches that formed cloud-like shapes on the van's ceiling, glad for the thoughtless distraction they provided as his eyes drifted over their meandering lines.

It was good to be alone. It had been a big day, and he was exhausted. With a bit of luck, he'd sleep for an hour and then he'd go over to the dining room and join the Skippers. Routine. That was what he needed. No more searching for Sofia. No more wallowing. He'd get back to work as soon as he could organise it. He liked it here at Montsalvat. He always had. The bush, with its swaying gumtrees, the whistling of birds, and the fragrance of eucalyptus offered peacefulness. He had friends here—the Skippers and Justus and Lil. The students would be up on the weekend. Their noisy banter and enthusiasm for the building projects would help take his mind off things. He would work alongside Matcham, the way they used to. Before… well… just before. Matcham's company would be excellent medicine for him.

A loud knocking startled Jack into alertness, and he was not sure where he was. Grey light filtering through a small window revealed shadowy outlines. The odour of bleach filled his nostrils, and it came back to him. Of course—he was in the caravan at Montsalvat—he must have fallen asleep.

'Coming…' He opened the door.

Lil's silhouette was barely visible in the deepening twilight, her hands full. 'Sorry to startle you, Jack. I just thought I would check that you're okay. It's good to have you back. The Skippers said that you were here. They'd thought that you might come over for dinner. I've brought you some soup and a bit of lamb casserole. Would you like it?'

'Thanks, Lil. That would be great. I thought that you had gone to San Remo?'

Jack wondered how long it would take for the sound of his voice to feel normal again rather than like an echo in his ears—disconnected, as though someone else was speaking.

'Not today, Jack. Today was a day in bed for me. Quite pleasant to have a few hours to oneself, really. I am sorry that I never heard you earlier. I would have come over to help.'

'Not necessary, Lil. Margaret was here, and she was like a whirlwind. There was barely room for me in here. Would you like to come in?'

He stood aside and Lil squeezed past him through the narrow doorway. It felt strange, her being in the confines of the small van. He could not remember a time when Lil had ever been inside here before.

'You have been busy—that bleach is strong. I can barely breathe! I don't know how you can stand it,' she said.

'Yes, it is strong, isn't it? I thought I must have slept heavy, but perhaps I was unconscious.'

'You have to wonder how good it is for you,' Lil said. 'I don't like chemicals much. Perhaps you should open up some windows.'

That was what Margaret had suggested. He opened them now and reached for the candle he'd set up, ready for nightfall. Its flickering light turned their forms into gigantic shadows dancing across the walls.

'Do you mind if I sit for a minute, Jack?'

'Not at all. I'd make you a cup of tea, but I haven't found my teapot yet. I guess it's buried in one of the boxes up at the Skippers.'

'Don't worry about that—I've drunk enough tea today to float the *Titanic*. I swear that I would spring a leak if you stuck a pin into me. You eat your dinner while it's still warm.'

'I will. Thanks, Lil.'

'So. Have you been able to find Sofia?'

Lil's question shattered the companionable atmosphere. He felt her eyes boring into him and knew that despite the dim light of the van, he was being subjected to the scrutiny of her psychologist's gaze.

'She's gone… back to Spain.'

'Spain!'

'Yes, Lil, Spain! I had a telegram from her. She could not forgive me for Scotty's death, and so she's gone. Now I just need to accept that, and get myself together, somehow.'

'Oh, Jack, no! It seems very odd that she would go back to Spain, but then she was in a terrible state after the accident. I don't think I have ever seen anyone in such a deep state of grief before. I am so very sorry, Jack. '

'Well, thank you, but being sorry is not helpful. I've had enough sympathy, and now I need to get on with my life. There's nothing more for it, really. So, Lil—that's how it is. Tomorrow I will go into Goldsbrough, Mort & Co, and arrange to get back to work. Get some routine into my life. All of this sitting around has been dreadful.'

'Are you sure? It seems very soon, after all that you've been through.'

'Yes, I'm sure.'

'Okay. You know best, I suppose. Just let me know if we can do anything…'

'How're the lessons in Queen Street going? Justus still inspiring the masses?' Jack tried not to feel rude as he changed the subject.

# CHAPTER 7

*I*t was Saturday morning. Sitting outside his van, as had become his habit on the weekends, Jack inhaled the sweetness of the morning air. Already, the bees were at work on the eucalyptus tree beside him, harvesting pollen from its wispy cream coloured flowers. It was comforting sitting in the morning sunshine, listening to the sounds drifting across from the kitchen. The murmur of female voices. The deeper tones of Justus; he always rose early and cooked his own bacon and eggs. Jack had once enjoyed joining Justus at this early hour, sharing a quiet chat and a cup of coffee before the work day began. He could hear the intermittent cries of the infants and smiled, picturing a mother—probably Sonia, for she seemed to be the one who undertook the early morning care of the babies—coaxing cereal into firmly closed mouths, their tiny heads stubbornly turning away from the spoons loaded with the grey gruel that she'd be offering them. Yuk. He wouldn't eat it either, he thought.

The squeaking brakes of a vehicle, followed by doors slamming, laughter and crunching gravel, drifted from the carpark. Justus' students arriving, as excited as he and Sofia had once been when they'd first starting coming here, back in the early days of building the retreat. Jack knew that today they planned to complete the stonework around the entry of the Great Hall, which was already looking a picture. Certainly, the building had lived up to its role as the jewel in the crown of Montsalvat, with its picturesque balcony, leadlight windows and its oversized front door with its iron bolts that looked like something out of a mediaeval fantasy.

Jack wondered if Matcham would come across for a chat. He often did. He'd probably want Jack to join everyone at the building site. Perhaps today, he might. He really should make more effort; but then again, there would be more of Justus' new students coming, and they were always so exhausting. Interested in everything, eager for him to answer their questions about his life here at Montsalvat—his art, the construction of the buildings, and the circumstances of when he first committed to living on the site. It would be easier for Jack to just stay where he was, out of the way of them all.

A magpie settled beside his outstretched legs. Watching Jack, the bird's head tilted from side to side as if assessing his mood. Jack flicked a piece of dried crust from the loaf beside him, and the bird's beak snapped as he leapt for it.

In honesty, Jack preferred weekdays to weekends. Then he had a clear routine. Wake up, splash his face in the cold water in his wash basin, get dressed and walk to the train station. After boarding the train, he'd close his eyes, lose himself to the rhythmic rocking of the carriage, enjoying the minutes of oblivion as it rolled along the tracks into the city. Jack found that feigning sleep was best, a good way to avoid the morning greetings from the fellowship of workers who shared the daily commute.

It had been three months since he'd returned to work, and he'd survived the initial awkwardness where neither he nor his workmates knew what to say. 'Sorry,' was perhaps the easiest conversation to deal with. Just the single word. Then he could nod in acknowledgement, and they could move on to talk about wool prices or account discrepancies.

It was the ones who wanted to say more that wore him down. Especially the women in the secretarial pool. He could always feel it coming. 'Oh, Jack…. It is so awful…. That poor little baby… I can't imagine how you are feeling...' How was he supposed to answer?

Some were at it for weeks. 'Jack, are you eating? Can I do anything for you? Have you heard from Sofia?' He knew that they meant well, but, their overtures of kindness were misguided. He came to work to escape his private life, not to expose his inner feelings. He'd discovered that by pasting a smile on his face and speaking first, bidding them good morning and asking if they had any messages for him, he had a better chance of deflecting comments of a personal nature. All day he was on guard—approaching every encounter with his workmates with caution. The last thing he needed was a probing comment at the wrong minute of the day, a "Poor Jack" coinciding at a time when all that was terribly wrong with his life bristled at the foremost of his thoughts, making his hands tremble, his eyes well and his throat close. A kindly enquiry at such a moment could bring his fragile façade crashing down.

At the end of each day, after the return train journey, he'd continued the long-held habit of the artists, dropping in at the Eltham pub for a couple of pints before dinner, and then walking back to Montsalvat. Sometimes he'd share dinner in the dining room with Lil and the Skippers, Arthur and anyone else who was staying at the retreat, but more frequently lately, he ate here at the van. It was easier. On Friday nights he'd stay at the pub for dinner, then pick up a carton of beer, and with the clinking bottles balanced on his shoulder, he'd make his way up the hill in the dark. A little weekend cheer.

The crunch of footsteps on gravel nearby caught his attention.

'Margaret! I didn't hear your car. Good to see you!'

'Hi to you, Jack. How are you?' Her eyes, from which nothing ever escaped, glanced around, and he knew she'd seen the pile of brown bottles heaped against the stringy-bark tree nearest the van. She'd be noticing the table that had tilted over, its contents—his washbasin and shaving gear—now strewn across the ground. A storm a few days earlier had created havoc around the van. Or perhaps it was last weekend. Jack couldn't remember. He'd get to tidying it when he had a minute.

Margaret had visited him each weekend when he first moved into the van. She'd coax him to go with her for a drive, or, when he resisted, she'd sit with him in the sun. Margaret talked too much… always full of advice. Lately her visits had ended in arguments. Well, perhaps not arguments. Just her leaving abruptly, irritated with him, frustrated by his inactivity. She didn't like seeing him at Montsalvat. She thought he was drinking too much and wasn't painting enough. In return, he'd get annoyed with her for bossing him. 'I'm fine,' he'd say. 'You worry too much. Leave me alone.'

That was it. He just wanted to be left alone. Today, he could see from the way Margaret stood, her body purposeful—her eyes shrewd —that she had a plan in mind, and she would not take no for an answer.

~

'Get dressed. We need to go to Melbourne.'

Here she goes, he thought. Going to Melbourne! He'd just spent a week travelling back and forth to Melbourne each day for work. Why on earth would he want to go to Melbourne now?

'I am dressed,' he replied.

'No, Jack. That's the suit you wore to work yesterday... you must have slept in it. Come on. I'll help you find something.'

It wasn't the first time that Jack had fallen asleep in his work clothes, and he didn't resist when she stepped around him and clambered into the caravan. He smiled to himself. *Won't she have something to say when she sees the mess in there?* he thought, waiting for a barrage of criticism to come hurtling through the van's open door.

To her credit, Margaret said nothing, and he listened to the sounds of her moving things about inside the van.

'So, these are the clean clothes?' she called out. He guessed she'd found the wash basket that Lena delivered to him every week—freshly washed shirts and work pants, his singlets and socks neatly folded on top. The arrangement had started with barely a conversation weeks earlier, and it suited Jack well: Lena slipping into his van to do a quick scan for his dirty laundry while he was at work, removing the soiled garments, returning them clean.

The only words ever spoken had been Lena's. 'Did you get your washing, Jack?' To which he'd replied, 'Yes, thank you, Lena.' She'd followed with, 'I'll pop over in a few days and collect your soiled clothing.' And she had. Good old Lena. That's what Jack liked about living here at Montsalvat. They left you in peace.

He followed Margaret's voice, heading into the van.

'Jack, put these on; we need to get moving.' She waved towards the clean underwear, a shirt and a pair of trousers that she'd laid out on the table.

'What's the hurry, Margaret? Where are you taking me?'

'There's a meeting. I think you might like it.'

Jack smiled yet again. It was a funny habit that he'd grown into, this smile that came from nowhere. It was as though deep within himself he was watching the outside world, the people in it, and found them amusing. Sometimes he amused himself. This time his smile was for Margaret; for her choice of words. A month ago, she'd have said, 'You need to get out, Jack. It would be good for you.' The type of phrase that raised his hackles—people telling him what was good for him. Margaret was doing better, he decided; and because of this, he felt inclined to humour her.

It took all of twenty minutes for him to change his clothes, splash icy water from the steel bucket onto his face and run a comb through his hair.

'You're off, Jack,' Mervyn commented as they passed him on their way to the carpark. Margaret answered for him.

'Yes, Mervyn. We are going to the meeting at CAS. You've heard of them? They're planning an exhibition.'

'Oh, good on you,' Mervyn replied. 'They are doing a good job, for sure—sticking it to Menzies.'

'Where on earth are you taking me?' Jack asked, as he settled into her little beauty, a flicker of curiosity stirring. Sticking it to the prime minister? What sort of rebellion was Margaret leading him into?

'The Contemporary Art Society's meeting, Jack. They seem to be an interesting mob. Another bunch of artists who are fed up with the National Gallery School's single-mindedness. And now, with Menzies on their side, sticking his bib into art policy, declaring that he wants to create an *Australian Academy of Art*.' Margaret tweaked her forefingers to emphasise the title, 'to preserve and protect traditional art and therefore, obviously, the status of traditional artists! What on earth will happen to modern artists? Who's representing them? Well, a group has decided to fight back. I was down at the Wattle Tea Rooms on Tuesday and met a lady, Cynthia, who was talking about it. When she noticed that I was listening, she gave me this… Apparently *The Herald* is sponsoring an exhibition of modern artworks, to be brought from Europe next year. It sounds really interesting.' Reaching into her bag, Margaret recovered a pamphlet and handed it to him.

Jack glanced at the crumpled pamphlet, titled, *To Art Lovers*. Just what Margaret would like. She was an art lover, there was no doubt. Was he? He'd been good at painting once, though he couldn't be bothered anymore. Certainly, he'd once loved the lifestyle of an artist. The life that he and Sofia and Andrés had shared in Malaga had been wonderful. And here at Montsalvat, beyond the building projects, he'd enjoyed Justus' demonstrations of the tonalist techniques beneath the gum trees on a Saturday afternoon. But was he interested in all the arguments about art anymore? The endless debates about the role of critics and the freedom of artists, of traditionalism versus new techniques, the vying for recognition of women and modernists? Really, did any of it matter? Not to him. Not today.

His head ached, and he leaned back, half-listening to Margaret while scanning the sidewalks, willing Sofia to appear. Perhaps he'd find her walking along Upper Plenty Road, a basket on her arm holding fresh bread and vegetables. Maybe she'd been living just streets away all this while. There was a line-up of people at a bus stop and he examined their faces. He shook himself. It had become a habit— perhaps even an obsession—this looking for Sofia. He couldn't help it. Even though he knew that she was on a ship to Spain—there by now, he supposed—this searching among commuters, peering into the backyards of houses on his daily train journey, looking through the open doorways of shops, never ceased.

The drive took barely thirty minutes and before he knew it, Margaret was settling her vehicle into a park in a narrow back lane and leading Jack to a second-floor office in Collins Street. Already, fifteen or more people, male and female, were gathered around a long table, while a few others sat around the periphery of the room. He and

Margaret quietly settled into the nearest vacant seats. Looking around, Jack did not recognise any faces.

~

The meeting was being run on formal terms, like one of the monthly meetings he used to attend at Goldsbrough, Mort & Co. A man stood at the front, clearing his throat, preparing to address the group.

'Let's get underway.' His voice was by nature soft, and he forced volume into his opening sentence to gain attention. He glanced across to Jack and Margaret, and then scanned those seated along the periphery of the room, before speaking.

'I'd like to begin by welcoming our visitors here today. I'm John Reed, secretary of our group—The Contemporary Art Society. Thank you for joining us... It is wonderful to know that so many people share our interest in the advancement of modern art in Australia.'

Returning his attention to those sitting at the table, Reed distributed a document for their perusal. For a minute or two he referred to various pages, paragraphs and sentences. It was a constitution of sorts; and from Reed's comments, Jack deduced that he had tabled a draft version at a previous meeting where they'd wrangled over the intricacies of the legal jargon framing its terms. Today, the re-tabled document was unanimously accepted, and *The Constitution for the Contemporary Art Society* was officially instated. To Jack, it felt like a momentous event where applause might be in order, but nobody clapped.

Reed then introduced a Mr Peter Bellew, who stood and spoke about the key agenda item—the art exhibition Margaret had mentioned that morning. Bellew was a young man, barely twenty, Jack guessed— and at possibly half the age of John Reed—appeared to have twice the older man's confidence and three times his volume. In Jack's opinion he was full of self-importance, reinforced as with a flourish the young man turned to those sitting along the edges of the room—including himself and Margaret—advising them that he was a reporter at the *Herald*, then describing Murdoch's plans to bring a series of important paintings from Europe. After being shown in Adelaide, the works would be transported to Melbourne, and then Sydney and perhaps even

Brisbane. The *Herald* hoped to acquire Van Goghs, Cezannes, Seurats, Picassos, Matisses and Gauguins for the display. It would be an extraordinary collection of paintings, the likes of which Australians had never seen. Bellew continued, using tones as though he were speaking to small children, that whilst Murdoch was sponsoring the exhibition, and the Herald's arts reporter Basil Burdett, was the key organiser, presently on a tour of London and Paris to search out paintings for the exhibition, the *Herald*—aka himself—was thankful for the Contemporary Art Society's agreement to assist in the planning for the event. Bellows then returned his attention to those seated at the table, and suggested that it was time they agreed on a working title of the exhibition, so that promotional activities could begin.

For the next forty minutes, considerable toing and froing took place. The CAS members firstly agreed the title should include a reference to London and Paris, ensuring that Australians realised modern artworks were not a mere local fad, but highly esteemed in the leading art centres of the world. A quietly spoken man introduced as George Bell—the president of the CAS—suggested that they'd do well to consider substituting the word 'Modern' with 'Contemporary' in the exhibition's title. He felt that while 'modernism' may be celebrated in Paris and London, in Australia it was viewed as 'the product of degenerates and perverts' as cited by the National Gallery's director himself. The director's description seemed to echo Jack's own shocked reaction to Salvador Dali when he'd seen his work in the Musee du Luxembourg, eight years earlier, and suddenly he felt like an imposter; the one person in the room who didn't wholeheartedly support the works of modern artists.

'Yes,' Bellew agreed with the CAS president. 'And moreover, last week Menzies was linking modern art to communism! Can you believe that even the prime minister would stoop to using politics to prejudice the public against anything with a whiff of "modernism".'

Jack nodded his agreement when Bellew added that since they were, in fact, the Contemporary Art Society, using the word 'contemporary' in the exhibition's title would strengthen the credibility of CAS.

Still on the subject of the exhibition's title, Bellew gathered steam, his confidence further increased by the success of his previous suggestions. 'I think it goes without saying that we include the word *'Herald'* in the title. After all, Keith *is* sponsoring the exhibition.' Jack couldn't help but smile. Anyone would think Bellew knew the owner of the newspaper—and one of Australia's richest men—personally. 'It's a real boon for us to have him onside. The possibilities are enormous, not only because Keith is influential, but also because it gives us tremendous opportunities for advertising as well as for controlling the reviews that are published.'

Jack nodded again. All Australians knew of the remarkable power Murdoch single-handedly wielded as publisher of Australia's largest newspaper group—a vehicle that was perfect for shaping and influencing attitudes towards contemporary art, or anything else that he chose. It made good sense to exploit Murdoch's endorsement of the exhibition.

And so, the vote on the title was unanimous: *'The Herald Exhibition of Contemporary Art of London and Paris'*. Quite a mouthful, but every word carried a weight that would surely further Australians' opportunity to appreciate modern art.

After confirming that despite the National Gallery flatly refusing to house the exhibition, Reed revealed that Melbourne's Lower Town Hall was available for them in October, and the opening date was set for the sixteenth. Finally, the meeting was over.

Within seconds, a woman with short-cropped hair appeared beside Jack and Margaret, accompanied by John Reed. She smiled broadly, greeted Margaret with enthusiasm, and turning, introduced herself to him as Cynthia Reed. Jack rightfully guessed that she was the woman whom Margaret had met the previous week—the one who'd given Margaret the pamphlet and invited her to this meeting.

'John, this is Margaret. Remember, I told you about her. She is very interested in what we are doing here. What did you think of our meeting, Margaret!'

'It certainly was interesting! Usually, the only artists that I talk to are the self-opinionated bores promoting their views at the pub. It's wonderful to meet a group that is actually doing something constructive. The exhibition sounds fabulous!' Margaret turned to

John. 'Let us know if we can do anything to help—you know, sell tickets at the door, anything. We would love to assist, wouldn't we, Jack?'

Jack smiled and nodded. Of course, what else could he do?

'Thank you. Margaret, is it? I will remember that. There'll be plenty to do as the date gets closer. Twelve months will go fast, I am sure. At present it is all discussions about packaging, transport and insurances. It's quite an ordeal to bring almost three hundred of the world's most famous paintings across the globe.'

Cynthia interrupted. 'I am glad that you came, Margaret and you too, Jack. I am sorry to be rude, but I have to dash, so I will leave you to it. Margaret, do tell John about your cousins! He will be fascinated.'

Reed laughed. 'Okay, off you go… catch up soon, love.' He then turned to them. 'So, you are both artists?'

'Jack is. He studied and exhibited in Paris, met Picasso and all.'

John turned to Jack with interest. 'So, you studied in Paris! Good for you. It sounds like the most wonderful of places. My wife, Sunday, has been there, but unfortunately I haven't yet made the trip. And you, Margaret? Did you also study in Paris? Are you an artist, too?'

'Oh, well. I paint, and yes, I did do a brief stint of lessons in Montparnasse. Unlike Jack, I'm not up to exhibition standard, but it's in my genes, you could say. Ness Bell's my cousin, and… well, she and her husband, Clive, they introduced me to painting when I was a child.'

'You are related to Ness and Clive Bell? Of Bloomsbury fame? Such connections! So that would make Virginia Woolf your cousin. My wife—both of us—are huge fans of the Bloomsburys. We love Virginia's writing. Wait till I tell Sunday that you were here today. She would love to meet you both. Could I entice you out to Heide? Perhaps sometime soon?'

Jack immediately observed the transformation in John. Though he'd been charming and polite in his preliminary greetings, his eyes had taken on the glint of a zealot when Margaret mentioned her family connections in England. As always, it surprised Jack to discover that the Bloomsburys' influence was so far-reaching.

'Why, thank you. We'd love to,' Margaret replied. 'You just say when, John, and we'll be there, won't we, Jack?'

Jack nodded, uncertainly. As often had been the case since he'd known her, Margaret's actions gained the momentum of a tidal wave, with him being swept along.

'Let's say next Saturday, then. Sunday will do us some lunch. She'll be thrilled when I tell her you're coming!'

# CHAPTER 8

The following Saturday, Jack's first conscious thought was of chilling moisture seeping through his body. Voices above him filtered through a foggy void, the sound contributing to a throbbing pain across his forehead. His effort to move incited a flurry of chatter.

'He's waking!'

'Are you alright, Jack?'

'Jack, sit up. You can't stay here. It's about to rain!'

Then came Lil's voice. 'Good Lord! He must have been here since yesterday. He came home from work on Thursday in a terrible state. Well, not directly from work, exactly. He'd had a few pints at the Eltham. We heard him come in. Could hear him from the dining room making a terrible ruckus. Mervyn and Matcham came over to see what was happening, but he just roared at them. They couldn't do a thing for him.'

'Yes, he lunged at us whenever we got close. We got him inside the van once, but he just came straight out again.' That was Matcham.

'And then, all day yesterday, he sat here in his chair. Quiet enough; subdued by the alcohol, I imagine. Sonia encouraged him to get changed—his clothes were soaking—and she brought some lunch across, and later some dinner. But from the looks of this, he hasn't eaten anything.' Jack pictured them looking at the enamel plate of cold mashed potato, beans and lamb chops he'd left sitting on the bench. He'd felt too ill to eat.

'What's that he's been drinking?' Margaret! Jack sensed movement close beside him and listened to the tinkle of glass fragments being dropped on the table. 'Whiskey! An entire bottle! Plus all of that beer. What was he thinking?'

'Yes... It doesn't seem right. When Justus got home last night, we coaxed him into the van... We knew that the rain was coming and we didn't want him outside for a second night, poor fellow. It's just awful, all that he's been through.'

Justus' voice chimed into the conversation, surprising Jack, who hadn't realised the Master was also there. 'Somehow he's got himself outside again. This is where we found him not five minutes ago.'

Jack squirmed, clarity increasing as the conversation filtered through. He felt uncomfortable, knowing that there was a crowd gathered above gazing down upon him.

Lil spoke—or was it Lena?

'This isn't right. Something must have happened on Thursday to set this off.'

Thursday! Something happened? Something happened alright. Jack had seen Sofia. Sofia and Scotty!

As always, the day in the office had been long. By two o'clock the rows of figures on the ledger had swirled before his eyes, making no sense at all. At five o'clock he'd been glad to leave, and on his way to the station a lady in the distance caught his attention. Small. Her dark hair was caught in a pony tail. Her dress was the blue polka-dot pattern that Sofia wore so often. Jack raced forward, excitement surging through him. It was hard to refrain from calling out. Before he'd covered the distance, a second woman arrived. A lady with a small child beside her. A little boy! The two women had embraced before transferring the child, and then the second lady departed.

Jack was amazed. Sofia and Scotty! Scotty alive! How this could be? But at that minute he hadn't cared. With his heart singing with joy, he'd closed the gap between them and reached out to touch her. 'Sofia! I have been looking everywhere for you!'

But it hadn't been Sofia. Nor was it Scotty. Lookalikes. There to taunt him. Shocked, he'd stood with his heart leaping in his chest, about to burst; a sob rising in his throat. He'd watched the mother pull her child close before turning and hurrying away.

'Are you alright, mate?' a man had asked, stepping around him.

Jack could barely remember the walk down the ramp to his train, or the journey home. He did recall stopping at the Eltham for a pint.

But he hadn't stopped at one pint. There had been a second and then a third. The regulars—Tom the plumber and Cecil, who was a mechanic—attempted conversation, but he'd been in no mood to answer them.

And then it was six o'clock. He had asked for a bottle of Johnny Walker.

'Are you sure, Jack?' the barman had asked. 'I'd say that you might have hit your limit today, wouldn't you agree?'

'It's for tomorrow,' Jack had assured him.

But that night, after drinking the dozen beers he'd had stored in the van, he had opened the whisky, swallowing glass after glass. Finally, he'd managed to obliterate the cruel vision of Sofia and Scotty—the false joy that had filled his heart for those few moments.

Jack had dim memories of the previous evening—the yelling and thrashing, stumbling around in the dark, Justus and Matcham trying to restrain him. He groaned, prompting further comments from above.

'He's opening his eyes.' The unmistakable deep tones were Mervyn's. When had he arrived? Jack wondered. Were all of Montsalvat's residents gathered around him?

'Come on, mate. Up with you now. Let's get you sorted.' Matcham, again.

The kindness in their voices was like salt to a wound, and Jack couldn't control the tears coursing down his cheeks. He didn't deserve their kindness. He'd lost his baby and his wife, and now he wanted to lose himself.

'Margaret, I doubt he will be going anywhere today, love.' That voice was Lena's. 'You go on. We'll look after him. Don't you worry.'

'But I hate leaving him like this!'

'It's alright. There is nothing to do but get him cleaned up and let him sleep it off. It's not the first time. He'll be okay. Matcham, go into the van and get rid of any beer. Make sure there is no more whiskey. I'd say our Jack has had enough drink for today.'

The van barely had room for two adults, and its small space was occupied first by Matcham, who, taking his detective duties seriously, opened every cupboard door in his search for liquor. When he emerged, Lena took his place, deftly filling her wash basket with dirty laundry and straightening the bed. When she retreated, Justus and Matcham helped Jack to stand, and half-pushing, half-pulling, they guided him through the narrow doorway and onto his bed. He lay still, listening as the van fell into silence and the voices outside faded into the distance.

While preferring the fresh atmosphere of the outdoors to the dank, cloying, mildewy confines of the van, Jack was thankful for the softness of the mattress and the pillow beneath his head.

'Jack?' It was Margaret speaking, and Jack didn't know what to say.

'I am worried about you, Jack.'

Jack ignored this, too. He could hardly defend himself and say that he was fine, could he?

'We need a better plan for you. This can't go on.'

Jack listened, his eyes tightly closed, not moving a muscle. *No*, he thought. *This can't go on.* Life—his life—was not worth living. But what could he do? Time heals, Lil had said to him. And yes, he couldn't deny, there were more moments of lucidity in his days. On balance, now, almost five months after the accident; perhaps eighty percent of the time, to all appearances, he was functioning. He could undertake tasks with sufficient aptitude to convince others he was coping.

Daily, he forced himself to rise from his bed, to put on the smile that was his mask; to adopt a polite, if not cheerful, voice, to provide appropriate responses to greetings, requests and instructions. But these actions were a façade adopted for the benefit of others. At night, visions haunted him—searing flames, billowing smoke, scorching eyes —blazed at him. And then there were the eyes—accusing and full of hate toward him. Jack hated himself.

Margaret's voice interrupted his torment. 'Jack, you need to rest. I'll go now, but I'll come back tomorrow.'

He sensed her pausing, the movement of her hand near his. He reached out, and clutched, gripping it tightly, as though it were a lifeline.

'Margaret!' Had he spoken? Warm tears trickled down his face and he felt them pooling against the pillow. Opening his eyes, he saw Margaret scrubbing her own face with the back of her hand.

'Oh, Jack! We will get you through this. You rest—I'll sit here for a bit longer.'

He nodded and closed his eyes, glad for the warmth of her hand in his as he retreated into the abyss that sleep offered.

When he woke late that afternoon, Jack felt embarrassed and tried to make amends by cleaning his van until it was spotless, and then taking a long shower. When Sonia offered to trim his hair, he accepted.

Evaluating his life, Jack resolved that the mid-week drinking needed to stop. From now on, he would join the Skippers and Jorgensens for dinner, just like he'd done in those first few weeks of his return to Montsalvat. Before he'd decided the evening gatherings were too difficult and avoided them by eating alone in the caravan, or at the pub.

He'd get more involved with the building projects, too. Do some carving with Sonia. She had less time for her stonework now that she had Saskia, and would be glad of some help. Fresh air, sunshine and physical work would do him good. He'd stop wallowing in despair. The third thing Jack planned was to visit his parents more frequently. He knew they worried about him. William called in to Jack's office twice a week and they'd eat lunch together, chatting about their work at Goldsbrough, Mort & Co, but he hadn't seen his mother for weeks.

He found the sadness in her eyes hard to bear; she too was heartbroken by the loss of Scotty, and though they'd never say it, he suspected that his parents blamed all that had happened on his and Sofia's choice to live at Montsalvat. As though they'd made an irresponsible decision and were now reaping the consequences.

The other thing Jack planned to do was to write a letter to Sofia. Not one of the rambling drunken letters that he'd started more than once, but a serious letter. Certainly, there were things between them that needed to be worked out. Her belongings, for one thing—not just her clothing, but there was also the issue of the tea chest, which was now in Margaret's care. He assumed that Sofia would make her way to Malaga, and so he'd write to Father Sebastian. He wondered why he hadn't thought to do it earlier. Of all the people in Sofia's life, she would surely turn to him. The priest had cared deeply for Sofia and been very suspicious of Jack's motives when he'd arrived at the finca with the twins eight years earlier. Jack would tell him how happy he and Sofia had been, assure Father Sebastian that he loved her, that he'd done his best to care for her. That he'd never meant to cause her this terrible pain.

~

'Just Jack! You are back,' Margaret said the following morning, grinning at him, using the nickname she'd given him on their very first meeting years earlier.

Together, they sat in the sun, making small talk. He felt embarrassed by yesterday and apologised for the state he had been in when she'd arrived to take him to Heide, but she waved his words away. He appreciated Margaret's capacity to mend things. She was never one to harp, but rather, she sought solutions. Made the best of things. He knew she'd have no more wish to revisit yesterday's nightmare than he.

'You should see Heide, Jack, it's beautiful! Like a paradise, really. And Sunday Reed! She's the most extraordinary woman I have ever met. Quite a stunner, too. Just like Cynthia—remember her? You met her at the CAS meeting. Sunday and Cynthia are sisters-in-law, though

81

with their willowy limbs and stylish haircuts, you could think they were sisters. Too thin, if you ask me, but that half-starved look is all the rage in Europe, and now it's trickling over here. Sunday's taste in clothes is exquisite—so very chic... I felt positively drab in her presence.'

Thinking for a minute, Jack realised that Margaret was referring to her visit to John Reed's house yesterday–to Heide. He was supposed to have gone with her.

He felt contrite, but Margaret was not seeking to make him feel guilty. 'You would love everything about the place... it's just your thing.'

'How so?'

'They are all about art there, too. Like here.' Margaret looked around dubiously—Montsalvat's rustic charm had never appealed to her. 'Perhaps not exactly like here, but Justus and the Reeds share the same objectives. They want to create environments that nurture artists. John and Sunday are very wealthy. I did a bit of asking around. And as it turns out, Sunday is a Baillieu—they are one of Melbourne's richest families. Perhaps even the richest! Her family home is not far from your parents, but, with all due respect, Jack, it makes your parents' home look like a shack. Sunday is their only daughter, and as you can imagine, she's been spoiled rotten. She comes from just the sort of people I usually hate. Like those rich young socialites we saw in London, running around like they owned the world. But here is the irony: not only are Sunday and John wealthy, but they are mad about art—live and breathe it—and what's more, it's where they put their money. And not the usual fuddy-duddy traditional works that rich people like to show off. Sunday and John are interested in new works. Unknown artists. Modern art.'

'Contemporary, you mean,' Jack added.

'That's right, contemporary. They are dedicated to developing a style of art that is uniquely Australian. One that will be identifiable and valued the world over. You should see their collection! They also support a number of artists. Financially, that is. They like to work really closely with them. "Co-creation," Sunday calls it. It's all quite unusual.'

Jack listened, but could not share Margaret's enthusiasm for this new group of artists she'd discovered. He'd drawn and painted his entire life, and look where it had gotten him. Just like art throughout history, it had taken far more than it had given. He liked living at Montsalvat, but it was not so much because he was with artists as because he felt like he was amongst family here. He was among people who cared, without intruding. He knew that they watched out for him. Lil popped over every few days, and Matcham and his sisters often brought the babies across to the van, along with a date loaf or something from their oven, and he'd make a pot of tea for them to share. In turn, he'd work on the buildings or take a shovel to the garden. At Montsalvat there was no judgement or expectations. But as far as actually painting was concerned, Jack no longer had the heart for it, nor was he interested in the many conversations it inspired.

Not so Margaret, though. She was clearly captivated by the Reeds.

'John is a lawyer. He and Cynthia come from Tasmania. They were raised in the strictest of conditions. Their father is a staunch Catholic and sounds truly awful. Selfish and self-seeking, John said. Full of religious dogma, but with no care for the poor or for the inequalities of society—only interested in preserving his wealth and status. John hates everything that they stand for. He's even considering joining the communists, and just to annoy his father, he goes to their party meetings.

Jack was surprised. The Australian Communist Party always came under fire in the newspapers. While many times he'd scanned articles which described modern artists as communists, he'd always been amazed. Nobody he'd known had ever shown the slightest interest in politics other than where the next government grants for the arts were being relegated.

'And Sunday?' Jack asked. 'What about her? Is she a communist, too?'

'Oh, Sunday is all about art and culture. In fact, she talked non-stop about books—asked a hundred questions about my cousins. She was particularly interested in Virginia—her writing, her inspirations and childhood. The truth is, I'm sure Sunday knows more about Virginia's writings than I ever will. She went on and on about how Ginnie uses "stream of consciousness," whatever that is, and was very impressed with the way she'd addressed "the implications of a person's sex" in *A Room of One's Own*. Good gracious, Sunday doesn't just read books… she studies them! Intellectualises about them. Not only did I feel drab next to her, I felt like a bloody clod-head for not even knowing about my cousin's writing.'

Jack chuckled, the sound of his laughter foreign to his ears. He'd like to meet the woman with the capacity to intimidate Margaret!

'They are keen to meet you, Jack. I said that we'd go out next weekend for afternoon tea. How does that sound?'

Jack nodded. In all honesty, the mere thought of talking to strangers exhausted him. However, after yesterday's debacle, it was time for him to get a grip on himself.

For an hour they sat in the sun and chattered, and then he accompanied Margaret on the drive back into Melbourne, where she dropped him, along with his overnight bag, outside his parents' home. She reminded him of his promise to visit Heide with her next week, and he agreed to be ready at two PM.

# CHAPTER 9

'Fruit Basket Country,' Margaret said, drawing Jack's attention to the neat rows of trees with their tissue-fine blossoms—pinks, yellows and whites—coating the spindly, leafless branches. Apples, peaches, plums and apricots. He identified each as they passed the chequered paddocks on their way to the Reeds.

'Soon, they will be laden with juicy ripe fruit! How lovely.' Jack supposed that Margaret's ceaseless chatter was intended to keep his mind focused on the present, to stop him from withdrawing into himself as he so often did.

'And here's Heide. By the way Jack, I must tell you, Sunday is a little bit hard of hearing. She is quite sensitive about it, too. Was sharp with me when she couldn't hear me properly a couple of times last week. She made it very clear that she doesn't like mumblers! Just thought that I'd warn you!'

'Thanks, Margaret. I will do my best! We don't want to go upsetting the wonderful Sunday Reed, do we, now?'

'No, Jack. It's not as bad as it sounds. Sunday is lovely! Just sensitive about her deafness, that's all. After all, it's not as though she is an old lady. I imagine forever having to say pardon to people is very frustrating for her.'

The first thing Jack noticed as they turned into Heide's drive was a sense of order. Lavender bushes in neat rows lined the driveway—not just randomly spaced bushes, but orderly hedges. The piles of iron, second-hand timber and rubble heaps that dotted Montsalvat's carpark were nowhere to be found here. Margaret brought the vehicle to a standstill alongside the porch of a cream-coloured house.

Roses surrounded the entrance, their sweet scent filling the air. His mother would be envious of these, Jack thought, admiring the near-perfect blooms. The sound of pulsing trumpets, a double bass, saxophones and piano, accompanied by gravelly voices, drifted through the open windows. Their sound was strange; Jack hadn't heard music for months. It was jazz and reminded him of Parisian nightlife.

Jack admired the sky-blue front door, the whiff of fresh paint lingering around it, and he'd barely finished knocking when a slim, fair-haired lady greeted them, kissing Margaret as one might a close friend even though they'd only met the previous week. Margaret was right. Sunday Reed oozed style. Not just in her apparel—slim-fitting slacks and tight shirt—it was something else. A subtle aspect in her presence, calm and poised but underpinned by a healthy vitality. She had tanned arms and bright, clear eyes. Her movements were at once delicate and yet commanding. When she turned to Jack, the eyes looking at him were candid, giving him the impression that she knew more about him than he would have liked. Squirming uncomfortably under her gaze, he nodded towards the roses.

'Beautiful gardens you have here.' Jack was conscious of speaking louder than usual, and hoped that he didn't sound like he was yelling.

He must have struck the right note, for her face lit up. 'Aren't they just heavenly? They're the delight of my life. The entire garden is, really. I can't get enough of it. I'll take you for a walk through it later, Jack, but first, come inside and we will have some tea. I have just taken a tray of scones from the oven—we must have them while they're warm!'

Sunday's voice was soft and feminine. Different to the brash tones of the Skipper women, who always spoke loudly, as though the people they spoke to were hard of hearing. Different to Sofia's lilting tones with her Spanish accent that had always sounded like music to Jack's ears. Different to Margaret, whose voice was… well… Margaret's. Sunday's voice was like honey. Sweet and seductive. Cultured. For the first time in years, Jack was reminded of Clarice Beckett, the beautiful woman and talented artist whose life had been steeped in thwarted love and denied opportunity, and then tragically ended in an untimely death. She had a way of speaking that was similar to Sunday.

It seemed odd, entering the Reed's home. Jack felt like an intruder entering a sacrosanct space to which he didn't belong. Beyond his parents' house, he rarely entered the privacy of other people's homes. Montsalvat had never had a sense of privacy; everywhere excepting Lil's House, was communal, shared not only by the Skippers and Jorgensens, but by any visitor who wished to arrive. Jack was familiar with the communal lifestyle. It was this quietness and seclusion that felt unfamiliar.

As though sensing his discomfort, Sunday linked her arm through his and led him down the hallway. The promise of her baking infused the air, its inviting aroma merging with a tangy floral perfume, and Jack noticed small bunches of lavender placed in glass jars and vases throughout the house. He also noticed, in addition to the paintings on the walls, dozens of canvases were stacked along the hallway and even in the sitting room. Margaret was right—the Reeds sure loved art.

'Oh, Margaret, Jack, you made it. That's wonderful. So lovely to see you again!' Like Sunday, John greeted Margaret with a kiss and then turned to Jack, shaking his hand. 'Nice to see you again, Jack. We were sorry to miss you last week.'

'John, how about you take Jack and Margaret to the dining room? I will fetch the tea and bring it through,' Sunday suggested.

'Let me help,' offered Margaret, and, without waiting for a reply, she followed Sunday out of the room.

'You sure have some paintings here,' Jack said, speaking first to avoid any uncomfortable questions about his absence the previous weekend.

'Yes, we do… wonderful, aren't they?'

Jack nodded. Indeed, some of the paintings were intriguing. Out of politeness more than anything, he moved closer to study an abstract. He couldn't help thinking that it looked like a piece of string had been loosely dropped onto the canvas and the spaces between painted in various shades of yellow.

'What do you think of that, Jack? "Organised Line to Yellow." One of Sam Atyeo's. We believe it is Australia's first modern painting. These here are also Sam's work.'

Jack moved along the wall, looking at the works John had indicated. They reminded him of the line paintings Sofia had in her chest by the Spanish artist, Miro.

'They're interesting, that's for sure. I can't imagine the traditionalists liking them.' Jack wasn't sure who would like them, beyond the Reeds. Not his parents, and neither did he think that he'd want them hanging on his own walls. He'd learned to like some abstract works, like those of Wassily Kandinsky and Paul Klee, but these paintings were far too strange for his taste.

He was relieved to avoid further comment when cheerful chattering, accompanied by the rattle of a tray, signalled the return of Margaret and Sunday. Within minutes, the dining room table was laden with a set of blue floral cups, saucers and plates and a matching sugar and creamer set. As Sunday lifted the cloth covering the scones, a sweet aroma was released. Jack couldn't remember the last time that he'd eaten home-baked scones, and the promise of these, slathered in jam and cream, was enticing.

As they ate, Sunday dominated the conversation. Since she'd seen Margaret last week she'd delved deeper into Heide's library, resurrecting two books written by Virginia Woolf, *To the Lighthouse* and *Jacob's Room,* which were now laid upon the table.

As though not to be outdone by Sunday's appreciation for Bloomsburys, John had unearthed a copy of Clive Bell's book with the simple title *Art.*

'I knew that I had this tucked away on our shelves, Margaret! Truly, your cousin's husband Clive is an extraordinary man. And to think he wrote this over two decades ago! Listen to this…'

In a warm, well-modulated voice that revealed an enjoyment for reading aloud, John recited, '… *The one good thing Society can do for the artist is to leave him alone. Give him liberty. The more completely the artist is freed from the pressure of public taste and opinion, from the hope of rewards and the menace of morals, from the fear of absolute starvation or punishment, and from the prospect of wealth or popular consideration, the better for him and the better for art, and therefore the better for everyone.*

Finishing, he looked up, expectantly, and Jack nodded. These were in fact familiar arguments to him.

'Isn't that exactly what we say, Sunday? Artists should be free to get on with expressing themselves, not forever combating critics or being forced to paint like trained monkeys. That's the problem with exhibitions—they force artists to focus on that which is sellable.'

Jack nodded, glancing at Margaret as if to say, 'See!', for Clive's words reflected Justus Jorgensen's criticism of exhibitions—how they resulted in reviews and judgements about paintings by people who knew nothing about art. This meant that in order to achieve success, artists were compelled to paint in styles that would please the taste of reviewers! Yet again, thoughts of Clarice Beckett returned to him; how male reviewers had repeatedly discredited her ability, as they did so many female artists. As if a canvas cared whether the hand wielding a brush upon it were male or female!

And hadn't the paintings he and Andrés created for the finca's gallery been tailored to tourists? Yes. Jack could see how painting for audiences limited an artist's creativity.

Listening to John's passionate analysis of Clive Bell's words transported him back in time, to the afternoon when he'd sat in the dining room of Charleston, holding his breath, while Roger and Clive had scrutinised his paintings. He'd listened as Clive shared his theory of aesthetic emotion, explaining how true art would move the hearts of its viewers.

As if sensing his reverie, Margaret turned the conversation back to that very time. 'Clive and Roger, Roger Fry—did you meet him, Sunday?—they were very impressed with Jack's paintings, weren't they, Jack?'

'Margaret, that was a long time ago.'

'Yes, but they saw that you had something… I saw that you had

89

something!' Margaret turned to Sunday. 'It was Roger who arranged for Jack to go to Paris. To have lessons at the Académie Julian.'

'Like I said, it was a lifetime ago, Margaret. None of that matters anymore. It doesn't bear mentioning….' Sitting in the Reeds' dining room, Jack had no interest in resurrecting discussions of that time, once so full of joy and now lost in heartbreak and ashes.

'Come on, Jack. Let's go out into the garden,' Sunday said, rising from her seat.

There was nothing for it but to follow. Jack stood and glanced back, expecting Margaret and John to join them.

'Don't worry about them,' Sunday said, leading him away. Despite Jack's wish to escape thoughts of his past, the cosiness of Sunday's kitchen, warmed by sunlight and with the lingering fragrance of recent baking, transported his thoughts to the finca, whose large windows had faced the orchard, where his feet had been cooled by terracotta tiles on hot summer days and the perfume of orange blossom and jasmine had filled the air. Heide's kitchen was clearly the much-loved domain of Sunday in the same way that the finca's kitchen had been loved by Sofia.

Once outdoors, Sunday led Jack to the side of the house, where they passed vegetables growing in neat rows, their beds edged with aromatic herbs as well as a grove of fruit trees. It further reminded him of the finca.

A man, who was vigorously striking his mattock into a patch of overgrown weeds, stood up at the sound of their voices, and stretched his back before giving them a wave. The three dogs lying in the sun beside him raised their heads lazily, their ears pricked, before standing and bounding towards them.

'Oh, come here you, silly poohs,' Sunday crooned as they jumped at her, threatening to knock her over. She scratched each behind the ears, which caused their tails to wag frantically. 'Boys, settle down and say hello to Jack… Jack, this is Karel, Tommy and Hank—three of the laziest lumps you are ever likely to meet.'

He reached out to pat them, enjoying the soft warmth of their fur in his fingers, comforted by the manner with which their trusting brown eyes returned his gaze.

'Have you got a moment, Sunday?' the man called.

'Sure, Neil. Jack, meet our garden guru—Neil Douglas. He's amazing. Knows more about self-sufficient gardens than anyone in Australia, and here he is doing wonders to get Heide sorted. The place has been transformed since he's been with us.'

Although bashfully waving away her compliments, Neil smiled at her words. 'Now, now, Sunday. I'll be getting a big head if you keep on like that. I just wanted to check if you still want me to plant those hydrangeas. If we don't get them in now, we'll have to wait until next year.'

'Of course, Neil. You decide what is best. You're the boss out here —we'll go along with whatever you suggest. Let John know if you need money.'

'That I will, m'lady,' he replied with twinkling eyes, and Sunday laughed. Jack could see that they worked well together.

It was as perfect a spring day as any, with the chirping of insects and the whistle of birds filling air that was replete with the scent of honey. A mother duck crossed the lawn, trailed by a dozen offspring. The concert of life amid the vibrancy of the colours was intoxicating, and Jack imagined that this place was what the Garden of Eden might be like.

Looking around, he felt guilty for comparing Heide's gardens with those of Montsalvat, but the contrast was extreme. While Justus definitely aspired to the same dream of self-sufficiency, the gardens at Montsalvat had evolved ad hoc, based upon ever-changing visions for the site, and a shoestring budget that meant all sorts of recycled materials had been used for fencing, trellises and garden edging.

Furthermore, the grounds of Montsalvat, with their accumulated heaps of gravel, stone and assorted supplies as well as the numerous semi-completed projects, gave the impression of a perpetual building site rather than the stately grandeur they'd all aspired to achieve. Usually whenever the mess grew beyond the pale, Lil or Sue complained, and a weekend of tidying would ensue. However, despite their best efforts, the outcome was invariably the creation of a dozen heaps of what looked like junk, and Montsalvat's overall effect was one of charming, rustic chaos.

Conversely, here at Heide, a sense of orderliness prevailed. The yard was a picture, with neatly sectioned beds connected by pathways that reflected an old-world charm.

'When we purchased the property five years ago, it was in shambles. A disused dairy. And the house was barely habitable. My father warned against our buying it, but when he realised our minds were made up, he lent us the deposit. John and I nearly broke our backs trying to get the garden sorted, until Neil came along. And now we are reaping the rewards. We have our own cow, who gives us milk, cream and butter; and I can just walk out and pick lettuce, cucumbers, radishes… anything I might want for dinner. And then, of course, there are eggs–both chicken and duck eggs–far more than we can ever use. It's wonderful!'

'It is very beautiful here, Sunday. You have done an amazing job.'

'We love it, Jack. It is nice to be out of the city, away from the crowds. It's peaceful… and the river—it's a bonus. Let's go down there.'

Taking his arm, she steered him to the left.

'So, Jack. John tells me that you lived in Paris for a while?'

'Yes, only for three months or so… Like Margaret said, it was her family connections that made it all happen. Clive and Roger Fry.'

'Oh, how wonderful Roger Fry is! Read is always referring to him.'

'Read?'

Jack's expression must have revealed his confusion. Sunday explained, 'R-E-A-D. No relation. Herbert Read's *Art Now*—it's our bible, so to speak. Read makes quite a few references to Fry. It says a lot about your ability, that Roger liked your paintings.'

'He liked some of my paintings. Not all of them.'

'Yes, but he did organise your lessons at the Académie Julian. That stands for something. I would love to see your work. Will you bring me some?'

'Perhaps I have something buried away. I haven't painted for quite a while.' Jack couldn't think of a single painting that he had to show Sunday—he was just replying out of politeness.

'Did you enjoy Paris?'

'Yes, it was wonderful.' He had loved Paris—that was where it all began for him. He'd savoured every minute of his time there—the art lessons, the Eiffel Tower and the museums like the Louvre, walking along the Seine. It had been a magical place, where he'd met Andrés and Sofia, where he'd fallen in love.

'La ville de l'amour!' Sunday said with a twinkle in her eye. 'The city of love,' she translated, and he nodded wistfully, reminded of his own love—the love that now lay in tatters.

'Jack, I am sorry! That was thoughtless of me. I did not mean to make you sad. You've been through a lot, I know. Was it Paris where you met your wife?'

Jack froze at her words, and then nodded.

They were quiet for a moment before Sunday spoke again, her voice soft. 'Tell me about her, Jack. Was she very beautiful?'

The question was one that few people would have dared to ask Jack. However, with Sunday's wide blue eyes firmly if quizzically fixed upon him, awaiting his response, it seemed right.

He turned his mind to Sofia as he'd first met her. That day at the Café Espanola, when she'd served olives and cheese to him and Andrés, her eyes lively as she'd bantered cheekily, taking umbrage at Andrés' description of her as his little sister.

'Yes, Sunday, Sofia *is* very beautiful. She has a glow to her. An energy. We had a wonderful time in Paris. She is very clever. She knows a lot about art. About painting. She curated her family's gallery in Malaga.'

As though a plug had been released, Jack talked. First about his time in Paris, and then of his and Sofia's life in Malaga. He described the olive and orange plantations perched on the steep slope where the land fell away to the shore; about the view from the finca, out over the Mediterranean Sea. The colourful fishing boats. The days he'd spent painting with Andrés before he died.

'How terrible for Sofia. I can imagine how she felt. My brother,

King, died unexpectedly when he was only twenty-five. Pneumonia! I was utterly devastated.'

Jack appreciated Sunday's understanding. He liked that her words were direct and unemotional, as though she knew that dripping sentimentality would pull him undone. Surprisingly, he actually felt comfortable speaking with her about his life with Sofia—the good and the bad—rather than burying their time together in the graveyard of unspeakable thoughts, as he'd been in the habit of doing in recent months.

'And so, of course... the civil war came upon you... you had left Spain by then?'

'Yes, we came to Australia before it started, thankfully. Andrés repeatedly told Sofia that Spain was in for bloodshed, that troubled times were ahead, but she refused to accept this. He made me promise that once he was gone, I would take her away from Spain; bring her here to Australia.'

'He was right. Franco's ruthless uprising has been terrible. So many people dead! John and I have been following it. Last year we lent some of our paintings to the Sedon Gallery; the Spanish Aid Council held an exhibition there to raise funds in support of the victims of Franco's purges. It is important to fight tyranny, don't you agree?'

Jack was surprised by Sunday's insight into the tumultuous events on the other side of the world. Even though it had often been mentioned in the newspapers, the Spanish Civil War was a topic that few Australians ever discussed in any knowledgeable sort of way. Again, he wished that Sofia was here to meet Sunday. The two women would surely have gotten along well.

'However did you come to live at Montsalvat with Norway and his followers?'

Jack was confused for a moment, then realised that it was Justus who Sunday referred to. 'Master' and 'Jorgy' he'd heard, often. Lil had sometimes called Justus 'Peachy,' which always sounded odd. Only a few people referred to him as Norway. Moreover, it amazed him that Sunday even knew of Justus—but then again, why not? One thing he'd discovered: the art circles of the world were invariably connected. He considered the Bloomsburys with their links to Paris, as well as their influence here in Australia; Gertrude Stein and her American friends; Picasso, whose paintings and personality had an impact across the world. And then, of course, dozens of Australians, including the Jorgensen, the Colahans, and even himself, had made the crossing to Europe. It was hardly surprising that the Reeds would know of the Meldrumite artists living barely twenty miles away.

'It was pure chance, really. We'd been in Australia for less than a year, and Sofia came upon the Meldrum Gallery when she was exploring Melbourne. Until then, we hadn't met any other artists in Australia. Nobody like the Meldrumites... a whole group of artists who shared their passion.'

'No doubt about it, Max Meldrum was a passionate teacher! I've spoken with him on a few occasions.'

Sunday's comment did not reveal her opinion of Max, his methods nor the Meldrumites, but even so, Jack spoke in their defence.

'They were friendly and full of big ideas. Justus has the most extraordinary mind. He's passionate about everything. Not just painting, but building, sculpture, ideas, life. I've learned a lot from him over the last five years.'

'And you have developed your painting using the tonalist techniques of Max Meldrum?'

Confronted by Sunday's questioning, Jack sought for the words to express what he had learned over the last five years.

'Well, yes, to an extent. But then again, no.' In honesty, Jack didn't think that his paintings had developed significantly at all in the last few years. 'The thing is, Montsalvat is about so much more than painting. It is about creativity, a lifestyle immersed in design. The buildings are incredible. It's as though every surface—the floors, the walls and even the ceilings—is a work of art. Justus wanted Montsalvat's atmosphere to inspire artists, not just painters, but sculptors, stonemasons and glassworkers.'

Jack suspected that his answer did not appease Sunday. She, like Margaret and even Sofia in the end, believed creating paintings on canvas should be the priority of an artist. For him, though, Justus' grander vision of Montsalvat had always been a worthy pursuit. By participating in the act of building, Jack had grown. By the very handling of mud and stone, by breathing in the eucalyptus-infused air —ever changed by woodsmoke, morning fogs and filtered sunlight— by digging his hands into the earth, feeling its weight on his shovel, observing the flickering retreat of worms and beetles through exposed soil, witnessing the scurrying of birds and lizards, he'd gained a far greater understanding of organic and inorganic form, of light and texture, than any artist would ever learn in the confines of a studio. And the communal living, the butting and blending of personalities, who at times dominated and hurt each other, but who were ultimately compassionate and caring, had deepened Jack's understanding of human nature.

Had his paintings evolved? Possibly not. But without doubt, Jack's intellect and emotions had been expanded; stretched to extraordinary lengths even as his body had been strengthened as he'd hewn timber, mixed mud and lifted and carried rocks.

How might this affect the way he approached painting? Jack didn't know. But he did know that the retreat, with its sculptures and stone carvings, its unique buildings and gardens, coarse as they were, was the art that he'd been creating over the past four years.

By comparison, a mere painting seemed to be a minor work. Instead, he and Sofia had been notes in a complex symphony, of which Justus had been the composer and conductor—the masterpiece of Montsalvat.

'But you were about to leave—you'd been planning to take a house in Eltham?'

'Yes… a few things happened. Justus can be very dominating at times. It's only that he cares. But we decided that we wanted a place of our own. And then there was the accident.' His last words came as a whisper.

To Sunday's credit, she didn't ask him to explain. In fact, she changed the subject.

'See here, Jack. Look at this tree. It's a river red—nearly five hundred years old! A songline tree for the Aborigines who walked these banks. Doesn't it make you wonder what it has seen, over time? What it might say, if only it could speak?'

Sunday reached out and touched the gnarled bark. 'To think the

Wurundjeri people lived on these very banks for thousands of years. Fished. Collected yams. Stood on this very spot. You can see how they've cut away a huge slab of bark from this tree. Probably made a canoe from it. It's remarkable, isn't it, the way life goes on? I often look at it and wonder, do trees feel pain? Did this tree feel the blade cutting into its flesh, the ripping away of its bark? Bark's a bit like skin, don't you think? But here it is. Still living. Survived. It serves as a reminder to me of what I must do. Pain, sorrow, they come and go, but I must survive. Continue to put down roots and grow.'

Jack's breathing all but ceased as he listened to Sunday. She reminded him of Justus at his best—the perceptive and skilful Master who had the ability to guide students with metaphor and parable.

'So, Jack. Are you painting at all?'

Somehow, Jack felt sure that Sunday knew he wasn't. 'Painting doesn't interest me these days.'

'Of course, it does. If anything, you need painting more than ever!

*Aha,* Jack thought to himself. As he'd suspected. Sunday knew more about him than Margaret had let on.

'No, Sunday. I have no desire to paint. What on earth would I paint? Gum trees? A river?' He cast his arm around the landscape. 'It's so pointless.'

'But you must use painting to heal yourself. Get your emotions out. Just like Clive said, "True art will move the emotions." Perhaps with your own emotions so moved, you could be painting your best work!'

From deep in his memories, Picasso's words returned, uttered all those years ago when he, Andrés and Sofia had visited the artist at his home. *"One day you will know grief, Jack. Then, you will understand how to paint truth. Then you will be great!"*

*Well, Pablo, you were right on one point, wrong on the other. I do know grief, but I have no intentions of painting anything.*

Sunday's words broke through Jack's reverie. 'I want you to come and live here, with us.'

'What?'

'We could be good for each other. You have been through a lot, and so have I. Lost love. Lost faith. Lost confidence. Lost a child....'

At her words, Jack inhaled sharply as he looked at Sunday. She held his gaze; her own was clear, warm and filled with sorrow. For him? For herself? She didn't expand on her loss or seek to know more about his.

'It's quiet here at Heide. Meditative. I like to think that we have created a place of healing through gardening, by growing our own food and eating well, by being surrounded with good books and music. You wouldn't even have to work if you choose not to. And I would get you painting again! What I have learned, Jack, is that you cannot control many things in life, but you can control the things that feed your heart and soul. A broken heart can be mended. Sometimes healing doesn't come from people, but rather from the arts. From music and literature. And, of course, from painting.'

They walked in silence for a few minutes before Sunday continued.

'You wouldn't be the first. We've had a few resident artists over the years. Sam Atyeo—you saw his works in the dining room? He stayed for almost a year before leaving for Paris. You could work in the garden; that would be helpful to us. In turn, we could sell your paintings. John and I, we have contacts. Money. It could be a very good arrangement.'

Jack stopped listening to Sunday's words as his mind grappled with the offer that she'd made. Certainly, the serenity of Heide was undeniable. From the minute that he'd walked through the house, he'd sensed its soothing effect. The place was a paradise.

Sunday's offer was tempting, but what if Sofia returned? What if she came looking for him?

Jack chided himself. Sofia was gone. She was in Spain. Maybe she would change her mind and return to Australia. But if she did, there were others who would direct her to him. His parents, for instance.

'Yes, Sunday. I think that I would like to come and live here, if you think it would be alright.' The spontaneity of Jack's decision surprised even himself.

'Wonderful!' Sunday clapped her hands together. 'When can you come?'

'Anytime… there is nothing to stop me.'

'Next weekend then,' Sunday said decisively, and Jack agreed.

Companionably they wound their way along the river, onto the path and back to the house in silence. It was as if their walk had served its purpose. The plan was made, and now it was time for practicalities.

~

'Guess what, love? Jack has agreed to come and live here at Heide with us,' Sunday exclaimed as soon as they entered the dining room.

'Excellent, Jack. It will be wonderful to have you!' John seemed genuinely pleased and not at all surprised by Sunday's comment. Jack realised that her invitation had been planned before his arrival at Heide today. Perhaps even the walk they'd just taken had been choreographed for that very purpose! Jack didn't mind. He felt sure that it was a good decision.

He glanced at Margaret, who was looking at him, wide-eyed. He wasn't sure whether it was because she had not expected such an offer to spring forth, or whether she had known but hadn't expected him to agree. Most likely it was the latter, and she'd anticipated that it would be her job to talk him into moving to Heide. He smiled. It felt good to see Margaret disconcerted for a change.

# CHAPTER 10

*P*reparing to leave Montsalvat for the second time seemed surreal. Repeatedly, Jack's thoughts returned to that time barely six months earlier when he and Sofia had packed their belongings. It hurt to recall how excited he'd been that week, how much they had looked forward to living in the cottage in Eltham, just the three of them—and then how, in a moment, it had all gone so horribly wrong. As quickly as the memories arose, Jack shut them out. Now was not the time to be overwhelmed with sadness so debilitating that he'd turn to alcohol to numb the pain. He needed to focus on getting his life together.

Last week, when she'd dropped Jack back at Montsalvat, Margaret had volunteered to drive him and his possessions to Heide, but he'd declined. She'd done enough for him. Too much, even. If he were to take control of his life, he wanted to do it alone. He needed to be strong, to stop leaning on Margaret, relying on her to organise his life and pick up the pieces when it fell apart.

Jack hoped that Heide would deliver the healing he needed. Maybe Sunday was right; he should be painting. Perhaps he'd take up her offer to get him going again. That week he'd seen Mr Macintyre, the Manager of Finances at Goldsbrough, Mort & Co, who'd agreed he could take leave. Three months would be a good break. A chance to restore his health. His holiday pay plus savings would see him through until February. At Heide, his expenses would be minimal, with a few hours' work in the garden each day in exchange for his room and meals. The prospect of working outdoors energised Jack. For the first time in months, the fog of depression and self-loathing that overwhelmed him each morning as he awakened was absent.

His parents had been thrilled when he'd told them he was taking leave from work, leaving Montsalvat and taking a room at Heide. His mother would have preferred that he'd come home, where she could care for him herself, though.

'No, Marian,' his father had spoken up. 'This is a good plan for Jack. The Reeds are respectable people.'

William had never met John or Sunday. However, merely knowing that Sunday was from the Baillieu family and that John was a solicitor provided reassurance enough for him. People with backgrounds of wealth and distinction invariably carried an aura of decorum in William Tomlinson's mind. Beyond that, Jack knew his parents were glad to see him living anywhere other than Montsalvat.

After packing his clothing and toiletries and tidying the van, Jack spent most of Saturday working with Matcham. Together they'd helped Sonia and Arthur install three of her stone finials onto the front eave of the Great Hall. The Gothic carvings looked fantastic when they were finally set in position. The sight of them made Jack glad that he'd been at Montsalvat to participate in the construction of the Hall. The building was a remarkable achievement, and for Justus' sake he was pleased that it had come together so well.

On Saturday night, it was with mixed feelings that Jack joined everyone in the dining room for dinner, sharing this last meal with the Skippers, Jorgensens, Arthur and Sue as well as Mitch and Dell, Cyril and Jim; a friendly group of young people who'd been travelling to Montsalvat from Castlemaine in recent weeks, keen to learn the techniques of building with *pisé* and mud bricks. Sue made a rabbit stew for dinner, knowing how much Jack liked it, and as usual, red wine flowed, though he limited himself to one glass. He did not trust himself to the dark moods that descended upon him when he consumed too much alcohol, these days. Justus was at his most charming, and the table was full of cheerful conversation, as if everyone had conspired to ensure that his farewell dinner would leave an impression of the Montsalvat community at their best.

Waking to the raucous cackling of kookaburras on Sunday morning, Jack dressed quickly and stepped out into the early dawn. Cobwebs glistened with morning dew and a fine mist lingered in the air as he crossed the grounds, treading a path that he'd avoided for months.

The cabins, now abandoned, their charred interiors filled with debris, the windows broken from the heat of the raging flames, were a grim testimony of that terrible day six months earlier. Jack inhaled deeply and tried to control his breathing.

Resting on his heels, he rubbed his hand over the wall beside the entry of the cabin he and Sofia had shared, and picked up a handful of the charred earth.

'I am so, so sorry, Scotty. I should have been there for you. For you and for Mummy…. Please, little man, forgive me!'

Jack wiped a hand across his eyes, not caring about the black trail it left across his face. He continued, feeling he should offer a message from Sofia to their baby, and yet in her absence what could he say? Honesty seemed to be the best approach.

'Scotty, I am not sure where Mummy is, but I know that she misses you badly. I promise, I will find her, make sure she is well. We love you, Scotty… please remember that. We love you!'

Standing, his heart heavy, Jack walked into the village of Eltham, a suitcase in each hand, and flagged the sole taxi waiting at the rink outside the station.

# CHAPTER 11

*A*s the taxi wove through the country roads, Jack felt sad to be leaving Montsalvat, yet sure that he'd made the right choice. He was even more sure when, arriving at Heide, he felt a sense of homecoming. Perhaps it was the calm orderliness of the gardens, reminiscent of his childhood. The rose beds and herbaceous borders were soothing; the warbling harmony of the magpies calling to each other, welcoming. The taxi rested at the front door, and the Reeds appeared, a two-person welcoming ceremony.

Grasping his hand, Sunday led him through the house, while John trailed behind with Jack's second case. 'Here, Jack—this is a lovely room, don't you think? From here you can see right down to the river.'

'It's very nice. Thanks, Sunday. I really appreciate you having me here.'

'Don't mention it. John and I are glad that you agreed to come! Take your time to unpack. No need to rush. It's such a beautiful day, I thought we would have lunch down by the river. Albert's coming over. You will like him. Joy will be with him, too. They are both artists. We've known them for years.'

After emptying the contents of his suitcase into the chest of drawers and hanging his trousers and shirts in the cupboard, Jack sat on the bed. Suddenly, it all seemed bizarre. What was he thinking, moving in with these strangers, living in their house? Perhaps he should have stayed in the van, straightened himself out at Montsalvat, remained among the people who understood him. He could have worked on the building projects that he was familiar with, perhaps even built himself a cabin on the grounds. Justus would have been thrilled to help him. Jack shook his head, reminding himself that this change was important. He just needed to take one day at a time.

Soon, voices from the hallway revealed that visitors had arrived. Determining to be more sociable in this new life, Jack rose to join them.

When he reached the door of the dining room, Sunday drew him in, her slender arm firm on his as she introduced the visitors—Albert Tucker and his girlfriend, Joy Hester.

'I know you,' Joy declared.

'Yes, you do. I was at the CAS meeting a few weeks ago.'

'You were! Now I remember. Albert, you really should come along to the meetings. You meet the most interesting of people!'

Jack felt warmed by the couple's banter. Albert was a likeable young man, perhaps a few years younger than himself, who was keen to chat, saying, 'So, Jack, John tells me you studied in Paris!'

While used to this fascination many young artists had with Paris, Jack frequently marvelled that he, who'd had no thought for travelling across the world to paint, had been fortunate enough to have lived in Montparnasse and study at the Académie Julian, albeit for a mere three months. Almost ten years later, the experience gave him the status of a celebrity in their eyes. He'd lost count of the times he'd answered questions about Paris from Justus' students, all envious of his adventure and determined to glean every ounce of information about it.

Jack answered their questions, describing the vast interior of the Louvre, the walks through the arrondissements of Paris, painting plein air along the Seine with his teacher, Monsieur Simon, and how by staying in Montparnasse, he'd lived among artists who'd travelled to Paris from across Europe. Thankfully, he was able to separate thoughts of Sofia and focus on the painterly aspects of his time in Paris.

'You certainly landed on your feet, by the sounds of things. Fancy meeting Roger Fry and him organising all of that!' Tucker said before turning to Joy. 'What do you think, love, do you think we should get ourselves over there?'

Before Joy could answer, Sunday intervened. 'Albert, don't be ridiculous. I don't know what is wrong with everybody. All so desperate to get to Paris and paint pictures of the Seine and the Champs-Élysées. Sit around in cafés all day, drinking absinthe, hoping to spot Picasso or Hemingway. Yes, granted, Paris is wonderful, but we need to learn from what Roger did and then adapt it to Australian culture. We don't want to churn out a bunch of artists who are all doing what the French achieved thirty years ago! We want our own contemporary art movement. Something unique.' The vehemence of her reply surprised Jack.

'Then why are we having the exhibition?' Joy voiced the question that had sprung to Jack's mind.

'The exhibition is not for us! It's for the public, to teach Australians that modern art is not the evil they are led to believe! To show them that it is highly respected in the art capitals across the world!'

'Come on, Sun, you're just annoyed because Sam got away from you,' Tucker teased.

'Yes, I am, actually. He could have been extraordinary. Unique.'

All eyes turned to Atyeo's paintings, and seeing them again, Jack wondered what the fuss was about.

'There'll be other artists for you, Sun. Jack here, perhaps he's the man you're looking for.'

They all laughed, and Jack shook his head, holding his hands up before him. 'Don't look at me—I barely pick up a brush these days. And really, modern art—abstracts and so forth—have never been my thing.'

'Don't be so sure, Jack. You might surprise yourself,' said Sunday.

'Come on,' John said. 'Let's head down to the river—it's going to be hot today. What would you like us to carry, Sun?'

Within minutes they'd gathered together baskets, blankets and towels. After following the same path to the river as he and Sunday had taken the previous week, they settled themselves under an enormous red-gum, its swaying branches offering welcome relief from the unseasonally warm rays of sunshine.

To Jack's surprise, John produced fishing handlines and a tin that was full of writhing worms from the canvas bag he'd slung over his shoulder. Jack accepted the reel he offered, and for the next hour the men sat half a dozen yards apart from each other, resting on various stumps and logs along the bank with their lines in the river. They caught dozens squirming, plump yabbies, which they placed in a bucket of water, ready to boil over the fire that Sunday and Joy were now feeding with small twigs as they chatted.

The shadows diminished into small pools at their feet as the noonday sun hovered directly overhead. Moving to the shade of the willow trees by the river's edge, they spread the blankets and set out the bowls and plates that Sunday drew from her picnic basket: an enormous bean salad, sliced carrots, fresh raw mushrooms, a rice mix and containers of cherry tomatoes, boiled eggs and lettuce.

Jack was used to eating salads; throughout his childhood Marian had often sliced tomatoes, lettuce, cucumber and radishes, over which she squeezed lemon juice and vinegar, and at Montsalvat salads often accompanied meals. However, he was surprised by the array of raw food set out before them.

John must have noticed his expression. 'Sun's got us all eating like rabbits,' he laughed. 'Ever since she discovered the Hay diet, I am not allowed so much as a lamb chop. These yabbies are about as close as I get to satisfying my carnivorous leanings. It was quite a shock to the system when suddenly we were banned from eating bacon for breakfast, and don't even get me started on the way her wonderful roasts vanished! Remember them, Tucker, the pork and crackling? All gone! Poor old Mrs Wells—she was our housekeeper—up and left! She couldn't keep up with which foods could be combined with what and all the talk of acids and alkalinity; the poor old thing was utterly confounded.'

'Mrs Wells did not leave because of the Hay diet!'

'If you'd like a T-Bone, you're welcome to my place anytime!' Joy offered.

'Thanks, Joy. I might take you up on that!'

'It's good for you to eat healthy, John… good for all of us!' Sunday chided. 'I feel so much better these days. Do you mind, Jack? I am sure you will get used to it.'

'No, it's fine,' Jack stammered, embarrassed for inciting the discussion about the food Sunday had prepared. For heaven's sake, he was their guest! The least he could do was be appreciative.

Their bantering continued throughout lunch, weaving from one subject to the next. Tucker launched into a discussion with Jack on creative minds versus rational minds; he extolled how, in his view, society was becoming increasingly dependent on scientific solutions to problems; people were ceasing to think for themselves and listen to their own instincts. His arguments appeared familiar to the others, and they teased him for his earnestness.

'I tell you what, Albert—you write the book, *How Science Kills Creativity*! The title sounds riveting; everyone's bound to read it! I just don't know who!'

'Alright, there's no need to be rude. All I'm saying is humans are becoming too dependent on scientific data to explain our behaviour. In the meantime, our instincts, and our capacity to think outside the square, are declining. We consult experts for every problem instead of being guided by our hunches. Just remember that you were forewarned by me, Albert Tucker!'

Jack was caught off guard when Sunday turned the conversation to him.

'Have you read Rimbaud, Jack?' she asked.

'No, Sunday, I can't say that I have.' He knew Dorothy McKellar's *My Country*, and of course, Patterson's *Man from Snowy River*. At school he'd studied some English poems, Chaucer's *Canterbury Tales* and Milton's *Paradise Lost*. They'd all bored him witless.

'I must get you reading him. He's extraordinary. Best read in French, of course. Perhaps I can teach you…'

*Laisse-le venir, laisse-le venir*
  *Le jour où les cœurs s'aiment comme un.*
  *Je suis patient depuis si longtemps*
  *J'ai même oublié*

She translated,
> *Let it come, let it come*
> *The day when hearts love as one.*
> *I've been patient so long*
> *I've forgotten even*
> *The terror and suffering*

'Are we swimming?' Joy asked, and Jack concluded that she did not share Sunday's fascination with poetry.

'Let's,' agreed Sunday, and to Jack's astonishment, the women stood up, peeled off their dresses, slipped off their brassieres and headed towards the river.

'Coming, Jack?' John stood up, shedding his trousers, but thankfully leaving his boxers on.

Jack tried to hide his embarrassment at swimming in the company of two bare-breasted women. Each time they climbed the steep side to take turns diving into the river, he'd time his paddling so that he'd be swimming towards the opposite bank. If either of the women spoke directly to him, he kept his eyes fixed upon theirs as he replied, and thought he did well to control his discomfort. Afterwards, lying under the trees, relaxed by the companionable murmur of voices in the background, Jack dozed. He awakened perhaps an hour later to find the others moving. Rising, he helped to pack the picnic before they returned to the house for arvo tea.

Late that night, lying on his bed, his hands behind his head, Jack stared at the ceiling. A volume of Rimbaud's *Illuminations* rested on his chest. Sunday had pressed it upon him a few hours earlier, insisting that once Jack'd read it, he would forever view the world differently.

Sunday was the leader at Heide, he decided. She was remarkable, what with her keen intellect, her skills in the garden, baking, making her own butter and cream, speaking French and who knew what else. He'd always thought Margaret was self-assured, but he'd never before met a woman with Sunday's confidence.

He wished that Sofia was here with him, that she too was meeting the Reeds. She'd like John, he knew, but was now less certain of her thoughts about Sunday. In the space of the morning, he'd concluded that Sunday was a woman who needed to be centre stage, especially where other females were present. While she didn't dominate conversations, she controlled them, pulling them up when she felt like it, changing topics at her whim. He suspected that she preferred the company of males; more than once she'd disregarded Joy's comments, deflecting the conversation back to himself, Tucker or John.

Waking at Heide was altogether a new experience for Jack. In the van at Montsalvat, he'd woken to the tweeting of birds, inches from his face as they'd tapped their beaks at their reflections in the van's windows.

The rustling of blue-tongued lizards, quails and marsupials living in the surrounding bush were constant companions. Sometimes too close, judging by the overturned pots and the nests made from dried gum leaves that regularly appeared under the van. Added to that were the scampering sounds on the roof—the scuffle of birds' feet, or falling leaves, or even the heavy tread of a possum, causing the van to rock as though a tremor had rippled across the earth's crust.

Here in his bedroom at Heide, under the iron roof buffered by plaster ceilings, surrounded by timber walls and well-sealed windows, the world outside was held at bay. He could hear the usual sounds of dawn—a rooster crowing in the distance, the harking of crows—but these were muffled through the solid walls. Even stranger was the sound of human activity close to where he lay. Footsteps in the hallway, taps gushing, a throat gargling.

A kettle's whistle rang through the house; and rising, Jack pulled his shirt and trousers on. He approached the kitchen, from which softly murmuring voices filtered down the hallway. John greeted him, waving a mug in his direction. He had been speaking with Neil, the gardener, sharing a pot of coffee, toast and cereal.

'Coffee, Jack. Shut the door behind you, will you? Thanks. We don't want to wake Sleeping Beauty. Sunday will sleep for hours yet. Best thing for all of us.' John winked.

'Is Sunday alright? Is she unwell?'

'Let's just say, sometimes it's better to let the kitten sleep, lest its claws draw blood.'

Neil laughed. 'You can say that again. Let Sun sleep until morning tea. That's the way. Then everybody's happy. And we can eat in peace, without her checking that we aren't combining our proteins with our starches.'

Over the next fifteen minutes, Jack consumed a bowl of muesli and a cup of coffee while he listened to John and Neil make plans for the day.

'We are just about to have a walk outside. Would you like to come along, Jack?' John asked.

Jack was glad to accompany them, keen to begin earning his keep by putting hand to shovel or whatever else was required of him. Neil led him and John from one spot to the next, assessing the progress of their current projects.

'I'll need to grab a few bags of lime today, John. The vegetables will struggle without it.' Neil stated.

'No worries, Neil. Just get whatever you need. I saw that the Johnsons have got some horse manure bagged up for sale, at their front gate. Perhaps we should grab some for the roses?'

'Yes. Jack, you ought to go down with Neil and meet the Johnsons. Great neighbours and excellent with cows. They are on the lookout for a good dairy cow for us.'

'I might get you to run the mower over the back-lawn when we get back, Jack. The grass is long enough to run half a dozen cows on it!' Neil laughed.

'No worries, Neil. Give me any job you like and point me in the right direction. It will be a pleasure to be working in these gardens.'

Jack quickly settled into the rhythm of Heide. He enjoyed the time spent with Neil, who he found lived at Heide a few days each week, immersing himself in the Reeds' garden before returning to his own home in Bayswater. Easy to work with, Neil had a way of chatting non-stop, which suited Jack because it saved him from speaking and prevented him from stewing over Sofia's whereabouts. Like Sunday said, the man was a wealth of information about self-sufficiency, but that was only the beginning of his knowledge. He was a born teacher and hard worker. It wasn't enough to simply do a job. Neil liked to explain what they were doing, why they were doing it, and what would happen if they didn't do it right. Jack discovered all sorts of things: the way plants responded to moon cycles, that aphids would leave tomatoes alone if they were planted alongside basil, and how if the compost heap was kept warm, microbes would break down organic matter and at the same time, undesirable seeds and bacteria would be destroyed.

Jack was not at all surprised to learn that Neil was not only a gardener but also an artist. He'd attended lessons at the Gallery School with Sam Atyeo, and it had been through Sam that Neil had met the Reeds. The layout of Heide's gardens—the verticals and horizontals, the shades of colour and the arrangement of blue against orange flowers—suggested the mind of a painter, and the result was exquisite.

With the warmth of spring, the plants had grown rapidly, and so too had the weeds. It was a full-time job weeding, pruning, planting and watering. Quickly, Jack learned that for all of Sunday's determination to identify as uniquely Australian, she wanted Heide's gardens to be like those she'd seen in France, with a potager, rose walk and discrete spaces that each had their own theme. She adored blue flowers, and so lavender, delphiniums, azaleas and bluebells grew everywhere. Sunday usually joined him and Neil in the garden about ten, arriving with a tray of biscuits and steaming pot for morning tea, after which she worked alongside them for an hour, digging weeds or putting on gumboots and gloves and clearing a patch with her mattock and hoe while the dogs bounced around her legs, eagerly waiting for a ball to be thrown.

It amused Jack to hear Sunday speaking to her plants. 'Oh, you little darling, haven't you done well?' she'd say as the first leaves emerged from the daffodil bulbs, or 'You naughty lavender. Last year you told me you liked it here, and now, look at you—all sulky and withered.' It was as though each plant were her own child.

'You just have to love them, Jack. Tell them you care, that you are going to look after them.'

Ever on the lookout for unusual species to be added to Heide's garden, Sunday invited him to join her and John on a plant hunt one Saturday morning. Jack was mystified as, armed with a basket of carefully prepared bulbs and cuttings, they walked through the streets of Brighton, spying out houses with attractive gardens; a sure sign that a keen gardener resided within. When a target was finally decided upon, Sunday boldly proceeded to the front door, her basket of cuttings in hand, whose contents she offered in exchange for cuttings of the plants she coveted.

～

In Jack's third week at Heide, he sensed rather than saw Sunday approaching him as he placed stakes against a shed wall, preparing to build a climbing frame for the beans that he intended to plant. He felt her eyes upon him, watching a while before she spoke.

'Jack, how's your painting going?'

'I don't know, Sunday. I just can't get interested in it. I'm not sure that I want to paint anymore.'

'I understand. You've been through a lot. I'd like to try something… it might help.'

Her cajoling intrigued him.

'Sure, Sunday, why not? What are you thinking?'

'Come on inside. I have some things set out.'

After washing his hands at the outdoor trough, Jack followed her indoors, where he found paints, drawing paper, writing pad and pens neatly set out on the dining-room table.

'Have a seat, Jack. Are you comfortable?'

'Yes...' Jack wasn't really. He wondered what Sunday had in mind for him.

'Now... first I will read to you.... You don't need to do anything—just shut your eyes and listen.... Let the words wash over you. Then, after I've finished, we'll see what happens. You could paint, or even write. As you wish. Just see what thoughts evolve—what creative urge springs forth—and let it flow forth.... Try not to overthink things.'

Jack nodded, although he couldn't imagine how listening to Sunday read could unlock his reticence to painting. But it wouldn't hurt, and she was only trying to help him.

He waited as she opened the book she was holding and began reading, her voice clear and modulated.

What? Jack looked at her, surprised, and she raised her hand to halt his interruption. As she continued reading, Sunday became animated, her hands fluttering, her words lifting and falling like froth on an ocean, clustered together on a rising swell, gathering speed and riding its crescent before cascading onto the shore—the words in fluent French!

Controlling his surprise, Jack fixed his eyes on the table before him, listening. Funnily, every so often a word was familiar—but mostly the passage was utterly meaningless. *How odd could life possibly get?* he wondered as he tried to focus on the task Sunday had set him.

Perhaps inspired by the French phrases, several images stirred in his mind: the delightful early mornings stepping out on the Passage de Dantzig, the evenings when he'd ridden his bicycle along the streets of Montparnasse, enchanted by the romance of Paris.

A dramatic deceleration of Sunday's monologue, her voice dropping to barely a whisper, induced feelings of sadness within him as he thought of Sofia and how happy they'd once been. By now familiar with unexpected emotional plunges, Jack deflected the memories before they could overpower him.

Finally, Sunday's recitation drew to a close, and she looked at him expectantly.

There was only one thing to do, and so he picked up a fine-tipped pencil and began sketching. Sam Atyeo's works loomed above and, inspired by the fluid lines of Sam's *Dancer*, Jack kept his pencil loose, deliberately aiming for organic swirls to suggest his subject, the semi-abstract form of a woman with a large hat. Around her, two or three lines implied a background of the round-backed chairs that were so common in Parisian cafés.

Whether it was because his mind had relaxed or because he was trying to please Sunday, Jack found the drawing exercise fun and was quite surprised by the charming picture that resulted. Sunday nodded as she looked at his work and smiled. She seemed to be pleased as well.

When Sunday appeared beside him the next Monday, Jack suspected that she had another drawing activity in mind.

'This is coming along nicely,' she said, admiring the birdbath that he'd cleaned and repositioned by the garden bed that held pride of place in the centre of Heide's front lawn.

'Yes, it is. Your garden is wonderful, Sunday, a pleasure to work in!'

'I was hoping that you would give me a hand to move a cupboard, Jack.'

'Sure, Sun. Of course.' Jack placed the rake against the shed wall and followed her into the house.

'Wait here, I'll just be a moment...' she said, leaving him standing in the hallway.

As he waited, he looked at a portrait on the wall. It sat in the shadows of a bookcase, and he hadn't noticed it before. The painting was of a young woman... Sunday?

'Yes... that's me!'

Sunday had glided up to him from behind and stood so close that Jack could feel her breath against his neck.

'Actually, it was painted in Montparnasse, possibly very close to where you stayed. The artist is Agnes Goodsir, another Australian seduced by the sparkling lights of Paris, never to return. Mind you,

Australia hasn't been particularly good to its female artists, so I don't blame her.'

'It's lovely,' Jack said, for want of a stronger response. It wasn't, really; the woman on the canvas was thin and pale, with overly large eyes and a haunted expression. She was barely a shadow of the Sunday he knew, with her sparkling clear eyes, tanned skin and lively personality.

Sunday must have detected the doubt in his tone. 'No, Jack. It's not lovely. Not lovely at all. Agnes painted it just after... well, let's just say I was possibly at the lowest point in my life... I don't know why I leave it on the wall, other than it serves as a reminder never to allow myself to be so foolish again.'

Her words roused Jack's curiosity. They seemed to be a reference to the scars that she'd referred to down by the riverbank, the first day he'd met her. However, Sunday changed the subject.

'Actually, you might be interested in these...' She beckoned him to follow, leading him through the door at the end of the hall. Into her and John's bedroom. The room was large, with a four-poster bed and a heavy-looking cupboard, whose doors were open. It was empty, the coats and dresses it held now draped over the chaise lounge beside it. Unsurprisingly, several paintings graced the walls of the room. Ignoring the cupboard waiting to be moved, Sunday led him to a pair of landscapes—paintings that were far more traditional than most of those displayed throughout the house.

'Why, these are Streeton's!' Jack was surprised; most of the modern artists he knew outrightly rejected Strecton's style.

'Yes, they are. In fact, I have a lot to thank Arthur for. He stayed with us for a while when I was young. My mother was mad about art. I suppose that is where I get it from. She painted a little herself, you know, seascapes and things. In fact, it was about the only work I ever saw her do.

'Anyway, the Baillieu and Streeton families were old friends, and my mother often invited Arthur to Merthon. That was our holiday home in Sorrento. I was only about five at the time and I thought it was wonderful, having him stay with us. I loved watching him work at his easel, and he was always patient… never told me to go away like most adults would have.'

Leaving the painting, Sunday moved across the room.

'See, this one—*Nocturne*—the child on the veranda there, that's me!' The wistful tones in Sunday's voice revealed her fond memory of a time long past.

'Yes, his paintings are wonderful,' Jack agreed. It impressed him to learn of Sunday's close ties to the famous artist. Arthur Streeton was a household name in Australia, and the Streeton on his parents' lounge room wall was Marian's pride and joy.

'I don't know—I am not so sure that his paintings are as wonderful as people make out. These are from his earlier works, his best period. See how fresh they are… organic. It's such a shame that he followed in the way of the traditionalists—turning our Australian landscapes into English fields with hazy skies and subdued green fields. Our landscape is bright with colour! Nobody seems to know how to paint our brilliant blue skies or deep red earth!'

Jack's breathing slowed in response to Sunday's bare skin against his as she linked arms. Although she did this often, today, with his sleeve rolled above his elbow from spending the morning working in the sunshine, their bare skin touching in the intimate confines of her bedroom—her and John's bedroom—made Jack feel uncomfortable.

Oblivious to his reaction, Sunday continued. 'Here is another that you may like—a McCubbin. He painted it at Mount Macedon.'

Jack could barely focus on the painting, an Australian bush scene with two children playing amid the forest, as he tried to ignore the distraction of Sunday's fingers, which were now lightly trailing along his forearm, causing his skin to tingle and his heart to knock against his chest wall.

'It's titled *The Rabbit Burrow. Jack…*' Her voice was low as she turned to him, her face close, her hands gripping his elbows. 'I feel so drawn to you! Do you feel it, too?'

Her parted lips were inches from his own, and Jack knew that they were within seconds of connecting. Blood pounded in his temples. That Sunday was lovely was undeniable, and he was not immune to her charm. To lean into her, place his lips against hers, was inviting; to lift his hands and run them through her sweet-smelling hair, tempting. To ease her back towards the empty bed, all of three steps away, promised delights he found hard to deny.

Jack swallowed and braced himself. Sunday was beautiful. However, she was not Sofia, and she was married to John. It was not complicated when he reduced this moment to these simple facts. Yes, she was attractive—and beyond her looks, she was extraordinary. But he did not love her. Notwithstanding, Sunday was a woman who expected her own way, and he instinctively knew this moment would be no exception. He would have to draw upon every ounce of tact that he could muster to extricate himself from her embrace without giving offence.

'Sunday, you are lovely. Beautiful, in fact. But this is not a good idea.'

'It is! We would be wonderful together.'

'No, I don't think so. I am married. I am Sofia's husband, and when she comes back, I plan to be here, waiting for her.'

'But you would be. Of course, you would be. I would love to meet Sofia. She would never know about… this.'

'There will be no 'this,' Sunday. There cannot be. I would never forgive myself if I betrayed her.'

'Darling, you're being silly. Sofia's in Spain. She may never come back. You just need time to think. Sleep on it, and we will talk about it again. I have just caught you by surprise.'

That night, lying in bed, Jack thought about the day—about Sunday, and the feeling of her in his arms. He couldn't deny that he was flattered by her offer. Sunday was a woman in a million. However, for all his fascination with her, it was the fascination one might have for an exotic creature. He was Sofia's husband. She was the only one he felt for in that particular way.

He considered his reply to Sunday, "… when Sofia comes back." Would she ever come back? Was that what he believed would happen? He longed to hear from Father Sebastian, but since he'd only sent his letter a few weeks ago, a reply would be months away. Yet it was not the mailman that Jack waited for, but rather the sound of Sofia's footsteps on the drive… the sound of her voice asking for him. Daily, he anticipated her return to him. Every time he heard the phone ringing, a vehicle on the driveway, a knock on the door, Jack's heart beat with excitement. He was sure that Sofia had recognised that leaving Australia—leaving him—had been a dreadful mistake, that she needed him as much as he needed her.

For the next few days, Jack felt uncomfortable in Sunday's presence and he could barely look John in the eye. Sickened about that moment in their bedroom, he vowed that he would never enter that private space again. Strangely, Sunday's manner didn't change at all; it was as though nothing had ever happened. After a few days, Jack began to question himself, wondering if he'd imagined those seconds where he'd held her in his arms—turned them into something they never were.

~

Jack needn't have worried, for the Reeds became distracted by a new excitement in their lives, which arrived in the form of a parcel delivered to Heide by Bellew. The large package wrapped in heavy waxed brown paper and tied with string was from Basil Burdett, the *Herald's* arts expert. The previous month he'd travelled to London, after which he'd crossed the Channel to France, where in both destinations he'd scoured both private collections and negotiated with the curators at various museums, searching for just the right blend of paintings that could be brought to Australia. The parcel that Bellew carried held photographs of the collection Burdett had managed to procure for the display.

John and Sunday could barely contain their excitement as they pored through the photographs. As well as half a dozen each of Picassos, Van Goghs and Gauguins, Cezannes and Matisses; there were also Mogdalinis, Chagalls and Derains; and they squealed their excitement as they explored the breadth of the collection. Amongst the British modern artists there was paintings by Mathew Smith, Richard

Sickert, and to Jack's amazement, a painting by Ness' lover, Duncan Grant. Jack could hardly wait to tell Margaret. She would be ecstatic to see Duncan numbered among the artists whose works would be exhibited in Australia.

Whilst many of the names held little meaning to Jack, equally many did; these were the giants of the modern art world, and it thrilled Sunday to know that many of the artists they'd be exhibiting were familiar enough to excite an Australian audience.

Burdell's successful negotiations exceeded their hopes. The exhibition was set to be the largest display of international art ever shown in Australia. There would easily be more than two hundred paintings as well as a number of sculptures. Many of the works would be available for purchase to Australian collectors. Although the exhibition was still many months away, there was much to be done. For its success, a careful promotion schedule was needed. Fortunately, with Murdoch owning newspapers, much of the hard work was overcome. All they needed to do was generate anticipation for the exhibition with feature articles and the commentary of carefully selected critics. Sunday and John were eager to get on with the task, along with Jack Bellew, who seemed to be at Heide the whole time, these days—always full of himself, and bragging about his encounters with 'Keith', as he liked to refer to Murdoch.

# CHAPTER 12

*T*he week before Christmas, the sound of a soft tinkling woke Jack and he leapt up. Was that Sunday, already up? Had he slept in? Did he sleep through breakfast?

With eyes barely opened, Jack pulled on his clothes and headed towards the kitchen. He paused at the lounge door, where a familiar looking woman sat at Sunday's piano.

'Good morning. And who might you be?' she asked authoritatively, and he stared back, confused. The young woman before him looked so much like Sunday it was disconcerting.

'I suppose, more to the point, you are wondering who I may be.' She continued with a chuckle. 'Since you appear to belong here, and I have just crashed in.'

'No—I know who you are.' It came back to him. This was the lady who'd invited Margaret to the CAS meeting—John's sister, Cynthia. He'd only met her briefly, just before she'd left the meeting; but he'd heard a lot about her since, for John and Sunday regularly mentioned 'Bob,' who he'd later learned was their name for her. He'd gleaned that John was exceptionally fond of her, Sunday less so.

'And I know who you are,' she retorted victoriously. 'You're Jack, Margaret's friend. I have caught up with her a few times since then. She's very nice. We get on well.'

Jack didn't know. He'd only met with Margaret once since he'd started living here at Heide. Three weeks earlier, they'd spent a pleasant day driving to St Kilda Beach and walking out along the pier, drinking cups of tea at the Pavilion before returning to his parents' for dinner. Margaret had asked a hundred questions about his life at Heide and been pleased to hear that he was painting again.

'So, Sunday moved you in?' The question had an odd intonation that Jack ignored.

'Yes. I've been living here for the past few months. It's lovely here. Peaceful. I try to do my bit to help.'

'Sunday and John have done a superb job with the place. It was falling down when they got it. Shambles, really. Sunday has a knack for making a place a home. How do you find her?'

'Why, good. Wonderful. She and John are very hospitable; it's kind of them to let me stay with them.' Jack deliberately expanded his response to include John.

'Kind...' Cynthia laughed. 'I suppose that's one word to describe Sunday!' Within a single sentence, she returned the focus back to her sister-in-law.

Jack remained silent. It felt wrong to be speaking about Sunday in this manner while he was a guest in the Reeds' home. However, Cynthia, had no such reservations.

'She's a man-eater, Jack... fancies herself as Lady Chatterley, I'm sure.'

Jack had no idea what Cynthia was talking about. Sure, he'd heard of Lady Chatterley. The wanton behaviour of the literary character had caused an uproar a few years earlier. No one could have missed it. The book was banned in Australia, although as Margaret's cousin Virginia once said, banning books simply guaranteed the author notoriety and sales. But Jack still did not see the connection between D. H. Lawrence's Lady Chatterley and Sunday. He shrugged, preferring to avoid the discussion, but Cynthia wasn't finished.

'You know. A rich woman, acting out her fantasies on the underlings in her life. Falling in love with whatever dashing young fellow takes her fancy. Have you taken Sunday's fancy, Jack?'

He shook his head. 'No, no. definitely not.' But he could feel heat rising on his face.

Cynthia laughed at his discomfort and continued. 'The problem is that while Sunday allows herself to fall sincerely and madly in love, she forgets that the triangles she creates are not equilateral, if you know what I mean.'

Jack had not the slightest idea, and his confused expression only fuelled Cynthia's analysis.

'It's her and John all the way. There is no question of that. They adore each other. No, I take that back—they need each other. It's like they are two parts that are perfect complements. Sunday, the colourful kite, fluttering high in the sky, dancing on the breeze for everyone to admire; John fixed to the ground, holding the string, the anchor who guides Sun's movements lest she crash. John can't bear it when Sunday's upset.'

Listening, Jack could not deny Cynthia's description. It was as though an invisible cord connected John and Sunday, binding them tightly together. Sunday's vivacious personality, her intellectual vibrance and boundless energy, held the attention of any room she stood in, while John's common-sense approach to life pulled her into check when she got emotional. He managed the big decisions around their life together and garnered respect from everybody, including Sunday. But Jack recognised the power of the two as they worked together, coordinating ideas and solutions; their achievements were a perfect blend of their personalities. Cynthia had described their relationship well.

'But still, they are not enough for each other, Jack,' she continued. 'Sunday becomes infatuated with her young artists. All dashing and bold and confident types who, like her, are full of energy and motivation. She lures them like moths to a flame. She bedazzles them, and they bedazzle her. It seems to go both ways. And then she draws John in too, because she can't manage without him. Why he puts up with it, I'll never understand. So then we have the triangle. They seem to find it fun at first, but then the bonds get tighter and tighter, until something invariably snaps and it all flies apart. Poor Sam—he had to leave the country to get away from her!'

'Sam! Sam Atyeo?'

'The one and same. I heard that Bellew—you know; that news reporter with the Herald—is the latest.'

'Yes, but I don't think there is anything in it…'

'Yes, there is, Jack,' Cynthia interrupted him impatiently. 'There is always someone in Sunday's life.'

'Good lord.' The words were out of Jack's mouth before he knew it. How had he missed it?

Jack had assumed that Bellew and Sunday were working on CAS' exhibition. Admittedly, he'd thought it odd when the young man had come over for lunch the previous weekend and John had steered Jack outdoors, seeking his help to collect some trees he'd purchased for the garden, leaving Bellew and Sunday alone for hours.

'I know,' Cynthia continued conspiratorially, misunderstanding Jack's shock for agreement. 'I've thought about it for years, tried to make sense of it all. I can only imagine it's a result of her upbringing—surrounded by males, indulged, raised to be a princess… You know Sunday was presented at the Palace, don't you?'

'Buckingham Palace?' Jack had heard of such things—society people travelling to London for their daughters to be presented at court. In honesty, he wasn't surprised. He'd expect no less for Sunday.

'But why would that make Sunday seek… lovers?' The word felt foreign on his lips.

'I suppose it fills her need to be admired—she thrives on the attention. And, as you may know, she's suffered terrible losses.'

Jack never got to hear the details of those losses, for the sounds of Neil and John returning from their morning walk interrupted Cynthia mid-sentence.

'Bob, love! You are bright and early. I didn't see you come in. We weren't expecting you until at least mid-morning.' John kissed his sister, stroking her hair, and she laughed.

'I am not a cat, John. Save your petting for Sunday.'

'Oh, she won't be up for ages. You must do.'

Seeing John beside Cynthia reminded Jack of images of John and Sunday. The women truly were remarkably similar.

As Christmas approached, Jack was filled with dread. Last year he and Sofia had spent Christmas Eve with his parents, enjoying the wonder of the celebration through Scotty's eyes. It had been his second Christmas, it had been fun to see the little boy excited by the idea of Santa Claus descending down the chimney during the night to leave gifts under the sparkling tree William and Jack had set up. After Scotty was asleep, he, Sofia and his parents had played cards and eaten chocolates until late, and rarely had Jack felt so close to them.

The next morning they'd all crept down the stairs with Scotty, thrilled with anticipation for the surprises that Santa might leave, and unwrapped presents before going into the yard to play. William had bought Scotty a pedal car and they'd taken photos of him, laughing at his serious expression as he'd tried to navigate the pathway, veering too far left, then too far right with the small steering wheel. Afterwards, despite the soaring temperature, they'd enjoyed roast vegetables and turkey and then searched for the silver coins hidden within their bowls of plum pudding and custard. Late in the afternoon he and Sofia had returned to Montsalvat, where they'd set the exhausted Scotty to sleep in his bed before joining the large gathering in the shade of the gumtrees, chatting and eating from the table of leftovers: cold meats, salads, pavlova and more plum pudding accompanied by icy cold glasses of beer.

As it turned out, Christmas at Heide proved better than he'd hoped for. Tucker, Joy, Cynthia and numerous others arrived on Christmas Eve, and with loud music blaring, they drank, danced, talked and ate and then drank some more. Jack and Tucker made a large bonfire down by the river; and as the night wore on, the revelry evolved into intense conversations, drunken canoodling or quiet introspection.

Leaving the heavily intoxicated Tucker, who'd launched into a convoluted rambling about his favourite argument—concern about how rational thought was disabling human ability to think creatively— Jack busied himself washing dishes in the kitchen, where his domestic skills were openly appreciated by the attractive young woman who volunteered to help him. He couldn't remember if her name was

Rosalie or Rosemary or Rosemarie. He suspected she would have been happy to pass the night in his bed should he wish to invite her, but of course he didn't.

On the morning of Christmas Day, Jack cadged a ride with Tucker and Joy into the city where they dropped him at his parents' home. Margaret had been invited, and when she arrived, they exchanged gifts of socks and chocolates and flowers. Over roast turkey, baked vegetables and plum pudding, they chatted about changes at Gainsbrough, Mort & Co., the uncharacteristic heat of the season, and Jack described the progress of Heide's beautiful garden. Nobody mentioned Sofia or Scotty, or referred to the previous year when Christmas Day had been a delightful affair. A wonderful day, enhanced by Scotty's excited chatter and games in the garden with the ball and toy car that Scotty had been so thrilled to receive.

~

The last weeks of January were noteworthy on two counts. The Archibald Prize, Australia's most prestigious art prize for portrait painting, had for the first time ever been awarded to a woman. Margaret was ecstatic, and she insisted that Jack come with her to see the painting. He met her under the clocks of Flinders Street Station, and together they walked to the National Gallery. It was the first time that Jack had ever seen the Archibald Prize exhibition, and the array of paintings present was astonishing.

'Jack, you should enter a portrait—you could win this, you know.'

Jack laughed at Margaret's enthusiasm. Once, he might have liked to try, but not now. He scrutinised the paintings. Most were of men—distinguished looking characters with sombre expressions as though they carried the weight of the world on their shoulders. The winning portrait stood out not only for its brightness of colour and attention to detail, or that the artist was a female, but because the image in the picture was a woman, too. It was very good, Jack agreed, noting the extraordinary skill the artist had demonstrated as she'd painted the gorgeous, ornately detailed jacket worn by the sitter.

The artist was Nora Heysen. Jack had never heard of her, but the surname was familiar, and from the chatter around him, he learned that she was the daughter of Hans Heysen—a man well-known for his extraordinary landscapes. In fact, by the dubious comments emitted from a number of attendees, more than one believed that the only reason Nora Heysen had been given the prize was that she was Hans' daughter. Furthermore, Jack realised that the blustering Irishman standing nearby, who was vocally discrediting woman artists in general, was none other than Max Meldrum.

'He's just got his nose out of joint because his own painting wasn't chosen,' Margaret said in a loud voice, drawing frowns from some people, nods of agreement from others.

That night, Jack returned to his parents' house, and he stayed with them for the weekend before returning to Heide on Monday. As soon as he walked through the door, he saw the crisp white letter with his name on the front, adorned with half a dozen stamps and heavily inked, revealing its lengthy journey across the world. Immediately Jack took it to his room, where, sitting on his bed, he opened it.

*Dear Jack,*

*It was with great surprise and sorrow that I received your letter this week. In answer to your question, Sofia has not, to my knowledge, returned to Malaga at any time over the past six months. Indeed, she has not been here since you left with her, all of those years ago.*

*Unfortunately,*

*Over the years since you left I have often thought of you both, and have been glad for the snippets of news that I'd gleaned from Jovita from time to time. However, two years ago Jovita and Stephan, along with many others, left Malaga following the troubles with Franco, so I am unable to seek information from them, with regards to Sofia.*

*Words cannot express how terribly sorry I am to hear of the loss of your child, Jack, and it grieves me to think that once again Sofia has experienced such a tragedy in her life.*

*If Sofia does return to Malaga, rest assured that I will do everything I can to comfort her, and regardless of her plans, I will make sure that you are advised of her whereabouts.*

*My thoughts and prayers are with you, dear Jack, as they are for Sofia. May God be of comfort to you and bring peace to your heart through this terrible time. I also pray that the weight of Sofia's grief is lessened and that when she is thinking clearly, she returns to your side.*

*God bless you.*

*Yours sincerely,*

*Johannes Sebastian*

Closing the letter, Jack sat very still, trying to digest the words he'd just read. For months now, he'd created enormous expectations for the message Father Sebastian would deliver, and now all of his hopes had come to nothing. Nothing at all.

Part of him could weep, but his heart felt numbed and his eyes were dry. He tried to grasp at a thought, to plan what his next move should be, but his mind was utterly blank. It was as though everything about Sofia had been erased from his life. He had been so sure that Father Sebastian would have news of substance, and he'd prepared himself to hear that Sofia was resolute in her decision to never see him again. Alternatively, he'd imagined the news he most hoped for—that Sofia was safely in Malaga, albeit lost and confused, and Jack should come to her immediately. What he had not anticipated was that Father Sebastian would have absolutely no knowledge of Sofia's whereabouts.

Sofia was gone. Vanished. If she wasn't in Spain, then where could she be?

Jack opened his drawer and pushed the letter deep into the back. Although the words were empty, the warmth of Father Sebastian's hand, extended across the oceans via the fold of paper, offered a degree of comfort. Jack could not bring himself to throw the page into the bin, but neither did he want to see it—the tangible evidence that Sofia was beyond his reach and his hopes had been futile. Everything about Father Sebastian's message had the potential to send Jack seeking the comfort whiskey could provide—an urge it took every ounce of his strength to resist.

Restless, he walked towards the back door. His legs felt heavy, as though they were someone else's, with a purpose of their own.

Outside, Sunday was throwing a ball to the dogs, and she seemed to sense the change in Jack's mood.

'You have news from Sofia?' she asked, her voice cautious. Of course, she knew of the letter from Spain—it was she who'd left it on the hall table.

'No, Sun. I received a letter, but no news.'

'No?'

'Sunday, if I talk about this, I will break. Do you understand? Something in me will fly apart and I'll never be put back together again. Please, can we leave it alone?'

She gazed into his eyes intently, as though weighing up her words.

'Jack. Come with me.'

To his surprise, she approached him and, taking his arm, she tugged him, entreating him to return inside.

'No, Sunday. I don't …'

'Shhh… Follow me.'

As they walked along the hallway, Jack remembered his vow never to enter Sunday's and John's bedroom again. He hoped that wasn't on her mind, for at this second, he felt disconnected from his body, his thoughts and certainly from his willpower.

She stopped and turned his attention to a painting on the wall.

'Remember this painting?'

He nodded. It was the portrait of her, painted in Montparnasse by Agnes Goodsir.

'You knew immediately when you first saw it that it was not me at my best, Jack. Not the portrait of a member of the esteemed Baillieu family. Anyone can see that. But like I told you, I hang it there as a reminder of my foolishness.'

'But what happened, Sunday? What foolishness?' Jack's voice was low, sounding like a stranger's to his own ears. Grief had filled his body, and he wasn't sure if he could bear another ounce of sadness.

'The foolishness of letting one person hold your happiness in their hands. Of letting someone who doesn't care for you, who doesn't love you, destroy you.

'That painting was completed just weeks after my heart was shattered by the man I loved. A man who was supposed to care for me. My husband. Instead, he cheated and lied and stole from me. And then, after filling me with the disease of his filthy behaviour, he abandoned me—left me broken and dying in a room in Paris.'

Sunday's words did not make sense to Jack. 'But you are married to John…?'

'Yes, now, but I am speaking of Leonard, my first husband. A man whose charm and promises were fulfilled by his putrid contamination. Who served his own pleasure and in doing so, infected me——my insides——and destroyed my unborn child. Thanks to his infidelity and gonorrhea, I will never have a child of my own. May the bastard rot in prison.'

'Sunday, I am so sorry. That's terrible. I feel dreadful for you!'

'As you know too well, all of the sorries in the world can't make up for the loss of a child, or the hurt inflicted upon you by someone you trust and love. But you can survive. What you need to do is walk down to the river…to that scar tree, you know the one? Lay your hands on it. Wrap your arms around it. Anchor yourself to something bigger than yourself, something that understands both the weight of pain and the power of regeneration. Draw from its strength. Learn the lessons it can teach you. Your scars will always be there, just as mine are. Every minute of every day, they'll cast a shadow on your happiness, but despite them you can grow and perhaps even become great. Just like that river red, the songline tree, down by the river. Or alternatively, you can wither and die, for heaven help us, we both know that would be the easiest thing to do.'

Jack swallowed and nodded. Waves of grief flowed through him, this time for Sunday and her losses. How dreadful! What sort of man could treat his wife like that? He looked at her. So strong and determined. So dignified.

'Thanks, Sunday.'

'And when you go down to the river, take your paints and easel. Trust me, there is no greater healing than through creation.'

Jack nodded, tears filling his eyes, not only for his own loss of Sofia and Scotty, but for the pain inflicted upon Sunday by her first husband, and for the deep scars she carried as a consequence. To think that because of that man's callous behaviour, she'd never have a child of her own! Hugging her tightly, Jack sensed that she understood his pain, and was comforted by her sympathy.

# CHAPTER 13

*T*hroughout autumn, Jack immersed himself into his work in Heide's garden by morning and painted in the afternoons. He sensed a change in himself—a hardening of his heart and a determination to get on with his life. Not that he had plans to do anything other than to get out of bed each morning, throw himself into clearing a patch of thistles, painting the back wall of the house or building a new run for the expanding brood of chickens. One day at a time, he repeated to himself as he tried to ignore the empty cavern within his soul.

Often, Jack caught himself comparing Montsalvat to Heide, as though his whole world was reduced to these two places. His mind was in a constant state of weighing and measuring, assessing and evaluating —as he grappled to make sense of them, to understand the power each place wielded.

He recognised that Justus and Sunday bore similarities and differences. Each were creators who understood the power of environment and its capacity to nurture artists. Each had a spouse to support and facilitate the realisation of their dreams. Although Justus was the dictator, designer and engineer of everything at Montsalvat— from the buildings and gardens to the very beliefs and philosophies for which the community stood—it was Lil who provided a firm financial base. With the Reeds, it was Sunday whose mind was ever churning with ideas for Heide's purpose; its gardens, its ethos, its usefulness for advancing modern art in Australia. It was John who refined her raw thoughts into practical application.

Montsalvat and Heide shared a common ethos of self-sufficiency—both having extensive vegetable gardens, cows, bees and chickens. Furthermore, their dinner tables were rich with conversations that could be as interesting as they were exhausting—dissecting and debating the works of philosophers, theorists and artists in intricate detail. However, there were also undeniable differences between Montsalvat and Heide.

Like the subtle ambience of an underpainting, Heide's tones were sweet and fragrant, colourful and imbued with light. Feminine, Jack concluded—its delightful atmosphere enhanced by Sunday's cushions and curtains, her flower-filled vases and antiques, the inviting aromas that drifted from her kitchen.

In contrast, the substance of Montsalvat was muted and organic: earthy tones, the greys and browns of stone and mudbrick, the hefty slabs of bridge timber and the piles of second-hand metal and wood for recycling—materials that were dense and heavy, that demanded physical strength to work. And the work involved wielding iron tools, chisels and axes, massive saws that forever needed sharpening. Montsalvat's interiors continued the rustic theme—its sturdy hand-hewn furniture standing on roughened slate floors amid chunky glazed pottery, heavy iron pots and skillets that could be set on open fires. If Heide's core—its very heartbeat—was feminine, Montsalvat's was surely masculine.

Jack found the most significant difference between the two places, the most welcome difference, was the sense of freedom that Heide offered. The Reeds had an inquiring approach to life and invited the opinions of others, and Jack always felt comfortable sharing his thoughts on any topic. He enjoyed the Reeds' manner of discussing all angles of an issue before reaching a well-considered opinion, of encouraging those around them to read and contribute their thoughts. Because of this, Jack was introduced to Mirsky's writings, which didn't overly interest him; Dostoyevsky's *Crime and Punishment*, which he loved; and the controversial Australian writer, Katherine Suzannah Prichard, who made him weep at the senseless tragedy of *Coonardoo*.

Conversely, although Justus exercised his own intellect through the writings of philosophers and theorists, he preferred to assimilate information and form conclusions alone which he later issued in the form of a lecture at the dinner table, representing himself as the all-knowing Master. To disagree and offer conflicting opinions was to invite the full force of his mockery and disdain.

A final difference between the Reeds and Justus was the way they viewed the outside world. The Reeds were vitally interested in international politics and economic forces. They rejected the ways that power served the wealthy at the expense of the poor, hence John's growing interest in the Communist Party.

In contrast, Justus' world was that of his own creation and he largely disdained mainstream society. Where Justus perceived a problem in someone's life, be it sickness, poverty or a broken relationship, he believed the solution was to reject social mores and instead submit to the lifestyle of the retreat: sure that the only world that made any sense, that would provide happiness and fulfilment, was the one of his own design. The world of Montsalvat.

Daily, as Jack set up his easel by the river, Sunday's insistence that he would find healing in painting played on his thoughts. He was reminded of Picasso, the message that he'd offered years earlier when Jack had visited him in his studio. Standing beside the great artist, looking at his painting of an old man and woman staggering along a roadway, Jack had been challenged to look beyond lines and colour, and instead to feel the story of drooped shoulders and shuffling gait. Picasso had pushed for Jack to see hunger and pain. To see grief. The great artist, who had lost his sister and dearest friend to early deaths, had insisted that Jack's own ability to be great would only evolve after he'd experienced deep pain himself.

'Well, Pablo.' Jack's words fell upon the ears of the birds and beetles in the bush as he dabbed titanium white onto his canvas, sharpening the sunlight that was reflected in the smooth branches of the ironbark—the focal point of the scene. 'I am not sure how much sorrow you think I must bear, but these days my work is far from great. In fact, it is barely good.'

Notwithstanding, Jack couldn't deny that, as Sunday had promised, the act of painting was healing. With the sun on his back and his thoughts consumed with getting the lines, angles, depth, shadows and reflections right, it was easier to block out the stray memories of Scotty's chatter and Sofia's smile which constantly crept into his thoughts when he least expected them, and so easily brought him undone.

Jack recognised that his style had reverted to the technically perfect scenes he'd painted a decade ago—the realism that always came so naturally to him. He tried to incorporate the loose brushwork and the bolder colours he'd learned in Paris into his skies and trees, but it never felt right. More than anything, Jack knew that his work lacked feeling. A reflection of himself, he thought. A symptom of his own emotionless state, for since he'd received the letter from Father Sebastian, his heart had become heavy, his thoughts broody. Happily, his works were just the type of landscapes that sold well to a public with conservative tastes, and now with livelihoods recovering from the hardship of the Great Depression, men and women alike enjoyed having a well-painted river scene grace the walls of their dining rooms.

As Jack completed each work, John transported it into the city on his way to his office, dropping it off at a small shop where it was framed for a good price and later delivered to the Somerset Gallery, where it sold within the month. Reassured by the regular cheques that almost equalled the wage he'd once earned, Jack was easily persuaded by the Reeds to relinquish his work at Goldsbrough, Mort & Co altogether. He did have thoughts of moving to a small studio flat in the city, but John and Sunday insisted that he should stay on at Heide for at least another six months or so, insisting that his work in the garden was invaluable; and furthermore, they enjoyed his company. Because it was the easiest thing to do, Jack stayed.

Jack was relieved when, in April, news came that the Spanish Civil War had ended. Even though it meant Spain had fallen under the rule of Franco, he hoped the bloodshed and brutality endured by the Spanish people for the past three years had ceased. For as much as Jack tried to forget about Sofia, he constantly wondered where she was. Had she been caught up in London or Paris, and never returned to Spain at all, as the letter from Father Sebastian suggested? He pictured her working in Paris, perhaps in a fancy restaurant like La Grande Colbert or a café like the one her Aunt Christina had owned. Or maybe she was in London and had found a position at one of the many galleries he and Margaret had visited. He was sure that Sofia would have tried to deal with the heartbreak of losing Scotty by immersing herself in work of some kind or another, and he was comforted by the knowledge that she still had money from the sale of the finca to provide for herself. For years Jack had resisted Sofia's offer to spend her money on their needs, but it saddened him to know the rainy day he'd encouraged her to keep it for proved to be one of tragedy and separation.

# CHAPTER 14

*I*n early May, as Jack painted in his usual spot, the sound of voices approaching caught his attention. It was John, accompanied by a young fellow with clear blue eyes and a shock of black hair.

'Jack, how's your day been? That's coming along nicely... What do you think, Sidney?'

The young man nodded acknowledgement. 'Good, mate!' But his words lacked conviction. Jack didn't blame him. The painting resting on his easel was hardly ground-breaking. A tinted photo might have achieved the same impact as the uninspiring scene.

'Sidney, meet Jack Tomlinson. Jack's being staying with us these last few months. Jack, this is Sidney...?'

'Nolan... Sidney Nolan.' The young man's grip was firm in Jack's hand and his smile friendly. Jack warmed to him instantly.

'G'day, mate. Pleased to meet you.'

'Sidney's an artist, too. He's very good! Well, I think so, anyway. I thought that we might subject him to Sunday's scrutiny... Is she about?'

'She slipped into town for the afternoon. Had a meeting with Bellew, but she thought that she'd be back for afternoon tea. She said that if you beat her home, there're scones on the bench. We should start without her.'

Since his conversation with Cynthia before Christmas, Jack felt uncomfortable mentioning Bellew's name so casually. However, John didn't so much as blink.

'Late? Never known Sunday to be late for arvo tea in her life.' He laughed, looking at Nolan. 'Mealtimes are like a religion to her.'

Jack agreed. In the same manner as Justus at Montsalvat, Sunday was strict about mealtime routines—even with the 'arvo tea' that she served every day at three PM—and she was invariably annoyed if anyone dared be late.

'Ah, here she is now...'

Sunday glanced at them as she steered into the driveway at speed, and Jack was reminded of the movie stars he'd seen on the covers of the magazines Sunday left in the lounge room, with her hair held in place with a scarf and large sunglasses obscuring her eyes.

They walked over to her.

'How are you, love?' John asked. 'Had fun today?'

The teasing glance he passed to Sunday confirmed Jack's suspicion. John was fully aware she was seeing Bellew for reasons beyond the planning for the exhibition. How bizarre!

'No John, the day hasn't been fun, actually. In fact, nothing has gone to plan.' She turned towards Sidney. 'And who have we here?' Today her voice lacked any sweetness of tone.

'I'm Sidney Nolan. John thought you may like to see my paintings.'

'Pardon? You need to speak clearly, for heaven's sake.' Sidney was a mumbler, and Jack felt sorry for him as he received the ire of Sunday, who was clearly in a bad mood.

'Sunday! I asked Sidney to bring his paintings for you to see. They are quite interesting. I'm sure that you will find his work fascinating.'

'Not today, I'm sorry. I've got a headache. In fact, you all go ahead without me. I think I will take an aspirin and have a lie down. Excuse me.' And with that, she was gone.

John looked at Nolan sheepishly. 'Sorry, Sidney. Sun does get these headaches from time to time. Bad ones. The best thing that she can do is rest. Come on in and we'll have a cuppa. Nobody makes scones, or jam, or cream quite like Sunday. What do you say, Jack?' Jack agreed. 'How about you, Neil, are you ready? It's just going three.'

John's artfulness as a host came to the fore as he thoughtfully made a cup of tea for Sunday and then returned to the kitchen, shutting the hallway door to stop their voices from travelling through the house and disturbing her.

For half an hour they made small talk, and Jack learned that Sidney had grown up in Carlton, the son of a tram-driver. Like himself, Sidney had always had a love of drawing and painting. He'd tried to make a living from it, but still relied on a range of income sources—wages from his job as a lunchtime cook at a Melbourne café and the money he earned picking asparagus—to pay his bills.

Over the next few days, Heide was cloaked in a veil of tension as the mood that Sunday brought home on Monday persisted. Bellew remained conspicuously absent, and Jack was glad. Whenever he'd been around discussing the advertising campaign, confirming copy he'd written and collecting photos for the exhibition, the young reporter's loud tones never ceased to grate upon Jack's nerves.

Bellew had become no less brash than he'd been the day Jack first heard him speak at the CAS meeting, and the manner in which he name-dropped the various artists as though their successful reception by Australian audiences lay with him alone was tedious. It riled Jack to hear him chatting about presenting Picasso's works to Australians as though the upcoming exhibition might enhance Picasso's career—as if Picasso would have cared! Jack would have loved to have told Bellew how he'd once spent an afternoon in Picasso's studio, looking through his drawing books, surrounded by his paintings and sculptures, drinking Picasso's tea and eating his biscuits. But he'd said nothing, instead escaping the dinner table by gathering all of their plates and busying himself in the kitchen.

Now it appeared that whatever had been between Sunday and Bellew was finally over, and perhaps they wouldn't be seeing him at

Heide any more. Nonetheless, it was awkward being in the house where Sunday had withdrawn to her room. Her wailing cries accompanied by the sound of John's calm voice attempting to pacify her filtered through the walls, whilst in Jack and Neil's presence John tried to keep a cheerful face.

Jack was glad Neil was there when on Thursday night, the sounds of Sunday's screeching and John's shouting echoed through the rooms. It seemed that Sunday's pain had evolved to anger and John's patience with her was wearing thin.

'Come on, Sunday. You knew it was only a fling for Bellew. He was out for a bit of fun, and so were you.'

'He's a snooty little upstart. He should appreciate the opportunity we've given him. Before us he was an unknown journalist. Now he's one of Australia's front reporters for modern art!'

Jack raised his eyebrows at Neil, who shrugged. 'That's our Sunday. When all is well, she's fabulous, but heaven help us when she's crossed. The plates will fly next, mark my words. Get ready to duck, Jack, and don't say that you haven't been warned!' Neil took a deep drag on his cigarette and chuckled softly. Jack was sure that he was joking.

Not so, however, for on Friday morning, after four days of seclusion, Sunday emerged from her bedroom, and her mood was volatile.

'John! Can't you even wash a plate properly?' she screeched, throwing a blue floral bowl across the room towards the rubbish bin.

'Come on, Sunday. Enough of that,' he barked in reply. Then, as if deliberately controlling his irritation, John's tone changed. 'Let's go for a drive, love. I'll take the day off from the office and we'll head down to Sorrento. The sea air will do you good. What do you think, Sun?'

Sunday assented, and Jack was thankful for the silence in the house after they'd left.

∾

The upset was all but forgotten a week later when, mid-afternoon Saturday, the young fellow—Nolan—sailed down the driveway on a

139

bicycle, followed closely behind by a pretty young woman who he introduced as his fiancée, Elizabeth Patterson. Sunday smiled broadly as she greeted them.

'I hope it's okay, us just turning up like this,' Nolan asked. 'John said that he thought it would be. I really don't want to bother you.'

'Of course, Sidney. Don't be silly. John told me to expect you. I wasn't well when you arrived the other day. I am sorry—it was terribly rude of me. We'll make up for it today, shall we? Have you got your paintings there? I would love to see them... Come join us for tea. I think we might have it outdoors. It's far too hot inside, don't you think? Just a minute and I will fetch it. John, you might give me a hand, if you wouldn't mind.'

As John followed Sunday into the house, Jack busied himself sweeping the leaves off the outdoor table, all the while answering the barrage of questions that Nolan directed at him.

'How long have you been living here for, mate?'

'Just over five months now, I suppose.'

'It's lovely. Look at this garden! It's a picture.'

'Yes, it's beautiful. The Reeds have worked miracles here along with Neil—he's the Reed's gardener. I help out for a couple of hours each morning before I get in a bit of painting.'

'John mentioned that you studied painting in Paris?'

'Yes, I did a stint there. Not for very long, though. Are you thinking of going?'

'Oh, well definitely. One day, for sure. At the moment, we're saving for our wedding, and one doesn't make a lot of money working at the café, nor from painting at present. Mind you, this week I have had a request to paint backdrops for the Australian Ballet Company. That should pay well.'

At the return of Sunday and John, cups of tea were poured; and scones, jam and cream as well as Sunday's lemon slice set out.

So, Sidney. What circumstances brought you to John's office last week?

Jack watched with interest as Nolan answered, surprised at how clear-sighted the young man was about his future goals.

'It was a bit of a journey, actually. I'd heard about some bursaries

—for artists to get to Paris—that were on offer. Beginning with the Herald offices, I was sent on a wild goose chase. Nobody thought that I qualified for a bursary, but they seemed to think that I might have something to offer. I was pushed from pillar to post, until I was told that yourself and John are keen on modern works, and I was given directions to John's office.'

'You are very persistent, aren't you? I like that.' Sunday replied.

Nolan continued, describing how he'd been creating letter-works and images for advertising for years; and more recently, he'd been attending classes at the National Gallery Art School, lessons that he found rather boring.

The intensity with which Nolan spoke suggested that he thought he had this one opportunity to sell himself to Sunday and needed to give it his all. His mind was quick, his voice clear and his ideas electric, crackling with intensity. He oozed a confidence that made Jack believe everything the young man dreamed of was utterly achievable.

'It all sounds very interesting. Show me what you have there.' Sunday's tone was cool, as if she doubted whether Nolan's artistic ability would match his verbal skills. She cleared the end of the table and invited Sidney to empty his knapsack. Turning the pages of the drawing book he gave her in quick succession, she nodded repeatedly, with increasing enthusiasm.

'These are very good! Look at these abstracts, John!'

Listening to Sunday's effusive trill, Jack checked himself... was that jealousy he felt? He looked at the series of paintings that Nolan had laid across the table. For the most part, they were geometric line drawings, some colourful, some plain, some with strange dots, and he wondered what Sunday saw in them.

A cold breeze rippled across the garden, sending several pages fluttering to the ground.

'Come on inside, Sidney. You and Elizabeth must stay for dinner, and we can talk some more.'

～

As they walked past the Reeds' library, Nolan's eyes lit up, and he turned to John.

'Wow…. Do you mind if I have a look in here?'

'Of course not. Do you like books?' John replied.

'I love books! I love reading! It's amazing how just a few words, a phrase here, a paragraph there, can alter the way you see things. How a single idea can set your mind off, leading to more ideas, until suddenly everything you ever thought you knew about the world is transformed.'

'Who do you read?' Sunday asked.

'Anything, really. The National Gallery Art School has a great library next door, and I also borrow from the State Library.'

'He goes to lessons and comes home with armfuls of books,' added Elizabeth. 'Buries himself in them. I hardly get a word out of him. And he writes, too.'

'Writes? My, my. You are quite the creative.' Sunday laughed as she watched Nolan scanning the shelves of the library.

'Yes, he's almost finished a novel!' Elizabeth was clearly proud of her multi-talented boyfriend.

'Rimbaud!' Nolan spied Sunday's copy of *Illuminations*, the one she'd lent to Jack when he'd first arrived. Jack was stunned. This young man—the son of a tram-driver who worked as a short-order cook in a city café—knew of the work of a French poet? Perhaps Jack himself was the uneducated oaf.

'You know Rimbaud's work, Sidney?' Sunday couldn't contain her excitement at finding a fellow enthusiast, and from that minute her rapture with Nolan began.

~

Over the next few weeks, Nolan was a frequent visitor to Heide, arriving at all times of the day, sometimes with Elizabeth, at other times alone. Sunday had finally found the protégé she'd been looking for: someone with whom she shared a meeting of minds, who loved painting, poetry and books in the same way that she did, and who she thought might be shaped into the artist that Australia was waiting for. It seemed that if Sunday wasn't talking to Nolan, she was talking about him.

'His writing is interesting,' she told Jack and John after having spent two days reading the novel that Sidney was writing, 'but really, he should focus on painting. I will tell him that tomorrow. He can't spread himself between both writing and paining—he must put all of his efforts into one or the other, and painting is his better skill.'

Forewarned by Cynthia's disclosure about Sunday's manner of attaching herself to her protégés, Jack watched with fascination as the relationship between her and Nolan unfolded.

On arriving, Nolan always made a beeline to Sunday, and together they studied books, analysed poetry, and dissected paintings. They were like two souls on a mission—each energised by the company of the other—and nothing could stop them from pursuing their goals; between them, anything was possible.

Throughout winter, John and Neil became used to working around Nolan's painting materials, which became a fixture on the kitchen sideboard, coming out onto the table when he arrived. There, he and Sunday worked, side by side, she sketching and outlining ideas, Nolan making marks upon canvas. All the while, they discussed and argued their way forward, he adding this, she that.

Their completed efforts were tacked onto the dining room wall, and each evening at the dinner table, Sunday explained the progression of 'their work'. John was always enthusiastic, asking just the right questions and offering praise. Jack found the way he and Sunday read all manner of ideas into the lines and shapes she and Sidney had created as fascinating. Nolan's style was utterly different to his own, and not at all to his taste, but Jack kept his thoughts to himself. Who was he to question the mysteries of contemporary art?

∾

Often, Jack felt sorry for Elizabeth, who at first accompanied Nolan to Heide on most of his visits, but quickly became bored with sitting around, waiting for him and Sunday to finish their collaborations. When she came outdoors, wandering across to pass the time with him while he worked, Jack was happy to chat with her. It was a shame to see her excluded from the tight unit that Nolan had formed with Sunday, and when she asked Jack if he thought Sunday might have bewitched Sidney, Jack didn't know how to answer.

Without doubt their relationship far exceeded the usual bounds of friendship between a young man and a married woman as their laughter and chat infiltrated every corner of Heide, and their energy charged the air from the kitchen where they painted together, to the dining room where they argued the nuances of the poets they loved, to the library which was scattered with the books that inspired them, and to the bedroom, where Jack suspected that they were looking at more than the Streetons and McCubbins gracing the walls. Furthermore, it became quite obvious that not only was John fully aware of Sunday's relationship with Nolan, but he was also a participant in their intimacies, and on more than one occasion Jack encountered the three of them leaving the Reeds' bedroom in the morning.

While once such behaviour would have shocked Jack, time and experience had revealed to him that other people's values could be very different to his own. He did hope that Nolan would do the decent thing by Elizabeth and at least tell her that he was intimate with the Reeds. Beyond that, he concluded that this tryst was not a case of young girls, like Helen and Sonia Skipper—being taken advantage of by older men —but the behaviour of adults in their own home, and he minded his own business.

# CHAPTER 15

*J*n August, with the *Herald Exhibition of Contemporary Art of London and Paris* barely six weeks away, final planning was stepped up, and Sunday and John seemed to be forever attending meetings to discuss the organisation for the event, while their dinner conversations became a constant assessment of the progress being made, and ticking off checklists. Who had written feature articles? Had final agreement on the layout of the proposed display been reached? If so, then was the program ready to be printed? Who was responsible for attending to the insurance required for transporting the paintings to Melbourne, and had all of the key guests been officially contacted with the final details for the Exhibition's opening night?

John and Sunday's conversations were not without trepidation, for a second event—one of world-wide significance—was unfolding. Daily the headlines of the *Herald* and *Sun* flagged warnings to their readers; their news reports outlining an emerging disaster caused by the actions of European dictators, that threatened to plunge Britain, into war. Adolf Hitler, the German Chancellor, had repeatedly ignored the conditions of the Treaty of Versailles that had been imposed on Germany at the end of the Great War by sending troops into the Rhineland and more recently, annexing Austria. And now the Italian leader, Mussolini, had joined forces with Hitler, and the two nations were operating in tandem to support each other's mission to increase their power in Europe.

Jack listened with interest to John's scathing analysis of the Treaty of Versailles and disdain for the British strategy of conceding to Hitler's demands in the hope of avoiding war. Like many, John believed that the vast loss of land and the heavy financial penalty extracted from Germany after the Great War had been overly punitive, and it was inevitable that the Germans would retaliate sooner or later. Now, it seemed, that time was upon them.

'It'll be like Franco all over again,' he told Jack. 'Untold brutality, innocent people imprisoned or slain. These dictators are monsters, and yet we stand by and watch and do nothing.'

Each evening, Jack joined the Reeds and Neil, tuning in to the BBC and listening to the broadcasts of the unfolding drama. On Saturdays, he, Sunday and John attended the matinee at the cinema, where the newsreels prior to the feature film provided visual footage of Hitler's growing popularity. A chill ran though Jack as he watched the thousands of Germans—perhaps even tens of thousands—gathered before the strange little man with a shrieking voice, waving hands and manic eyes, with their arms raised to salute their Fuhrer amid the billowing swastika flags. It was easy to feel worried.

Each morning, Jack and Neil searched the *Sun* and the *Argus* for updates of the growing unrest. Increasingly, the Allie's strategy of appeasement—keeping Hitler happy at all costs—was being questioned.

'All very well for us to stick our heads in the sand, Jack, but while we are doing nothing, the Nazis are gaining in power,' Neil said. 'Britain may not want a war, but I can't see how they can avoid it.'

At Neil's words, Jack's thoughts turned to Sofia, and he prayed that she was safe. He thought of Aunt Elizabeth and Uncle Robert, reminding himself to ask his mother how they were. He wanted to believe that Neil was wrong, that war might be averted, but the gardener remained adamant that war was necessary, and eventually Jack was persuaded that he was right; Hitler needed to be stopped.

Throughout August, the papers reported on the British and French leaders' continued negotiations with Hitler and Mussolini, describing the pledges and promises that were being made, and then broken. They reported how Hitler's demands for Czechoslovakia's Sudetenland had been granted. It was after all, they felt, largely populated with German citizens; and surely now the German Chancellor would cease his aggressive stance. However, when he brazenly claimed the remainder of Czechoslovakia, and then threatened that he would also take Poland, it was obvious that there was no satisfying Hitler's hunger for power. He had to be stopped.

And on the third of September, Jack, Neil, Sunday and John gathered around the radio, to hear the words of Prime Minister Menzies they'd been expecting; his voice purposeful as it was sombre. '*Fellow Australians, it is my melancholy duty to inform you officially that, in consequence of the persistence of Germany in her invasion of Poland, Great Britain has declared war upon her, and that, as a result, Australia is also at war.*'

Jack glanced at the others as the words sank in. It was as though time had been suspended. Could this be real? Australia was officially at war! Neil shook his head in disgust. The news was no surprise to him; his disgust was for mankind and the impossible situations it created. John's back straightened, taking on the stoic bearing of a man who had an important duty to attend. Sunday gasped, her hand to her mouth, shocked by the announcement that had turned months of speculation into reality in the space of seconds. She might well retire to her bedroom for a few days, Jack thought. Emotional events had that effect on her.

Despite his own anticipation of this announcement, the reality of Australia being at war seemed surreal. He felt as though he were swimming underwater, perceiving the world through a lens. He glanced outside the kitchen window, as if he might see a rush of the RAAF's Hawker Demons, Bristol Bulldogs and Avro Ansons hurtling northward to drop bombs on Germany; but in the dusky twilight, the dreadful news held no interest to the inhabitants of Heide's grounds.

At the height of spring, the garden was at its most beautiful, an explosion of colour. The warmth of the days invigorated the plants, abetting an eruption of blooms, seeds, sticky pollen and sweet nectar designed to attract bees, beetles, grasshoppers and aphids, whose presence nourished the birds that scampered from branch to branch, building their nests. The orchard's trees were abundant with fruit, ripening in readiness to be picked and stewed or pickled or turned into pies and jams. The chirping of a thousand cicadas filled the air—their shrill chorus adding to the sunset cackling of kookaburras and the mournful cry of a flock of cockatoos as they perched on the trees along the riverbank, ready to settle for the night.

While the natural world responded to instincts to grow and multiply, humans were preparing to destroy or be destroyed.

Finally, they were at war! Who could believe it? Jack wondered.

In bed that night, a restlessness descended upon him, and he found it impossible to sleep. Thoughts of Sofia consumed him; she was in Europe, and war was imminent. How could he get to her? She was alone in the world, and whether she wished to see him or not, Sofia was his wife. It was his duty to ensure her safety! He needed to be over there, and enlisting in Australia's armed forces seemed to offer the best solution.

The day after Menzies' announcement, Jack visited his parents. As he'd anticipated, they were in shock. His own hazy memories of the Great War were fashioned through the obscure lens of childhood, when he'd been sheltered from stories of bombs exploding, shattered buildings and the deaths of a generation of young Australian men. However, for his parents, the announcement of war resurrected memories of four years of horror, death and destruction, the effects of which still lingered for many of their friends.

Marian was convinced that this time, Australia would hold back. 'Certainly, we might send a few enlisted soldiers to Europe, but that would be all. We couldn't possibly risk the lives of tens of thousands of young boys the way we did in the Great War.' Her words were as much a question as a statement.

'But Mum, what if the Germans come here? Surely it is best to stop them in their tracks while they are in Europe.'

'Yes, but haven't we got the Militia to do that? They will protect our borders. That's what they're there for!'

'Marian, how on earth could the Militia protect Australia's borders? We have thousands of miles of unoccupied land. An enemy could gain a foothold anywhere they liked, and we wouldn't even know about it for a month!'

'Do you think that you should get your old job back at Goldsbrough, Mort & Co., Jack? Then you might be spared from being called up!'

'Mum, no. I won't be doing that!' It horrified Jack that his mother could even suggest such a thing. During the Great War, his father had been spared active duty—his work deemed essential—a fact that his mother was thankful for, but which Jack knew had sat heavily on William's conscience. More than once he'd heard his father state his regret that he'd been at home listening to news of the terrible losses of young men in Gallipoli and the Western Front and not alongside them, shouldering his share of the burden.

Before he left his parents' house, Jack spoke to his father alone. 'Dad, I intend to go when we get the call.'

William nodded, and said quietly, 'We won't worry your mother about that for now. Perhaps things won't come to that after all.' His hollow tone suggested that, like Jack, his father doubted war was avoidable.

Although the talk of war, followed by Menzies announcement, dominated most people's thoughts and conversations, it seemed that for John and Sunday, Menzies announcement acted as a catalyst akin to a starter gun in a foot race. A race to get the CAS exhibition over and done with before Australia was totally swamped by the war that was surely coming. It was as though they believed that by stepping up their preparations for the exhibition; making posters, submitting the final news articles, discussing rosters for the door, selecting the clothing they would wear and the champagne to be consumed, then perhaps they could thwart Hitler's relentless quest to drag the world into war.

Jack listened to their plans, offered his opinion when asked and agreed that he'd be happy to man the door and escort dignitaries to tables, along with Cynthia and Margaret. However, of far greater importance to him were the updates of the nations' impending commitment to the war. Daily, he and Neil discussed the issues, although they seemed to raise far more questions than answers. What would the war mean to the everyday lives of Australians? When would they enter the battle? Where would the fighting begin? When and how would Menzies raise troops to be sent to Britain's aid? It was obvious, by the newspapers' articles, that others shared their concerns. And even though people dreaded the thought of a war, waiting for answers to these questions proved equally frustrating.

Many believed that Australia should be sending troops to Britain immediately, although there was confusion about the nature of such a force. At present, the only army Australia had was the Militia—a force of peacetime volunteers, whose role was limited to defending Australian soil. And for all of the enthusiasm of those who believed 'we should get over there', when the British Parliament passed a bill for conscription, a second wave of debate arose about Australia's ability to support a war in Europe.

'They'll be useless, Jack,' Neil insisted. 'The service has never been trained for overseas action, and most of the men will have far too many demands on their personal lives, what with their work and families, to agree to fight a war on the other side of the world.'

Certainly, the newspapers described the Militia as utterly ill-prepared and under-equipped.

'Maybe they will call for conscripts,' said Jack.

'Yeah... well, that will be a circus. We've never accepted it in the past, so I can't see it working now. It will be a brave government to suggest it.'

Many shared Neil's view. A widespread argument went that conscription ballots were rigged, skewed to send the sons of the less affluent into battle, while the sons of wealthy families were spared. And those of the Militia who'd stepped forward and volunteered themselves as professional soldiers, equally opposed conscription. They argued that if you were going to stand in a trench with a gun in your hand, you wanted someone beside you who'd chosen to be there, not some snivelling coward who'd been forced into the battle against his will.

Jack conceded that the view of the Militia had merit, and henceforth his mind was made up. He would not wait to be conscripted into an Australian army and forever be viewed as an unwilling participant to the battle! He'd step up and enlist at the first opportunity. He wanted to get to Europe and stop the Germans in their tracks. And also, by getting to England, he could stop the constant worrying and wondering about Sofia and instead find her.

And when Jack saw an article asking volunteers for the Second Australian Imperial Forces to present themselves at their nearest recruitment office, of which a number of addresses were included, he never hesitated.

# CHAPTER 16

*J*ack rose early and was on the train and travelling into the city after John had left for work, but before Sunday rose. Beyond telling his father the previous month, Jack had not discussed his intention to enlist with anybody; he wanted to be sure that he was eligible before sharing his plans.

Descending the stairs, Jack had paused under the clocks, checking the torn newspaper article for the street number of the recruitment office for the dozenth time. He needn't have bothered, for as soon as he turned onto Elizabeth Street, he saw a crowd of men gathered outside a grey building. Men of every size, shape and age: young, old, short, tall, bespectacled or not. Some—surely they were merely boys—had arrived in groups. Listening to their banter, Jack could tell that they were excited about the prospects of an adventure in the offering. He smiled as they ribbed each other about heroes and cowards: Who was the best shot and who was likely to run home to their mothers at the first scratch. They reminded him of times past—his senior years at school—when such teasing had underpinned the bonds of friendship.

An older man stood to one side; he was also watching the young lads, concern in his eyes. He must be at least fifty, Jack thought, surprised. The advertisement cited the age bracket for those enlisting as eighteen to thirty-five years. From the man's grey hair and trimmed moustache, upright stance and resolute expression, Jack suspected that he was a man who'd served in the military before—that he knew the call to arms was no laughing matter, but a duty not to be shirked. He was right, of course. The city was full of diggers of the Great War, with broken bodies, missing limbs and only a bottle of whiskey to cheer their damaged souls—leaving no doubts that the battlefield created far more casualties than heroes.

'Next!' The female voice echoed through the open doorway, and it was Jack's turn to step through. Inside, the lady ushered him towards her desk.

'Welcome, sir. Before we start, I need you to fill out this form.' Without waiting for him to speak, she gave him the cream-coloured paper and waved him towards a trestle table at the side of the room. 'You will find a seat over there. Pen and inkwells, too. Let me know if you have any questions.'

Seated, Jack glanced around the room, where other men were in the process of completing their forms. He focused on the paper before him, reading the ornate heading—*Attestation Form*. In the spaces indicated, he recorded his name, age, address, occupation, religion, educational qualifications, previous service experience. He added 'yes' to Married, and 'Sofia Tomlinson' in the space titled Spouse. Children—Yes? No? There was no provision to acknowledge Scotty, to recognise a child who was no more. Swallowing hard, he left it blank and returned to the lady seated at the desk.

'That was quick. Looks good. No questions? Okay, that's step one completed. You must pass a medical examination now. It should only take a few minutes. Go through that door, you'll see a bench. Wait there and one of the doctors will call you when he's ready.'

Jack nodded at the two men already seated on the bench seat as they made space for him. After light chat about the surprising number of blokes who'd turned up and where they were from and how bad the troubles in Europe were, he found himself called into the office of a smiling-faced doctor.

'Good morning, young man. How are you? All fit and ready to

serve your country? Well done. We need more men like you—eager to take on the enemy. Let's just slip your shirt and trousers off, can we? Down to your underwear. That's right.'

Standing in his singlet and underpants, Jack followed the doctor's instructions to breathe and hold and bend and stretch.

It only took ten minutes to record his baseline details. Height and weight—a bit thin, the doctor told him; chest—clear; eyes—twenty-twenty; hearing—excellent, he'd be able to hear the footsteps of a beetle from a hundred yards away. Next, Jack answered a series of questions regarding his medical history. Past illnesses? Hospitalisations? Family history? And then it was over.

Nodding approvingly, the doctor signed his form. There were no impediments; Jack was fit and ready for duty.

All that remained were the signatures—the official recording of his acceptance of enlistment—and for that, Jack was shuffled to another bench, where, again, he waited for his name to be called.

This time, it was two men in uniform who greeted him; again, cheerful types who were keen to welcome him into the brotherhood of the military.

'G'day, mate. You've joined up. Well done to you. We're very grateful to have you on board.'

'Yes. Thanks. It's all new to me, of course, but I have been keen to enlist ever since I heard that we were at war.'

'That's the way. You're almost there. The medical went well; that's the main thing. Now we just need to complete the official pledge and signing. Are you ready?'

Jack was, and following their instructions, he looked at the last paragraph on the Attestation Form, "The Oath of Enlistment."

He never faltered as he read the lines.


*'I, Jack William Tomlinson, swear that I will well and truly serve our Sovereign Lord, the King, in the Military Forces of the Commonwealth of Australia until the cessation of the present time of war and twelve months thereafter or until sooner lawfully discharged, dismissed, or removed, and that I will resist His Majesty's enemies and cause His*

154

*Majesty's peace to be kept and maintained, and that I will in all matters appertaining to my service faithfully discharge my duty according to law.*

*So help me, God.'*

'Good work, Tomlinson. Now all that's needed is your signature. There. That's the way.'

He signed, they signed, and then there was a shaking of hands.

'Congratulations, Recruit Tomlinson. It's official. You are now enlisted in the Second Australian Imperial Force's 17th Brigade. Further details of your appointment will be mailed to you in the next few days. Pleased to have you on board, Recruit Tomlinson!'

Their jovial tone was underpinned by officialdom, and again, Jack accepted their handshakes. He glanced down at the completed paperwork, the ink wet upon the page, and knew he had done the right thing. A new chapter was about to begin and he was ready for it. For twelve months, his life had been on hold. He'd restored his physical health, and his mind had become much clearer. Losing Scotty remained ever painful, but it had lost its gut-wrenching punch. Now, each night as he prepared for sleep, Jack had adopted the ritual of first thinking of his little man, picturing him as one might a cherubic angel, sweet and whole, with laughter and mischief in his eyes. He'd bid him good night before turning his thoughts to Sofia— thoughts which varied from week to week, from an internal cry of *where are you?* to hoping she was safe, to imagining her in his arms. Sometimes he whispered to her, promising that he would find her, that he would never hurt her again. Other times he'd feel bitterness, frustrated that she'd abandoned him and their marriage, vanishing and leaving him helpless to do anything. Mostly, though, he was worried for her safety and state of mind, and despaired at the tortured thoughts that had led her to flee from himself and from Australia.

But living at Heide was a temporary arrangement; Jack knew that. He neither could, nor did he wish to, live in the Reeds' spare bedroom forever. The onset of war offered the impetus for change. He'd get to

Europe and once there, he would find Sofia and see what the future held for them.

⁓

As he stepped out into the sunshine, Jack was surprised to see the swell of men had almost trebled from what it had been an hour earlier. Already he felt different as he wove between them, nodding and smiling, replying 'Thanks, mate,' to the comments of 'Good on ya, cobber,' and 'Well done, mate.'

Walking back to Flinders Street Station, Jack felt energised and keen to share his news with somebody. He phoned Margaret from the station and could tell from her voice that she was pleased to hear from him. Usually, it was she who did the contacting.

'Fancy you ringing me, Jack—to what do I deserve the honour? It's not bad news, is it? Is everything alright?'

'Of course everything's alright,' Jack gave the obligatory response, although he knew that, of all people, Margaret was least likely to take the news of his enlistment well. 'I was just wondering if you'd like to catch up for a pint after work.'

'Sure—the Latin? We'll have a pint and some fish and chips, shall we?'

They agreed to meet at five thirty, and hanging up, Jack decided that at the end of the evening he'd return to Copelin Street and spend the weekend with his parents.

When he got back to Heide, Sunday and Nolan were in the kitchen, chattering with excitement. They'd decided to paint a series of paintings depicting Ned Kelly.

'What could be more Australian than a series of our most famous bushranger?' Sunday exclaimed, clearly thrilled with the project.

'Sure, Sunday. That would be interesting.' Jack found it best to go along with whatever Sunday's ideas were, although he could hardly imagine how Ned Kelly, a murderous bushranger of the previous century, could be incorporated into a modern art style. Glancing at the table, he saw their sketches. Bold images of the unusual steel helmet that Ned Kelly famously wore. Backgrounds in strong colours. It would be interesting to see what she and Nolan could do with the theme. And there was no argument from him that the idea was both original and Australian.

'What have you been up to?' Sunday squinted as she quizzed him. Her curiosity wasn't surprising; it was almost unheard of for Jack to leave Heide for a whole morning without mentioning his plans.

'I've joined the army, Sunday! I couldn't help myself. Ever since Menzies announced that we were at war, it's played on my mind.'

Their responses came in a blur of each other's words.

'Wow, Jack. That's a big step... You are a better man than me!' Nolan offered.

'Oh no, Jack! Why? Who would have thought? I don't know what to say! I hate to think of you going to war. Don't you get any ideas, Sidney! Now it feels like it's really happening. As if our lives will never be the same! Are you sure you'll be okay, Jack? And what about the exhibition?'

'I'm not sure if anything about war is safe, Sun, but the point of enlisting is so that our homes here in Australia can be safe. And the exhibition is only two weeks away... I don't expect they'll have me facing the Jerries before then!'

'What will your parents say? Poor things. And you their only son. How awful for them!'

'Hey! Don't write me off, Sunday! I plan to be a hero—I am not bad with a gun, you know!' He laughed as she rolled her eyes at him. 'I'm going to stay with Mum and Dad this weekend; I'll tell them then. I am more worried about telling Margaret this evening. If I survive her reaction, I'll survive the Germans, that's for sure!'

Margaret, as he'd expected, was furious.

'Enlisted! For heaven's sake, Jack, why? This is not Australia's war! Menzies can say what he likes about the Mother Country and our duty to the Empire, blah, blah blah. Just because they've chosen to start a war, I don't see why we have to be dragged into it, too.'

157

'Yes, but if we don't get in and help now, the Germans might end up on our doorstep!'

'That's ridiculous. Why on earth would the Germans invade Australia? We are thousands of miles away—a bloody little island on the other side of the world. What on earth could they possibly want from us?'

'World domination! Plus, Australia has resources: Iron. Copper. Gold. Land! And, in any case, we need to support those people in England. If the Japanese should invade us, well, we'll be wanting the help of Britain, so it's only fair that we are there for them against the Germans. Besides, most Australians have family there. You included! Don't you want to keep them safe?'

Jack knew that using Margaret's family was scant defence; she came from a line of pacifists. Vanessa and Virginia and all the other Bloomsburys had been conscientious objectors throughout the Great War and Ness had lost Julian to the Spanish war. He wondered how Ness and Duncan, Clive and Roger were coping now, with war yet again threatening their country.

Margaret changed her tack. 'Regardless, Jack, even if Australia wants to send its army, you are no soldier… You're an artist!'

She had branded him with the same title aboard the *Ormonde* almost a decade earlier, a phrase that catapulted him into the world of painters and led him to Paris.

'I can play soldiers as well as the next man, Margaret! You watch me.'

His playful pseudo-sibling teasing did not have the desired effect. Tears suddenly erupted and she did not seem to care who overheard her as she shouted at him, her voice thunderous and her face red, punctuating the phrases of her tirade with her fist against the table.

'Let the British fight their own damned war! For heaven's sake, Jack. People get killed in wars. People die! If Menzies wants to fight, well, he can take himself and his cabinet to London and pick up a gun himself. They're always so bloody quick to send our young men off to do their dirty work, but you can bet the politicians and their sons won't be standing on any battlefield facing the enemy's bullets!'

Jack was shocked. He had expected opposition, for Margaret to give him a hundred reasons why he shouldn't enlist. He had prepared for her to beg him not to go—to be frightened for him. What he hadn't expected was the cold fury, the berating, the tears. Her tears were not for him, he knew, but for the young man that she'd lost in the Great War. Her beloved artist who'd put duty before love... and despite his promises to return, had got himself killed.

'Margaret, I will be alright, I promise! I need to go—I need to find Sofia—be sure she is okay. She's right in the middle of this, you realise. And after all, she is my wife.'

Margaret's face fell, defeated. She nodded, hugging him.

'Yes, I know, I know... It's just... please be safe. Please make sure that you come home.'

'Sure, I'll come home. You'd probably kill me if I didn't.'

'That is not even funny, Jack. But you are right. I will. With my bare hands.'

Telling his parents was easier than Jack had expected. He wasn't sure if his demeanour had changed since that morning, but it was as though they knew the minute he stepped through the front door.

'You've enlisted! Already!' His mother had tears in her eyes, but she held them back.

William's response betrayed a gruffness in his voice. 'Good on you, son. I can't say I am happy to see you go to war, but I agree, Hitler needs to know that Australians are not prepared to put up with his nonsense, and we need to be there for Britain. God help them, they've barely recovered from the last war. Hopefully this will be over quickly.'

Over dinner they discussed every scenario they could imagine—both for Jack's immediate future and that of the world's stage. When would he be called up and where would he go? What training would he need? Where would he be posted? Would he be able to send letters home? William and Marian drew on their recollections of the Great War, and Jack could see they were trying to be positive. From her controlled reaction, he realised that his father had prepared his mother for the likelihood that Jack would enlist, and he was glad to see them take it so well. What choice did any of them have?

~

A week later, the letter he'd been waiting for arrived—crisp, cream coloured and important looking. Jack's appointment to the Second Australian Imperial Force, Sixth Division, 17th Brigade was official. Of the Brigade's four infantry units, he was allocated to the 2/5th and was to report for duty at the Brigade Headquarters, the Melbourne Showgrounds, on Friday, October 20th. Considering the date, he was pleased, for it meant that he'd be available to attend the Town Hall for the *Herald* Exhibition of Contemporary Art of London and Paris as he'd hoped.

~

They were strange for Jack—the days leading up to the exhibition. His mood felt unsettled, as if he were living between two worlds, which of course he was. He was about to step into a world entering a war, threatening and uncertain; but coupled with the thrilling possibility of being united with Sofia. The other was the pre-war world of Heide, which was fixated on the exhibition that would commence that very weekend. Preparations were all but completed, and conversations had come down to the simple things like which clothes to wear and the transport arrangements for the evening.

A sense of celebration filled the air, and although Australian towns and cities everywhere held men who were packing their bags and farewelling their families in readiness to take their place in the various army training camps dotted across the nation, the residents of Heide had more important things at hand. Cynthia had arrived for the weekend, and Margaret joined them for the Sunday evening before the opening. They sat around drinking wine and cocktails, and eating cheese and olive canapés—all of them thrilled that finally some of the world's most extraordinary and significant modern artwork was about to be revealed to Melbourne's public.

On Monday the 16<sup>th</sup> they were up early and full of good humour as they manned the door of the Town Hall, happily chatting with the guests and handing out programs that listed the paintings on display. It was interesting to see the celebrities of the day arrive and the men from the *Herald*. Bill Burdett, the man responsible for selecting the paintings, was congratulated by everyone, as was Keith Murdoch for his role in sponsoring the event. It irked Jack to see Bellows clinging to the coattails of both men, smiling and nodding as if he alone was responsible for the success of the event.

Jack, Cynthia and Margaret manned the doors on and off throughout the week, and Jack enjoyed the exhibition far more than he'd anticipated. Cynthia was terrific company—witty and well-travelled—and as it turned out, the three shared much in common. She'd spent time in London a couple of years earlier, where she'd met Roger Fry and even been to the Burlington Gallery to attend an extraordinary surrealist exhibition that Roger had organised.

'Surrealism! Truly, I ask you, what does anyone see in it? Modern art, yes, the impressionists and even some of the abstracts are interesting, but I just can't understand the fuss about surrealism,' Jack said, thinking of Salvador Dali's strange concoctions, and remembering Monsieur Simon's unflattering descriptions of the conceited artist.

'You need to be open-minded. Surrealism portrays the subconscious mind, our dreams and fantasies,' Cynthia explained.

'Well, some people's dreams are downright weird. I don't think that surrealism helps the cause of modern art at all.'

'Yes, Jack, but you always were such a conservative,' Margaret teased, and he laughed, remembering how she'd taken him through the galleries of London, teaching him about the various art movements, and how he'd mocked some of the ridiculous works she'd shown him. She was right. He was a conservative. Essentially, the paintings that he appreciated most were traditional, although he now loved the impressionists like Renoir and Monet, and he didn't even mind the strange colours used by Cezanne and Matisse.

It was wonderful to have the works of artists he'd seen on the walls of the Louvre here in Melbourne, amid the chattering Australians—

vocal in their opinions, laughing and analysing the works with gusto. The atmosphere of the display was utterly unlike Paris, where he, Sofia and Andrés had frequently been shushed by frowning museum staff. In quiet moments, Jack looked around the room, his thoughts turning to Sofia. How he wished she were here with him! She would have loved this exhibition, and he felt sure that John would have found a way to include her in the organisation of this landmark event.

Manning the door was interesting, Jack found, for it was fun to see the arrivals. The vast majority of people knew little about modern art, but they were full of curiosity. In addition, it seemed that everybody connected to Melbourne's art world was there, even those who openly abhorred modern art, and Jack was surprised to see Max Meldrum and numerous dignitaries from the National Gallery. He wondered if their opinion of modern art would be improved after they viewed the exhibition. Also surprising to him was the arrival of the Jorgensens and Skippers along with a group of Justus' pupils. Lena was trailed by Mervyn, whose pencil worked furiously, filling his notebook—no doubt preparing an article for *The Bulletin*. The Montsalvat artists were equally surprised to see Jack at the door and keen to hear about his life at Heide. They were pleased to see him looking so well, although shocked when he told them he'd enlisted in the AIF and was reporting for duty later that week.

Fobbing off their concern, Jack enquired about the latest happenings at Montsalvat and learned that the babies had grown fast; now they were almost walking, and Sonia had settled into a small cabin with Arthur after all. Jack was pleased for Sonia and her daughter, sure that their lives would be much easier living within the semblance of a family, even if there was no ring or certificate to formalise the arrangement.

From the outset, the exhibition received wildly opposing reviews. Burdett and Murdoch were lauded as visionaries and geniuses for allowing Australians the opportunity to experience modern art, whilst the denigration expressed by Melbourne conservatives descended to new lows as they described the exhibition as 'putrid meat' and called modernism 'a disease'.

Notwithstanding, it was very possible that their negativity served to support the goal of the exhibition's organisers: to provide widespread exposure of modern art to Victorians. Throughout the week, over twenty thousand attendees walked through the doors of the Town Hall, and so popular did the exhibition prove, that its duration was extended by four days. Nonetheless, Jack had to withdraw from his door duties, for on Friday he was due to report at Melbourne's showgrounds for his initiation into the Second Australian Imperial Force.

# PART II

*MIDDLE EAST*

# CHAPTER 17

*B*oarding the train to the showgrounds, Jack noticed the buzz of excitement that filled the air immediately. The carriage was full, with far more young men on board than he remembered seeing in times past when he'd travelled from Eltham to the city on his way to work. At Flinders Street Station, he joined the dozens of men now striding along the platform with purposeful gaits, each gripping bags or small suitcases, converging on the central console. Like a multi-tailed snake, they wove towards the sign indicating Platform Four and descended the long ramp to board the train resting there. Soon, it was full with standing room only, and men squeezed into the doorways to watch as the train rolled through the rail yard, barely exceeding a walking pace, creaking along the intersecting web of rails until it finally came to a standstill at Richmond Station, barely five minutes away.

On disembarking, Jack gave himself over to the human tide, allowing it to direct his footsteps towards their common destination: the Melbourne Showgrounds.

The showgrounds had the atmosphere of schoolboys arriving for a camp—albeit an adult version—and as they approached the makeshift buildings, his footsteps stalled along with the crowd around him, uncertainty setting in. Although no one seemed to know what to do next, the air was alive with expectancy and chatter. Many of the lads, judging from their rough clothing, were labourers from farms or perhaps factory workers, and excited for a change from their otherwise dreary lives.

In the distance he could see a series of tables set in a row, and already men were forming lines behind them. They were guided by officers in uniform, who weaved among the new arrivals, calling directions—'Fifth/Sixth this way… Seventh/Eighth that way… The tables are in alphabetical order for your surnames. Check the letter you received if you are unsure of your unit.'

Jack had been allocated to the 2/5th unit, and so he turned to the right accordingly. Moving along the rows of tables, he read the sign, *2AIF 6th Division 17th Brigade 2/5th Battalion N–Z*. He joined the queue and quickly arrived at the front desk, where a tick was placed against his name; and he was given a sheath of papers, including a map of the showgrounds. He noted the cross that marked Hut 87—the large rectangular tent that he would call home for the next few weeks—and made his way towards it.

The tent was sparsely furnished with rows of canvas stretchers set out along the perimeter. Half a dozen men stood in a circle in the centre, chatting and laughing. Their belongings had been neatly set beside camp beds, as if they had anticipated the army's stipulation for orderliness and weren't going to be found wanting.

A stretcher in the corner of the room appeared to be unclaimed and Jack ventured towards it, nodding at the tallest man in the group, who'd caught his eye.

'G'day, mate. Welcome to the Bat Cave.' The men laughed, pointing to the decomposing remains captured in the tent's top rail. The man speaking was about thirty years old—and at least six foot six, with shoulders a yard wide. Huge, by any stretch of the imagination, Jack reached out for the lump of a hand extended toward him and felt welcomed by his hearty greeting.

'Shorty.' The man gestured to himself, chuckling before turning to the others. 'Snowy and Macka.' He pointed to the two men on his right. 'We're from Horsham. Came down on the train last night. And here we have Johno and the Doc. They've just arrived from down Frankston way.'

'Jack,' he replied. 'Pleased to meet you. I am from here— Melbourne. Heidelberg.' He shook hands with each of the men in turn, listening as Shorty bantered.

'Watch out, boys. We've got another city-slicker here. Better keep our heads low. If Jacko here gets a gun in his hand, he's as likely to blow our heads off as hit the Jerries.' Their laughter was good natured, and so it began: Jack became Jacko, and a city versus country rivalry was launched. For half an hour the men chatted, and Jack learned that Shorty and Snowy were brothers, and Macka their friend. They were sons of men from a Light Horse Brigade who'd served in the Great War and determined to do their bit to keep the world free of the likes of Hitler. Like Jack, they'd joined up at the first opportunity and were ready for anything. They told him that they were only sorry that they could not bring their horses along.

Over the next half hour, another dozen men stepped into the hut. It became a ritual that each would be greeted by Shorty, who demonstrated an astonishing memory for detail as each time he repeated introductions on behalf of the whole group before bestowing the new arrival with a nickname and making him feel welcome.

Together they chatted until a loud siren sounded through the grounds; and guessing it was a call to assemble, they left the bunkhouse and headed outdoors.

'Hey, hup,' said Shorty as they shuffled into a ragged line and straightened their backs. Winking at Jack, he chuckled and glanced at his watch. 'O nine thirty hours and reporting for duty.'

'Hmph…' the uniformed man standing on a makeshift stage tapped on his microphone to get attention. 'Good morning, men. It's wonderful to see you all here, so bright and early. We welcome you and are very glad for your decision to join the Second Australian Imperial Force. Believe me, Australia needs men exactly like you— men who show initiative and commitment to duty.'

The man speaking introduced himself as Major General Thomas

Blamey, the commanding officer of the Sixth Division. He was immaculately presented; his uniform freshly pressed, his shoulders square, his khaki-clad breast a fine backdrop for the multitude of colourful ribbons gracing it, an array of stripes on his sleeve: irrefutable evidence that he bore an impressive military service history. Blamey's voice was firm and authoritative, and Jack had no doubts as to the man's proficiency as leader of the Australian military. He spoke to them at length, describing the virtues of life as a soldier and the enormous pride that their government and country bore for each of them for volunteering themselves to the AIF in their country's hour of need. His words drew to a close with a final statement, accompanied by a smile.

'You may be raw yet, and you will have much to learn. Nonetheless, you are good material and it is our intention to train you until you are Australia's finest army—as fine as our Diggers of the Great War.'

Clapping erupted at the words, and Jack looked around him, detecting the ripple of pride now swirling through the lines—just a mild current, but discernible. He felt it rise within him too and was glad of his decision to join up. There was something about being here, together with so many types, all sharing a common purpose. Men from rural villages as well as the bigger country towns and those, like him— from the city. Men who were educated and others, possibly illiterate. Men who showed determination and savvy, like the fellows from Horsham. A mix of nationalities gathered here also, judging from the various accents he'd heard since he'd arrived, and even a few Aborigines' dark features stood out among the rows of pale-skinned faces.

Jack watched as a second officer took the podium, who introduced himself as Brigadier Stanley Savige, General Officer in Command of the 17th Brigade. He welcomed them and explained that they were just the first five hundred of those who'd be arriving to the camp. Over the next two days the remainder of the 17$^{th}$ Brigade would arrive, and by Sunday night in excess of three thousand men would be in residence at the showground. Looking around the lines, Jack was amazed. As it was, the five hundred or so fellows gathered together felt crowded. To think that their numbers would be multiplied six-fold seemed incredible.

The man continued to speak, advising that the weekend's timetable was written up on the blackboard outside the canteen, and then he followed with a brief outline of the events that they could expect. And in a single sentence Jack felt the thrill of transformation from civilian to soldier, ushered by one of the most fundamental features of language —the words pertaining to the measurement of time. They would reconvene on the oval for some basic training at 1030hrs, break for lunch at 1230hrs and resume afternoon training activities at 1330hrs. For the sake of organisation, they would be divided into groups of twenty-five—each led by men of the Militia who would supervise their activities and answer any questions they may have regarding military protocol. The real training would begin on Monday; however, they should use the weekend to learn as much as they could. Additionally, they'd have time to get to know each other and familiarise themselves with the resources available to them at the showgrounds. Immediately following the meeting, they would be issued with some basic supplies, following which, morning tea would be available at the canteen.

After being dismissed, Jack joined with the men from the Bat Cave, lining up for their provisions: two pannikins, a knife, fork and spoon, two blankets and a paillasse stuffed with straw. 'So far, so good,' they all agreed, as they headed across to the canteen.

Morning tea was plentiful. Steaming cups of Bushells, accompanied by bread and jam of every type imaginable: fig and apple, quince jelly, raspberry and apricot. Judging from the comments Jack heard, the jam was a real treat for some of the lads.

The men from the Bat Cave were pleased to find that they were to be combined with the men of Hut 88 for training activities, and a good-natured competitiveness developed between the two groups as they followed the instructions of a dour, nervous type, a Private Johns, who'd been given the task of guiding the new recruits through the weekend's activities.

At 1230hrs, Jack, Shorty, Snowy and Macka filed into the mess hall, where lunch was being served. Ham and pea soup was followed by generous slabs of mutton, well boiled vegetables and to finish, a baked rice custard. After almost a year of eating a mostly vegetarian diet at Heide, Jack enjoyed the mutton and had to acknowledge that despite being spoilt by Sunday's baking, he found the meals tolerable. Very likely they were more than some of the men were used to.

～

Throughout the afternoon, evening and into the night, a constant stream of men arrived at the showgrounds, all bearing confused expressions as they wandered around, adapting to the strange new world.

On Saturday morning, huddled around the benches in the canteen, full from the porridge, toast and tea he'd eaten, Jack felt like an old-timer. Barely twenty hours in, he was already familiar with the layout of the camp, the location of the canteen and restrooms; and he was developing a fast-growing network of new mates.

The weekend's routine was much the same as the previous day—a morning's muster followed by exercises, morning tea, more exercises and lunch and then still more exercises. The only difference was that the numbers of men increased almost by the hour, and the oval became full as groups of twenty-five vied for space to conduct their activities.

At the end of each day, Shorty and Macka were quick to organise teams for football, inviting anyone within earshot—who thought they knew one end of a ball from the other—to the far end of the showgrounds, where goal posts were created from rubbish bins, and opposing teams were distinguished by their jumpers: sleeves up versus sleeves down. Quickly, there were over forty players to a side. Needless to say, the games were riotous.

On the first day, Jack joined the men on the football field for a short time; but as the teams' numbers swelled, he left them to it, choosing instead to stroll around the camp. He was surrounded by men of every description, using their free time to either socialise with the others, or to escape to a quiet place for a few minutes where they could sit back and watch the world around them. Some, Jack noticed were using the time to write in journals, or perhaps they were writing letters to their girlfriends or families. Card games sprang up everywhere, though uniformed men were quick to shut down games where the jingling of ha'pennies was heard. No gambling was allowed, much to the disappointment of some of the men.

As the weekend wore on, Jack enjoyed the activities and the camaraderie of the men in his team. He was conscious of feeling different—independent—and he liked it. Nobody really knew him here; sure, they called him Jacko and everyone was friendly, but here relationships were superficial. His grief and losses were private, as were any burdens the other lads may carry. In some ways, everybody had the chance for a fresh start. A blank slate on which all of them were equal and each could rebuild their lives into a new and better version of himself.

Like so many times in Jack's past when he'd found himself amongst strangers, a desire to sketch took hold of him. It was as if, amid the men in this camp, he'd reverted to a Jack of old, the schoolboy who'd sat in parks or down by the river with his pad and pencil poised. Who'd enjoyed watching the people around him—family groups playing cricket or fishing, boats on the river, children flying kites—bringing the scenes to life with deft movements of his pencil on the page.

His thoughts turned to Sofia, wondering what she would make of all of this, and it shocked him to realise that he found it difficult to form a clear picture of her face. He decided that it must be this overwhelmingly masculine environment that obscured her image from him.

On Monday morning, following the relaxed introduction to army life over the weekend, the men of the Bat Cave were keen to commence preliminary training, learning the basic skills: lining up and saluting, marching, and body-strengthening exercises. Quickly their friendly rivalry intensified, each determined to run farther, carry more weights and do more push-ups than anybody else. Whilst giving it his best, Jack accepted that nobody had a chance of outdoing Shorty and Snowy. Coming from a large sheep property, the whole of the brothers'

lives had been committed to running, lifting and carrying; and each had the strength of an ox. Nonetheless, Jack was satisfied with his progress and thankful for the years of shovel work, lifting beams and climbing around scaffolding with Matcham at Montsalvat, as well as for his last twelve months working in the garden at Heide.

Each afternoon ended with a game of football on the back oval, which became a gathering place to end the day before they lined up for showers and headed to the dining room for dinner.

On the first of November, the men were called to the quartermaster's hut to receive their khaki uniforms. With much hilarity they dressed in the ill-fitting garments, swapping slouch hats until they found a size that fit, and strapped on thick webbing belts to hold up the oversized waistlines of the baggy trousers. To Jack, it seemed that they were more like boys playing dress-ups than soldiers, and it had been fun.

When they were issued with Lee Enfield .303 rifles, albeit without bullets, Jack watched the manner in which the Horsham boys handled the weapons, weighing them in their hands, peering through the sights, turning them over with casual nonchalance before slinging them onto their shoulders with the ease of lads who'd been shooting rabbits since they were ten-year-olds. In Jack's hands the weapon felt awkward, and he resisted the irrational feeling that it might discharge in his hand despite its empty chamber. He'd never held a gun in his life, and even devoid of bullets, it felt like a killing machine that could explode at any second.

Shorty evidently picked up on Jack's caution. 'Come here, city boy. We better show you how this thing works before you shoot our nogg'ns off.' Finding a place to squat, he spent fifteen minutes explaining how Jack needed to hold the rifle against himself as though he were caressing his sweetheart, the butt of the stock firmly fitted into his shoulder, the barrel against his cheekbone. He pointed out the sights, one near the stock, the other at the end of the long barrel, and demonstrated how Jack should line them up to be sure that his aim was true, then showed him how to work the bolt and how to slowly squeeze the trigger. For as casual as the lesson was, on the bright sunny day in the back corner of the showground, it shook Jack to think that one day in the very near future he might be pointing this very weapon into the face of the enemy; that by his hand, it may kill another human being.

~

Although Jack and the others had commenced their training at Melbourne's showgrounds, the site was only ever intended to be a temporary measure. In mid-November, it was announced that the men of the 17th Brigade were to be transported by rail to the camp that had been built especially for them, seventy miles north of Melbourne, near the township of Seymour.

William and Marian, accompanied by Margaret, were amongst the families at Richmond Station on the morning of their departure.

'Heavens, Mum. You'd think we were heading off to war to be slaughtered, with all of the tears going on here!'

'Jack! No! It's just that we don't know when we'll see you again. Who knows what the future holds? We just have to make the most of these moments while we can.' She gave him a large brown envelope. 'Don't open it now,' she said, but Jack couldn't resist.

It held three photographs. One of himself and his parents, taken immediately after his graduation—he had no recollection of ever seeing it. The next was a photograph of himself and Sofia on their wedding day—a copy of the one that his mother kept on the mantelpiece in her dining room. He gently touched the face of Sofia, whose smile was full of the joy of their marriage, and wondered how on earth he could ever forget her features. The third was a photograph of Scotty, taken in the back garden of Copelin Street. His boy was sitting in the small tin truck his grandparents had bought him two years earlier, and the sight of it brought tears to Jack's eyes.

'Is it okay? I hope you don't mind! I thought that you might like to have it... you know... when you are so far from home. I know it is sad and all, but I just thought you should have it.'

'Thank you, Mum. Thank you!' He hugged her. 'I'm going to find Sofia, you know!'

'Of course you will, love. Bring her home to us all, please!'

A whistle blew, and as they boarded the train, Jack compared the

175

men around him to the motley collection of lads who'd gathered at the showgrounds barely a month earlier. Now they wore their uniforms with ease; the slouch hats looked worn and comfortable and he couldn't imagine them dressed any other way. They looked like… well… an army, prepared for battle, and he felt proud to be numbered among them.

After the initial excitement of boarding, the men settled into quiet groups. As the train crept through the city of Melbourne via Spencer Street and wove its way northward, their mood seemed to grow sombre, imbued with a sense that the fun and games were over—that action was imminent.

Two hours later, they arrived at Seymour Station, from where they were transported via lorries to the camp seven miles out of town. Much had been said of this purpose-built camp, that had been constructed in the space of a month, designed to accommodate twenty-thousand men. Jack had been quick to join in the jests: joining the city boys in their teasing of the country lads, bantering with Shorty, Snowy and Macka about the expectation that there would be a bunch of sheep sheds for them to sleep in; how instead of a lavatory, they'd be issued with cut-up newspapers and a shovel; and how for meals they'd take a sheep from a neighbouring paddock and would make damper over open fires.

Now, finally they were here, and Jack could not deny Camp Puckapunyal was nothing less than impressive. Three hundred and twenty huts, as well as kitchens, showers, meat houses and stables had been built from timber that had been transported from mills across Victoria, and its water supply was pumped directly from the Goulburn River. It was astonishing—a whole brand spanking new village risen where barely a month earlier, only virgin bush had stood. It must have cost thousands of pounds, and Jack couldn't wait for an opportunity to climb the rise that overlooked the camp and sketch it from the elevated position.

Weeks at the camp turned into months, and while Jack was pleased to be given leave to spend Christmas with his family he couldn't shake the feeling of being a soldier who was walking among civilians—a man who bore knowledge that was to be kept secret—and when it was time to return to the camp on Boxing Day, he was ready. Whilst it had been wonderful to spend time with his parents and Margaret, he'd found their endless questions exhausting. He limited his replies to the extraordinary resources that the soldiers had been provided with and the magnitude of the camp, rather than discussing the nature of the training activities. For whilst training routines at 'Pucka' were similar to those at the showgrounds, now their activities had a far more deadly intent. Bayonet drill, weapons training and toughening-up exercises seemed endless. Jack learned about the sorts of artillery the units would have access to, and beyond their .303s they were trained to use Webley revolvers and Mills bombs. The details of war machines such as Matilda tanks and Bren Carriers were demonstrated, and they were all taught how to manage machine guns such as the Owen and Bren— weapons that would be handled only by the gunners—and additionally, they were taught how to work as a team to setup, feed and fire the largest of machine guns—the Vickers. In addition, there was marching and marching and marching some more. Many of the younger men grumbled, but Jack knew that these preparations were not just about fitness and order, but also about mental strength. The refusal to give in. Jack was intrigued by the way the men in his unit garnered the tenacity to maintain the stringent training regime. For some, like Shorty and Snowy it was about a hatred for the Germans, a determination to take them down. For others—like the Doctor and his friend, George—it was about the competition, the notion that the battles ahead of them would be defined by the victors and the defeated, and that they had no intention of being the latter. Jack had his own source of motivation: each time he endured yet another dozen push-ups followed by jogging ten laps around the oval, his thoughts were for Sofia. For her, he'd train twenty hours a day if he had to. Nobody knew what was ahead of them, but if they experienced anything like the Diggers did in the Great War—where troops had spent months holed up in trenches and walked ten days at a time with minimal rations—he was determined that he would survive for Sofia.

# CHAPTER 18

*I*n early April, the prime minister's order came—the 17th Brigade was to embark within the month, crossing the ocean in readiness to support the French and British in their fight against Hitler and Mussolini. Where they were destined for exactly, nobody knew. Jack accepted that during wartime, many things were held secret for fear that the enemy would take advantage of the intelligence, but ignorance didn't stop him from weighing in on the various discussions. A bloke called Pete heard that they were going up into the Pacific, while The Doc's father was attached to the British Foreign Office; and he'd told his son they might be heading for somewhere near Russia. Others thought that they might be going directly to Poland to wrestle it back from Hitler. Jack remained convinced that they'd be posted somewhere in the United Kingdom, or even France; surely each were under threat and needed reinforcements. He hoped he was right because as soon as he got leave, he intended to search for Sofia.

It was strange, Jack realised, to be so confident that he would find her; so sure even, that she wanted to be found. It was illogical, perhaps, but ever since Menzies had announced that Australia was at war, it had seemed that Jack's whole purpose in life had been clarified. As Sofia's husband, it was his duty to ensure that his wife was okay. And in being sure of finding Sofia, he was even more sure that at last, they would be reunited. Jack constantly imagined the moment when he would finally lay eyes on her; perhaps a chance meeting with her at a railway, or across a café, or perhaps he would bump into her while walking in the streets of London or Paris. It was fanciful, he knew, but in his mind it seemed utterly feasible, and more than that, the thrill of his imaginings became his daily inspiration and hope for the future.

~

Before they were to travel across the world, the men of the 17th Brigade had one last duty: All 5000 troops would march through the centre of Melbourne. It was on a Saturday, and the autumn sky was clear, the air crisp. The march had the atmosphere of a fair. The army's brass band took the lead, footsteps striding to the 2/2 beat of the drum, trumpets and coronets weaving bright tunes—*Roll out the Barrel* and *Tipperary*. Thousands of people—citizens, as Jack now viewed them—lined the streets, and it was touching to be on the receiving end of their show of appreciation. Children waved their small flags, and the adults clapped and called out words of encouragement.

'On you, boys!'

'Stay safe!'

'May God be with you!'

'Go get 'em!'

'Come home and I'll marry you!'

Jack nodded as he caught the eye of ladies dabbing lace handkerchiefs to their eyes, smiling bravely through tears. He smiled at the dozens of young women who ran forward, pressing small slips of paper into the hands of troops—which he later found to be postal addresses where a lonely soldier far from home might like to send a letter. He returned the grim gaze of the older men who stood silently, unsmiling, their brows furrowed, offering barely perceptible nods of their heads. Jack had no doubts that these men were Diggers from The Great War. The war that was supposed to end all wars. What must they be thinking today, he wondered? The Diggers knew the horrors of the trenches. They knew that not all of those marching past them today would come home, and truth be told, so did those marching. However, these were reflections for another day. Today, every single lad felt invincible. They'd be home in no time for sure!

~

After the parade, Jack joined the hundreds of soldiers who'd packed into the main bar of The Young and Jackson, the hotel directly opposite Flinders Street Station—one he had passed possibly a thousand times in his life and never once thought to enter. The mood was celebratory and Jack joined in with the men as they toasted each other, toasted their anticipated victory and toasted Chloe, the beautiful woman depicted standing in all of her naked glory—her luminous curves and silky skin the closest that some young soldiers would ever get to the charms of a female.

'She's splendid,' Jack commented to Shorty, who was standing with him, waiting to have his photograph taken beside the girl.

'Hey! I thought that you had a girlfriend,' Jack teased.

'Oh, well. If you don't tell, nor will I,' Shorty laughed.

'She sure is gorgeous,' slurred Macka lasciviously.

Jack laughed. His own comment had been that of an appreciative artist rather than an adoring male, although without question the girl was beautiful, and the enormous painting—over eight feet high and three feet wide—stunning. He looked at the signature. *Jules Lefebvre, 1875.* A small poster was pasted to the wall beside the frame describing how *Chloe*, the Melbourne Icon, had hung on this wall for over forty years. Jack read how the model was a young woman named Marie, and how she'd died after taking poison, her heart broken by the artist, Lefebvre, because he'd married her sister. He went on to read how, throughout the Great War, soldiers had come to Young and Jackson, for a final beer and to farewell *Chloe* before sailing north and then on returning, they'd come back to greet her. According to the notice, more than one soldier from the trenches of Turkey had even sent her letters. Jack looked at the lineup of young men waiting for their photographs to be taken, and had no doubts that visions of *Chloe* would enliven the hearts and fantasies of more than one soldier today, as they ventured towards an uncertain future. He raised his glass—not to *Chloe*, sweet as she was—but to Lefebvre, the artist of the previous century—congratulating him for the stunning result he'd achieved with his painting.

~

The day of the Seventeenth's departure from Australian shores came at short notice when at the sound of the morning bell, they assembled and Brigadier Savige told them that they were to have a quick breakfast, pack their kits and then reassemble at 0900hrs. Then, they would march to the train station where they would board carriages that would take them directly to Port Melbourne, and from there they'd board a waiting troop ship. To where? Savige did not say and the men weren't even sure if he knew. Needless to say, Jack, Shorty and Macka could barely contain their excitement. At last, after months of training, something was happening.

Even though the movement of the 2AIF was meant to be a secret, the sight of carriages full of soldiers thundering through the sleepy country towns of Victoria raised excitement amongst the public, who undoubtedly raced to their telephones to share the news. By the time the troops arrived at Station Pier, thousands of people stood waiting, and as the trains emptied, they waved and cheered to the soldiers as they marched onto the ship.

Once the troops had boarded, the jostling crowd was released onto the dock where calls of good wishes and colourful streamers reached the soldiers who stood lining the ship's deck. Jack suddenly became conscious of the actions of the men around him, as they climbed onto the ships stairwells and searched the crowds, desperate for a sight of their wives and girlfriends. Some had been clever, evidently conspiring with their loved ones for such an occasion, and when Shorty pulled out a bright lime green piece of fabric from his pack, Jack was amazed.

'What on earth are you going to do with that,' he shouted, trying to make himself heard above the noise.

'Not sure, mate… It was Evelyn's idea. Her mother and father did the same in the Great War... signalled each other to say hellos and goodbyes, or to find each other on crowded stations.'

Leaning over the rail beside Shorty, to watch the sea of faces below that now jammed the pier below, Jack wondered that anyone could be found. He wondered if there was any chance that his own parents or even Margaret might be there. Planning signals for such an occasion had never entered his mind.

'There she is, there she is,' said Shorty, as he waved his green fabric furiously. 'Hi love, can you see me? Here I am, here, here!' he shouted into the distance. Jack looked at him in amazement. His giant friend with the easy-going manner seemed to have lost his mind with his frenzied shouting, and Jack swore that tears were streaming down his face, even as he frantically called to a woman in a crowd who had no chance of hearing him.

Looking in the direction that Shorty was waving, Jack saw it. A lime green piece of fabric that matched the one Shorty held, flapping furiously; and suddenly he found himself waving and calling in the same direction.

'Here he is, Evelyn... over here...' War certainly had the effect of turning everybody mad, he thought, even as he smiled, pleased for Shorty that he had a chance to farewell his girlfriend.

It was mid-afternoon when the ship finally loosened its ties to the dock and set out into the bay. Brigadier Savige called them to attention and after expressing his pleasure in the smooth embarkation, advised them that they would be out in the open waters soon, where they'd be joined by troopships carrying soldiers from Sydney as well as New Zealand. Together the flotilla would cross the Indian Ocean, however for now their destination would remain hidden, lest the enemy be warned to expect them.

Jack breathed deeply, absorbing the moment. He felt that he was part of something much greater than himself—greater than any single one of them, yet as a whole, the men of the 17th Brigade were a force to be reckoned with. He was sure that in no time they would crush the Germans for once and for all, hence finishing the job that the Diggers of the Great War had started.

As Brigadier Savige had promised, within twenty-four hours three other ships appeared on the horizon, and travelling a few hundred yards apart, they motored across the ocean. Jack often joined Shorty, Snowy, Macka and Doc, leaning against the ship's rails, gazing at sunrises, sunsets and starry nights, trying to ascertain the direction they were travelling. Certainly, it wasn't east—the shadows were wrong— were they travelling due north? They had lost sight of land days ago. One of the men, Frank from Bendigo, understood astronomy, and he fascinated them by describing the features of the night sky: how the brightest star was Venus, and the direction in which the largest planet, Jupiter, could be seen. He pointed out the constellations—the Big Dipper and Orion—and explained how the Southern Cross could be used to locate due south should they ever get lost.

As it emerged, the troopships were travelling northwest on a route not dissimilar to the one Jack had taken a decade earlier. As the ships steamed along, their formation steady, the men wavered between desperation to arrive and get this thing finished and a respectful apprehension. Their conversations turned to the circumstances of the battles ahead of them. What weapons might be used against them, how strong might the German army be, and how long would it take to subdue them? Some men thought they might be back by Christmas whilst others thought it would take a bit longer. Jack wondered if it were all over in a month or two and the troopship was returning home, perhaps they would let him stay on in Europe so he could find Sofia.

Jack had always resisted the habit to smoke, but with the long days at sea, the habit of dragging on a cigarette while leaning on the ship's rails and gazing into the horizon seemed enticing. He reasoned that the daily allowance of tobacco, provided by the Australian Comfort Fund, was free, so why not use it? And in no time at all, he mastered the art of rolling a wad of dried and finely cut tobacco leaf between the fine slips of rice paper that were issued to him each week.

Between ongoing target practice, physical training and formal parades on the ship's deck, there were still copious amounts of free time which Jack used to sketch or even paint. Perched on the stairs, or tables in the mess room or on the deck, a smouldering cigarette dangling from his lips, he created drawings of his fellow officers, gulls perched on the deck rails, and in the evenings, of the accompanying flotilla of troop carriers in waters that glistened with the quivering reflections of crimson and silver and purple as the setting sun's rays danced upon their dappled surface.

~

As they moved into the Northern Hemisphere, the threat of enemy attack increased. Although watch duties were in place, Jack constantly scanned the skies for swooping aircraft, the rolling ocean for the funnel of a submarine and the horizon for puffs of smoke. Emergency drills were practiced daily, and additionally the men began their own fitness regimes; doing push-ups, chin-ups and sharing in the arm-wrestling bouts. No private wanted to be panting for air or lacking the strength to carry his pack or scramble across a fence should a time when his life depended on his fitness arise.

~

It was mid-April when, finally, land appeared—a hazy strip on the horizon that quickly took shape and form. Jack and the others lined up along the deck rail, watching, and as they got closer, some boys let out a battle cry. The lone voice that shouted 'Watch out, Gerry, the Aussies are here!' was rewarded with whistling and cheering.

'Where the hell are we?' more than one man asked. Jack scanned the horizon; red sand was visible for as far as his eyes could see.

They didn't have to wait long to find out. The siren rang—the signal for them to assemble on the deck, where Brigadier Stanley Savige once again addressed them.

'Good afternoon, men. You will be pleased to know that finally we have reached our destination—Kantara, Egypt. At approximately sixteen hundred hours you will be disembarking, and we will maintain lines of three and march to the station, where awaiting trains will transport you to Gaza. Stand easy for further orders.'

So, despite all the entertaining bragging that had taken place over the six past weeks, when they'd almost believed they'd be leaping off the carrier with arms drawn, their bayonets poised, ready to deflect an onslaught of bullets raining upon them, the day of their arrival on land was long and boring. The oft-repeated joke was that they'd finally made it across the world, and the only scenery available to them was some bastard's back. It was true, for their first day on foreign soil was spent in hours of forming lines as they waited to board the train to Alexandria and then again forming lines to wait their turn to be loaded onto the backs of lorries and transported to their new home—a training camp known as Beit Jirja.

As the lorry slowly rumbled down the ribbon of roadway, Jack felt like he was in a dream. He'd spent weeks at sea; and now perched in the back of the swaying vehicle, his pack between his legs, his shoulders bumping one minute against Macka and the next against Shorty, as the vehicle rolled towards a featureless horizon, nothing seemed real. Adding to the dreamlike atmosphere, a gigantic full moon was making an early appearance on the horizon. Its large, almost transparent disc appeared fragile against the deep blue, cloudless sky. Jack laid his head back, closed his eyes, and tried to capture Sofia's face, as if by seeing her, he might bind her to him so she too might accompany him on this strange journey, but today she was elusive.

Like at Puckapunyal, the daily routine at Beit Jirja was of training exercises, but although the men talked, laughed and entertained themselves with cards and games, everyone knew that the action was drawing closer.

When he thought about it, a lump rose in Jack's chest. Was he scared? He guessed he was, for despite the endless practises and marching around, he couldn't help but wonder if any of them was truly prepared for the reality of war. Had they all been kidding themselves, full of bravado as they'd imagined victory—like children playing war games in the safety of their backyards? Now that war was imminent, the severity of their situation was impossible to ignore.

Beyond training, camp life offered plenty of opportunities for fun; and the men enjoyed piling onto the Brens, whose tracked wheels gripped the sand as they veered over the dunes, precariously twisting and turning in pursuit of an imagined enemy; or took it in turns to man the guns and fire at targets which they'd set up. Additionally, they played cricket and football, and at night they played cards or 'two-up'; a game that could be played anywhere, anytime by flicking two coins high in the air, summoning calls of 'come in spinner' and the rapid cry of bets on whether the coin would land heads up; and although the exchange of coins for prizes was forbidden, most times their senior officers looked the other way.

Although it was winter, a few of the men took to swimming, agreeing that despite the cold, the minutes spent splashing underwater were perhaps the only minutes of their day when they didn't feel that they were being inundated by sand invading every orifice of their bodies.

Jack, Shorty, Snowy and Macka seized every opportunity available to leave the camp. They caught the bus to Alexandria, where they partook of copious amounts of cognac and camel's piss—as Shorty called the warm, cheap beer served at bars where belly dancers writhed in impossible contortions for the men's entertainment—or they sat in cafés drinking bitter coffee accompanied by delectable slices of kunafa —a sugary pastry that they all loved.

In their third week, they caught the bus to Cairo. Jack was amazed to see the historical home of the Great Pyramids of Giza and surprised to find modern buildings alongside the ancient temples, mosques, citadels and markets. The twisting streets were full of stores offering fascinating produce, and Jack purchased gifts for his parents and brooches for Margaret and Sunday. He was thrilled to discover art supplies tucked into the dark corner of a store packed with vases, statues and beads. Selecting a drawing book, block of canvas and oil paints, Jack happily replenished the supplies that he'd used on the ocean crossing.

He found the exotic scenes of Cairo, the play of sunlight and shadow on the windswept sand dunes and the astonishing vibrancy of the sunrises and sunsets, to be endlessly alluring; and for the first time in years he was excited by the thought of mixing colours. Here he wanted to duplicate the glorious desert skies. The second time they went to Cairo, they accepted a tour guide's offer to show them the ancient city of the dead and then the pyramids. Jack sketched a series of postcards to send to his parents, and later in the day he set himself by a water fountain in the marketplace, sketching men and women as they shopped and young children playing in the square. The boys and girls were fascinated by the images of themselves, and Jack purchased another sketchbook and spent an hour creating dozens of quick portraits, which he passed to the eagerly waving hands of children calling, 'Me, too, soldier—me too!'

Each night Jack gazed at the photograph of himself and Sofia on their wedding day. Some nights he felt comforted by the sight of her smile. On other nights, it troubled him to feel that he was looking at two strangers, and he knew that he'd made a terrible mistake thinking that the war would deliver him to her. He'd always envisaged that the Australian units would go to England before getting further orders, and he'd pictured living amid the British towns with railway links. He'd thought he'd be able to slip into London or Paris and retrace the steps that he, Andrés and Sofia had taken. Never in his wildest imagination had he thought he'd be posted to a remote desert outpost in Egypt.

Mail from Australia was the highlight of the week; and when it arrived the camp became quiet as men withdrew, their thoughts full of families and sweethearts. From some came joyous cries in response to a baby born, a sister being engaged or a parcel of fruitcake or knitted socks unwrapped. For others, there was silence or anger—a girlfriend or worse, a wife with doubts about their future, children who were ill and financial concerns that from ten thousand miles away could not be fixed. Jack always received a letter from his mother, often two, each with a note at the bottom of the page from his father.

Reading the mail, Jack often sensed Shorty's eyes upon him. His friend was curious; he had seen Jack's photos, the wedding picture and the toddler in the car, and yet Jack never spoke of his family. Only very occasionally did he allow his mind to meander to Montsalvat, and the students' cabin where a small dark-haired boy crawled around his legs, playing with the wooden train that his grandpa had bought him. Whenever the memories arose, a terrible stabbing sensation racked Jack's chest. Even though two years had passed since Scotty's death, he still found it impossible to think of his little boy without hurting.

It seemed to Jack that now they'd crossed the world, Shorty spoke of Evelyn constantly, clearly missing the girlfriend to whom he'd waved the green fabric furiously as the troopship had left Melbourne. Jack learned that they'd spoken of marriage; and now that he was so far from home, Shorty was even more sure that he wanted Evelyn for his wife, declaring his intention to marry her as soon as the war was over. She was a nurse whom he'd met at Horsham Hospital when he'd gone in to visit a mate who'd been thrown from his rearing mare after a wallaby had startled the horse by dashing between her legs. Shorty was forever writing postcards to her and was thrilled when Jack offered some drawings he'd made of the camp to send to her.

As days in Beit Jirja turned into weeks and then months, boredom seeped across the camp and into the minds of the men, leading to an increase in complaints and more than one bout of fists let loose as tempers frayed. Their thirst to enter the war had been whetted; hadn't they travelled across the world to crush the enemy? Surely their families thought that they were sending their men to squash the Germans, not to a Boy Scout training camp where they'd play war games. Jack understood the rising frustration caused by the lack of action. He too was feeling it.

A move to Cairo in September relieved some of the tensions, and then in early December it was as though London's War Office understood that the Australian lads of the 2nd AIF's 6th Division had run out of patience. A rumour emerged that was quickly verified by an official statement. The 6th Division would march to Alexandria any day now. From there a ship which would carry the Australians to the location of their first skirmish—Bardia. The boys cheered when they got the news. Finally, it was time for action.

# CHAPTER 19

$\mathcal{E}$xcitement ran high as their training regime escalated to fulfil plans for the upcoming battle, which now had a location and their enemy a face—not the Germans whom they were rearing to fight, but rather Italians, for Bardia was an Italian fortress town situated on the Mediterranean Sea over three hundred miles west of Alexandria. The 2/5th waited anxiously for the details of the battle that was being planned by the division brigadiers and Major General Iven Mackay, who was in charge of the whole operation. Their daily training took on a whole new level of seriousness, and Jack listened carefully to the discussions of the proposed artillery attack from the sky and sea before the land troops breached Bardia's double fenced and heavily guarded perimeter. They were told to expect heavy resistance from the thousands of Italian troops within, who'd already experienced a number of attacks in recent months, and so would be prepared to react quickly. As well as fitness and artillery training the troops studied the maps of the town. Also, they learned essential Italian phrases: *Mani alto*—hands up; *apri li mani*—open your hands; and *lascia le armi*—leave your weapons, and they entertained themselves as they practiced the commands on each other.

It came as a surprise to Jack when two weeks later, just as he finished washing-up duties, he was approached by a young private.

'Private Tomlinson? You're wanted over at headquarters.'

'This minute?' Never, in all of his time in the army, had Jack been singled out for anything. The only troops called to headquarters were those whose pranks had gone too far.

'Now you've done it, Jacko,' Macka teased. 'They've heard about your lover hidden away in Cairo. I told you that you'd be caught!' The boys laughed, and Jack shook his head, smiling. It was pointless to deny the fabrications; they would only add more stories which would be doubly damning to his reputation.

'What do they want with me, do you know?' he asked more seriously as he wrung out his wash cloth and hung it on the rail before following the young man out the door.

'I don't know, mate.... I'm just the messenger. Come along and find out, and then you can tell me!'

Arriving at the Administration Headquarters, the private pointed towards a bench. 'Have a seat, and I will let the major know you're here.'

Mystified, his mind churning, Jack tried to imagine a single reason that he'd be called to Headquarters. Was there bad news from home? Something about Sofia!

'Private Tomlinson, the major's ready to see you now.'

The room he entered was distinctive for its sparseness—furnished with only a desk, a filing cabinet and half a dozen chairs, and a framed photograph of the king mounted on the wall. Jack affected the perfunctory salute that was offered to superiors. Brigadier Savige sat at the large desk, a second man in civilian dress opposite him.

'Stand easy, Private Tomlinson. No need to look worried, lad. Nothing's wrong. I don't expect that you will have met this character? John Treloar—Secretary of the Department of Information?'

'No. I haven't, sir.'

'He'd like to speak with you. I will leave you to it, John, if you don't mind. I have a battle to organise. Thankfully, this one is with Mr Johnny Walker. Come over and join me when you've finished here.'

As the major left the room, Jack looked at Treloar expectantly.

'How's army life going, Tomlinson?'

Jack wondered if there was a right and wrong answer. Should he be adopting a formal title of military address? The man's relaxed demeanour and casual attire suggested that he need not bother, so he stayed with 'sir'.

'Good, sir. Not that we've seen any battles, yet, sir.'

'I guess they will come soon enough. So, how have you been passing the time?'

'We haven't done much of anything, really, sir. Just continued the training exercises that we were doing in Puckapunyal. The dust gets tiresome. Word is that we will be on the move any day now.'

'You are an artist, I hear.'

Jack looked up sharply, surprised by the comment. How on earth did this man know he painted? Was it against the rules? Was he in some sort of trouble? 'Yes, I guess so, sir. I do a few sketches of the lads, occasionally, sir.'

Treloar nodded. 'I don't suppose that you've heard of the Department of Information?'

Jack hadn't and shook his head.

'We're new. Our job is to monitor communications—censorship and propaganda, mostly.'

'Yes, sir.'

'Unfortunately, Murdoch's been in charge of it all until recently. You've heard of Murdoch? Owns the *Herald* and *Sun* newspapers? The prime minister commissioned him to report on the war in such a way that the public would support Australia's involvement, be happy for the government to spend money on armaments, etcetera. It was Murdoch's job "to keep the public smiling".'

'Hard for anyone to be smiling during a war, sir.' Jack didn't disclose that not only had he heard of Keith Murdoch, he'd even spoken to the famous millionaire on the opening night of the *Herald* Exhibition of Contemporary Art of London and Paris, when he'd escorted him to the table set aside for the dignitaries.

'Well, as strange as it sounds, we do need to highlight the successes of the war—you know, good news stories. Conversely the bad news stories, the ones where our troops take losses, tend to be downplayed. It's not good for the Allies if the enemy thinks they've had a win, nor is it good for the morale of Australians. If the public thinks the war is going badly, we'll have mothers marching on the streets, insisting that their boys be brought home.'

'But shouldn't newspapers be reporting the true facts about the war, the good and the bad? Inform the public and let them draw their own conclusions?' As soon as Jack spoke, he realised how simplistic he sounded. He'd merely echoed the complaints Neil used to make when they'd read the newspapers at Heide over their morning tea. Nonetheless, war was serious business. Surely it was one thing to present limited perspectives on a matter, another to be telling blatant lies to the Australian public about the war that they were fighting.

'Ideally, yes, Jack, and in honesty, I don't like propaganda either. Foremost, I am a historian, and it offends me that the propaganda we include in newspaper articles and pamphlets today undermines the reliability of these artefacts for future use. Because of this, it is vital that we create a sound record of wartime experiences; information based on truth. Not just for academics, but for war generals and the like.'

Jack nodded.

'Now Murdoch has gone, and I'm looking after things. Additionally, I am tasked with gathering resources for the war memorial that we are building in Canberra. We have access to documents, and I am gathering photographs and film, but it is my intention to expand our collection to include artworks—primary documents that are created in the field by eye-witnesses to events.'

Jack nodded. Treloar's objective made sense.

'Our best source of information will come straight from the battleground. The experiences of the troops. The daily lives of civilians. Events that are captured while they are fresh. Factual information that speaks the truth of war. The good, the bad and the ugly. The perspectives of men and women. Allies and the enemy. I have seen your work, Jack. You've certainly got an eye for detail. These are yours?'

Jack was astonished when Treloar laid three of his drawings onto the table. Children climbing over a fountain in the central square; soldiers playing cricket with half a dozen young lads; the portrait of a small girl holding the hand of her tiny sister. All sketched in Cairo just over a month ago. Jack remembered the day.

'I was just passing time.... You know, it was a day off.... I am sorry if...'

Treloar laughed, waving his hand. 'No, Tomlinson. Don't apologise. This is war. It's not all heroic battles and victory marches. Civilian life goes on. Troops interact. Soldiers get bored. Dare I say, soldiers even play up a bit, from time to time. Have you always drawn?'

'For as long as I can remember. I've also painted in oils, and even had a stint as an art student in Paris.'

'Perfect. You will do the job nicely.'

'What job?'

'Why, don't you understand? I want you to be an artist for the army. We had them during the Great War—mind you, they painted most of their work from photographs, long after the war was over. And because the artists themselves hadn't been to war, the paintings aren't primary documents. I want us to do it properly this time. You are my first appointment. And as a professional artist, your rank will be reassigned to captain. On a captain's wage.'

It sounded strange to hear Treloar describe the sketches Jack had amused himself with as work. Furthermore, it was incredible to think, after training for almost a year for war, he was now being asked to exchange his rank of private to that of captain, all for doing a few paintings!

'So, what will I do with myself?' he asked.

'Just draw, Jack. Do what you do best. Have you got materials? What do you need? You'll need a backpack... something light to carry.'

'I've got a drawing book.'

'How about I pick up some supplies for plein air oils? There is a good little kit available, I've heard. Perhaps some ink. I managed to get these in Cairo.' Treloar passed over a metal cylinder that was about twelve inches long and three inches in diameter, as well as a thick block of paper and a set of graphite pencils.

'You can store your work in the cylinder—it's light and should fit into your pack easily. When you get a chance, submit your drawings to me via your unit's headquarters. They may want to do a bit of censoring, but they'll keep them safe and get them to me when they can.'

'Sir, I don't think I can do this. We're just about to go into battle. The word is out already—I didn't join up to be sketching and painting! I can't let the lads down! That's not to say I won't do some sketches. I'll do what I can for you, of course.'

Treloar was persistent. 'Jack, recording the facts about war is important work! You must have seen Bell's paintings from the Great War at the National Gallery. And have you heard of Charles Bean— he's possibly Australia's greatest war historian? He and I worked together in London. The British were planning their own war memorial, and it was Charles who insisted that we must have ours, and what's more that it must include paintings. I don't know how many times I've heard him say *"Art expresses the inexpressible—helps us make sense of the utterly senseless".*'

Jack could see that Treloar held his workmate in high regard.

'You would be joining the likes of McCubbin and Streeton as well as Bell, but where their work was painted after the battle and based on photographs, yours will be done on the field!'

McCubbin and Streeton were war artists? Jack thought about the war scenes he'd viewed in London and Paris, enormous seventeenth-century battle scenes. Horses rearing, soldiers with bright red and gold jackets, their swords and muskets poised. Some of them were so large that they covered half a wall.

Treloar was quick to take Jack's silence as assent. 'Then it's agreed? I will pay you two guineas per day. Don't you worry about anything. I just need you to sign here so I can organise your new rank with the Pay Corps. Well done, Jack. Trust me, your work will be highly valued and it will add to the annals of Australian history!'

Stepping into the darkness, Jack looked at the brilliance of the desert stars. He felt dazed. For months he had worked tirelessly, preparing himself to participate on the battlefield. At the first sound of the morning siren, he'd leapt up, ready for the daily exercise regime. He'd enjoyed the cheerful banter of his unit and was very aware of the delight they took in teasing anyone who faltered, or was a bit sickly, or who was a braggart or even worse, a snob. What would they make of an artist? He'd cheerfully developed an infantryman's skills alongside his fellows in the 2/5th, becoming an Australian Digger, disciplined and fit, with an alert mind and a watchful eye—prepared to do what was required to protect his fellows' backs from enemy attack.

Now, at the stroke of a pen, he'd been relieved of his soldier duties. His rifle was to be replaced with a paintbrush, his grenades with an easel. He had no idea how he was going to tell the boys.

Jack didn't have to tell anyone, as it turned out. The next morning, as he stood at attention during the early parade, the voice of the sergeant rang out. 'Captain Tomlinson, step forward.'

It took a second for Jack to realise that it was himself the sergeant referred to.

'Yes, sir!' He shouted the obligatory reply. Only when he stepped forwards did he notice the makeshift easel set up in front of the parade. The sergeant was only beginning with his fun at Jack's expense.

'Men, let me introduce you to our resident artist, Private Tomlinson —henceforth to be known as Captain Tomlinson. Captain Tomlinson will no longer be joining us in our preparations for war. Instead, he will be sketching us as we go about the business of defeating the enemy! Line up, boys, and make sure your hair is neat and your sideburns are trimmed. We want to look pretty for our portraits, don't we?'

Hundreds of men laughed uproariously while Jack squirmed with embarrassment. However had he allowed Treloar to talk him into taking on the role of a war artist?

Later in the morning, during their tea break, numerous men approached Jack, keen to hear the facts of his story. Very few had ever heard of such a thing as a war artist, although more than one had seen paintings of battles. It had never occurred to them that the army actually employed artists. As he answered their questions, Jack felt embarrassed by both the change in his appointment and by his new rank, but he needn't have worried. Most of the men were curious and pleased for Jack, admitting that they'd grab at the opportunity in a moment to relinquish their guns for paintbrushes, if only they had the skills.

~

When the men heard that they were to celebrate Christmas Day four days early, they knew that the command for them to depart for Bardia was imminent. Whilst a spirit of good humour and bravado prevailed, Jack wondered if others, like himself, harboured fears that this Christmas might be their last, spent as far away from their homes and families as a man could possibly be, and that the only thing to do was make the best of it. Together they joked as they opened the extra tin of bully beef and sipped on the tots of rum that they'd been issued, cheering as boxes were brought to the dining room and opened, to reveal hampers donated by the Australian Comforts Fund. With the excitement of children opening presents, they were delighted at the contents: plum pudding, fruit cake and tins of fruit and cream as well as an assortment of razor blades, tobacco, boxes of Minties and Anzac biscuits. The men were vocal in their appreciation, raising their glasses to toast the women at home who so badly wanted to make 'their boys' Christmas dinner nice, and who'd dedicated hundreds of hours to raising money, knitting socks and collecting books to improve the lives of troops.

That week's mailbag was jammed with letters and parcels, and more than one man had tears in his eyes as he read letters from families that he hadn't seen for six months. Now, so far from home, the time and distance suddenly felt both incomprehensible and intolerable.

Jack had his own package of letters—messages from his parents as well as from Sunday and John and from Margaret. It warmed him to hear about their lives. As he read, his thoughts turned to Sofia, and he hoped that she too would receive messages of goodwill from somebody this Christmas.

# CHAPTER 20

On December 28th they received the news that they would be moving out the next morning, and what's more, that they needed to smarten up, for Lieutenant General Blamey was arriving at the barracks to inspect them that very afternoon. The news that they were being paraded before the Australian Commander of the AIF was both a shock and an honour, and boots and guns were polished and uniforms tidied in preparation. It was hard to describe the pride they felt as he congratulated them for their preparations and wished them well, before reminding them that the mission at Bardia was Australia's entry into the war; all eyes would be on them. And then, following his speech, they marched five abreast past the General, receiving his salute in return for theirs, and it was impossible not to feel the pride of being an Australian soldier. Indeed, it felt like Australia's image on the world stage—the image that the Diggers had created by their service in the Great War—was about to be tested, and they were determined that they would not let their country down.

As he prepared to leave the next morning, Jack felt mortified by the metal cylinder and sketching pens in his pack. What if his mates needed cover, or if he encountered an enemy gun pointing straight at him? At the last minute, he grabbed his rifle. Sure, he would fulfil his duty and capture the unfolding battle through 'artist eyes' if that was what Treloar wanted, but there was no way that he was going to stand back, helpless and unarmed, should he be needed.

～

Three days later, joining the combined force of Australian and New Zealand troops as they moved in silence through the open desert crossing the border from Egypt into Libya, Jack could not shake the feeling of being an imposter. He was surrounded by men with a life and death mission, yet was excused from participating in his appointment as War Artist. Regardless, he was determined to be as useful as he could, and under no circumstances would he shirk the hardships of those facing the battle.

The night was freezing, despite the protection of their greatcoats and leather jerkins, and very few of the men had slept. At 0300hrs, the Comforts Fund staff issued stew and coffee. A round of rum was distributed by one of the sergeants, who claimed that a couple of sips of the syrupy mixture would provide relief from the cold now seeping into their bones and would strengthen their spirits in the face of fire.

At 0430hrs Jack waited with the men of the 17th Brigade, watching as the 16th Brigade quietly moved west under the cover of darkness, in preparation for their dawn attack and the 2/6th take a position to the south, their task being to create a diversion at the point where the Italian defence was deemed to be weakest. Much to the disappointment of the men of the 17th Brigade, they were to stand aside for the first few hours, waiting for the moment when they would be needed.

Nothing could have prepared Jack for both the speed and the ferocity of the attack when it came, right on time at 0530hrs as planned. Beginning with a sea and air assault, the Navy opened fire from the coastline while the RAF roared overhead. Jack watched the torpedoes tumbling from the sky, where they collided with the ground in thunderous explosions that shook the earth. He noted that the Italians wasted no time in reacting, for almost immediately, colourful flares were visible from their quarters as they returned fire.

The sound was stupendous as a series of explosions occurred to the far left, and Jack guessed that the outer wire fence that surrounded

Bardia had been breached by the Bangalore torpedos. Now the infantry would be able to enter and advance on the Italian defence posts that surrounded the perimeter.

Seizing the freedom of his newly appointed status, a role for which no one really seemed to know the rules, Jack left the men of the 17th, and moved closer to the battle field, where he could see the buildings of upper Bardia in the distance, the lighthouse dominant on the horizon. He knew that below the cliff sat a second cluster of buildings, the headquarters of the Italian military garrison.

Within an hour, a group of about five hundred men were marched from the field—Italian prisoners—and Jack thought that the battle might be over quicker than expected. However, over the next few hours the noise only intensified as various skirmishes occurred on both to his right and left, as the Italians resisted with ferocity. Through the dusty haze, Jack watched the sappers—an advanced foot-team of engineers—working with picks and shovels to remove debris, ever watchful for enemy land mines. As they cleared the way, he saw a dozen Matildas advance. He'd once heard these described as the Queens of the Battlefield, and could see why. Their progress was stately, like a fleet of battle cruisers advancing, with turrets high, one or two with pennants fluttering in the breeze, their guns menacing. It seemed that nothing would deter them from their duty, and with shellfire pinging as it bounced off their armour, they forged through the eight-foot wire fences. Their targets were the Italian gunners who were stationed every few hundred yards along the boundary fence; if the Matildas successfully disabled these, the 17th's job would be easier.

By mid-morning, thousands of Italian prisoners had been taken, and Jack knew that many of the Allied soldiers would have fallen. He was thankful that at least the men of the 2/5th weren't among those, for still they were being held out of the battle.

It was late in the morning when, with mixed feelings, Jack saw the men of his unit enter the battlefield—the first that they would fight on together. Led by the tanks, the lads jogged in line abreast formation. Shorty stood out—a head taller than most—and Jack could see Snowy and Macka, a few lines back. They jogged forward, with faces grim, their rifles gripped firmly against their chests, ready for action. A wave of regret washed over Jack as he watched them with a mixture of admiration and nervousness. The jovial rascals he knew were now a formidable group of trained professional soldiers advancing forth on a mission that he should have been part of.

The thudding of artillery escalated as the 2/5th made their presence felt, and then dozens more men entered the field—the 19th Brigade— who provided further reinforcement. Jack was glad to know that his mates had backup.

During the second day, Jack was able to get closer to the township where beyond gunfire, he heard shouting—mostly cursing, or the frenzied voices of the sergeants bellowed orders as they attempted to bring sense to the chaos. Other sounds came to him also. The surprised cries of the injured, the rattle of a woman's voice, angry and frightened, and the wailing of a baby. He hoped that the civilians in the town had found safe places to hide for the duration of the battle's deadly course.

Over three days, the battle raged. There were moments of hope that it would be over soon, as white flags appeared and prisoners were taken, but on it went. In that time Jack produced dozens of sketches, first focusing on the overall shapes of the landscape and the advancing units, and then picking out details. He sketched the plumes of smoke bursting from the Vickers and Brens as they released their fire; an abandoned Italian tank resting on its side; an advancing infantry unit silhouetted against the dunes. He could see how these small sketches would contribute to a larger painting of the battle, a massive canvas like those he'd seen at London's National Gallery, portraying the desert landscape, its gently rising hills, the huddle of buildings, and the carnage now being inflicted on this Italian outpost on the Libyan coastline.

Mid-morning on the third day, Jack noticed the barrage from the Tommy guns and rifles subsiding and the seconds between shots lengthening to minutes until only the occasional single shot was heard. More white flags appeared, and then there were more—small strips of white cloth tied to guns or poles and held aloft. Lines of men came forth, dusty and weary, their arms raised in surrender. An important image, Jack was sure, and he repositioned himself closer to capture their expressions. Row upon row of Italian soldiers, five to a line, passed within yards of him. Some staggered, supported by mates, their blood-soaked clothing a sure sign that they'd taken a hit.

Jack was shocked as he looked into the smooth, dirt-coated faces of the soldiers, with lank hair and ragged uniforms. Their foes were a bunch of boys! Some glanced towards him and smiled tiredly, their relief to finally submit after forty hours of relentless fighting, evident in their eyes.

Jack considered following the endless stream of prisoners now filing past him, but decided there'd be time enough to see their destination later. First, he would investigate the scars of the battlefield, where smouldering debris and lifeless bodies lay amid abandoned vehicles and weapons. Already, he could see Allied soldiers moving among the buildings, some with weapons poised as they did a final check for snipers, others speaking to a frightened-looking huddle of citizens in the town square, doubtless in shock from what had just taken place. He held his rifle before him as he approached, a gesture that seemed somewhat belated, but nonetheless sensible, given that he was entering a battlefield.

There were surprises. A small wire-haired dog lay beside its dead master; a second sniffed amongst the debris with interest. Slinging his rifle over his shoulder, Jack's hand moved over his drawing book as he created quick sketches of the desolation around him—outlines with enough details to help him recall this moment at a later date.

Not everybody was lifeless, and Jack paused beside a young man who lay on his back in a small alleyway, surprised by the movement of a head turning towards him. The young man's eyes were not fear-filled, as may have been expected, but rather steeped in fatigue. Weary and accepting the fate that would come quickly, judging by a jagged wound at the base of his shin, now absent a right foot. A dark crimson stream seeped through a cloth where someone had attempted to bandage the stump. It was easy to see that the soldier had little chance of surviving. Squatting alongside him, Jack positioned himself so that he cast a shadow over the lad's face, relieving him of the harsh sunlight. The irony of the action did not escape him; thirty minutes earlier, the Allied forces were raining bullets upon the boy. Now here was Jack, protecting him from rays of sunshine.

It was a small gesture to a fellow human, Jack felt. Certainly, in a political sense, the lad was his enemy, and unarguably the gun he carried was intended to maim and kill the Australians he'd just been fighting. Perhaps he'd even landed a mark on a few. But luck had been against him today. Retrieving a water canteen strapped to the boy's pack, Jack offered him a sip, and for his effort received a tired smile and a grunt of thanks, a foreign 'humph' sound.

Reminded of Andrés, Jack found it hard to leave this boy in his last few minutes of life, and so he didn't. What the hell. He was an artist at this minute, not a soldier, and nobody was depending on him for fire cover or support. Pulling out his pad, he held it close to the young man's face, watching as he grasped the pencil. The blackened hand trembled, but was not beyond scrawling a few words until weakness set in and it dropped from the page. Jack could feel the eyes fixed upon his face, as the man slumped backwards.

'I'll see it gets home, mate,' Jack said, offering him another sip of water. It was all the young Italian could do to swallow a mouthful, and then that was it. It was over for him.

Had this been the young man's first battle? Jack wondered. Was he like Margaret's Jim? Had he signed up in a fit of nationalistic fervour, to last only a couple of months? Would his family be proud of his sacrifice, or just confused by the waste of it all? For it was a waste of a young life, Jack had no doubts. But that was war. Invade or be invaded. Kill or be killed.

Just as Treloar had said, war wasn't pretty—and surely this recognition of a young man's life was as worthy a record as any. Jack quickly sketched him: now still, his eyes staring unseeing into the sky, a thick pool of crimson around his lower leg, flies gathering to take advantage of the windfall. Jack flicked them away. It should have been terrible, and in a way it was, but it was also a moment of kindness and opportunity, and Jack felt humbled as, bending close, he placed the lad's beret over his face before making a quick record of the badge, carefully noting the number printed beneath it.

Standing, he glanced around the battlefield, at soldiers now sorting through guns, ammunition, food supplies and vehicles, some of which had been abandoned, others of which held drivers who'd been shot mid-battle. Their bodies were roughly pulled aside and the vehicles driven to a clearing. Later they'd be collected by the Allies. The spoils of battle. Jack noted that war was as much about accumulation of resources as it was about destroying lives.

In the distance, Jack saw injured soldiers being loaded into ambulances for transfer to the field hospital. Packing away his pencils, he went across to assist. As well as the injured, there was the dead, both Italian and their own. The bodies were carefully laid in neat rows, hats covering their faces, awaiting the lorries to collect them. Jack was thankful that none of them was exceptionally tall or bore a shock of fair hair.

He thought about the families—the mothers and fathers, wives and sweethearts—about to have their lives destroyed by a postman arriving on their doorstep with a telegram in his hand, and his heart felt heavy for them.

That day, thirty-five thousand Italian prisoners were taken. The troops of the 17th gave three cheers the next morning after being told that *London's Daily Express* had described the Australian soldiers at Bardia as 'the cream of the Empire's troops–the finest and toughest fighting men in the world!'

Soon after their success at Bardia, orders for the 2/5th's next mission came through: they were to seize a town called Tobruk farther to the west, which, like Bardia, was being held by Italian troops. The men were still jubilant following the success of their first battle, and ready for anything. Even though they'd travelled across the world to knock the Germans off their perch, for now, they were happy to practise on the Italians.

Like Bardia, Tobruk was a coastal town on the desert fringe where the sand met the sea. For days the men of the 6th Division waited in the featureless landscape, enduring a battering of dust storms intent on redistributing sand into their food, clothing, mouths, noses and ears. The heat was dreadful, and flies were everywhere. However, the spirits of the 2/5th remained high; a few flies could not crush them. Waiting, they entertained themselves with cricket, card games and two-up.

The good humour of the troops in the face of the harsh conditions of the western desert earned congratulations from Brigadier Savige, and whilst the men shrugged off the praise from their commander for their cheerfulness and daring, Jack had no doubts that inside, each one of them was gratified by his encouraging words.

The battle of Tobruk was almost a repeat of that at Bardia three weeks earlier, only made easier by the fact that the British had managed to cut the town's telephone lines, preventing the Italians from alerting their command of the attack. Like Bardia, the assault began before sunrise, and Jack watched the British planes dipping in the sky as the RAF pilots skilfully dropped bombs to soften the targets. In the grey light of dawn he could see movement from the sappers as they cleared the way for the tanks. The first group of tanks to enter were the L3/35s, Italian tanks that had been salvaged from the Bardian battle, and which were now being driven by Australians. He cheered as they advanced. A few days earlier he'd been asked to put his brushes to work to Australianise them, and now images of kangaroos decorated their sides. However, rather than leaping forward like 'roos in flight, their movement was more like that of slowly ambling tortoises as they waited for sweepers to carefully search the sand ahead for tell-tale signs that a landmine was planted beneath the surface.

As in Bardia, heavy artillery fire was exchanged with the Italians for most of the day, with the addition of a flight of Italian airplanes that were quickly shot down by the RAF. Again, the men of the 2/5th had to wait their turn, as the sixteenth brigade entered the battle first, followed by a British Tanks regiment. It was after 1000hrs before the 17th Brigade finally entered, and within half an hour, many of the Italian strongpoints within Tobruk had been taken. Throughout the afternoon the air attack continued as Blenheims and Hurricanes patrolled the skies whilst the Australian infantry pushed forward.

The Italians fought valiantly, but the allied attack was strong, and Jack watched with surprise when late in the afternoon they turned their gunfire onto their own harbour and its stores. He realised that they'd accepted they were defeated, and intended to deny the Allies the spoils of war.

And early the following morning, white flags were raised and the gunfire ceased. Jack watched as hundreds of Italian soldiers emerged with their hands held high. He was thrilled for the victory as he advanced into Tobruk's narrow streets, where he paused and sketched the battered Digger's slouch hat that had been raised on the centre flag post, replacing the green, white and red Italian flag that lay in tatters on the ground. It was the 17th Brigade's second victory in the space of a month, and the men cheered jubilantly.

In the early evening, Jack sketched scenes of the enclosure holding the prisoners—another twenty-thousand of which had been taken. Listening to the sounds from within, where officers of 2/7th Battalion supervised the prisoners, he smiled. Good-natured in their supervision, they were encouraging the Italians to sing along with them to the tunes of 'Waltzing Matilda' and 'The Wild Colonial Boy'.

The 17th Brigade remained in Tobruk, helping the villagers re-establish their water supply and clear debris. It was a relaxing time, and the men were glad for the opportunity to assist the locals to make the village livable before returning to Egypt. However, when in late March, instructions came through that the 2/5th were to be deployed to Greece, the boys were ecstatic. At long last they were being given a chance to fight the Germans!

# CHAPTER 21

*A*s ever, confusion reigned about the state of Greece and the battle ahead of them; factual information about the various battlefronts was invariably scant, and frequently complicated by rumours and updates of events that were long over. The BBC was the 2/5th's most reliable source of information, and even it was subject to propaganda, misinformation and confusion.

Fortunately, one of the chaps, Harold Green, who prior to the war had been a school teacher with a passion for history, made it his business to stay abreast of the various battles that were being fought across Europe. Harold was a wealth of information regarding the international overview. Some of the chaps teased him, calling him 'The Professor'. Ever patient, and happy to answer the smallest of questions, Harold was a whiz at creating outlines of countries and mountain ranges that they'd never heard of, explaining the political motivations of the Italians, Germans, Russians and Albanians as they were drawn into the action, and suggesting possible scenarios based on the outcomes of the various battles. On occasions, when the sergeant gave his morning briefings, Jack noticed him glance at Harold as if to confirm the briefing had been in full accordance with Harold's research; and Jack developed the habit of looking for Harold's response, his rapid nod or perhaps a frown, suggesting the sergeant's information was flawed.

The morning after the news that the 2/5th would sail to Greece, Jack joined the others gathered around Harold at the breakfast table. 'What are the Germans doing in Greece, Professor?' Snowy asked him. Jack listened with interest, for not only had they been told that Greece was a neutral nation, but that the Germans were concentrating their efforts in northern Europe.

Harold was happy to clarify the latest political shifts that had forced Greece into the war. 'What's happened is that Mussolini has seized an opportunity to expand Italy's power by taking Greece for himself,' he explained. 'You know, extend Italy's presence in Southern Europe. Mussolini thought subjugating the Greeks would be easy, but not so. They've put up a good show in holding the Italians off in their northern mountains. However, weeks have turned into months and now the Greek army is exhausted. You can imagine what it's like, the snow and blistering winds in the mountains. It must be dreadful—freezing, starving and ready to drop. I wouldn't like it.'

For the soldiers around the table, who'd been subjected to the open desert and relentless sand storms for months, cold they could understand, but imagining snow covered mountains was difficult. Nonetheless, they nodded for Harold to continue.

'Yes, but what has that got to do with Hitler?' Jack asked.

'It's not Mussolini's plight that Hitler's worried about. He'd probably be happy to ignore the Italians, let them sort out the mess that they've started in Greece. However, a new problem has arisen because Churchill—the canny bastard—has taken advantage of the fact that the Greeks are exhausted, and offered to come to their aid. By sending us and the New Zealanders to support the Greek army, Britain stands to gain a military presence in Southern Europe.'

'But does it matter to Hitler, if the British have a base in Greece?' Shorty asked.

'Well, in fact, yes, it does. It's all about resources,' Harold said, seamlessly shifting the conversation from battlefronts to politics and then to economics with authority. 'Oil, to be exact. If the Allies get a foothold in Greece, it puts us in range of the Romanian oil fields: the oil supply that Germany depends on. So, as annoyed as Hitler may be, he has no choice. He has to send troops in to finish what Mussolini started. And that is where we come in, laddies! We are going to kick Hitler's sorry arse all the way back over the Rhodope mountains and into Albania!'

Jack considered his options and was determined that he would be numbered amongst those advancing to Greece; it was surely a step closer to Paris or Spain than Palestine was. There was every possibility that after they'd finished with the Germans, he might be able to get leave. Perhaps he could get across to Italy, and from there, to France, where he could make inquiries about Sofia's whereabouts.

Days later, Jack was glad to be on the troopship travelling to Piraeus, a port city on the outskirts of Athens. The mood of the 2/5th was euphoric. After weeks of rest, they had finally become bored with the cricket, two-up and gin rummy and were eager for their next campaign. More importantly, they were finally getting a chance to quell the Germans, and they couldn't wait. Although the word was that the Germans had already achieved what the Italians had failed to do— force their way across the mountains and towards Athens—this news did not phase the 2/5th at all. Hitler hadn't met with Australians yet, and his soldiers were in for a hiding the likes of which they'd never encountered!

Nightly, they gathered in the ship's dining room, where Brigadier Savige went over the maps of Greece, reiterating the proposed plan of attack. Preparation was everything, he insisted, emphasising that they were meeting an advancing enemy head-on, a formidable enemy, the power of whom shouldn't be underestimated. Each time Savige warned them of the might of the German army, the troops reacted with a show of bravado—no German army was going to defeat them—and Jack suspected that their brigade leader feared that his unit had become overly confident following their successes at Bardia and Tobruk. Nonetheless, the proposed strategy seemed simple enough—following an air attack from the RAF, the 17th Brigade would approach from the south, and push them back over the mountains. All being well, they'd have the Germans retreating within the week.

~

Arriving at Piraeus, all they could do was gaze longingly at the turquoise of the Mediterranean Sea lapping the shore, beckoning them to throw their sand-infused bodies into its sweet waters. But there was no time to waste. Immediately on disembarking they were hustled into lines and marched through the town to the cheering and clapping of the locals. Accepting the flowers handed to them by young women, the glasses of water and small bags of food that children ran forwards to offer, they found it hard not to feel inspired. That night, they stayed in a nearby village, Daphnis, and the following morning they marched with the confidence of an already victorious army—eight miles to the railway, where they boarded creaking carriages and commenced a journey through some of the most beautiful countryside Jack had ever seen.

Flowers lined the roadside and filled the fields. Every few miles they passed through tiny hamlets, where farmers paused from their work to raise their hands in greeting.

Bound for Larissa, some two hundred miles north, they settled in for the journey. Between dozing and gazing at the scenery, the time passed uneventfully until the train drew to a halt. The sound of yelling drew Jack to the window. Numerous soldiers, their uniforms in tatters, their faces desperate, were trying to board the train. Greeks?

'By golly, they are trying to take the train! They want to turn us around,' said the man beside him.

Jack listened to the raised voices.

'Flee, flee! The Germans, we cannot defeat them!'

Jack jostled for position with hundreds of men, who leaned out of the windows, watching as a sergeant stepped forth and shouted at the men to move, angered by the obstruction to their journey.

'Cowards,' said the man beside him, and he nodded in agreement. What sort of soldier fled before the enemy? he wondered, although since his own role had changed from Private Tomlinson, 2/5th Infantry to Captain Tomlinson, Official War Artist, he was self-conscious of his own non-combative role.

All around him, the men expressed disdain for the Greeks who'd abandoned their post. The Australians had only just arrived to the battle and were in no mind to give up without so much as bloodying a bayonet! When shots rang out, Macka, who was watching at the window, gasped.

'We fired at them! Not at them directly, but a warning message! The CO has just given the order: if the Greeks don't step back from the train, they will be shot! Heaven forbid, I think he's serious. Here we are in Greece, protecting the Greeks, and the first shots we've fired are at them!'

The threat seemed to work, for within minutes, the train continued its journey, and two hours later, they arrived at their destination, Larissa.

When barely an hour later they'd disembarked from the train at a small station nestled under the shadow of Mount Olympus, and watched as eighteen Messerschmitts tore across the sky toward them—their rapid gunfire destroying anything in their path—the bravado of the men was dampened. Their bullets had just missed one of the lorries that the Australians were about to board, commissioned to take them to the east of the advancing Germans.

Jack glanced at Macka and Shorty, then gazed northward, where plumes of smoke rose amid deafening explosions. Their long-awaited opportunity to take on the Germans was upon them. However, judging by the thundering barrage ahead and the vision of dozens of airplanes —not the RAF's Vickers Wellingtons—but instead, the Luftwaffe's Junkers and Messerschmitts, it was clear that this was not going to be the pushover they'd anticipated. Inhaling the cool evening air, heavy with moisture and filled with the acrid smell of gunfire, it occurred to Jack that in Bardia and Tobruk the Allies had the benefit of well positioned surprise attacks on sleeping villages. Here, as Savige had warned, they faced an enemy in full throttle that was advancing toward them, mercilessly.

The men were quiet as they approached the positions that had been planned from the comfort of the ship's dining room. In the broad light of day, nothing about the cataclysmic conditions that they'd entered related to the clear pathway to victory that had been laid out on the sergeant's large blackboard in the preceding week.

Jack didn't have to think; he knew that this was no moment to be a war artist. Instead, he checked his .303 and joined Shorty and Snowy, jogging towards an outcrop of jagged rocks to their left.

As the Germans came within firing distance, he shot round after round from his rifle before grabbing a machine gun that had been relinquished by the blood-splattered body of one of his own unit, lying barely a dozen yards away.

This time, Jack had no opportunity to ponder the tragedy of war and the grief of families as he'd done at Bardia. Instead he grasped the Bren, determined to continue where the young soldier had left off, releasing hundreds of rounds as quickly as he could load them into the magazine. He was thankful for the diminishing light that sent the armies to bed, allowing time for troops on both sides to tend to wounds, reconsider their positions and rest their weary bones. Jack wondered if the German soldiers found the same relief in the silence of the night as he did.

For four days Jack and his unit pushed forward—their determination firm—matching machine gun fire blaze for blaze, setting their rifles' sights on anything that moved, but making little ground.

More than anything, they waited for the air support, forever scanning the sky, desperate for sight of the British torpedo bombers; but all that they could see was Goering's air force, the Luftwaffe. If it wasn't his Messershcmitts, it was his Stukas, and if it wasn't his Stukas it was the Heinkels. Twice the infantry units had to retreat as the German guns closed in.

On the fifth day, the order came for the Allies to withdraw. They were to retreat to Kalamata immediately—ships had already been dispatched from Palestine and were now on their way to perform an evacuation. Greece was being forsaken to the Germans!

While none of the men mentioned the Greek soldiers they'd ridiculed for fleeing the Germans a week earlier, Jack felt terrible for them. To think of how those lads had been fighting for months—fending off first the Italian army and then the Germans, of how they'd endured the worst of a freezing winter to protect their country in a war that they'd never wanted, and been exhausted and starving. How harsh the Australians had been with their scathing criticism! Their unfounded confidence had filled them with a bravado that was disproportionate to the might of the German army. Their threats to shoot those young men who'd fought so bravely for their country had been abominable. They should have cheered them and given them some rations to see them through. More than anything, Jack hoped that somehow the lads had made it home to their families safely.

# CHAPTER 22

*A*rriving at the small coastal town of Kalamata eighteen hours later, Jack looked around the beach, now crowded with thousands of men waiting to board the ships that would carry them back to Alexandria. The ringing of axes belting against motors filled the air as the lorries which had transported them from the battlefields were being destroyed. The Germans already had enough resources at their disposal—the Australians didn't need to be adding to their strength with salvageable vehicles. He looked at the hundreds of troops who'd gathered on the beach, some in groups quietly chatting, others alone, taking deep drags from their cigarettes, attempting to steady their nerves and make sense of the last week. He felt their shock. That the Allies might be defeated by the Germans had never been considered. Worse, that they'd actually turn on their heels and flee in the face of the enemy, had been unimaginable.

Jack, Shorty and Macka gathered together, along with Green and Doc; and a few troops of the 2/7th joined them. Shorty was worried about Snowy; he hadn't seen his brother since they got separated at Larissa but Green felt certain that he'd seen him on the beach, barely an hour earlier. They made a tally of who'd seen whom, and worried for a couple of the men who were unaccounted for. So far the men of the Bat Cave had been lucky, surviving Bardia and Tobruk with only minor injuries.

As they revisited the events of Larissa, the men grasped to restore their sense of pride—insisting that the Allies had done everything anyone could possibly have done to push the Germans back. However, as Shorty said, they'd been like ants trying to turn a boulder; the strength of the German army had been totally underestimated by the Allied command. Across the beach rang voices that were bitter in their criticism of the London Office, who was responsible for providing intelligence about the German Army.

'And, where were the RAF when we needed them?' Macka added as he wrapped a bandage around his shin, where mercifully flying shrapnel had caused only a minor flesh wound.

Everyone had their own ideas of how the Australians could have pulled off a victory with proper planning and a dash of luck on their side.

Even now the fighting was not over, and Jack wasn't sure if it was echoes of the last five days or the actual thud of gunfire in the distance that rang in his ears. He knew that rear-guard men—the 2/19th and the New Zealanders— had stayed behind to provide cover to the allies as they'd retreated. Jack thought about the young men who'd volunteered for what could only be a suicide mission, for it would take a miracle for them to escape their posts. Again, he listened to the rat-tat-tat of gunfire—louder than ever. He was sure it was them, with their Bren and Vickers machine guns. At least the rattle was evidence that it was not over for them yet, and miracles were not unheard of.

Restless, Jack searched for a quiet spot, thinking he'd ease his mind by adding to the bundle of sketches he'd accumulated in Tobruk. A soldier in the distance hugged a dog close to his chest: a good subject, he thought. Was it Jim and Horrie? Jim Moody had found Horrie in the desert, and the little pup became a mascot among the men, accompanying them through all their battles, and was even credited with warning them of attacks from approaching aircraft. Jack had wanted to sketch him for a while. That the dog remained with Jim despite the smoke-filled air, the roar of engines and the thundering of bombs was remarkable—the horror of it all was enough to have anyone with two legs running, let alone four.

Moving amongst the soldiers on the beach were Greek civilians: ladies with baskets, distributing food to the troops; men asking questions about the front, begging for weapons with which to defend their families when the Germans arrived. Jack thought how different this scene was from that a week earlier, when the troops had arrived in Greece to cheering and clapping and flowers. It felt terrible to have let them down.

The beach was eventually cloaked in darkness, and soon after, pinpricks of light approached—the destroyers, arriving to collect them. Within an hour the convoy of ships rested offshore. Maintaining order, the troops lined in groups of three and prepared to board. Jack searched for Shorty, Macka and Snowy but could not see them. He found a small group of others from the 2/5th and sloshed through the cool waters to board a destroyer that transported them out to a Dutch ship resting further out—the *SS Costa Rica*, which was already heavily loaded with men of the 2/6th and 2/7th.

'Up you come, now.' The accent was distinctly Irish. 'You may as well join us and be bombed here as on dry land out there. I always think a sea burial is better than bones scorching in the sun.'

'Danny, put a sock in it, will you?' The words came from an older man who emitted the aura of a commanding officer.

'Yes, sir. Up you come, lads, we've got you now. Not to say that you'll be any safer with us. In fact, you may have stepped out of the frying pan and into the fire.'

'Danny!'

'Yes sir, sorry, sir… but you must acknowledge, there is truth in it.'

Jack learned that there was certainly truth in Danny's comments, for over the past forty-eight hours, their rescuers had endured two attacks as they'd travelled from Alexandria to Kalamata for the evacuation. The first came from a couple of Italian bombers, who had been easily deflected when Danny and his unit fired their personal weapons into the sky. Danny was sure they'd tipped the wings of at least one of the low-flying planes and sent it to a watery grave. The second attack had been even more thrilling and not without irony.

'Here we were,' Danny explained, 'tuned in to Westminster's Anzac service, our voices lifted in praise to the Lord.' Danny's voice burst into tune. "*For those that peril on the sea...*" What we didn't know was that we, along with all of those kindly souls in London gathered at the abbey, were in fact singing a blessing to our own sweet selves, for out of the blue, the screaming tones of Italian Stukas joined the choir. Utterly out of tune, they were, and directly above us—seven of them—and they weren't praying for our souls, that's for sure!'

'Don't worry lads, we're here now—you'll be right!' The comment came from Jim, and Jack was glad to see the moist black tip of Horrie's nose peering from behind his legs. He reached out and patted the dog, who whimpered. Perhaps Horrie'd had enough adventures, Jack thought. He certainly had.

'They be strong words from someone who has just run from the Germans and needed to be evacuated, but full marks for bravado, because we aren't home yet!' Danny laughed at Jim, then glanced between his legs. 'And what's that you've got there? A wee dog! Well, I'll be. Here, champ... would you like a bit of jerky to tide you over?'

Danny was a character, Jack decided, as he settled against the side of the deck, using his pack for a pillow and the stars for a blanket. Within minutes he fell into the heaviest sleep. By the time he awoke, the scorching sun fell onto the deck, and he sat up to rummage through his pack for some biscuits and a swig of water.

'Want a mouthful,' Jim must have noticed Jack had come up empty-handed from his search into his pack, for he held out a glass bottle toward him.

'Thanks mate... mouth's dry as a sheet of sandpaper.' He accepted the bottle and sipped the aniseed flavoured liquid.

'Raki?' he asked Jim in surprise.

'No, Ouzo... Not bad, is it? Not quite as refreshing as a Fosters, but then you can't even get a decent beer over here. Spirits will have to do us, I'm afraid!'

Jack smiled and watched as Horrie wriggled from behind Jim, and walked across the deck to where a sleeping soldier lay, lifting his leg to pee against the man's pack. Jack held his breath as he watched the man stir from his sleep and mumble, before sinking back into oblivion.

'Horrie! Show some manners, will you!' Jim chided, as the pup returned and snuggled against his leg. Jack laughed and laid his head down again before raising it and shaking his finger at the dog.

'Don't you go peeing on me, you cheeky little bugger,' he said, and then exhausted after the week in the Greek mountains fighting an unwinnable battle, he slept, lulled by the lapping water and the hum of motors as the flotilla commenced its retreat from Kalamata.

Jack woke with a start to the sounds of yelling and the sight of men leaping to their feet and scrabbling for weapons. A shriek from above revealed two Italian planes swooping and diving in the sky above them. He joined with the other men to support the ship's gunners by spraying ammunition skyward from anything they could find—rifles, pistols and Tommy Guns. Their barrage forced the attackers higher and higher, until finally they became defeated black specks retreating to the north.

The cheers from the *Costa Rica* were echoed by those of the other ships who'd joined the return fire, as they continued their zigzagging journey across the Mediterranean. Yet they remained on high alert, and responded with the same frenzied defence to each of no less than seven attacks that followed.

Between the bouts of return fire, they snacked on biscuits and chatted. Some of the men still relived the events of the past week that had them fleeing the Germans, while others were pleased to forget the whole sorry mess and talk of other things.

On reflection, Jack wondered if they'd all gotten too relaxed, or too confident or even too tired, following the repeated attacks, for at mid-afternoon a lone Stuka flew out of bright sunshine and landed two bombs to the side of the *Costa Rica* before anyone had a chance to raise their weapons.

# CHAPTER 23

*T*hankfully, it wasn't a direct hit, and the ship's gunners were quick to return fire. They chased the Stuka away even as the vessel reared up like a bucking bronco, with men, packs and equipment sliding precariously across the deck. Jack was quick to grab the rail beside him, but he feared that they'd all be cast into the sea.

No sooner had the ship settled than its whistle blew—the command for everyone to assemble on the deck. Jack waited for the captain to speak, noting how despite their irreverent humour and penchant for horsing around, Australian Diggers always knew to a man when business was business. Within minutes they stood in silence, shoulder to shoulder, barely breathing. In the stillness, Jack was conscious of the slight sway in the ship and the absence of the steady hum of thudding motors vibrating through the hull. He listened as the captain spoke.

'Men, thank God, the *Costa Rica* is still afloat. However, there is damage to the plates; the engine room is taking water. We are now waiting for a final assessment. Until then, I ask you to stand quietly and wait for further orders.'

As the words sank in, that they were on a vessel possibly about to sink, a call came from below. 'Sir, we've got no lights down here.'

Jack was relieved that he'd been one of the last of the men to board this vessel, and as a result had been forced to remain on the open deck.

He could only imagine the scenes below when the ship had taken the thud of the Stuka's bombs and lurched. And it didn't bear thinking how the men below must be feeling now, trapped in the darkness, knowing that the *Costa Rica* might sink at any minute.

Danny, who Jack now realised was not a man to be quietened in any situation, launched into a monologue, contemplating which was their greatest threat—the ship about to become a steely coffin as they were swallowed by the innocuous-looking waters, or the clear blue sky which might at any second reveal a squadron of enemy aircraft hurtling towards them.

Another man began to offer bets—he thought the sea, and believed it to be the better option, for at least one might swim.

'I can't swim,' said another. 'I'll be fish food for sure!'

The banter was interrupted by a message from the captain.

'The *Costa Rica* is beyond repair, but thankfully, we are not alone. We will use the lifeboats to transfer you to the destroyers accompanying us—the *Defender*, *Herewith* and *Hero*.'

'What do you think?' Jack said to Stevo, one of the men from the 2/5th. 'Could be a long wait!'

'Long wait! Why, we'll all be dead of old age before they get us off using those lifeboats,' Danny exclaimed, as they watched twenty men fill up the closest boat before it was lowered into the sea.

The ship's captain must have shared Danny's view, for fifteen minutes later a second announcement was made. There was to be a change of plans: the men would be transferred directly, ship to ship. The troops of the *Costa Rica* would be distributed amongst the remaining five ships that were now circling them.

Again, to a man, they conducted themselves with restraint, falling in and holding position, not moving a muscle even as their breaths quickened and their heartbeats pounded in their chests until given the command to move.

How long would it be until the *Costa Rica*'s lower decks flooded and they were swallowed up by the lapping waters? Jack watched as first the HMS *Hero*, then the *Defender*, moved against the *Costa Rica*. The skills of their respective captains were impressive, he thought, watching as the hulls gently bumped together to enable the men to leap across the decks. This was easier said than done, Jack noted, for the swell of the sea caused the decks of the two vessels to rise and fall across each other, meaning that the troops were in for a climb or a jump of perhaps twenty feet, with care being taken not to fall between the vessels and risk being crushed between the steel hulls.

The method proved to be reasonably effective, and quickly Jack found himself within a few feet of the rails. He calculated the rhythm of movement, hoping to jump rather than climb when it came to his turn. His thoughts were interrupted by sudden gasps around him accompanied by a cry.

'Ho—man down!'

The shout came from Teague, the man standing in front of Jack, as Stevo, the man standing two in front, mistimed his step and plunged between the ships, falling over forty feet into the sea.

Thinking quickly, Teague launched overboard, calling for a rope even as he jumped. Jack leapt to action, working with the surrounding men to uncoil the nearest of the heavy ropes positioned at intervals along the deck. They heaved it over the side and held their breaths as Teague hooked the rope around the hapless Stevo—who'd be teased forever for creating the drama—then attached himself before waving a signal to bring them up.

They all pulled on the ropes, their raising of the two men dictated by the rhythmic movement of the hulls.

'Up…. Wait…. Up…' Jack called to the men behind him. If they got this wrong, Teague and Stevo would be crushed in a second.

Finally, the men tumbled back onto the deck of the *Costa Rica* to cheers. Jack was sure that Teague's spontaneous action was the bravest thing he'd ever seen, and he wondered if he'd have had the foresight to do the same.

'Nice swim, mate?' Danny asked. 'You might have chosen a better time for a dip, don't you think…'

'Okay—let's go, men!' Their minds returned to the job of evacuation. After all, they were standing aboard a ship that was about to go under!

Following Stevo and Teague, Jack jumped as he'd planned to the welcoming committee of a bunch of men with the brown-over-red badge of the 2/7th. They helped each of the new arrivals to their feet before readying themselves for the next man to jump or be hurled up on the dangling ropes. Looking around, Jack realised that most of the faces surrounding him were unfamiliar. Again, he searched for Shorty's broad shoulders and Snowy's fair hair, but found neither. He hadn't seen any of the men from the Bat Cave since he'd left the beach at Kalamata.

These men seemed to be a friendly bunch, and shaking hands and introducing themselves, they may well have been men from his own division for all of their jesting and irreverent humour at yet another mate's brush with death. They teased the men that they'd rescued off the *SS Costa Rica* for wasting their time, hoping that they didn't have targets on them, lest the Stukas come looking for a second chance, and in doing so bomb the living daylights out of the *Defender*.

It was all over in barely forty-five minutes. Two thousand and six hundred men safely transferred off the *Costa Rica* and distributed amongst the accompanying war ships. As the flotilla regrouped, Jack looked back just in time to see the damaged ship's bow dip below the surface and continued to watch as minutes later the remainder of the ship was swallowed up. Thank goodness they'd been part of a fleet, he thought, and thus rescued so efficiently!

The flotilla continued its south-easterly journey without event until late in the afternoon when the *Defender* and three other vessels broke from the group and veered towards a large island. They entered a sheltered cove with a picturesque beach and a small settlement against the backdrop of a mountain range. The bay was dotted with relics of naval vessels abandoned from a previous battle. The island was Crete; the beach, they quickly learned, was Suda Bay.

# CHAPTER 24

'What the hell are we doing here?' The words came from a tall man with sandy hair, who Jack recognised as one who'd been rescued from the *Costa Rica*, and he looked as confused as Jack felt.

The reply came in the tones of the cheeky Irishman, whose original journey from Alexandria to Kalamata on the *Costa Rica* had always been intended for this destination. He seemed to be very pleased that the disruption of the Stuka's bombing and the subsequent sinking of the vessel had not interfered with the plan.

'Oh, we are the reinforcements. The British have a station here—set it up months ago, but the word is out that the Germans are coming, plotting to take the island for themselves. The British soldiers aren't up to the job, so they've called for some serious muscle to throw the Germans back into the sea.' Danny swaggered as he spoke, looking for all the world like he'd be happy to throw the Germans into the sea himself, one by one.

'But I thought we were going back to Alexandria.' The tall man sounded aggrieved.

'We will, for sure. Just after we sort this wee problem out.'

Exhausted, Jack tried to make sense of events. In the space of a week, he'd endured the horror of the German attack in Greece and the subsequent evacuation, multiple air raids, a sunken ship; and now here he was, being set down on an island in the middle of nowhere. It was like a dream. One thing about it, the men from the 2/7th seemed to be a decent bunch, and Danny was certainly good fun and quick to liven up any situation. He watched as the Defender anchored, and quietly waited in line for his turn to be ferried to the beach, along with enormous boxes; supplies of tents, food rations and blankets that they would be needing for the days ahead.

As he waded through the knee-deep water, his boots tied together by their laces and slung over his shoulder, the beauty of the bay was undeniable. Jack remembered the little beach on Malaga's shoreline where he, Sofia and Andrés had spent hot summer afternoons. The water lapping his shins was crystal clear and warm, and the sand felt soft beneath his feet. Walking up the beach, Jack noticed the brilliant red flowers nestled against dark green foliage—hibiscus, he thought. And were those olive groves in the distance?

Beyond the haven of the bay, mountains erupted skyward, and their ragged peaks looked spectacular against the deep blue sky. Searching into their reaches, Jack could spot an occasional building and grassy knolls descending at impossible angles before vanishing into deep, inhospitable crevices.

A steep cliff rose immediately behind the beach, which Jack imagined would provide an excellent view of the Germans when they arrived; surely they could easily be picked off as they approached the beach. This battle shouldn't be difficult, he thought, and it would be good to have a win after the horror that they'd just experienced in Greece.

'Captain, you're off the *Costa Rica*—how about you join my unit here?' The offer came from the commander of the 2/7th , who'd also been transferred from the sinking ship to the *Defender*, Battalion Commander Colonel Walker.

Jack nodded appreciatively and picked up his bag before joining them, relieved that it had been slung on his shoulders when the *Costa Rica* took the hit from the Stuka's bomb. He would have been sorry to have lost his sketches. He was also pleased to see that Danny and Teague were part of this group.

'Okay, boys. Let's get away from the mayhem—we'll head up to the hill there, see, near the vineyard. That should do us. Danny, you lead the way. With a tongue like yours wagging, you'll be able to guide us in the dark.' Jack was glad to see that his new commanding officer was a purposeful leader, who'd summed up the chaos on the beach and responded accordingly. He was one of the rare kind who had the capacity to maintain both discipline and good cheer among his troops without fuss. The type of leader who inspired confidence.

As they settled on the hill, Colonel Walker continued to direct their actions. 'It'll be dark before we know it, lads, and I'm sure that you're all hungry. Just see what we can slap together to keep the pangs down before we get a good night's rest. Can you pool your resources for now? That's the way. I'll get supplies for us all tomorrow.'

Over the next hour, the men tallied their food, weapons and bedding while Colonel Walker made notes in his diary.

It took less than a minute for Jack to tally his own belongings—his backpack, which held some tinned beef, a spoon, the cylinder containing a few dozen sketches, his drawing book, the stump of a pencil and a dozen or so bullets, but little else. The clothes he was wearing were ragged, but more than some of the others had, and he did have his greatcoat, which offered welcome warmth. The .303 he'd carried from Bardia to Tobruk to Greece had vanished. He must have lost it on the *Costa Rica*. No great loss, Jack thought. It had a dent in the magazine and one of the sights was damaged, rendering it almost dangerous to use.

Jack was not the only one travelling light—the unit quickly realised that they were short on virtually everything. Despite the lack, their spirits remained high. Here they were, nestled on the prettiest of beaches and hopefully away from the immediate threat of gunshots and bombing for at least a day or two!

As the final rays of the sun cast long shadows across the island, the men divided their meagre food supplies. They laughed as they claimed the empty tin cans as substitutes for missing plates and broke twigs from an ancient vine to serve as forks. Afterward they lay against their backpacks and chatted as they gazed at the night sky. In preparation for sleep, woollen coats were spread on the ground, and they divided the few blankets that they could find between them. Despite the warmth of the day, the air had cooled, and amid much joking about who was going to sleep with whom and cuddle who, they lay in groups, sharing their limited resources.

'Over here, Jack,' Danny called. 'Your skinny bones shouldn't take up much space—you, me and Leo can snuggle here together and keep each other warm!'

〜

The next morning, Jack listened to Colonel Walker's update, keen to learn what he could about the battle ahead. Overnight Crete—the tiny island in the Mediterranean virtually unknown to any of them a day earlier, had garnered such strategic importance that it seemed they were defending the nerve centre of the war.

'Churchill says that if we can hold Crete, we can control the Balkans. In controlling the Balkans, we can starve the Germans of oil! That will pull them up in their tracks—and then the war will be over for sure!' Danny's excitement was both palpable and contagious.

'Yes, well, we won't be pushing anybody anywhere if they don't get us some weapons,' replied Colonel Walker dourly. Overnight, their leader had been in meetings with the other senior officers on the island, including men of the British and New Zealander troops as well as Major General Weston who commanded the British Garrison on the island. Jack learned that the entire Allied forces' presence on the island was being led by General Freyberg, a New Zealander who was none too happy about the situation they'd been placed in, but was trying to make the best of it. Walker explained how, with over ten thousand troops landed on the island, there was a shortage of food; advising them that they'd have to make do with what resources they could acquire from the Cretans. Of further concern, Walker explained, was a lack of weapons; the weapon shortage the 2/7th had identified the previous evening had proved to be widespread, and they could only hope that replacement weapons might arrive on the island, soon. The men looked at each other, happy to blame the shortage of weapons on the sinking of the *Costa Rica*; nobody was admitting that during their

225

retreat from Greece, dozens of citizens had asked for guns, and many of the men had obliged, feeling bad for leaving the Greeks at the mercy of the German army, and anticipating they'd soon be at Alexandria where replacement weapons would be available.

'We can only keep our fingers crossed that the replacement weapons arrive before the Germans do,' Walker said, adding that General Freyberg had placed a request to Alexandria that weapons, food and bedding be forwarded to Crete as a matter of urgency.

The carefree ambience Crete offered, with time suspended between battles of the past and those of the future, soothed Jack's mind and body, and he was glad for every day that the Germans delayed their arrival. Waiting, they took advantage of the time to rest, explore the island and meet the inhabitants. Jack wondered how Shorty, Snowy and Macka were faring and hoped that when this campaign was over, he'd be reunited with them. Nonetheless, the men of the 2/7th had made him welcome, and he was also getting to know a few of the New Zealand soldiers, including some Maori fellows. Much like the Australian boys, he found them to be larrikins who shared the same irreverent humour. Furthermore, there was an undeniable bond between the Australians and the New Zealand soldiers, a legacy of the Great War, where troops from the tiny nations had proved themselves brave and resilient in their support for Britain in her hour of need, almost three decades earlier.

Jack tossed up whether he should come clean with Colonel Walker and explain that his true commission was that of war artist, that he was not in fact, the captain of an infantry unit. He concluded it would be barely worthy of a conversation—the CO had far more important things on his mind. Besides, since the 2/5th's evacuation from Greece and the sinking of the *Costa Rica,* the work of a war artist had become utterly irrelevant. There was of course, the question of his captain's wages, now being received under false pretences, but Jack decided he would sort that out with Treloar at some time in the future. Only a few men here on the island even knew of Jack's promotion, and with the pending battle—now being referred to as Creforce—he didn't imagine anyone would insist that he should be wielding his paintbrushes instead of a gun.

The Cretan people were delightful, and like the Greeks at Piraeus, were overwhelmingly grateful for the Australians' and New Zealanders' presence on their island. Jack hoped they wouldn't be disappointed. Each day groups of women approached the camp, carrying fruit, eggs, chickens and wine in their baskets, encouraging the men to eat; and the troops were grateful for the additions to the paltry army rations they were receiving.

Moving into summer, the days were warm and easily passed, with swimming in the bay, attempts to catch fish from the rocks, or walks into the village of Chania, where the grocery store was well stocked. Jack was able to buy a razor to scrape away the raggedy beard matting around his chin, a hairbrush, a small drawing pad and four pencils.

Like most of the men, he all but gave up the battle for cleanliness; after weeks of travel, every article of clothing that he owned was encrusted in salt, filthy—and worse still, crawling with the lice which seemed to have enlisted with the enemy in plague proportions and now conducted their own insidious battle with his flesh.

He'd happily relinquished his shirt and trousers when, amid much laughter, the Cretan ladies had gestured for him, Danny and the others from their group to strip down to their underwear. The women took away batches of shirts and shorts for laundering and returned them clean and neatly folded the following day.

Of note was the number of troops continuously arriving on the island; and the numbers quickly exceeded thirty-thousand as soldiers from the AIF, New Zealand and the British military arrived, as well as soldiers from the Greek Army who'd managed to escape the mainland using all manner of vessels. Suda Bay now bulged with immense destroyers, barges, caiques and fishing boats responsible for transportation. There were other arrivals, too—men with heavy moustaches, wearing baggy pants and headscarves, who slipped across the sand and into the hills like shadows; a group of well-dressed dignitaries who greeted the troops as they passed through; and, to Jack's amazement, a group of giggling females dressed in glamourous evening dresses, escorted by fellow troops from the AIF. The Australian soldiers were teased mercilessly when they'd stepped ashore with the women, and defended themselves, insisting that they were not taking advantage of them but rather the women had begged to be taken away from Athens. They were cabaret dancers and feared for their safety when the Germans arrived. What choice did the Australian soldiers have, but do the gentlemanly thing and assist these damsels in distress?

'I wonder if they'd like to do a bit of a show here,' Danny suggested. 'I'm sure that we could find an audience without looking too far.'

'Come on, Danny. Keep your eyes on the war, not the women,' Jack teased. He liked the Irishman with the laughing eyes, greased-lightning wit and a tongue that could ooze liquid-honey charm in one minute and fiery indignation the next. Somehow, Danny reminded Jack of Sidney Nolan, with the same shock of black hair, blue eyes, effusive chatter and twinkling humour.

By the end of the first week, it emerged that the Allied military units on the island—now exceeding thirty-thousand men—were not the only ones planning to defend Crete. Rumours abounded that important people had sought refuge on the island—senior members of the Greek Cabinet, possibly even the prime minister of Greece, himself: Emmanuel Tsourderos, a Cretan who'd been appointed recently following the suicide of his predecessor. Supposedly he'd arrived by night, as had dozens of members of the KKE, the Greek Communist Party. And then there were the locals: the old men, the women and children all united in their determination to seek vengeance for the sons, husbands and fathers now either lost or slaughtered on the Greek mainland. It was hard to know whether these disparate combinations of formal and informal resistors would aid in the battle against the Germans, or merely add to the chaos.

Every morning and evening Jack's unit clustered into a low, cave-like formation on the far left of the beach, which they'd claimed as their own. Here they listened to Colonel Walker's briefings, updated with the facts that he'd gleaned from Brigadier Vasey and Major General Freyberg, the sour-faced man appointed with the formidable task of commanding the troops now occupying the island. Jack quickly learned that Freyberg's dour expression was not without reason.

First, the officers of the British Garrison based on Crete, whom they'd arrived to support, were making little effort to cooperate with Freyberg: and so the Major General had to lead and direct the thirty-thousand troops now gathered around Chania single-handedly. And worse, although Freyberg assumed their plans to resist the German invasion were to be supported by the British air force and navy, all his attempts to gain the details of a coordinated battle plan were fruitless.

'You've got to be joking!' Danny cried in outrage when Colonel Walker outlined the challenges that they were facing. 'How on earth can we bumpkins hope to win a war when you clowns at the top can't organise your own game plan? Not you, sir. I don't mean you, boss— you're tops. I mean those fools that sit on their backsides in Whitehall, gazing at the wall charts and maps, their fingers plucking at their coloured pins and moving us around the globe as if we're pawns on a chessboard.'

Danny's indignation increased when Colonel Walker announced that there were ongoing problems with accessing resources—sufficient food supplies, guns, transport and even senior officers with the skills to command the excessive numbers of troops that had been sent to the island, as well as a breakdown of the communication between the army, navy and airforce leadership.

'Surely a few educated men—some of the overpaid top brass from the army, navy and air force, might find their way into a room and talk some sense to each other. And what's more, while they're considering how they might get a few weapons across to us so that we can do the job they've sent us here to do, they might like to consider providing us starving fellows with a sweet pot of stew or a couple of legs of mutton. Even a wee scone and jam would be appreciated! And think about it! If they got that part right, then we might even attract a few officers to our sojourn to keep us all in shape.'

Jack was not surprised when Colonel Walker called a special meeting to emphasise the importance of maintaining the AIF's good name, adopting a high standard of conduct and policing each other to negate unseemly behaviour. With too much time on their hands, some of the men were becoming unruly, drinking vast quantities of the potent Cretan raki, fighting amongst each other and even being nuisances to the local residents. He finished with a stern order to restrain their tomfoolery lest they shame the Australian flag and give the Germans a chance to overwhelm them while they were being fools.

'Well, what do those in authority expect? They dump us here, undernourished, unarmed and unsupported and expect us to say yes sir, no sir.' Danny winked at Jack even as he spoke, and Jack knew that the Irishman enjoyed the chance for a theatrical protest.

Of all the problems on the island, the lack of means to communicate during the pending invasion was perhaps the most serious. At the height of any battle, it is essential that messages are transmitted in a timely and efficient manner—the sharing of information about the enemy's movements, calls for reinforcements or requests for medical assistance need to be communicated. While there were dozens of skilled signallers on Crete, it emerged there was an abysmal shortage of wireless transmitters. In the end, it was agreed that runners would have to be used in addition to the Cretan public phone network. Both had their problems. Runners were slow and could get lost in the wilderness or captured by the Germans. The public phone system was at risk of messages being intercepted or the lines cut.

Even Colonel Walker smiled when Danny couldn't be quietened following this announcement.

'What about pigeons, boss? Has anybody thought of that? We could make little notes and attach them to their wee legs and they could flap across the island, delivering critical messages pronto to help us win the war. Or better still, geese. Surely a flock of geese would be helpful, although if our command don't lift their game, they won't be needed—we'll all look like a bunch of bloody gooses!'

'Now, now, Danny. The only thing flapping on the battlefields will be your tongue, and I have no doubts that if we could attach it to an electric turbine, we could power the whole island. But I will pass on your suggestions to General Freyberg, mark my words. Now, how about we put that energy of yours into some work?'

Glad of something constructive to do, the unit spent the week mixing concrete and gelignite in jam tins to make grenades, as well as setting wire on the sand to hinder German soldiers arriving by sea and prevent aircraft from making a beach landing. Preparations for the coming battle were further accelerated when a young German soldier was found washed upon the rocks by a fisherman. Believing his rescuer to be sympathetic, the boy revealed the German attack would occur within the week. His information verified the facts that had been gleaned from "Ultra", the secret code used by the German army that had been cracked by the British Intelligence Service months earlier, and now regularly provided insightful intel on the German plans. Between the German lad washed ashore and Ultra's intelligence, they now knew that Operation Merkur—the German name for their proposed invasion of Crete—would commence on May 20th.

# CHAPTER 25

*J*ack studied the hand-drawn maps of the island that had been made available, familiarising himself with the proposed strategy to defend Crete. He saw that the island was long and thin, shaped like a flattened bowl, on which they were now located on the top left-hand side, the island's north-western region. Four locations along the northern face were marked, each identified as a likely point of entry for the Germans when they tried to take the island for themselves. The first point, to their immediate left, was the British Administrative Area at Chania, the source of endless frustration to General Freyberg, for the British officers who were stationed there continued to demonstrate reluctance to cooperate with him or assist in the management of the thousands of allied troops on the island, despite his desperate pleas for senior officers to support him. Still farther west was the Maleme Airfield, while to the east— midway along the island—was the Retimo Airfield, and to the far east, the Heraklion Airfield. Colonel Walker repeatedly reiterated that their success in securing the island relied on effectively defending each of these targets.

'Okay, men. Our job is Retimo. We will cross the island to there as quickly as possible. It's going to have to be a walk, I am afraid, for there are no vehicles to take us. With the way the roads are, it'll probably take us two days. Never mind. Let's just get on with it and make a good start, and then we'll be able to get home.' As always, Colonel Walker was clear sighted and optimistic as he encouraged the unit.

On the map, the Retimo Airfield looked close—a half-day march under normal circumstances—but Jack knew that the Colonel was right. Travelling anywhere across Crete's mountainous terrain was bound to be slow.

With good spirits, the men joked as they packed the old rifles they'd been issued and divided up the ammunition. Water bottles were filled, bully beef distributed, groundsheets were argued over and by those who were lucky, spare sets of socks were grabbed.

Walker, ever strict, insisted that they maintain lines and march in an orderly fashion. As they set off, Danny led them in song, beginning with '*Waltzing Matilda*' and quickly following with the favourites —'*Mademoiselle From Armentieres*' and '*Lili Marlene*'. Jack smiled to himself as he listened to the lads join in, thinking that it was a good thing that their mothers weren't here to listen to the bawdy lyrics their sons sang with such gusto to keep their steps in unison, their spirits high and their minds alert.

Retimo Airfield was a small open space close to the beach, and the 2/7th was delegated the task of creating obstacles to prevent the enemy from making a beach landing. For two days they set up wires, laid mines and dug trenches in readiness for the German attack.

When all there was left to do was look to the skies, the commanding officers allowed some recreation, and Jack took the opportunity to sketch the airfield as it was before the battle, thinking that it may be of value to John Treloar's collection in the future.

'Jack? You're Jack from Melbourne?' The question was delivered cautiously, from a British officer of about twenty-five years old. Jack tried to ignore the blazing red scar that started at the centre of the lad's forehead, crossing the corner of his eye before vanishing into the hairline above his right ear. It was only freshly healed and evidence of a recent close call, and despite its grotesque appearance, it was clear that the man was lucky to be alive.

'Yes, mate, I am. Mind you, there are probably a hundred Jacks from Melbourne floating around these battlefields at present.'

'But you are an artist, right? I saw you drawing this morning. You have a Spanish friend? Sofia?'

Jack froze.

'Sofia! You've seen Sofia?'

'Yes... a Spanish girl. A nurse at the military hospital in Alexandria. It was her who got my eye right—saved it, really. The doctor wanted to take it out—reckoned that I was going to get an infection in the brain if he didn't—but she begged him to let her work on it for longer. Three times a day she cleaned it; morning, noon and night. It was putrid. The smell alone nearly knocked me out. But she didn't let that stop her. Hurt like the blazes—all of her poking and prodding—but if I so much as whimpered, she told me to bite my tongue and toughen up, that it would all be worth it. And she was right —now my eye is as good as new!'

'What did she say? Why was she there?'

'I don't know. She was a nurse. She never said much about herself. Stern, really. For all the lads teasing, we could never get her to crack a smile. She always pushed us beyond our limits. Insisted that if we would just walk another lap, breathe a little deeper, try a little harder, we'd have a better recovery. She was deaf to our complaints, even to those who screamed with pain, and she copped more than one mouthful of abuse. We called her the Merciless Matron.'

The words tore at Jack's heart. It saddened him to think of Sofia, once so full of joy and laughter, now so grim.

'All in fun, like. We knew that she was good for us! And she never rested. Every time I opened my eyes, she was there. The men loved her... not because she was particularly friendly, but because she worked so hard. It was like every wound was her personal battle. It was her mission to see us walk out the door, healed. The other thing I noticed was how she asked everybody who came in if they'd come across a soldier who sketched that was called Jack. Didn't say a lot more. When we teased her, she clammed up. Just said she wanted to know that he was safe. Hell, who could say that anyone was safe? This was war!'

Jack was beside himself. Sofia was barely two hundred miles away! Over the next few days, it felt like he was conducting a military interrogation on the young man, who he learned was named Leonard, from North London. Repeatedly he asked the same questions only to receive the same answers. And for all of his questions, he learned nothing about Sofia other than that she was working alongside the British nurses in Alexandria. Over and over his mind churned with what-ifs and if-onlys—the workings of time and chance and fate. If only the *Costa Rica* hadn't sunk, if only he hadn't been rescued by the one ship that was diverted to Crete. If he'd stuck with Snowy and Shorty, he'd be in Alexandria now, and perhaps at this very minute he'd be with her. But then again, it was only because he was here that he'd finally learned of Sofia's whereabouts.

For all that Jack was consumed with thoughts of getting to Alexandria, war was imminent, and he anticipated the invasion with equal doses of hope and fear. The sooner the battle was done with, the sooner he'd be on the ship to Alexandria and to Sofia. However, another part of him worried that his reunion with Sofia was somehow doomed. He'd spent so long trying to find her, searching across Melbourne and facing one disappointment after another, and now here she was, barely a couple of hundred miles away. Would fate have him killed on the battlefield, forever robbed of the opportunity to hold her close to him, denied the chance to make amends? Having witnessed the strength of the German army firsthand in Greece, Jack knew that for all of Danny's bravado and the optimism of the 2/7th, the battle ahead wouldn't be easy. Holding the position on the island was an advantage, he told himself, but the German Luftwaffe was extraordinary, and an air attack was inevitable. He prayed that this time, the British Airforce would provide the reinforcement that they'd omitted in Greece.

~

It was at 0800hrs on the twentieth of May that the cry, '*Ehronte*', the Cretan word for 'They're coming', echoed around Retimo Airport. Jack joined with the others of the 2/7th looking northward as a thunderous rumble filled the air, his eyes widening in astonishment at the black cloud advancing towards them from the north.

As the aircraft drew closer, even more surprising was the appearance of tiny specks launching from them—black dots which blossomed into colourful balls as though a bed of flowers were blooming in the sky. Thousands of white chutes interspersed with others, green, yellow and brown—all drifted towards them. Jack watched, stunned as the scene gathered focus. His mind turned to the works of Salvador Dali—those surreal paintings where the lines between reality and fantasy were blurred. He had never experienced a more surreal moment in his life than now.

'The Fallschirmjäger,' Danny whispered, his voice a combination of amazement and awe. Jack nodded in agreement. These were surely the German paratroopers that they'd heard about—an elite force selected from Germany's best soldiers. Until now the unit had seemed almost mythological; to Jack's knowledge, they hadn't appeared in any of the battles across Europe so far, yet here they were, at the forefront of the invasion of Crete.

Strangely, the artist within Jack emerged, for immediately he knew that this scene was worthy of an oil painting for Treloar, and while it was not a moment for sketching, he committed the vision before him to memory.

Movement from Danny jolted him back to reality. Positioning the sights of his .303 onto the falling targets, he timed the soft squeeze of the trigger, listening to the splitting sound as the bullet was released. If the sight of thousands of delightfully coloured objects drifting towards them was surreal, the carnage caused by gunshots firing into the sky only made it more bizarre.

'Yes!' shouted Danny as he and Jack lined up one parachutist after another. It was ridiculously easy, for the men were trapped by the cords and billowing fabric, the design of the apparatus rendering them helpless to manoeuvre effectively while the colourful chute acted as a bulls-eye, assisting the most poorly skilled rifleman to find a target. And of the chutists fortunate enough to escape the gunfire, many suffered the humiliation of being caught in tree branches, dangling for all of the world like Christmas decorations. All they could do was raise their hands in surrender, allowing the Allies to cut them down, relieve them of their weapons and take them prisoner.

After the sky cleared, soldiers and civilians alike worked together—old men, women and children, even dogs scampered through the fields, checking bodies.

Colonel Walker was generous in his praise. They'd held the Retimo Airfield with relative ease against the terrible cloud that approached them so menacingly only hours earlier. Jubilantly they walked the fields, admiring the Schmeisser sub-machine gun they'd seized from the parachutists and discovering that some of the parachuted targets were not human, but rather large boxes, which on opening revealed still more weapons and ammunition. It was certainly a victory for the Australians, and they grinned from ear to ear. Over the day, runners arrived from across the island, providing updates of the German invasion, including the pleasing information that the Allies had also held firm at Heraklion.

Morning had just broken when a runner arrived from the west, declaring that Maleme was in trouble. New Zealand's 22nd Battalion had fought hard, but the defence of the western edge of the airfield had proved to be weak and the Germans had gained a foothold on the island. Help was needed.

There was no shortage of volunteers, and it took all of Colonel Walker's authority to restrain his troops, reminding them that even though a first wave of Germans at Retimo had been defeated, there may well be a second onslaught. Jack admired the calm and considered bearing of their commanding officer as he digested the runner's information before selecting a group of men to join him, of which Jack was glad to be numbered. Despite frequent interruptions from Danny, eager to be off to crush the Germans, Colonel Walker sketched detailed diagrams in the sand, discussing their best approach to Meleme. While the CO's methods seemed slow, they made sense. Jack knew that the likes of Danny would have gathered a posse and hurtled towards the Maleme Airfield like Celtic warriors charging into battle, without thought, and quite likely with dire consequences.

After an hour's journey bouncing along in the back of a creaking lorry, it was late morning when Colonel Walker led the unit across the ridge, where they had an unrestricted view to the beach. It was obvious to Jack that they were too late. Below them, Germans, tens of thousands of them perhaps, were like ants constructing a nest, systematically unloading supplies from the hulls of the giant aircraft now resting on the airfield. Motorcycles, troop carriers and jeeps had been set in neat rows. In a stupendously large pile, Jack saw hundreds of wooden crates, no doubt filled with food, weapons and ammunition. Worse, though, was the sight at the far end of the beach: a fenced-off area patrolled by armed German soldiers. Within its bounds, groups of men in the familiar khaki of the AIF and New Zealanders were seated on the ground, defeat in their bearing.

A group of Maori soldiers joined them on the ridge, and together they searched for a weakness in the German position but could find none. Finally, with darkness beginning to fall, Colonel Walker gave the order for them to retreat to higher ground—he didn't want them to be trapped by Germans and added to the POW count.

Just as darkness fell, they arrived at the cliff top. Called "42nd Street", it was the stretch between two olive groves that the 42nd British Battalion had named after themselves weeks earlier. Suddenly, one of the men—an Aboriginal named Saunders, who always walked out in front—gave a sharp wave of his hand, indicating for them to be still, and they discovered that they were not alone; a German patrol was camped on the road ahead of them.

Jack wasn't sure who was more surprised, as he could hear the grunts of the Germans as they struggled upright, grappling for their weapons. Following a split second of silence, the New Zealand Maori reacted, erupting into bloodcurdling shrieks as they forged forward. Without thinking, Jack pulled his rifle off his back and entered the melee, swinging his gun in all directions, shooting wildly. The skills of hand-to-hand combat, developed on the training fields of Puckapunyal, came to the fore as the unit launched themselves upon the Germans in a frenzy. Nothing could describe the carnage of the next half hour, as close contact fighting continued until the Germans broke and ran into the bushes, the noisy sounds of their departure receding into the distance.

Of all Jack's experiences to date, this battle ranked as the most truly grotesque. The hacking into bodies, blood streaming, shouting and grunting. The sense of being half-human, half-animal, locked in a fight for survival, not nation against nation, not army against army, but man against man. Kill or be killed, Jack had repeated over and over to himself as, with red splatters washed over his face, he'd attacked.

Knowing that the Germans would be regrouping, possibly returning for them at that very moment, they responded to Colonel Walker's signal to retreat at speed. In the twilight, they had to feel their way forward among rocks and trees. Jack touched his left arm, sticky and moist. Blood. He hoped that the wound wasn't too bad. Judging by men about him, some limping, some being supported as they walked, he wasn't the only one injured, which was hardly surprising.

Jack thought about the battle just fought. At both Bardia and Tobruk, he had managed to hold back from the fighting, although he'd kept his gun at the ready should it be needed, and he'd maintained his role of observer and sketcher. In Greece, most of the fighting had been from a distance, and while Jack had added his bullets to the assault, there was no surety that he'd hit any mark. At Retimo, certainly he'd fired into the air, his gun pointed at the hapless parachutists, and he'd even suspected one or two of his targets had crumpled in the restraints of their chute harness, but distance had obscured the emotional impact of the killing.

Nothing in those experiences had prepared Jack for the battle they'd just fought in the small clearing high on the cliffs of Crete. Picasso's *Guernica* filled his mind. He'd seen a photograph of the painting in the morning newspaper the previous year. At the time it had been a sensation, firstly for its size, and for the fact that it had been rendered in Picasso's fragmented cubist style. But, mostly, it was the subject of the painting that caused a stir: the carnage Franco's troops had wrought on a small Spanish town. When Jack had read the article's damning depictions of modern art and studied the photo of *Guernica* the newspaper had published, he'd been so disappointed. The painting seemed wild and fragmented. Where was the talented artist of the early twentieth century? The artist who'd painted such beautiful portraits when he was a child? The artist whose paintings through his Blue Period had depicted pain and sorrow so clearly that it could make you weep? The artist who'd told Jack that only when he experienced grief would he be able to paint truth? What truth was to be found in Picasso's nonsense of *Guernica*, Jack had wondered.

Only now did Jack understand Picasso's intent. No 'realistic' painting could evoke the brutality and horror he'd just experienced. Certainly, it had been staged within a physical world, but the stony ground, flailing limbs and the metallic thud of crudely employed weapons were a mere backdrop to the real battle: one of savage desperation to survive. Jack now could see that Picasso's *Guernica* was a brazen shout to the world—war is not a compilation of neatly fired bullets and strategically placed bombs detonated from impersonal distances. Rather, it's a terrifying chaos. A barbaric confusion of flailing and scrabbling, the wild discharge of bullets, the swinging of bludgeons whose purpose is to maim and kill. War slaughters and maims humans and beasts, the innocent and the guilty. One day, Jack thought, he would draw this battle, fought between the olive fields along the stretch called 42nd Street. Already, he had the image of the painting in his mind. Picasso would be proud of him.

Colonel Walker insisted that in view of their meagre firepower, famished state and utter fatigue, it would be best to seek refuge in the hills nearby until further orders could be sought.

Jack was relieved. The sides of his feet burned with each step forward. His socks, more holes than knit, seemed barely worth wearing. Each time he had a moment he'd reposition them, shift the pressure of his shoe away from the raw skin where blisters had formed. He had two plasters left in his kit and wanted to make them last for as long as he could.

Over the next forty-eight hours, dispatches came in fragments. A Cretan runner, moving through the trees like a shadow, delivered his message with breathless urgency. It had been issued by the battalion's headquarters. An evacuation was being organised; they were to make their way to the south of the island, to a place called Sphakia, immediately. Leading them to the edge of the forest, the man pointed to the left, and signalled that they must go quickly and remain silent. He wished them well before vanishing into the forest.

If one good thing came out of the daylight for Jack, it was the discovery that his arm injury was insignificant, a slash which had bled profusely, but proved to be superficial. Others in the unit weren't so lucky. Danny had received a slice across his face, which he bragged only added to his good looks. Jack gave him a swig of rum from his canteen to lessen the pain as a medical orderly from the New Zealand battalion attempted to stitch the wound. Far more unfortunate was a young man called Curly, who had taken a bullet to his knee that had left him in agonising pain and unfit to walk. Jack took his turn along with the others to carry him on their journey south, full of admiration for the young fellow's determination to maintain cheer as they jostled him along inhospitable bush tracks.

'Oy, oy, go easy, you bastards,' Curly repeated for the hundredth time as he was dropped to the ground. He had to stand and use his gun as a crutch while those who'd supported him scrambled down almost vertical banks before raising him onto their shoulders again.

'Ah, that's better. I feel like the prince of Arabia, floating along on my magic carpet. Anyone got a smoke for me?' Every few hours his bandages were checked and tightened and a large dose of rum was poured down his throat.

They'd anticipated that the walk would be tough—sixty miles across wild, rugged country. However, crossing the precipitous White Mountains with little food and scant water, with the ever-present threat of German sniper bullets sailing towards them from across the valley, interspersed with intermittent bombing from the skies above, was beyond anything they could have imagined. To add to their difficulties, no one knew whether the path they followed was the right one; they just forged in a southerly direction, navigating near vertical banks and crossing rocky streams from which they filled their water bottles. The track was so narrow, windy and precipitously steep that the journey was nothing less than a nightmare, and they were relieved when locals appeared from out of the bushes along its edge, pushing loaves of bread towards them, smiling encouragement, nodding and pointing the way. As the days wore on, more and more aircraft appeared in the sky, and they could hear the spluttering sounds of vehicles chugging along the pot-holed roads nearby. In addition, single shots and the distant rattle of submachine guns each acted as reminders of the peril they faced. There was nothing to do but keep moving.

Jack realised that they were not alone as they journeyed through the mountains. For whilst the troops responded to the order for evacuation, numerous others had learned that the Allies were leaving, and now the forest tracks swarmed with Cypriots and Palestinians, all straggling through the forests and making their way to Sphakia, hoping they too might be transported off the island.

Colonel Walker, ever vigilant, refused to let his men disintegrate amid the disorder surrounding them. Instead, he insisted that they stay tight, maintain discipline, look to the men directly in front and behind them and move quickly. Every few hours he allowed them a five-minute break to drink from a stream and regain their breaths, rebandage wounds and share tots of rum.

Despite the summer heat, Jack was glad for the quick pace their commander set. When he was not taking turns floating Curly along on his magic carpet, he strode forward, near the front of the group. Mostly, Danny walked behind him and was good for his banter, but

Jack was determined to keep his eyes on the broad back of Reg Saunders, for the Aborigine's instincts for pending trouble proved infallible. Jack learned that by watching the man's left hand, he could interpret the silent signals that indicated they should slow down, or stand stock-still while Saunders evaluated the direction of a motor vehicle or a distant airplane that only he could hear. More than once, he turned around to Jack, his fingers to his lips, before leading the unit deep into the bushes, where they'd wait quietly as a German patrol passed by.

~

That they'd been forced to evacuate, yet again defeated by the German army, was a bitter pill for the troops to swallow. While proud of their efforts, the boys rued the lack of support from London. The lack of food, adequate weapons and means of communication was one thing, but to be denied air cover when they needed it most was another! Just as in Greece, the Germans had once more controlled the sky to gain advantage. If the RAF had come in over Maleme, how different things might have been!

They knew that Colonel Walker was also furious about the lack of support from the Royal Air Force, but ever the disciplined leader, his mind remained on the here and now rather than worrying about what could and should have been.

Nonetheless, he was quite outspoken about the lack of food or weapons available for his men, and throughout the last weeks, when rations finally arrived, he insisted that the gunners be given the greater share.

~

It was his excitement at the thought of seeing Sofia that kept Jack's spirits buoyant. Once on the ship, it would be barely a day's travel to Alexandria, and his mind was filled with anticipation of their reunion. Would she be pleased to see him or still be so angry that she'd turn away? No, the British officer had said that she'd sought news of him, asking everyone if they'd seen an artist called Jack. How lucky it was that he'd taken his pencil out that morning in Retimo so that the young man recognised him. What a chance event that was! This war seemed to be full of chances, some drawing him towards Sofia, others pulling him away from her. Perhaps the odds were with them after all, and soon they'd be together. Jack's heart thudded with hope.

~

Finally, the settlement of Sphakia appeared—a cluster of buildings nested against the coastline at the base of a steep mountain range, with a series of small bays and a protrusion of land shaped like the foot of a goanna reaching into the sea. As they approached the descent, their path was blocked, not by the enemy but rather by a unit of British soldiers who'd set themselves up as gatekeepers, monitoring those who approached the beach. As they questioned the unit's activities over the last week, Jack grew furious. He wanted to be onto the beach and into the waiting barges as quickly as possible, not standing here arguing with these pompous British idiots. 'What do these rags and bloodstains tell you?' he replied when they asked if they'd engaged with the enemy or been shirkers?

Danny shared Jack's frustration. 'Can you bastards just step aside? Because now that I've asked you polite-like, if you don't move, I'm going to throw you over the edge.'

'Danny!' Colonel Walker's voice was commanding, but he stood a few paces behind. Pretending they hadn't heard him, Jack and Saunders stepped forwards to join Danny, and the three of them looked menacingly at the British officers whose uniforms looked far too clean for soldiers who'd been involved in recent battles.

'Down you go, then, and perhaps your commanding officer might teach you a little respect,' was the reply of one officer as Jack, Saunders and Danny pushed through. Danny veered precariously close to the man, now foolishly balanced on the edge of the steep bank.

'What the heck do you think you're doing?'

'Mind your footing, now, mate… if you are not careful, you might take a tumble over the edge,' Danny suggested.

Laughing loudly, the three descended to the beach, where thousands of people—civilians and soldiers alike—were gathered, with no apparent order among them and barely an officer in sight.

Colonel Walker passed them, growling, 'Mind your place, boys, and stay with me,' before leading them at a brisk march to join the tail of a long line of soldiers. Jack looked anxiously at the string of barges at work, ferrying groups to a huge naval vessel whose decks were already crowded. He scanned the sky for German bombers before shifting his mind to calculating the number of men lined up before him. He estimated there were approximately three hundred. It was going to be close, he realised, breathing deeply, fearing that the odds were against them. And forty minutes later, as he'd suspected, the ratio did not fall in their favour, for as the last barge filled, it was obvious that it was not going to fit them all in. A sombre Colonel Walker, in a tired but firm voice, pointed his finger towards them. 'Private Sweeny and Private Murphy, off you go now. Best wishes to you both. May God keep you safe.'

They were the youngest of the group—Curly, of course, with his damaged knee, and Murphy who'd bravely staggered the last five miles across the island even though he was clearly finished. Fair decisions in impossible circumstances, Jack knew, despite his frustration at being thwarted at the last minute when he'd been so close to returning to Alexandria and Sofia.

Bitterly disappointed, he contained his emotions. He could hardly have stepped forwards and say that he must go—he had to find his wife,—or all the men were desperate for the arms of their loved ones. No one here knew that his situation was different. That his wife had been missing for two years and was now found. That she was over in Alexandria, barely four hundred miles southeast! He clung to the hope that another chance to leave the island would present itself soon. And, watching the barge as it left, he kicked himself for not having the foresight to pass a message through to her!

~

Jack joined the remaining men and followed Colonel Walker back to the protection offered by the dunes. He paused, however, surprised to hear the soft sound of singing. A sweet melody drifted across the water and grew louder. Turning, Jack realised that it was the voices of a New Zealand unit—their mighty Maori contingent—rising loud and clear, singing a familiar tune in their traditional language. It was a poignant gesture, and as if in reply, a chorus of voices on the beach united and joined them, singing in English. '*Now the hour when we must say farewell.*' It was an incredible moment, one worthy of a painting, Jack thought as he inhaled deeply and wondered if he was the only one with a tear in his eye. He imagined the scene on canvas: the over-full troopship, ready to receive its last passengers before departing, the ragged men remaining on the shore, disappointed at being left behind, the steep cliffs behind them, a trio of Stukas menacingly flying in the distance. He could even place himself on the shoreline, wistfully gazing out at the barge receding into the distance, his thoughts for Sofia.

*Will we ever see Curly and Murphy again?* he wondered. The threat to all of them was far from over, for out in the open sea, the ship would be vulnerable to enemy bombers, even as those remaining on the island were vastly outnumbered by the Germans; and with supplies low, weapons in poor shape and little ammunition left, it was hard to say who had the better chances for survival. At this moment, after their days of marching on near-empty stomachs, food and sleep were all that really mattered.

The afternoon was long, and spirits were low as they scavenged the fields for corn, dates and olives before preparing for their nightly ritual —drawing straws for watch duty, laying out the greatcoats to rest upon, and collapsing into uneasy sleep—none too comfortably.

At 0400hrs, Jack rose to see Colonel Walker already up. He had news to share, and it wasn't good.

He'd just returned from a meeting with the British General, where they'd been using a transmitter to communicate with the London War

Office about the situation at Crete. They'd learned that the Navy was not planning on returning anytime soon. They believed that too many ships and too many men had already been lost to the Germans. If they were to attempt a second evacuation, the Germans would surely be ready for them and more lives would be lost.

Colonel Walker's next words came as a surprise.

'So now, boys, it's to be every man for himself. You can surrender to the Germans, let them take you as prisoners, and hope that they will treat you well, or test yourselves against the mountains of Crete. The decision is yours to make.'

The men looked at each other, speechless. This was certainly a turn of events. Here they were, over six thousand men huddled on a small cove in Southern Crete and being told to fend for themselves! Looking around, Jack thought the bewilderment showing on the men's faces would be funny if their circumstances weren't so dire. Certainly, their training had included the actions that they should take if captured or perhaps surrendering to the enemy, or should they become separated in enemy terrain, but it had always seemed terribly unlikely. They were Australians. They didn't plan to lose battles, or be taken prisoner.

Again, Colonel Walker spoke, this time with firmness in his voice. 'Men, this is serious. We are now members of a surrendered army. You need to break into small parties and either wait for the Germans to pick you up, or strike off—perhaps you might find a way off the island. There is nothing else to be done. Good luck to you all. You've done a mighty job here in Crete, under very difficult circumstances. You can be proud of yourselves. I am certainly proud of you. I only wish that things had turned out differently for us all!'

Within minutes, patches of flames appeared across the beach and Jack looked on as thousands of men threw their papers, followed by their weapons and ammo into fires. Hundreds of white flags appeared, created from singlets or canvas bags. It was clear that the majority of men intended to offer themselves to the Germans when they arrived.

'I don't know about you jokers, but I'm not giving myself over to any Germans. If they want me, they'll have to come and get me, and they'll have a fight on their hands if they try!'

Jack agreed with Danny. He'd far sooner take his chances in the forests than be locked up behind barbed wire or worse.

Within minutes, over a dozen of the 2/7th had reached an agreement—surrender was not an option.

They bandied a range of suggestions about where they could go and what they might do.

'How about we grab a barge?' That was Jack's preference—taking a boat across the Mediterranean to the mainland, and from there, making their way to Alexandria. However, a glance at the bay indicated that already hundreds of men had lined the shoreline with the same idea.

'I think we need to head into the mountains.' Jack was not a bushman like Shorty and Snowy, but his years at Montsalvat had given him a range of skills for living rough.

'Definitely,' said Saunders. 'And soon. The Germans are likely to be here any minute.'

Jack was pleased to have Saunders join them. The walk to Sphakia had been tough, and it had been Saunders heightened senses that had detected the enemy's presence, hence saving the unit, more than once.

In the end, fifteen men of the 2/7th formed a group; Danny, Saunders, Roger, Leo and Greaves were numbered among them, and Jack was glad, for they were solid dependable men, who kept a steady head when things got tough. They agreed to stay around the foothills of the beach for a day or two longer, just in case the Navy had a change of heart and decided to rescue them. In the meantime, exhausted after ten days of almost no sleep, they trekked a couple of hundred yards up the cliff where they found a clearing that offered both protection and a view of the sea. There they created roster system, allocating two men to keep lookout along the cliff face for the arrival of Germans whilst a second pair would sit on a rocky overhang overlooking the sea, where they'd signal Morse code into the inky black night while the remainder collapsed into a deep sleep.

When early the next morning, a contingent of Germans was visible stepping onto the beach, they knew that it was time to move. At Saunders' suggestion, they decided to return to Suda Bay—he knew of a hoard of food that had been buried there two weeks earlier, before the German invasion had begun.

'Find that food? You gotta be kidding,' laughed, Roger, incredulous at the suggestion that the food cache could be located by them amid the forest around Canea. However, as Saunders wordlessly returned Roger's gaze, Jack had no doubts that the Aborigine knew to the tree exactly where the buried food would be.

And, eight days later, after long days of walking in the sun, with senses on constant alert for bombers overhead, snipers in the bushes and Germans approaching, Saunders led them to a tree where they unearthed a large timber box loaded with tins of beef, rice, jam, cocoa, tea and a dozen packets of dried biscuits, earning the rest of the men's praise and acclaim.

Long discussions ensued about their next move. The men knew that they couldn't aimlessly roam across the island; they needed to find shelter and a sustainable food supply, and with summer upon them, a water supply was important. The mountains to their right, toward the centre of the island seemed to be the best option, offering cover by day, the possibility of a cave for shelter at night and streams that would provide fresh water. Jack hoped that they might find somewhere near a village, where they could communicate with the Cretans, who'd hopefully be able to suggest ways that they could leave Crete. A second concern was the size of their group. Fifteen men moving through the wilderness was too many; they'd be conspicuous, and therefore easily captured. They agreed that once they'd reached the shelter of the mountains, they'd disband into groups of three or four, and that as soon as any of them made it off the island and back to unit headquarters in Alexandria, they would report to the authorities that not all of the troops that had been left behind on Crete had surrendered to the Germans; that a number of Australians were hiding in the mountains. Hopefully, when things settled down, the British would send a vessel to rescue them.

Even before they reached the mountains, their group diminished in size. Saunders was the first to go, after a surprise attack by a low-flying Stuka raining bullets from the sky. Although all fifteen were accounted for following their dive into the bushes, somewhere over the next hour, Saunders melted into the forest.

Good luck to him, Jack thought. He hoped he'd make it. Of all of them, he was sure that the Australian bushman had the best chance.

A few days later, Greaves was next to go. He'd always loved the Cretans and everything about their lifestyle and had even developed a knack for the language. Repeatedly, he'd suggested that their best chance of survival was if they blended in with the Cretan population in one of the larger villages.

'If we blend in with the villagers, then the Germans will leave us alone,' he argued.

'How many Cretans have an Irish accent?' Danny replied.

'Perhaps you could be a mute Cretan.'

'Mute, ha—I'd pay to see Danny mute for a day! It'd give my ears a rest,' Jack offered.

Nonetheless, when Greaves turned up in baggy pants, a rough shirt with a wide belt and a head scarf, they had to agree that he looked every bit like he belonged on the island. Wishing him luck, they watched him set off with a wave and smile towards the nearest village.

For five days the men continued their walk, avoiding the main roads as they ventured into the mountain, sharing the food supply which was rapidly diminishing and drinking water from the creeks. Their passage was slow. Despite the seclusion offered by the forest tracks it seemed that gunfire, the movement of vehicles and planes thundering through the sky was ever close, and many hours of the day were spent laying low under the cover of trees. Jack's nerves were rattled by the constant threat of enemy attack; and from the quiet seriousness that had settled over the others, he knew that they were feeling it too. He was convinced that despite their camaraderie, their risk of capture whilst remaining in such a large group was high. It was only a matter of time before a Germans sniper noticed the rustling movement of the bushes or saw the glint of a weapon in the sunlight. And when Jack saw a path—barely a goat track—leading off to the right on a steep ascent, he decided the time had come to separate.

'How about we see where this takes us?' he suggested, pointing out the track to Leo and Danny, and they agreed. The three of them would stick together and find themselves a hideout in the mountains towering above them.

'Yes, Jack. This looks perfect. We'll get an excellent view of the sea from up there—see if the Navy reconsiders and arrives to rescue us.'

With good wishes and farewells to the remaining men, and ignoring the pangs in his belly, Jack took the lead, scrambling up the steep bank and weaving along the path for almost two hours until the light faded and they decided to rest for the night on a broad open ledge, where lights below indicated a village close by.

As uncomfortable as the hard ground beneath him was, sleep came easily and Jack did not move until a glimmer of dazzling red and orange revealed the sun was just about to rise.

A few minutes later, with Danny and Leo now awake and loading packs onto their backs, Jack was shocked to see an old man with thick grey hair, a heavily bearded face and black pantaloons emerge from the bushes only feet away.

Instinctively, Jack's hands reached for his gun. The man frowned at them and shook his head, holding his fingers to his lips, entreating them to remain silent.

They stood still and listened.

'Come,' he mouthed, beckoning them to follow him. 'Too many Germans… This way…' While his words were difficult to understand, his gestures were universal, and Jack gladly followed. It seemed sensible to place themselves in the hands of someone who knew the island.

# CHAPTER 26

*J*ack did his best to maintain the pace of the man in front of him, who despite his age navigated the wilderness with ease, first scrambling down a bank which led them onto what was little more than a goat track meandering through the trees. It was a slow journey and Jack realised they were not alone; four young boys, aged about fourteen, intermittently appeared for brief periods before retreating into the bushes. At first he thought it was just the one boy, but as the morning wore on he began to notice variations; the worn, oversized shirt on one was a small, torn undersized shirt on another. One lad was tall and slim, another tiny. Common to all were shiny bright eyes alight with enthusiasm for their task and the manner in which they walked, adopting the stealth of soldiers stalking an enemy.

They were runners, he realised, taking turns to advance along the track, checking to see that the route before them was safe, and passing messages to contacts along the way. Apprentice guerrilla soldiers, honing their skills under the guidance of men who'd protected their island for centuries.

The walk seemed endless, the sunshine intense, and they were glad for the opportunity to fill their water bottles from the fresh streams that they crossed from time to time. Morning turned to midday, and then it was afternoon before finally the man slowed at the juncture of a cliff face. Without hesitating, their guide turned right; and following, Jack took a deep breath as he observed their position. They were high on the mountainous track—their path alongside the wall of a near vertical cliff face—and although they were shielded by the cover of the tree line, Jack could see that the forest fell away below them into a deep abyss. After walking a hundred yards, their guide paused and then beckoning them to follow, with a nimble manoeuvre, he vanished under a rocky overhang.

Remaining close, Jack ducked low and followed the leather boots vanishing into the cliff face. As he crawled into the cave, darkness enveloped him, but Jack sensed that the space he'd entered was large. He heard a scratching sound, and squinting, tried to make sense of his surroundings by the dim glow of the flickering match which had suddenly sputtered to life a few yards in front of him. Leo added a beam of torchlight, which he directed to the left and right, to reveal a broad cavern, an area about six yards deep and four yards wide. Their guide nodded approvingly and motioned that they must remain within the cave. Modelling with the universal sign of hands against cheek, he advised them to sleep.

As rough as the cave was, Jack was glad of the shelter it provided. Despite the summer heat, it felt cool, and the floor looked clean. He, Leo and Danny spread their packs and arranged their greatcoats before lying down and marvelling at their luck in being led here by the Cretan. They knew that they could have passed by a hundred entrances leading into a cave like this, and never noticed. Within minutes, Jack gave into the exhaustion caused by weeks of walking through the mountains with his senses ever strained, the nights of watch duties and restless sleep, and the day they'd just spent endlessly ascending steep tracks at speed. That night he slept with a sense of safety that he hadn't felt in weeks.

∼

As light seeped across the floor of the cave the following morning, a rustling from outside caught Jack's attention and suddenly his senses were on high alert. Was it an animal? Had the Germans discovered them? Leo, lying next to him, stirred, and Jack shushed him before easing towards his backpack to reach for his gun. Lying on his stomach, he peered towards the entrance, where a pair of worn leather boots shuffled along the track, their tread uneven, the left foot dragging to keep up with the right. The human legs were accompanied by the slow, heavy tread of four hooves. A mule? Jack held his breath, waiting for it to pass, and then after a minute of silence, he wriggled forwards and peered to the left.

Jack jolted when he realised that the traveller remained close by. It was a woman, who now sat on a rock barely a dozen yards away. She was leaning forward, her black shawl draped over her head, her shoulders bowed. He exhaled; it was only an old woman resting. Perhaps she had a hut nearby, and was travelling down to the village for supplies.

'What is it?' Leo whispered, and Jack leaned back, making space for him to see.

Barely breathing, they lay together, keeping watch while Danny slept. Jack hoped that he wouldn't wake, because it would be impossible to keep the Irishman quiet.

Five minutes passed, and then another five.

Jack looked at Leo with raised eyebrows at the sound of a low whistle from farther down the track. Surely that was not the call of a bird.

A clear ringing emitted from the woman as she returned the call, and within minutes, a young boy appeared. Jack watched the woman stand and speak with the lad, surprised when she indicated for him to sit on the rock that she'd just vacated. He nudged Leo, again holding his breath, as she returned along the track towards them.

～

'Hello… It is safe for you to come out now.' The woman's voice was low, her tone far more youthful than Jack had expected.

Jack crawled through the opening, followed by Leo and a confused-looking Danny, and they watched warily as she pulled back her shawl, revealing the face of a woman perhaps in her mid-thirties. She smiled at them.

'Did you sleep well?' The glimmer of amusement in her eyes suggested she was enjoying her subterfuge.

Jack nodded cautiously, still surprised by her presence and wondering why she was there.

'My uncle sent me here. It was he who led you here last night. He thought that you might be hungry.'

The woman returned to the mule, now nibbling at the grass that edged the stony track, and she reached into a bag slung beside the saddle. Drawing out an enamel pot, she held it towards Jack, who took it. Next she fished out two loaves of bread and a bag of nectarines, offering these to Leo. She then turned to a second saddlebag and retrieved a sack of potatoes and onions as well as a jar of olive oil and a hessian bag of dates, which she placed into Danny's open hands.

'These should keep you going for a day or so. You have a burner?'

'We certainly do, and thank you for this! My, it's a feast for sure!'

Jack and Leo nodded, agreeing with Danny, who'd been the first of them to speak.

'We sure haven't eaten this well for weeks, ma'am.' Leo's words reflected an old-world charm, surprising Jack.

'You need to stay quiet. There are Germans everywhere… they are very suspicious. Very… what say… bossy.'

'And who do we have the pleasure of meeting?' Danny asked, as if they were standing at the bar of the Watson and Young and introducing themselves to an attractive female.

'Me? I am Marita, from Astikas.'

Her wry expression made Jack wonder if Marita was, in fact, her proper name, or Astikas the place where she lived.

'Come, let us go into the cave and talk.'

'Is the boy okay there? What if German soldiers come past?' Jack asked.

'Yes, he is fine. He knows what to do.'

'Throw them over the cliff, I'd be thinking,' said Danny.

'Oh, no! He won't do that.' The feminine sound of her laughter was unfamiliar to Jack's ears after months in the company of men. 'No, he would continue walking, luring them away from here. Tell them he's visiting his grandfather in the next village. That he'd just sat for a minute because he needed to rest. I will hear his whistle if there's a problem.'

Slipping into the cave, they gathered within its entrance, where the shadows played across Marita's face as she spoke. She quizzed them for fifteen minutes, and Jack concluded that not only had she come to replenish their stores, but also to undertake a fact-finding mission.

'You've been to Maleme? What is happening there?' she asked, and they told her about the German stronghold—how thousands of prisoners had been taken and were now held in barbed wire enclosures guarded by armed sentries.

'And the rest of the British? I heard that the Germans sent parachutists to the airfields.'

'Yes, and we shot them out of the sky like clay ducks! Mind you, we aren't British. We are Australians—called in especially, to give the Pommies backup.' Danny's chest seemed to broaden, and if they had been standing, Jack was sure that he'd be three inches taller.

Jack chuckled. 'It's true. We did down the Germans at Retimo and also at Heraklion. It was all too easy, really, but there were problems at Maleme; and once the Germans got a foothold in, there was nothing anybody could have done to stop them. By the time we arrived to provide backup, it was all over.'

'And then there was an evacuation?'

'Yes—at Sphakia, where perhaps three-quarters of the troops were evacuated, but the rest of us were left behind to surrender or fend for ourselves. Thousands chose to surrender, but there was no way we were going to hand ourselves over.' Danny was at his most talkative.

'Your information supports what I have heard. Most of them … submitted? … surrendered? The British… and their allies… they are now being held across the island. Under German guard in churches and halls. They had a dozen men in our little school building for a few days, but they have now been moved. The Germans tell us they are waiting for the ships to take them away—perhaps to Italy or Africa.'

'Are they being treated well?' Jack asked, thinking with concern about Colonel Walker and the men of the 2/7th.

'I am not sure. Perhaps, those who do as they are told. I've heard that some of the men have tried to escape, which made the German's very angry. At present, German patrols are scouring the island for the allied troops that they know are hiding in the mountains. There are many threats. We need to be very careful.'

Marita laughed when they told her about their surprise attack at 42nd Street.

'Well done! These Germans think that they can slaughter our men and take our island, but soon they will learn how wrong they are! You said that you are not British?'

'No, Ma'am. We are Australian.'

'You are from Australia! I'd heard that there are many Australians here! It is unbelievable to think that you crossed the world to help us save our little island!'

'That, we have, ma'am. At your service!' Danny's chivalrous charm was entertaining and Jack smiled as he listened to his bragging.

'We will push those Germans off the island in no time and you'll be able to live your lives in peace again!'

This time Jack did laugh. Danny's bravado, which was utterly incongruous given the reality of their circumstances—three starving Australians, two guns between them, dressed in rags and with barely enough ammunition to shoot a kangaroo, let alone rid the island of ten thousand Germans. Marita showed more respect.

'Thank you, but not yet. For now, you must stay here,' she replied, her words serious but the twinkle in her eye revealing her amusement at the Irishman. 'This cave is well hidden, and the only passing traffic should be goats and sheep. We'll get food to you. If the Germans find you, they'll take you as their prisoners. Perhaps even shoot you. At present, the island is very unsettled and there are no routines. Germans arrive at Astikas at all times of the day and night. We expect that soon they will realise that there is nothing in our little village to interest them, and they will go away.'

Jack, Leo and Danny agreed with Marita that they needed to lay low. The cave was large, dry and cool, and the ledge offered a clear view over the valley, with visibility to the left and right of about a hundred yards. There could be worse places to stay. Over the next few days, Jack, Danny and Leo slept a lot. Each morning when they woke, they found a bag of food had been slipped into the entrance of the cave. As alert as they tried to be, they never saw the person who'd placed it there. Leo took on the role of chef each night, using his small oil cooker to fry potatoes and onions. Jack was sure that he made some of the best meals he had ever eaten.

On their second day and thereafter, when they arose, they left the cave and checked around their immediate area, each day moving a little further, cautiously venturing below the tree line and along the track to the east and west for a couple hundred yards, taking care to avoid the bare escarpment where their movement could be easily detected by a sniper's keen eye.

The days were long, and with little to do, they rehashed the events of the last week a dozen times, their conversations meandering to sharing their reasons for enlisting, and their lives before the war.

Jack discovered that both Danny and Leo had also been based at Puckapunyal before they'd been sent to Egypt, and like the 2/5th, had fought in Bardia and Tobruk. Danny worked for the railways—he'd been a station manager at Frankston—and as transport was viewed as an essential service, he had no need to enlist.

'Imagine, me, turning up to work each morning with my shiny blue uniform and neat badges, as if there wasn't a care in the world,' he said. '*Ma'am, would that be a single or a return... Begging your pardon, but did you say Brighton, or was it Highett'* He shook his head in disgust. 'No, that wouldn't have done at all, what with Hitler the murderous bastard, threatening to bomb the daylights out of London and Paris. Not to say that there's many an Irishman who'd be happy to obliterate the British cabinet, but not me.'

As Jack had suspected, Leo was a country lad, he'd been raised on a wheat farm in the western district of Victoria and loved the bush. However, as much as Leo enjoyed working on his family's farm, the effects of the depression had forced him to find other work. These days he helped his parents where he could, and in addition, spent his days driving trucks, loading and transporting grain from the farms to the railway stations.

Neither of the men had wives, or even girlfriends, although Danny frequently referred to various past loves, entertaining Jack and Leo with tales of numerous near perfect romances that had been thwarted when his wondering eyes and soft heart were beguiled by a new love.

In return, Jack provided scant information about his own life, other than that he'd been married, however, he and his wife were now separated. He could not help adding that he had hopes that they'd be reunited in Alexandria. Jack also spoke little about his life as an artist. However, in the boredom of their long days in the cave, he frequently drew, and both Leo and Danny were impressed with his sketches of the battles that had been fought on Crete, and of the landscape and their cave.

While Danny and Jack still had torches and Leo had his army issued cooker, water was an issue. Leo reasoned, with the common sense of a man who'd grown up in the bush, that there would be dozens of springs in the crevices below them; all they needed to do was descend into the valley and find one with a decent flow. With their water bottles hooked to their belts and the enamel pot Leo used to cook for them swinging, Leo led the way while Danny and Jack followed, rifles in hand should they be confronted by enemy soldiers. As it turned out, the only enemy they found was the corpse of a Fallschirmjäger, who'd somehow drifted off course and now dangled in the branches of a pine tree by his parachute cords. Ignoring the stench, they cut him down and thanked him for his Schmeisser, ammunition, knife, rations and boots.

Sure enough, Leo's skills proved fruitful. In no time they found a discharge of moisture seeping across a rock face, which led them to crystal-clear water accumulating in a shallow pool. A trickle continued overflowing from it down the escarpment to a creek far below. From then on, each morning they trekked to the pool to wash their bodies and clothing and to fill their water bottles and the enamel pot. Leo was pleased; he would now use the water to boil the lentils or potatoes when they wanted a change from eating them fried in oil.

They did not need a reminder to be cautious in their movements; the sky was a constant testament to the Germans' relentless activity, with dozens of Junkers circling the island daily, preparing to land at the Maleme airstrip to the west of the valley, no doubt strengthening their troops with a steady supply of weapons, transport and food. In addition, Heinkel bombers roared through the valley at regular intervals, flying so low that Jack could see the outlines of pilots sitting in their cockpits.

On the sixth morning, shattering explosions rang out just after dawn, drawing Jack, Leo and Danny to the mouth of the cave. For over two hours they lay watching plumes of smoke rise above the treetops, and the acrid smell of smoke and cordite filled the valley as a constant stream of Heinkels roared above, releasing bombs with an explosive force, until eventually it was quiet again.

Fearing for the village below, Jack suggested that they go down to investigate. Perhaps Marita and the villagers of Astikas might be injured and could use their help. Danny and Leo agreed, and dreading what they would find, they left the cave and ventured down the mountain. The track was steep, zigzagging across the mountain side through cypress and maple trees, the path adorned by clumps of colourful flowers—daisies, orchids and even gladioli. He was surprised when it suddenly ended, opening up into a long roadway, where a huddle of buildings balanced on a steep ledge that offered views of the ocean in the distance. The yellow clay houses were picturesque, with a small church at the far end and a village square at the centre defined by a small row of shops, their doors closed.

Remaining under the cover of the trees, Jack tried to make sense of what was happening. There was no sign of humans—either villagers or enemy soldiers—and the buildings appeared intact, raising the question of where the bombs had landed, if not here. A movement far along the dusty road caught his attention, and he nudged the others as a jeep entered the village from the far end, roared through the town, then turning, it retreated through the town and came to a rest outside a building at the far end of the street.

Within minutes a deep rumbling came from above, growing closer and closer until the air vibrated with the thunderous roar of engines so loud, it threatened to rupture their eardrums. Was an airplane about to land? Surely not—there was no runway here! Yet the shadow of a low-flying plane preceded its arrival.

The enormous craft passed overhead so slowly it seemed to appear motionless. It was a Stuka, whose mission today was not to drop bombs, Jack realised, as he watched hundreds of papers fluttering from its belly. Captured by the air rushing from its rotating propellors, many drifted into the forest, and Danny scrambled to retrieve one. It was a pamphlet of sorts, its Greek symbols meaningless to them.

Soon, the aircraft drifted off, and as the rumble of its engine faded, Jack was relieved to see movement from the houses. A man appeared in his doorway, scanning the roadside. A young boy dashed out onto the street and scooped up a handful of leaflets before returning to the safety of his home. A lady with a crying baby balanced on her hip, and two more children clinging to her sides, stepped out and collected a sheet of paper lying close to her door before retreating, slamming it behind her.

Over the next hour, villagers, one after the other, snatched the papers from the ground. Jack resisted the urge to engage with one of them and seek clarification of the events that had taken place—to check that everything was alright. He knew that would just add unnecessary stress to the people of the village. Worse, if a German officer were to see them, he, Danny and Leo would be taken captive in no time. As the shadows lengthened, they knew their only course of action was to return to the cave, with the satisfaction of knowing the village residents, for the present at least, were safe.

Nobody visited them that night, nor the following day until late afternoon. In the fading light, they were startled by rustling at the mouth of the cave, followed by two young men, perhaps sixteen or seventeen years of age, sliding through its entrance.

Grinning, they introduced themselves as George and Michael and explained that they'd been sent by their aunt to deliver dinner. Opening a rucksack with extreme care, they set out a heavy pot emitting a mouth-watering aroma, along with a loaf of bread and a bag of oranges.

Fishing deep into his rucksack, Michael retrieved a half a dozen batteries which he handed to Danny, and a flashlight, which he positioned on a ledge beside the entrance. After obscuring the mouth of the cave with their backpacks, Jack, Danny and Leo ate. As they did, they listened to George and Michael stumble over each other's words in surprisingly good English, providing updates on the latest events of the island.

As Jack had feared, although Astikas had been spared, other villages had not been so fortunate. The bombing Jack had seen had been at Kandanas, which according to the boys had been razed to the ground.

Jack was shocked to hear of such an outright assault on civilians by the Germans. It was one thing for the Germans to attack allied soldiers, but to bomb a village of innocent people was unthinkable.

George explained that the Germans were angered by the ongoing resistance of the Cretans. They knew that the islanders were hiding soldiers and conducting sabotage missions to hinder the Germans. As a consequence, they'd embarked on a brutal retaliation campaign against them

The boys shared stories they'd heard about the growing anger and brutal reactions of the Germans toward the Cretans circulated across the island. They'd heard that a week earlier, German soldiers had stormed the village of Kondomari, banging on the doors of the houses and calling everyone outside. The residents had been herded to the village square, and for hours they'd been shouted at. The Germans accused them of torturing and mutilating paratroopers and supporting the Allied forces. The soldiers had rampaged through the village, forcing their way into houses, destroying furniture and stealing food. They'd then marched everyone to an olive grove, and before the eyes of the women and children, they'd lined up and shot over forty men.

And then, the day after the attack on Kondomari, German

headquarters had decided to warn the people of Crete for once and for all what would happen to them if they continued their acts of insurrection. Hence the bombing of Kandanis, that Jack, Danny and Leo had witnessed, that had been followed by the leaflet drop, informing the residents of Crete of the rules that the Germans had put in place. The pamphlets had been delivered by air all over the island.

George retrieved a scrunched paper from the folds of his shirt and, displaying a flair for the dramatic, adopted a German officer's barking tones as he read it. While the leaflets did not bear weapons or grenades, they were no less deadly in the message that they carried.

'No Allied soldiers should be given refuge. Penalty—death.

'All weapons must be handed over, including hunting rifles. Punishment for failure to do so—you will be shot.

'All livestock, including donkeys, mules, sheep and goats, must be made available to the German army if requested.

'All Cretan men between sixteen and seventy years of age must register with the village council and be available for work duties if requested by the German army. Should they fail to report for duty, their village will suffer severe reprisals.'

'Sheesh, it's a right old bloody mess, isn't it?' Danny exclaimed. Jack agreed.

Following the cold-blooded killing at Kondomari and the devastating bombing of Kandanis, there could be no doubts about the swift and brutal retaliation that the Germans were capable of. It horrified Jack to know that he, Danny and Leo might be placing the lives of Marita and her family at such risk by living in the cave, dependent on them for supplies.

'Boys, you must not come here again! You are putting your lives at risk, perhaps the lives of your families! We will fend for ourselves from now on.'

'No, no. We will work something out,' Michael replied. 'It is impossible for you to leave here. Much too soon. I will talk to Marita. She will know what to do.'

As he and George prepared to leave, Jack asked them to pass on his thanks to their aunt for the delicious food that she had provided.

'Yes, tell her that chicken was beautiful…' Leo added.

'Chicken?'

'Yes, it was lovely and moist—perfect!' Danny said with an exaggerated kissing of his fingertips.

George laughed loudly, shaking his head. 'No, no…. not chicken! That was kohli—snails!'

'Snails! No way!' Danny grimaced in shock, no doubt picturing the pesky slugs that left slimy trails across the pavements in Australian gardens.

'No! Really! Snails?' Leo was equally surprised.

'Yes, kohli.'

'Mate… to be honest, chicken, snails, grasshoppers—I'd eat anything, that is cooked so well!' Leo said. 'You tell your aunt that her kohli was delicious!'

Jack laughed at Danny's gape of astonishment and agreed with Leo —the meal had been delicious. Memories of other times when he'd partaken of snails flashed through his mind. The first was in Paris, seated across the table from Sofia at Le Grand Colbert, with white linen serviettes and polished silver cutlery set out before them. They'd received table service from a waiter wearing a gold-buttoned jacket. Then there were the numerous occasions in Malaga when Sofia had fried onion and garlic and herbs from her garden, then tossed a handful of plump escargot into her pan to sauté them in the spicy oil mix. Memories of hot summer evenings in the finca's courtyard, its air sweet with the aroma of orange blossom, swept over him. Memories from a time long ago in a place far away.

'You will be able to tell her yourself! She will be up in the morning,' George replied, and for a second Jack actually thought he meant Sofia—that she was coming here to the cave! But of course, she wasn't. It was his aunt who George referred to. Marita was planning to visit again.

Leaving them with more potatoes, eggs, a bag of lentils, onions and some soft cheese to add to their store, the boys departed. Jack sat on the ledge and watched them make their way along the path until the pinpricks of their lanterns vanished amid the trees on the mountain, hoping their return trip would be safe. He wanted it to be all over—the fighting and the war. Suddenly he felt desperate to get off this island and back to Alexandria where he could resume his search for Sofia.

∽

Jack slept badly that night, with his dreams set in Paris. In them he searched lanes and blind-ended courtyards, running anxiously along the Seine and peering into the faces of women, none of whom were Sofia.

He was still sleepy when Marita arrived the next morning. She repeated the pantomime of the previous visit by dressing as an old woman and resting on the rock, waiting for the whistle to come, not moving until she was assured that the track was clear.

This time her visit was brief. Reiterating descriptions of the German soldiers' horrific actions, she again encouraged Jack, Leo and Danny to remain in the cave's shelter for at least the next few days. German patrols were everywhere, frequently arriving at Astikas, where they had claimed schoolrooms to use as a base for whenever they were in town. It left the villagers feeling uneasy, as if everything they did was being scrutinised.

'Marita, do you think there is any chance for us to leave the island?' Jack asked. 'Are there any boats that we could board? Perhaps if we were to disguise ourselves as fishermen or something.'

'No, no… you must not think to do this. The beaches are watched constantly. Every boat leaving the island is now checked. You must stay here, in the mountains, for now. The coast roads, the beaches are swarming with German soldiers. Nowhere is safe for you!'

'Well, it's too dangerous for you to be coming up here. It would be terrible if you got caught. How about we come down and get food under the cover of darkness? Would that be okay? If we are caught, we can say we're stealing food. Your villagers can't be accused of helping us that way. We will repay you someday, when this is all over.'

Marita nodded thoughtfully, although her grim expression revealed concern for them. 'Yes. We do not want to risk our people—it is terrible what the Germans are doing. They want total obedience and for

265

now, that is what we must show them. Otherwise, we too will suffer as Kondomari has suffered, or even worse, be bombed like Kandanis!'

Using a twig, she sketched the road through the village in the sandy soil, then marked the site of the schoolhouse where the Germans occasionally stayed overnight. At the opposite end of the town, she marked the site of an old shed, explaining that it was about twenty yards behind the town's dairy and well out of the schoolhouse's view. The shed had both a rear and a side door; Marita instructed them to take a broad sweep around the perimeter of the village and approach the shed through its back entry. She was confident that under the cover of darkness they could easily avoid drawing the attention of the Germans, should they be in town.

Next she marked the route of the track down to the village, noting the point where the forest ended and the village began. She drew an X to mark a house to the left of the base of the mountain track.

'This house, here, it is Uncle Giorgo's. You've met him—he's the one who brought you to this cave. He has a window... here...' Marita sketched out the front of the house, and then detailed the side facing the hill. 'This is his spare bedroom. If he feels that the village is unsafe, I will see that he puts a light on. If you see the light, you will have to go hungry.' She smiled. 'Really, you should be fine. The German soldiers, they will soon realise that there is nothing for them in our sleepy little village. They will leave us alone soon.'

Jack, Danny and Leo agreed to follow Marita's advice and remain in the cave during the daylight hours. Every second evening, they would make their way down the hill. She would make sure that food was placed in a cupboard in the shed.

Despite their reassurances that they would find their way back up the mountain in the darkness, Marita wanted to help with that, too. She explained that kohli gatherers went out each evening after dark; they would act as guides. Their lanterns would follow the route up the hill and along this track before their cave. Marita insisted that they were not to speak to them, just quietly follow from a distance and slip into the cave when they reached it.

Before departing, she unloaded her bag, leaving them with more torch batteries, matches and oil for their stove and three old sacks they could use as ground covers; they'd provide a buffer against the hard stone floor of the cave.

~

And so it was that two days later, Jack, Leo and Danny ventured down the mountain at sunset. Carefully, they followed Marita's instructions, first checking the side window of the house near the track to be sure there was no warning glow, then remaining under the cover of the trees, circling to the back of the village before approaching the shed on a path barely visible in the veil of descending darkness.

Slipping through the shed door, Leo lit his torch and held it low for a few minutes so that they could get their bearings. A wooden cupboard sat beside the back door, and on the lowest shelf rested a large wooden box. In this they found two loaves of bread wrapped in a towel, an enamel pot—its contents still warm—and a jumble of enamel plates and cutlery. Wasting no time, they dished out the enticing meal and ate it quickly before filling their packs with the vegetables and fresh fruit that had been left out for them.

As Marita had organised, when they left the shed barely twenty minutes later, the glow of four lanterns hovered in the distance, and Jack could hear the laughter and chatter of their bearers. They must have sensed the men's presence, for quickly they approached the mountain track and began their ascent, with Jack, Leo and Danny following about twenty yards behind. For over an hour they followed the chattering Cretans, resting while they stopped to collect snails from the base of tree trunks, then continuing on. He was thankful for their presence. By night, the track was totally unfamiliar, and when a shadowy figure placed a lamp low and whispered, "Here is your entrance," he knew they would never have made it to the safety of their cave without the guidance of the kohli gatherers.

They continued with this pattern—going down to the village for sustenance every second night—grateful for the spicy lentils, salads and cheese pies as well as bags of fresh fruit and vegetables that were left for them. Only once did they find the lamp in the bedroom window shining its warning into the night, and although they watched from the trees for signs of German soldiers menacing the town, all appeared quiet. Nonetheless, they returned to their cave with stomachs rumbling.

On their fifth visit, Jack was startled to see a man leaning against the wooden bench in the shed. To his relief, he realised that it was George, who was relaxed and in high spirits and keen to update them on the latest events of the war-stricken island.

As Marita had predicted, visits from the German soldiers to Astikas had diminished. They only arrived once every two or three days, roaring through the main street on a half-track or a motorcycle with side car, staying a few minutes and then departing again. Regardless, the village council had decided to set up a sentry on the southern road at the point where the patrols entered and exited the village; and by using a series of whistles, they always knew in advance if a German patrol was about to sweep into the town.

George was highly amused by the strategy their mayor had adopted, pretending to cooperate with the Germans, when really he abhorred their invasion of the island. Like an actor, he demonstrated the bombastic tones of the German commander who'd met with the mayor the previous week.

'You must ensure that all weapons in the village are collected and submitted to the German army promptly. No guns are to be withheld, or there will be severe consequences.'

'Yes, yes, certainly,' their mayor had agreed. Then he'd joined the elders of the village in gathering every broken and ancient relic that could be found, adding a couple of reasonable hunting rifles to the cache to allay suspicions. When a unit of Germans arrived late one afternoon and requested a fat lamb for their dinner, the mayor had offered two, and also a flagon of oil, bunches of freshly picked comfrey and a bottle of their strongest raki. When a labour team was summoned to mend a damaged bridge two miles down the hill, the mayor wasted no time in assembling a dozen good men, who'd worked well. Not only did they fix the bridge, but they'd tried their hardest to assist a hapless German officer repair his wireless transmitter, which had unaccountably lost reception repeatedly during the week when the bridge was being worked on.

In this way, by appearing immensely cooperative, the villagers hoped that the Germans would never learn how the villagers spent hours huddled in one house or another, discussing strategies to sabotage German operations or relaying messages across the island via the young shepherds who acted as runners. Nor, they hoped, would the Germans suspect that dozens of sub-machine guns, rifles and handguns lay hidden beneath floorboards of houses throughout the village, or that a jeep lay concealed down a forest track barely two miles away.

George told them that the Germans' main efforts were still focused on the airports, but that troops were now positioned all along the island's coastline, monitoring the movements of seafaring vessels and prepared for a British naval assault. Almost daily, the Germans were intercepting rafts and barges loaded with Australian and New Zealand soldiers—men who'd hidden in the mountains like Jack, Danny and Leo, but who'd seized an opportunity to escape, with unfortunate results.

'Yes, but maybe some are making it off the island?' Jack couldn't keep himself from being hopeful. Surely there was one way or another that they could get to the mainland!

'Perhaps. I don't know. Word is that a few days ago, a submarine slipped in under the cover of dark and rescued a few dozen men, but I don't know if this is true.'

As frustrating as it was, Jack had to acccpt that he, Leo and Danny were stuck on the island for the time being at least. It felt like they'd been there for months already, and calculating the dates in his notebook, he realised that it had been. Following the sinking of the *Costa Rica*, they'd landed on the island in late April, and the German invasion of Crete had begun on the twentieth of May. Then there'd been the walk to Sphakia followed by the weeks in the hills before they'd come to the cave. With the days now cooling, he knew that autumn was upon them, and, confirming the date with Marita the week later, it was no surprise to find that it was now September.

They stayed with the routine of going down to the village on alternative evenings, enjoying the meals that were left for them, and ever hopeful that the news Marita provided to them on the occasions when she met them would be positive. When, in mid-December she advised them that the Japanese had entered the war with an attack on the American naval base at Pearl Harbour, they were shocked and could speak of nothing else for days. The war in Europe had become a world war, and they feared for what this may mean for Australia.

George, sometimes accompanied by Michael, was a frequent visitor to the shed, also. The boys were both fascinated by the culture and political freedoms of England and Australia, and they asked endless questions about life in 'the western democracies', as they referred to the nations of the British Commonwealth. America, and especially Hollywood, fascinated them also; and they loved to hear about talking films and glamorous stars, of which Danny proved to have expert knowledge. George, in particular, loved to discuss books of any description, and Jack thought it a shame that it was he rather than Sidney Nolan, who was called upon to answer questions about Tolstoy, Dostoyevsky and Rudyard Kipling. George and Sidney must have been born under the same star—each from humble beginnings and yet harbouring cravings to know everything he could about writers and poets.

Jack was curious about how George, Michael and Marita had learned to speak English so well, and George explained that Marita's husband, Henry, had been a British soldier. She had met him in Greece during the Great War. Together, they'd lived in England for a short while, and then in Greece; and then, with their son Manos, they'd returned to live in Crete. Twice weekly for over a decade, either Henry or Marita had given English lessons at the local school, and many of the adults in the village had also learned some phrases. Both Henry and Manos, who was now nineteen, had left with the men from Crete to assist the Greeks resist the Italian invaders.

On learning about the bravery of Henry and Manos and of their commitment to supporting mainland Greece, Jack stewed about their own inactivity—hiding in the mountains, doing no more than passing time sitting against the ledge and watching the planes circle the sky before landing at their airfield to their east, wondering what the occasional bomb or plume of smoke might mean, and spending his days sleeping or sketching. He discussed his concerns with Leo and Danny and the next time they saw George, they insisted that they needed to see Marita, and to come up with a plan for action. They were soldiers, after all. Surely there was something they could be doing.

# CHAPTER 27

'You are getting restless, George tells me?' Marita asked them, a week later.

'Sure we are, ma'am! We are at war, and it is time for us to be doing a little more,' Danny replied, his chest puffed out, his shoulders straightened, looking every bit a soldier who was ready for action.

'Surely we could be doing something to slow down the Germans. Perhaps we could study their movements at the airfield at Meleme. That seems to be their major entry point. If we could disable the airstrip, that would stop the Germans from landing their supply planes.' Danny shared the plan that had dominated their conversation over the last week. Now the idea that seemed to have such merit in the cave sounded ridiculously improbable to Jack as Danny spoke the words to Marita, and judging from her reaction, she thought so too.

'No, no! You must understand, it is still very dangerous for you to upset the Germans. They are very strong and vastly outnumber our defences. Their vehicles and weapons command the roads.'

Jack, Leo and Danny listened dubiously as she continued.

'Now the war front in Russia is escalating; it will only be a matter of time before most of the German soldiers are called off the island to go and support them. Then we will be able to put our plans into action.'

'Our plans?' Jack wondered what plans the villagers had made.

'Yes, Jack. Our plans. Crete has been at war for centuries. We have defended our island—our way of life—in the past, and we will defend it again. It is all a matter of patience and timing. Daily, our resistance is gaining strength. Some important men have returned to Crete, and now we have the EAM—that is, the communists—as well as the EOK, who are non-communist, working together to rid the island of our invaders. However, it is essential that when we do retaliate, our efforts are effective. Our response needs to be like that of a tiger pouncing on a sleeping elephant. We need to play the Germans' own game of blitzkrieg. If we simply buzz around like mosquitoes biting, blowing up bridges and immobilising their vehicles, certainly we will draw some blood; but we will just irritate them and make them suspicious. Particularly now with the Hitler Youth on the island, whose punishments for such irritations are particularly nasty.'

'Hitler Youth? Who are these boys?' Danny's quick bark suggested that he was ready, willing and more than able to squash any German youngster if she would just point her finger towards them.

'Danny, these are not ordinary boys. They are truly dreadful. Malicious and without honour. Far worse than the German soldiers. Hitler Youth are thugs who take pleasure in cruelty. Because of this, we must make sure that our own actions are coordinated, foolproof, and most of all, do not provoke their barbaric retaliations.'

Jack nodded despondently. The last week's plans to attack the airport had filled him with excitement. For a few days, he'd felt that they were taking control of their lives, living up to their training as Australian Diggers. It was hard to call themselves professional soldiers when they were hiding in a cave and dependent on the people of Astikas to feed them. Nonetheless, he accepted Marita's point. It would be terrible if they acted in haste and somehow their actions brought retribution to Astikas.

Marita paused, as if she had an idea, then continued. 'The village is mostly quiet these day. How about you join us for dinner? Lots of people would love to meet you. Next week would be perfect, if the Germans keep away.'

Looking at Danny and Leo, who nodded, Jack replied, 'We'd love to. Thank you, Marita. Are you sure it will be safe? We'd hate to cause any trouble.'

While it was not action that would defeat their enemy, anything to relieve their boredom was welcome, and the invitation to take part in a civilised meal proved irresistible.

~

The following Friday, Jack, Leo and Danny arose as excited as sixteen-year-old lads going out to their first dance—full of chatter about the night ahead. Just after midday, they walked to their pool to wash and returned with water, which they boiled before shaving, combing their hair and scratching around for their cleanest shirts and trousers. There was nothing Jack could do about the flapping sole of his left boot other than tie string around it, and he wondered if the village might have any boots for sale.

As the sun sank, they made their way down the track. Jack noticed Danny lagging.

'What on earth is he doing?' he said to Leo, pausing to wait for him to catch up.

'You didn't think we could turn up without a gift, now, did you?' Danny grinned broadly, waving a bunch of colourful flowers towards them.

As soon as they stepped off the mountain track, Jack guessed their destination would be the house halfway along the road, where laughter and the strumming of a guitar drifted onto the street. By habit, they checked the front upstairs window of the house nearest them, then proceeded forward. No warning lamp had been lit, and remaining in the cover of the street's shadows, they advanced towards the sounds.

George appeared out of the darkness and led them through the front door. Immediately, a dozen faces turned towards them, curiosity in their eyes. As George commenced a rapid circle of introductions, Jack nodded at the men and women and winked at the children, who smiled shyly at him. He followed George to a dining room, where still more people were gathered, and a central table was heaped with delicious-looking platters of pies, fried pastries, salads and fruit.

A glass of raki was thrust into Jack's hands by a very elderly gentleman whose repeated nodding and gesticulations for them to eat and drink suggested that he'd not availed himself of Henry's English lessons. Jack sipped from it while George began a second round of introductions, and he discovered that most of the villagers were related to each other.

It emerged that the occasion for the dinner was a birthday celebration. Marita's Uncle Manoussos, the man who'd offered the spirit to them, was seventy years old. Shaking his hand, Jack offered birthday greetings, and in return Uncle Manoussos gestured for him to drink again. However, after barely half a dozen mouthfuls, Jack's head was spinning and he knew he should be careful—his stomach was empty, and the raki very strong.

Marita appeared through a doorway, bearing a large platter of cheese pies, which she offered to them.

'It's very noisy here. Are you sure there won't be any unfriendly visitors?' Jack was more worried for the townspeople than he was for himself. It would be dreadful for Marita's family if allied soldiers were found in their living room.

Marita nodded. 'Yes, definitely. Today has been a big day for the Germans. This morning they loaded hundreds of captured soldiers onto ships. Apparently they're being taken to Galatas, in Greece. Because of this, all the Germans are in Maleme. No one will be coming this way today.'

'But what if you're wrong?' Jack insisted. It occurred to him that it had been an omission not to plan for the contingency of German patrol arriving to the village unexpectedly.

'Okay, Jack. If we do get a surprise visit, you can slip out the back door—here, let me show you.' Marita led them through the kitchen and out into a scullery, where she opened a door.

'See that pathway?' A strip of pale gravel leading away from the house glowed in the moonlight. 'You will follow that path for about twenty yards and then climb over a fence. Stay there until you get a call that it is safe, or a false alarm. If there is no call, make your way down along the fence and turn to the left. When you reach the last house, you will recognise that it is my uncle's. Then you will know where you are. The path on the right leads up to the cave.'

Reassured that at least there was a plan, Jack, Leo and Danny returned to the crowded living room. After months of living outdoors, it was impossible to describe how wonderful it felt to be within the walls of a house, absorbing its warmth and cosy hospitality, surrounded by the welcoming faces of villagers who treated them like royalty.

Repeatedly they were questioned about their experiences in battle, and particularly about their time in Greece. That the Cretans held depths of bitterness for both the Italians and the Germans, to whom they'd lost husbands and sons, was evident. Jack realised that for these people, the fight was deeply personal, not just for liberty of Crete, but also revenge for their lost men.

The other information Jack gleaned was that as much as the Cretan people valued the efforts of the British, Australian and New Zealand forces on their island to save the island from the Germans, they did not view the soldiers as protectors, but rather, as comrades; and not withstanding their deep appreciation for the ongoing efforts of the Allies, they were confident of the strategies they had in place to resist the Germans when the time was right.

Jack did not doubt the strength of their conviction. In the aftermath of the parachute landing at Heraklion, he'd been astonished by the sight of old men, women and children moving around the airfield, wielding any weapon available, including their bare hands, to rid their island of the invaders from the sky.

The following week was Christmas, and although arrangements had been made for Jack, Leo and Danny to join the villagers in their celebrations, the arrival of a patrol of Germans to the village a few days earlier ruined this plan. Nonetheless, the soldiers weren't forgotten. When George appeared on Christmas Eve with a basket laden with treats, they all but cheered. Enjoying the almond short bread and honey glazed walnuts, which he explained were traditional Cretan Christmas fare, they watched as he set an ornately carved ship against the wall of the cave. Unlike the English tradition of Christmas trees, he told them, the houses of Crete bore decorated ships in commemoration of St Nicholas, the patron saint of the sailors and seamen of Crete.

Stretching out on the floor of the cave later that evening, Jack tried to make sense of the passing of time. A year earlier, they'd been making preparations for the battle of Bardia at this time, a battle they'd won with ease. Their victory at Tobruk had soon followed before they'd been sent to the disaster of Greece, after which they'd been brought here to Crete. He calculated that they'd now been on the island for over seven months, which seemed astonishing. And Sofia? He wondered how she was coping. Could she still be at Alexandria? Had she continued to ask the soldiers she treated if they knew of a Jack? In the darkness of the cave, they were big questions with no answers; and unable to sleep, Jack crawled outside to the ledge and lit a cigarette. It was a cloudless night, and the stars in the sky were dazzling. He gazed at them, captivated by their mystery, then searched for the familiar sign of the Southern Cross. Of course it was absent; it was a constellation for the Southern Hemisphere. What on earth was he doing here? He breathed deeply, and then dragged on the cigarette, trying to ward off the heaviness that was descending upon him. Scotty, Sofia, the things that had once made his life make sense were now as unreachable as the stars, and he wondered if he'd ever again find that deep sense of completeness that had once made him so happy.

Two weeks later, with the German patrol packed up and gone, Marita suggested to the men that they might like to join her family for another meal, and henceforth it became their habit to join the villagers for a meal at least once a week; and following a meal of souvlaki or lamb and rice accompanied by mugs of raki, they'd stay overnight, sleeping in the shed at the back of the dairy.

It was hard not to be frustrated by their predicament, and for all of Marita's warnings that they remain low throughout the winter, they entertained themselves by creating endless wild plans to hinder the Germans, or to escape the island and make their way to Africa. Occasionally, when they really thought that a plan had merit, they raised it with Marita; but as always, she insisted that they must bide their time, with hints that activities were underfoot.

Frustrating as it was, they had little choice but to take her advice, and increasingly spent nights in the shed in the village and days helping out by collecting firewood, repairing water pumps and entertaining children. And when Marita suggested that they replace their clothing that had been reduced to rags from months of rough living with the shirts, pantaloons and boots worn by Cretan men, they were grateful. Jack found that by dressing like the locals, he began to feel like a Cretan. He even adopted a number of greetings and common phrases as he adapted to the rhythm of village life. He, Leo and Danny were quick to learn the system of warning whistles the villagers used to flag the sighting of German soldiers who were about to enter the village. Whenever they heard the call, they were quick to melt into the forest and make their way up to the cave, where they remained for a few days, to avoid the risk of being caught or even worse, inciting the fury of the German soldiers upon the villagers.

The young children loved their presence in the village and sought their company at every opportunity, especially when Leo found a small piece of timber and fashioned it into a bat so they could play games of cricket.

For all of Danny's Irish charm, it was not he who found love in the village, but Leo and increasingly the quiet man vanished for hours on end, often staying out late and creeping into his bed long after Jack and Danny had retired. The quick smile and sparkling eyes of Marita's cousin, Theresa, when she looked at Leo made Jack wonder if she might be the distraction, but Leo never mentioned anything, and Jack didn't ask.

The small village general store was well stocked, and Jack was pleased to find a half a dozen reasonable quality sketch books on its shelves, for which the store owner was happy to accept Jack's handful of Egyptian bronze 5 and 10 millieme coins for all of them. From then on, he frequently drew scenes around the village and found that young and old alike enjoyed receiving pictures of themselves from 'the Australian soldier'. Without thinking, he began adding brief messages on the backs of the drawings and felt foolish when Marita pulled him aside and chastised him.

'Jack, no, you mustn't use names! If the Germans find these drawings with messages on them that are signed "Jack", what will they think?'

From then on, Jack added his own mark: a discreet symbol within the drawing, concealed in such a way that no one would ever notice unless they knew what they were looking for. Five small dots—the stars of the Southern Cross, Australia's most recognisable constellation, which Jack could hardly wait to see again.

Marita was constantly on the move, donning her old woman costume to connect with others on the island, gleaning what information she could about the Germans' activities. She liked to deal in facts—if she heard a rumour, she set out to investigate its truth, and Jack learned that she was very active in passing information to the Cretan resistance movement. Sometimes she was away for weeks at a time.

Jack felt Marita's absence when she was gone, for her company was a pleasant change from Danny and Leo's. He found her easy to talk to, and occasionally they sat in the moonlight, smoking and chatting together. They spoke of the war, of his drawing and of his appointment as a war artist. He asked about her time in London; about her child, Manos; and about her and Henry's life in Athens. She explained how they'd loved living in Athens, but once they'd had their baby, they liked the idea of raising Manos in the village amongst her family. She spoke of Henry, telling Jack of his work as a botanist, and how since he'd been on the island, he'd focused on studies of the wild date palms of Crete, conducting tests that he hoped might improve opportunities for the Cretans to cultivate and harvest the wild dates, and then to sell them to markets beyond the island.

Nonetheless, she told Jack, Henry had never hesitated when Greece had been invaded by the Italians the previous winter. Having fought for the British in the Great War, he'd believed his experience on the battlefield would be helpful. And Manos, who'd turned eighteen two weeks earlier, insisted that he should go with his father.

'All the men were going,' Marita told Jack. 'How could I stop them? Like they said, it was our duty to support Greece. It was no less than we'd expect if it had been our own home under attack. I was so naïve—waving them off with all the other men. It was if they were going away to play a game of football, and they would return later that day with the winning trophy. And now, of course, Crete has been invaded, and we have no men to protect our island.'

While several women had received formal notice from the Greek army that their men had been killed in action, Marita had not received such news regarding Henry or Manos and so remained hopeful. She was sure that Henry would have done anything that he could to protect Manos, and she speculated that they might have escaped to Palestine or Egypt, or perhaps they'd become prisoners of war.

'And you, Jack. Do you have a wife? Children?'

These were familiar questions, and Jack answered them in different ways—depending upon the circumstances. With Marita, however, he was honest, holding nothing back of his story; and he even shared with her his photos of Sofia and Scotty, something he'd never done with anybody before. At the end of his story, she patted him on the hand.

'Jack, I will pray for you. For you and for your Sofia. That out of this terrible war, you will find each other, and then, out of your grief, you will find your love again. This will be my prayer for you.'

'And I will pray for the return of Henry and Manos for you,' Jack replied, remembering his own prayer in the grandeur of St Patrick's. His promise to God that if he could find Sofia, he'd attend church every week. The problem was that he wasn't so sure if he believed in God anymore.

⁓

In early March, Marita returned from a trip to the east of Crete, excited.

'Jack, I think that I have found a way to get you off the island!

280

There is a monastery in Prevali. The abbot there, he has been helping to support allied soldiers all through winter… many of them have been living in the hills in southern Crete. Before winter, a number of small rescue operations took place. An Englishman came across in a submarine and took a few dozen men off the island. The word is that he intends to return as soon as the weather warms.'

Jack's heart beat with excitement. After months of inactivity, of being holed up in the cave and passing days around the village, the option to escape had become nothing more than a wishful fantasy. The Germans' presence on the island was too strong, and although the escapades of allied soldiers sabotaging enemy operations or attempting to escape the island filtered through to them, so also did stories of the reprisals. Of shootings and bombings. Of villages where dozens of men were slaughtered before their families, and their food supplies were confiscated because they'd been caught aiding Allied soldiers hiding in the mountains. But finally, here was news of an organised effort to evacuate the soldiers who'd been left behind.

To be part of the rescue, Marita told them that they'd need to get to Prevali, make themselves known to the abbot and put themselves in his hands. This was no small feat, for Prevali was over one hundred and fifty miles away—weeks of walking with a constant threat of being discovered by Germans. These days it was hard enough for Cretans to move around the island without raising suspicions. Careful planning would be necessary. They would have to cross whole mountain ranges, avoiding the main roads and instead using the paths of shepherds.

Days were spent planning the trip, envisioning the various scenarios that they might encounter along the journey and preparing the stories to which they would adhere, should they be interrogated.

In the end, it was decided that Marita's uncle, Giorgis, her nephews George and Michael, and four of the younger village boys would act as guides to see Jack, Danny and Leo across the mountains.

The boys, between thirteen and sixteen, were chosen for their quick-wittedness and speed. They would walk out ahead, guiding a small flock of goats, and take turns running back and forth to relay information to the others. In this way they'd know whether up ahead lay a hut or village, a German patrol or a major intersection. The men worked with the boys to develop a repertoire of distinctive whistles which they'd use to transmit messages.

George and Michael would follow the goatherd, accompanying their uncle, who would pretend to be ill—suffering from an abdominal malady. As they proceeded across the island, they would maintain the fiction that they were going to Dr Tsoulous, whom they'd heard was well regarded for his capacity to treat abdominal conditions.

Jack, Danny and Leo would tail the group, following whatever instructions they were provided with by the young shepherds each day —information that would lead them from one safe shed or cave or hut to the next. As Allied soldiers, they were most vulnerable, and at risk of being shot should they be caught. It was agreed that should they be intercepted by the Germans, they would admit that they'd been living in the mountains, eating olives and wild dates and trapping birds and stealing food. They would claim that they were starving and now wished to surrender themselves. Repeatedly, Marita insisted that they must not attempt to evade arrest. To do so would undoubtedly lead to being shot or possibly worse, subjected to the terrible punishments of the sadistic Hitler Youth, with neither judge nor jury available to ensure that they were treated fairly. They'd have a better chance of survival if they offered themselves as war prisoners.

Leo, who'd always been the fittest of the three, shamed Jack and Danny into joining him in daily exercises. He insisted that if they didn't, they wouldn't have to wait for the Germans to capture them; instead they'd die of exhaustion on the mountain crossing. Even though Danny and Jack returned the jibes, Jack knew that Leo was right. They needed to be fit if they were going to walk one hundred and fifty miles across Crete, through inhospitable mountainous country.

# CHAPTER 28

*I*t seemed that the whole of the village of Astikas turned out for the farewell dinner that was held for Jack, Leo and Danny the night before their departure; and with sadness Jack said his goodbyes, promising that after the war was over, he would return to the village one day.

Before he left, he made up two packages. The first was a flat bundle of a dozen oil paintings that he'd spent the last few weeks working on each morning, outside the cave. They included images of the village, including the games of cricket and the evenings where they'd gathered around Marita's dinner table and shared meals. He'd painted a scene of the shed at sunset, with an outline of three soldiers furtively entering its back door, and one of the cave where an old woman stood at the front beside a donkey. Each painting held the symbol that served as Jack's signature—the image of the southern cross amid its lines and shapes.

'Hide them for now, Marita,' he told her. 'Keep them until after the war, when it is safe to display them. They are mementos of our stay here. The boys and I will never forget how you have cared for us, kept us safe for the past twelve months.'

The second parcel included his metal cylinder—now full of loose-paged sketches—and three drawing books, also full. While they were rough, the hundreds of pieces provided a visual record of his time in Greece: of their evacuation in Kalamata, and the disembarkation at Suda Bay. In his months of boredom in the cave, he'd recreated the battle on 42nd Street and their long walk to Sphakia from memory, and more recently he'd added sketches of their life in the cave and around the village. Should he ever be called to paint his experiences for the army, these sketches would prompt his recollection of events. While he'd been lucky to hold the cylinder and those early drawings despite the sinking of the *Costa Rica* and the battles on Crete, he didn't want to take a chance of losing them on the trek across the island and back to Alexandria; and although he didn't like to think about it, there was always the chance that he'd be caught by the Germans or even killed.

'I have included the address, Marita, but don't worry about sending them anytime soon. If you could just hide them somewhere until the end of the war, that would be wonderful.'

Finally, the moment arrived for them to be on their way. As Jack farewelled his Cretan friends, he hoped that no German soldiers would visit Astikas over the next few days. Anticipation of their journey had captured the villagers' imaginations; their excitement was palpable and would surely raise suspicions. The young shepherds left first, and George and Michael were about to depart with their uncle. Jack looked at Danny as they waited for Leo at the end of the roadway. They were to set off in about thirty minutes. Could he have made a last-minute decision to remain behind? Jack wondered. However, Leo eventually appeared, accompanied by Theresa, and the first thing Jack noticed was a gold chain peeping from beneath his shirt—no doubt a parting gift from the woman he'd fallen in love with.

Jack smiled back at the villagers and gave a final wave. At last, something was happening! In a few weeks they would be off the island and he could find Sofia.

Jack was glad of Leo's insistence that they undertake an exercise routine in preparation before they left, for by the end of the first day—after climbing steep banks and walking paths that meandered in all directions, ascending and descending one mountain ridge after the next—he was beyond tired, and thankful when they finally collapsed in a vacant shepherd's hut that smelled more suitable for sheep than humans.

Each day was the same: relentless walking, with frequent interceptions from the smiling runners, who advised them of changes in direction or a hut for them to rest in for the night. The boys seemed to have boundless energy as they ran up and down the mountains, delivering souvlaki, fruit and cheese pastries which they'd purchased or acquired from the network of Greek resistance spread across the island. For company, most nights they had only themselves and the kohli gatherers moving in rows along the hills, distinctive for their bobbing lamps in the distance. Occasionally, they met with those who'd provided them with shelter for the night and shared a meal and a stilted exchange of information. Few of the Cretans they met spoke English, but their welcoming greetings and broad smiles offered reassurance that the Cretan resistance movement was achieving pleasing results. After ten days of walking, Jack, Leo and Danny were taken to a farmhouse at the end of a long day. There, they enjoyed a pleasant meal with a man called Demetrios and his wife, Evanthia, who greeted them warmly.

The couple lived in the mountains, where they raised quite a large herd of goats as well as two small children, a little boy, Pétros, who was four years old, and their daughter, Maria, who was just crawling. Like the other places Jack, Danny and Leo had stayed, they learned that they weren't their first visitors. Demetrios and Evanthia, who spoke English very well, told them that they'd frequently offered their shed to Allied soldiers to hide in, as they moved across the island. It was from Demetrios that they learned more details about the Greek resistance that was operating in the southern end of the island; how it was being led by the Doundoulakis boys, who they saw as heroes for their efforts to support the Allied soldiers that had been hiding on the island over the past year. Jack was amazed to learn that the brothers were in direct collaboration with the British SOE—a Special Operations Executive, which Churchill had established to liaise with resistance groups, and whose operations included rescue missions to bring the allies who remained hidden in the mountains of Crete off the island. It seemed that they hadn't been abandoned by the allied administration, after all.

After a meal of moussaka, hummus and yoghurt, they were shown to the shed to the left of the house, which provided clean comfortable conditions for them to sleep. Demetrios showed them the loose cladding at the back of the shed, designed to allow for a quick exit, should German soldiers appear to search the farm, as they'd done from time to time. If such an occasion arose, he told them they must scramble through the opening and make their way to the wood heap a few dozen yards away, and then to the gully below, that would lead them downhill to the edge of a forest. From there, they needed to turn left; make their way along the forest edge in an easterly direction.

In no time at all, Jack fell into a heavy sleep. The next morning, however, he was woken early by the sound of German voices ringing across the yard. Exactly the circumstances that Demetrios had prepared them for!

'Where are they?'

'Who do you want? We are all here! What are you asking this for?

'The British! They have been here!'

'What British? There are no British here, look around and you will see for yourselves!' The volume of Demetrios' outraged response was undoubtedly meant as a warning to the soldiers hiding in his shed, and Jack, Leo and Danny grabbed their packs, ready to lunge through the gap in the wall, and retreat to the woodstack at the first opportunity.

Before leaving, Jack peered through the side of the shed door where he could see a motorcycle, complete with side car, parked near the front entrance of the farmhouse, and the backs of two German soldiers speaking with Demetrios. Leo peered over Jack's shoulder to see what was happening, before pointing to the exit at the rear. Jack nodded, agreeing that they should make their move immediately, for who knew if the soldiers would decide to search the property.

As they prepared to leave, they looked at each other as chilling words from one soldier were followed by screams from Evanthia.

'Tell me now—where are they?'

Putting his fingers to his lips, Jack returned to the door, where through the crack he saw Pétros being held in the firm grip of one of the now red-faced German soldiers. His whimpering cries drifted across the yard.

Fury swept through Jack. He gestured for Danny and Leo to leave without him, waving his arm in a circular motion, indicating for them to take a position at the side of the house. Understanding his intentions, they slid through the gap in the wall; and from there, they sprinted to the side of the house, while Jack raised his rifle in readiness.

When they reached the cover of the farmhouse, Jack clanged the door open and stepped forward, his .303 held aloft.

'Leave them!' he roared. 'These people don't know that I've been camping here at night. It's been cold. I was just needing shelter.'

As Jack had expected, his outburst surprised the soldiers, who swung towards him. He levelled his rifle at their faces, praying that should he fire, his aim would be steady.

'Put down your gun!' the taller man screeched.

'You release that child first—then, I will put down my gun!' Jack's words carried the force of his anger, and when he cocked the trigger of his gun, its click echoed across the yard.

The taller soldier nodded at the other, and Jack watched Pétros stumble into Evanthia's arms and be pulled through the door.

As it slammed behind the family, the taller of the Germans raised his gun towards Jack, and without thought, Jack squeezed the trigger of his own weapon.

The sound of two loud cracks echoed in his ears, and a sharp pain tore through his left shoulder. He lurched backwards just as Danny and Leo burst from the side of the house, guns aloft, and he heard them releasing a barrage of bullets and hoped that they would be alright.

Within seconds, they were at Jack's side, prodding at the injury that had bright red blood seeping through his ragged shirt. Demetrios and Evanthia appeared behind them.

'Quick, Jack, you must get up. Let me see your shoulder.'

Evanthia's words prompted the men into action, and they lifted him to his feet where he clutched his left arm and followed her into the house, stepping over the body of the taller of the German which now lay slumped beside the one Jack had hit, and he listened as Evanthias spoke sharply to her husband. 'Demetrios, hurry! Take care of them!'

Stepping through the doorway, Jack almost tripped.

'You are weak, Jack. You're bleeding heavily. Sit here and I will get you some rum.'

As Evanthia tended to his shoulder, all the while thanking him for saving her son, Jack watched out the window as Danny, Leo and Demetrios dragged the lifeless bodies of the Germans across the yard. It was a nasty gash, and knowing that a bullet was lodged in Jack's shoulder, Evanthia considered aloud whether she should try to remove it. She probed the wound, apologising for the pain she was causing.

'Jack, I am going to have to leave the bullet. It has lodged deep in your shoulder. I fear that I will add to the damage if I dig around too much. For now, I will pack the wound to stop the bleeding, and then I will bandage it. When you get to Prevali, they will see that you get some medical attention.'

Jack nodded. He was happy for Evanthia to proceed as she saw fit. In truth, he was too dazed by the events of the last few minutes and the loss of blood to care what happened to his shoulder.

'Are you alright mate? We must get moving. If we stay around here, anything could happen,' Leo called from the doorway, and Jack knew that he was right. As much as he wanted to lie down and sleep, another group of German soldiers could appear at any minute. To stay in the house was to put Evanthia and Demetrios at terrible risk.

Evanthia rummaged through her cupboard, filling a bag with food for them to take, whilst Demetrios gave instructions.

'You must go this way,' Demetrios pointed towards the back of their property. 'If you follow those trees to the right for about two miles—see there, at that point where they dip— you will find a pathway leading down the valley. Wait at that point; hide in the bushes to the left of the path. I will get word to your escort party, and they will come and collect you. In a few days you will reach Prevali—once there, you will be safe. The abbot is an extraordinary man. He will look after you!'

Jack tried to ignore the burning in his shoulder as they made their way towards the trees and turned to the right, as Demetrios had instructed. There was no path, but rather dense forest. Weaving through the trees, and keeping the open fields to the right in sight, it took them almost an hour to travel the mere two miles to the dip, where a small creek flowed with crystal clear water. Without thinking, they crossed the stream and continued along the path, and before they knew it, found themselves on the verge of entering a busy thoroughfare, largely a bush track, but wide enough to take vehicles; and within minutes a jeep load of Germans careered into sight. Deciding that this was the junction which Demetrios had advised them to wait, they returned to the stream and sought shelter under the trees to the side of the track, glad for the bread and cheese that Evanthia had given them, before settling deeper in the cover of the bushes to rest.

Two hours later Jack woke to a sense of throbbing in his shoulder, and a short sharp whistling sound in his ears. He peeped through the bushes to see George looking bewildered in the clearing.

'Oh, thank God! There you are! Michael and I have been scouring the bushes a hundred yards farther down the track. Uncle is up at the next village resting. The boys couldn't find you, so Michael and I came back for you.'

'Sorry, mate,' Leo spoke for them. 'It's been a big night. We've been hiding in here waiting for you. I guess we fell asleep!'

'What is that, Jack? You've been injured! Is that a gunshot wound?' George's alarm at the sight of the bandage on Jack's shoulder was evident, and he and Michael launched into a conversation in Greek, their concerns for Jack's wound apparently impacting on their plan. Turning to Jack, George explained.

'Jack, this is very serious. If the Germans see you, they will be very angry. They are not fools. A gunshot wound will only mean one thing to them!'

'Yes, especially if they link it to the two bodies, buried under the wood heap back there!' Danny's information had the overtones of a braggart, and Jack knew that for as minuscule as the victory was in the

289

grand scheme of the thousands of Germans who'd invaded Crete, they'd all been thrilled to have had the opportunity to knock a couple of Germans off their perches before they left the island. George and Michael were less impressed.

'What! There are dead German soldiers!' Again they conspired, their faces grave, as they considered the situation.

'This is very serious! German patrols may be looking for you this very minute. We have to go!'

'Come, I will check the intersection, and will call for you when it is clear. You will see me ahead... I will point to the right, there is a track that you must follow. Michael and I will stay on the high road, you take the low track. We cannot afford for Germans to make a connection between us, lest they know we are leading you across the island... come on, this way! We have a long way to go today.'

George went first, waiting for a quiet moment to signal to them that it was safe to cross the intersection, and as they crossed and meandered along the track, they found he had waited for them. Jack listened as he pointed out a distant ridge where a church's steeple marked the village where they'd regroup for dinner, explaining how one of the runners would await their arrival in the woods behind the church and inform them of where they should camp for the night. George then pointed out the track to the right, apologising to them that their route would be long and difficult, but explaining that it was the best option, given the possibility that German soldiers were looking for them.

It was nightfall before they finally arrived at the village where they were quickly shown to a shed with a clean floor and a small canvas sack of bread, cooked lentils and potatoes. However, it was all Jack could do to stagger through the door, and drop to the ground, where he fell into a deep sleep without taking a bite.

Unlike the hospitality they'd enjoyed at Evanthia and Demetrios' home, the following week consisted of long days of walking through forests or narrow ridges, or separating as they crept across open fields, regrouping under the cover of foliage before continuing their journey.

The days were warm and some nights were spent sleeping outdoors, other nights in shepherd's huts or wood sheds at the back of farms where bags of fruit, loaves of bread and pies were left for them, but rarely did they speak to anybody. After almost three weeks of walking, they were in a state of constant exhaustion, and Jack's shoulder throbbed continuously, but he said nothing, for what was there to do but get to Prevali, where perhaps he could get some medicine to relieve the pain, and some fresh bandages. Mindlessly, he followed the steps of the others, concentrating on placing one foot in front of the other throughout the long days, before collapsing into dreamless sleep at night.

And when, after walking for a number of hours on a fine sunny morning, a blanket of glorious blue sea opened up before them, he, Leo and Danny stood gaping in astonishment. Small colourful vessels could be seen–fishing boats, they assumed—bobbing on the rolling swell of the ocean's surface. After weeks of trekking along forest tracks and crossing rocky fields, they'd finally arrived at the southern end of the island! With renewed energy and a burst of excitement, they scrambled along their path which now fell away into an almost vertical descent, and the narrow tracks they walked became a series of zigging and zagging stretches across the cliff face. Halfway down, they reached an outcrop of rocks, from where they could see a cluster of buildings nestled against the cliff below. They had reached Preveli!

# CHAPTER 29

*A*s they followed the stony path that meandered down the cliff to the beach, Jack couldn't believe his eyes. Amid the village, the Preveli Monastery was unmistakable—a large fortress like, clay-coloured construction with an extensive array of courtyards connected by walkways and stairs, that appeared to be built directly into the rocky cliff-face. Arriving at the foot of a stone stairwell, they were greeted by a tall heavily bearded man with piercing eyes, who introduced himself as Abbot Agathagelos, and offered them a warm welcome. He beckoned for them to follow him into a large room with a number of tables, and showed them to a bench where a pot of lamb stew emitted an enticing aroma, and crusty bread looked inviting. Additionally, there were dates, fruit, salad, cheese and wine, and he encouraged them to take their fill.

Suddenly, Georgios, George and Michael burst into the room, smiling broadly at the sight of the new arrivals and hugging them with delight. The men from Astakis, along with the youngsters, had arrived at Preveli two days earlier, their journey made easier by accessing a more direct track to the village than the one Jack, Leo and Danny had been forced to use. As they sat discussing their journey, a number of the monks joined them, and for an hour they shared raki, dates, cheese and stories of the events that had taken place on Crete over the past year. Their mood was victorious; rescue missions to remove allied soldiers off the island were complex, and each one a cause for celebration. Jack was amazed to hear how the monks had played an integral role in facilitating the return to safety of hundreds of the allied soldiers before winter, and now with the summer months upon them, would recommence their activities. Jack wondered if any others of their original fifteen—Roger and Saunders and Greaves and the others —had made it off the island. When Danny marvelled at the commitment of the monks, they replied with a shrug of nonchalance, and the abbot explained how for centuries the monks of Preveli's primary task had been to work with resistance movements during episodes when Crete's independence had been threatened. Whilst there had been numerous times where the monks had paid with their lives and the monastery had been destroyed, this had never stopped the monks of Preveli from fighting for freedom; they would rather die than submit to an enemy.

A smiling monk who sat between Jack and Abbot Agathagelos spoke up;

*"Saint John, there's a little dust in your courtyard, go in and out and clean it!"* He smiled and explained.

'This is our prayer for whatever enemy or problem comes along; get busy and fix it! This is what we do, and Saint John smiles at us, as he watches over us.'

The timing of their arrival was perfect, the Abbot was pleased to tell Jack, Leo and Danny. Any day now, he expected to hear the final details of a trawler that was being sent by the British Special Executive Operations unit; in three nights, a full moon would provide the perfect opportunity for the escape. Jack, Leo and Danny would board the trawler under the cover of darkness, along with over seventy men, who were now presently hidden in the outlying villages.

Jack avoided the eyes of Leo and Danny as they absorbed the news, for he was certain that like himself, theirs would be moist with emotion. It was almost impossible to take in, that finally, after almost eighteen months on Crete, they were leaving the island that very week!

At nine, the Abbot rose, and noticing the bloody stain on Jack's shoulder and his faltering energy, he led him to a small room, a monks

293

cell, Jack imagined, where his wound was cleaned and redressed by a kindly man, who expressed concern at the mangled raw flesh which was now inflamed and shrouded in a purulent discharge. As he offered Jack a dose of Laudanum and a sip of Ouzo to help relieve the pain, he sternly insisted that Jack must seek medical advice immediately on arrival at Alexandria, before leaving him to rest.

The following morning, with mixed emotions, they farewelled Giorgo, George, Michael and the youngsters who'd escorted them to the monastery. It was an emotional farewell, for how could they ever repay not only Marita and the villagers who'd cared for them for almost a year, but also these men who'd crossed Crete on an impossible journey to lead them to safety. Jack hoped that their return trip might be made easier by road, hopefully even aboard a vehicle.

And so it was that three nights later, Jack, Danny and Leo sat on the stony beach of Prevali waiting for the *Hedgehog*, the trawler coming to rescue them, alongside dozens of men, who like themselves had been living in caves supported by villagers all across Crete, waiting for the day when they would finally leave the island. Although the men tried to be quiet, a nervous excitement filled the air, for as close as they were to being rescued, there remained a fear that German soldiers might pour onto the shore with guns poised at any moment. Danny was beside himself with excitement for being reunited with some of the men from the 2/7th, and weepy with nostalgia for the time he'd spent living out the last eighteen months with Leo and Jack. Jack searched the men's faces, but didn't recognise anyone from the 2/5th. He was pleased to see Saunders; he'd always been sure that the Aboriginal man would have survived, although he didn't have good news of Roger and Cecil, who'd been captured by the Germans soon after the original fifteen soldiers had separated for fear of being caught.

At around eleven, the men went silent as the chugging of the trawler sent to rescue them could be heard closing in to the shore. Before they could climb aboard, there was work to be done to transport its full load of supplies that were being delivered to the monastery. The injury to Jack's shoulder prevented him from assisting, and for over an hour he watched as the men formed a human chain, lifting boxes and handing them along until they reached the beach, from where they were loaded onto donkeys and carted up the steep tracks by moonlight. Rations, clothing and rifles that would be distributed to the underground units on the island and gold sovereigns were given to the abbot, which he would distribute as compensation to the various agents who'd cared for the soldiers. Jack hoped that Michael and George would receive some coins to take back to Marita, for their support for himself, Danny and Leo over the last year.

Finally, they boarded the *Hedgehog*, and just after midnight, its engines thudded to life and started its journey southward. Looking back at the island, Jack watched as the mountains—their silhouette clearly visible by the light of the moon—receded into the distance. He was quite sure that if he never saw another mountain again, it wouldn't be too soon.

Onboard the *Hedgehog*, he was grateful to receive a change of clothing—the first clean clothes he'd had in months. Fruit and rum were quickly distributed; and together the rescued Allies sat, trying to muffle their laughter as they ate, drank and shared stories of how they'd survived the German occupation on Crete.

Despite his excitement at finally being rescued, within an hour, Jack felt the familiar throbbing in his shoulder accompanied by a flush of warmth, which radiated down his arm. He balled his left hand into a fist, and squeezed it a number of times, knowing that his hands too, were swollen. Taking a final deep swig of rum, he sought the welcome escape of sleep.

# CHAPTER 30

'*M*ate, we'd better take a look at that wound, don't you think?'

It was the next day, and the sun was high in the sky, its heat causing a lather of perspiration to form on Jack's forehead.

He heard the voice as though from a distance, and found the rocking motion of the boat comforting. Only when Jack felt the pull against his shirt did he realise it was to himself that the words had been directed.

Opening his eyes, he glanced towards the hands now tugging at the bandage on his shoulder.

'Roll over, mate.'

He noticed Leo sitting beside him—a frown of concern on his face, and looking down, he watched as the shirt which he'd been issued was pulled clear and the once white, then grey and now blackened bandage that he'd been wearing for the last few days was removed, exposing his shoulder. He crammed his head to see the wound; a mass of glistening flesh, red and white and raw, looking nothing like his normally smooth skinned shoulder. A tell-tale trickle of a greenish fluid seeped down his arm. At the sight of the wound, along with its rancid odour, Jack knew a serious infection had taken hold.

'Frank, can you get the medical kit?' the voice called, and Jack felt movement around him as the man studied the filthy dressing, before throwing it overboard.

'Shush… this is nasty. Hold still, now, while I get some iodine into it… Get ready for the sting.'

Jack jumped at the touch of the cold fluid against his skin and braced himself as the diligent officer probed his shoulder. As he pushed down on the wound, a thick green discharge emerged.

'My… it's a deep one! I'm no medic, but I reckon that you've got an abscess brewing here. The smell is enough to knock me out! I'll clean it up as best I can; the doctors at Alexandria will have to sort it out.'

*The doctors? What about the nurses? What about Sofia? She'll be waiting in Alexandria, and she'll get me better.*

Jack slumped back onto the deck, glad for the cool breeze wafting over him, while the man pushed, prodded, cleansed, dressed and bandaged his wound. As he encouraged Jack to lean forward so that he could place a sling around his neck to hold his arm firm, Jack started to shiver uncontrollably.

'Mate, we can't leave you here. Come on. We'll find a hammock below. We've got a couple more days before we get to Alexandria. You'll be more comfortable in a bed. Over here, private, we need to move this one—he's pretty ill.'

Jack felt himself being stood upright, and did his best to support himself as they half-dragged, half-carried him down a dark stairwell.

For the next two days, the officer fastidiously tended to Jack's arm, washing the bandage and hanging it off a rail to dry, administering iodine to the wound, water to his forehead and whisky to his lips. Little helped to lower Jack's temperature, and when the *Hedgehog* finally arrived at Port Said, he was barely conscious as they loaded him onto a stretcher, placed him in an ambulance and transferred him to the hospital.

# CHAPTER 31

*T*hree things assaulted Jack's senses as he drifted into wakefulness. The first was a feeling of coolness against his skin. No, not coolness, but bareness, softness,... tenderness, even. He was clean! Clean in a way that he hadn't felt in months. Perhaps years, even. Not only his body was clean, but so were the cotton pyjamas he was clad in, and the sheets that were draped over him. Then there was the odours. Jack felt as if he'd been immersed into a bath of antiseptic, and the pungent aroma of Lysol was almost overpowering. Finally, as he opened his eyes fully, Jack was conscious of the vividness of his surroundings. Crystal-clear, as though he were looking through a highly magnified lens. The predominant whites were brilliant, contrasted with a surgical green— deep and important looking—and the black curves of his iron bed frame gleamed; the glow that emitted from the lamp dangling from the ceiling was warm. It was an absence of dust, he realised, that had sharpened the details of the world. The lack of gravel and grit offered a cleanliness that felt utterly unfamiliar to him after months of living in caves and wandering the dry tracks of Crete, where the cleansing of body and clothing occurred in mountain pools and creeks, or leaning over a bucket of water beside an iron tank, as had been the case in Astikas.

He tried to lift himself, but his left shoulder was heavily bandaged and movement near impossible.

'Whoa, there, soldier. Here, let me help you. Where are you trying to go, exactly?' The voice was female, with a strong accent.

'I just need to move,' Jack said, his voice echoing in the large room as if it, too, had transformed into something utterly unfamiliar to him.

'Okay. We need to take this slowly, though. You have been very ill, you know, and your left side is out of action, what with the way that arm has been bandaged. How about we sit you up on the side of the bed for a couple of minutes? That might just do you for now.'

Jack nodded, already tired again. Sitting on the side of the bed suddenly seemed like a monumental effort. He slumped back.

'Perhaps I might just rest here for a bit....'

Later that afternoon he stirred again, and this time when he opened his eyes, his surroundings made more sense. The strong smell of disinfectant was offset by other odours: the rancid smell of infection, the fetid odour of a bowel movement—surely not his own, he hoped with alarm. And then there was an inviting smell of roasted potatoes and the sweetness of apples and custard. The latter, he realised, wafted from a covered plate set on the table next to his bed. He studied the row of beds along the wall opposite, each draped in white linen and containing a man in varying positions. One lay so still, Jack wondered if he were breathing; another, leaning up on his elbow, was shovelling food into his mouth hungrily with a fork. Another, sitting on the side of his bed, heaved heavily into a large silver dish. Jack recognised that he was in hospital.

'You awake, love?' The nurse was pretty, with a friendly smile. 'Hungry?'

Jack nodded.

'Of course you are. A silly question. You haven't eaten for three days—you must be famished. We'd better start with just a few mouthfuls lest you bring it all up again. Sometimes that happens, you know.'

Jack nodded, his mind trying to come to terms with his changed circumstances. The last things he remembered were the hours of hanging on to a rope and wading through salty water, emptying the trawler that was their rescue boat, of its supplies, before boarding it for the journey to Alexandria, he'd presumed. He'd been so pleased to be leaving the island. Pleased and tired, and he recalled slumping onto the deck, where he'd listened to the chattering of men even as he'd succumbed to sleep.

He recalled the kindly face of a private who offered sips of whisky and bandaged the wound on his shoulder.

Jack groped, his right hand reaching for his left shoulder. He could feel nothing other than a bulky dressing. Looking down, he saw the fingers of his left hand protruding high on the right side of his shoulder —held in place by a tightly bound sling.

'Don't try to move yourself,' the nurse said to him. 'I will get someone to help me. It's best we have someone on each side of you, lest you fall flat on your face.'

'Sofia?'

'No, I am Betty,' the nurse said.

'No, not you. Is Sofia here? Can I see her?'

'What do you mean? There is no one called Sofia on staff.'

'She is. I was told that I would find her here.'

'Where do you think you are, Jack?'

'Alexandria. That's where I was told that we were going.'

'Well, yes, you've got that right. We are in Alexandria. But there are no Sofias here that I've ever heard mentioned.'

'She's got to be… Please, can you go and check?' Jack could hear the warble in his voice and tried to control it. Here he was, finally in Alexandria, desperate to see Sofia, and this nurse was telling him that she'd never even heard of her!

'Look, Jack, let's get a few spoonfuls of this into you whilst it's warm, settle you back into bed, and then we can talk some more. I just need to find someone to help me.'

Half an hour later, the nurse sat beside Jack, a notepad in her hand.

'Tell me about Sofia, Jack. What was she doing here in Alexandria?'

'Nursing, I think.'

'You think?'

'Well, I was told that she was here.'

'And she is your sister...? Fiancé...?'

'No, no. My wife.'

'Your wife? Are you sure, Jack?'

'Yes, she's my wife. Of course I'm sure.'

'No, I meant, are you sure that she was here? Not many married women come out into the field hospitals.'

'I was told she is here. That everyone knows her. That she helps lots of men get better.' Jack could hear a shrillness enter his voice and took a deep breath.

'Who told you that, Jack?'

'Well, it was when we arrived at Crete. In those first few weeks. A young British private who'd almost lost his eye. She saved it. He told me so. He said it was Sofia, and she was asking after me.'

'What, you are one of the men who was taken off Crete last week! We heard that a few evacuations had taken place. Gosh. It's unbelievable. We thought you were all dead. Or that the Germans had taken you prisoner.'

'Not all of us,' Jack replied.

'True. Every so often we get a soldier from Crete admitted. No one for ages now, though.'

Later that evening, Betty was excited to report to Jack that not only had the AIF deemed him missing, but he had in fact officially been recorded as dead six months earlier.

Again, Jack could barely believe that he'd been in Crete for over twelve months. Certainly, it had been the beginning of summer when he'd arrived, and he had certainly experienced the cold of winter.

'So where is Sofia?' he asked yet again.

'Jack, the medical units here are constantly changing. Just because Sofia was here in 1941, it doesn't mean that she's here now. Which unit was she with?'

'I'm not sure,' Jack answered, convinced that the nurse was judging him for not knowing the whereabouts of his wife. Not to mention because his wife was on the frontline of a war zone, nursing out of canvas tents and inefficient makeshift wards in old buildings, rather than in the safety of a house with solid walls and a warm fire.

'So, she's with an Australian unit?'

'I just don't know,' Jack replied disconsolately. 'Perhaps French? Maybe British? She was travelling through Europe when war broke out.'

'Well, we have the Australian nurses, the London girls, even some from Ireland.'

'She'd be with the London girls, I suppose.' Jack heard the uncertainty in his own voice. Sofia was Spanish, and more recently, Australian. The thought of her now numbered amongst the British was difficult enough, without beginning to imagine that she'd gone beyond London.

'You aren't sure? Didn't you say that she was your wife?'

Jack groaned and rolled over.

~

Later in the evening, he spoke to the charge sister, who seemed more informed about the war hospitals.

'So, Jack, in January last year, we had the 133rd British General Unit, and after that the 148th, but they are war units. They follow the fronts and stay close to the fighting to receive the wounded soldiers directly off the battlefields. From here, the 133rd went on to South Africa; but really, it could be anywhere now; and of course, there's no saying that Sofia is still with them.

'The most important thing for you to think about is getting yourself better—doing everything possible to save that arm. We plan to get you back to Australia as quickly as we can. Your shoulder will need surgery and that is best done in Melbourne. There's a corvette heading there sometime next week. We'll get you on it, and have you home before you know it.'

'But I don't want to go to home. I need to stay here and find Sofia.'

'Jack, like I said, there is no Sofia here. I'll tell you what I will do. I'll put out a few memos. You can even write a letter and I will hang on to it until I can make contact with someone who knows about her.

That's the best we can do for now, I am afraid. There are people through here all the time. Somebody's bound to know something about her.'

Jack stared at her in disbelief, searching for a reply. How could he go home? He had to find Sofia. His mind whirled with ideas. Perhaps he could find a way to South Africa... follow the route that the British Medical Units took. As it turned out, Jack was going nowhere. Infection coursed from his shoulder to his fingertips, causing his arm to double in size; and he could barely move his fingers, his hand was so swollen. From this wound, the infection invaded his bloodstream, and with his body wracked with fever and delirium, the doctors battled, not just to save his arm—but to save his life. Hence, it was not until August that he was deemed fit enough for the sea journey, and early December, 1942, before he arrived in Australia.

# PART III

*MELBOURNE*

# CHAPTER 32

*J*ack squinted at the bright sunlight filtering through tall, narrow windows—one to his left, another to his right. Rippling flashes of gold and silver bounced off the walls. Tinsel? Christmas decorations? An overwhelming odour filled the air. Was it bleach or antiseptic?

A cheery voice startled him, and he turned to find a female wearing an apron and a nun-like white veil standing beside his bed. 'So, he's decided to come back and join us at last.'

It was then Jack realised that the source of the pungent odour came from a swab the woman held between the prongs of tweezers, and she was attending to his shoulder, which was draped in surgical green linen. A nurse? He tried to turn more, to see what she was doing.

'Don't move,' she said abruptly. 'I'll be finished here in a mo.'

'Where am I?'

'Melbourne, Australia. You are in Ward Six, the surgical ward of the Heidelberg Repatriation Hospital. It's Christmas Day, so Merry Christmas to you. You've been here for over a week now. That infection really had a hold on you. Mr Martin insisted that you go to theatre the minute he saw your shoulder; he wanted to clean your wound properly. It was touch and go for a while. You've been very ill. Mr Martin is good, though... saves dozens of lives with his endless fussing about antiseptics and hygiene. You've been lucky to have him. Your shoulder was a right old mess.'

Jack thought that the nurse sounded as if she was thrilled by the right old mess of his shoulder, enthused by the challenge of getting it better.

'Thank you.' He was surprised by the rasp in his voice.

'Our pleasure! We want to get you fellows well again, you know. This incision is pretty deep. But then again, Mr Martin had to go in a long way to remove a bone fragment and fix the damaged tendons. He couldn't stitch it properly—too much infection. He did what he could, but we've packed it with gauze, and now we have to let it heal from the inside, so it will take a while. You're actually doing quite well, all things considered.'

Jack nodded appreciatively, but he was too dazed to comprehend the details she'd just described. Her words became muffled, and he closed his eyes to escape the brightness that was giving him a headache.

Later that afternoon, Jack was again awoken, roused by the movement of two nurses who together encouraged him to sit upright and at least try to nibble on the plate of sandwiches they offered. This time, his mind felt a little clearer, and he did his best to assist them by leaning forwards as they packed pillows behind him. Despite the dryness of his mouth, Jack attempted to chew the food on the tray, alternating with sips from the cup of water they offered him. He felt like he might topple over at any minute; his sense of balance was upset as his left arm was rendered useless, now supported by a sling which had been bound firmly against his chest.

Jack tried to make sense of his surroundings. Melbourne? Australia? He was home!

Shortly after his lunch, he watched as an elderly couple entered the ward, their gait slow, the man shuffling on a walking frame. Tears sprang to his eyes as they approached his bed; it was his parents. He looked at them, and they at him, as if each barely believed what they saw.

It had been three years since they'd last seen each other, and clearly, much had changed.

'Jack. You are awake, at last! What a wonderful Christmas surprise this is!' His mother was the first to speak, wiping her eyes and gazing at him in disbelief. He felt her hand reaching for his forehead as though she were checking his temperature, a habit she'd had since when he was a small child. 'Thank God! I knew that you would return, despite... well. Never mind, you are here now and that is all that matters.'

Jack wondered what they had been told, and he felt pangs of guilt. He should have contacted them. Worked harder to get a message home to assure them he was okay. He tried to apologise, but Marian waved his words away.

'No, Jack. What are you apologising for? You have been terribly ill. Don't be so silly.'

He turned to his father, whose face was familiar, but his body that of an elderly stranger. The once-broad shoulders now slumped forward; the hands that had deftly worked his fountain pen and manipulated garden shears now grasped the handles of the metal walking frame as if that was their sole purpose. Tears streamed down hollowed cheeks, channelling towards the creases surrounding his mouth, and the rivulets flowed onto his chin. Clutching a handkerchief to his mouth, he attempted to speak.

'Ja...' he whispered.

'It's okay, William.' Marian patted his hand. 'Jack's awake now, and he's looking well, don't you think? Come now, let's sit for a minute.' She assisted William to sit on Jack's right, and Jack reached out and clung to the hand stretched towards him. He smiled at his father before turning back to his mother enquiringly. What had happened, he wondered, to cause William to be so debilitated?

Marian ignored the question in his eyes with a brief shake of her head. 'The matron has only given us half an hour, but still... its good of them, because it *is* outside visiting hours. They are usually terribly strict

309

about these things. We've been coming in each day to sit with you. We were in earlier, weren't we William, but you were still out to the world, Jack. We had to come back, though, when they phoned to tell us that you had woken. It's been over ten days since you got here. We've been waiting for this moment. I can barely believe that you are finally awake!'

'It's so good to see you both.' Jack's voice quivered with emotion as he looked between them. 'How is home? The garden? Your roses must be in bloom by now?' *What a funny thing to ask*, he thought.

'Yes, they are,' his mother replied. 'That's the thing about roses. The whole world goes to war, bombing and killing each other, and the roses—well, they just continue to form their perfect buds and burst into wonderful perfumed blooms, as if nothing's changed. They've been hard to appreciate, though, what with you missing and all. Mind you, on that Thursday, when we got the call that you were here, and… well… after laying eyes on you and learning that you were going to be okay, we went home and I made us a cup of tea, and we sat in the garden, inhaling every ounce of the sweetness of the air, and we thanked God, didn't we, William? And I am telling you, Jack, even though it's overgrown and the weeds have gone mad, my garden has never looked more beautiful than it does now that I know that you are home and safe.'

Jack nodded and again turned to his father.

'Dad! It is so good to see you!'

William nodded, his blue eyes sharp, albeit watery, and more tears spilled down his cheeks.

Jack looked at his mother. 'What has happened?' he asked.

'We got a letter that you were missing, Jack. It came last June. It didn't offer any words of hope and… well, of course, we were shattered. Dad took a little turn, but you are getting much better, now, aren't you, William dear? It's wonderful to see Jack looking so well, isn't it?'

William nodded, again grunting, trying to speak words that refused to form, and Marian intervened on his behalf. 'Dad's so pleased to see you, Jack. We both are. It's an answered prayer. I kept saying to William, "Our Jack is fine. He will be home soon." I just knew it, Jack, the same way that I know that the sky is blue and the grass is green. And here you are!'

~

Jack's second visitor for the day was Margaret, who arrived minutes after his parents left, flying into the ward, accompanied by the strident tones of a none-too-happy charge nurse calling, 'Five minutes and not a second longer. These men need their rest!'

Flinging her arms around Jack, she hugged him tightly.

'Jeez, Margaret! Watch a man's arm, won't you? You'll open my wound and then I will be back in surgery, being put back together again.'

'What happened to you? Why didn't you write?' Margaret sounded at once annoyed and relieved.

'Well, darn the war, I told myself. Why dodge bullets and throw grenades around when I could camp out on a tropical island in the middle of the Mediterranean and leave the world to deal with the craziness all to itself? You know, palm trees swaying... great food... swimming and fishing. It was like heaven on earth! No post office, though, I'm sorry to say!'

'You're lying, Jack. That was no tropical island holiday, that's for sure! You were on Crete, forced into hiding from the Germans. I have my information. I was sure that you had been taken prisoner—heaven forbid! When we didn't hear from you... well, I wrote to every person I could, trying to piece together what had happened. I traced you from Bardia to Tobruk and then to Greece. They told me about the sinking of the *Costa Rica:* and given that only one death was reported, I was confident that you had survived that. But then all the information got a little obscure. It took ages to work out whether you managed to escape to Africa or Palestine or wherever. No one would tell me anything. To be honest, there were so many mixed stories, I think that even the army is in a state of confusion about it all. A bit embarrassing for them to lose so many men.

'I finally concluded that you were most likely on Crete, one of the thousands left behind after the evacuation. Damn the army for leaving you! You were abandoned as far as I am concerned, and I let them know it, too. The whole operation sounds like it was a first-class disaster. They would have got you out, they told me, but what with the Japanese entering the war, all attention was turned to the Pacific. It was near impossible to find out anything from them after that, and they as good as told me to give up, implying, of course, that you had probably been killed. God, I hate war!'

Margaret's tone reeked of bitterness, and Jack did not smile. He knew that his circumstances—missing in action—would have been an awful reminder of the love she'd never forgotten nor replaced, when over twenty years earlier he'd been killed in the Great War. Jack also knew that, had he not come back, she would have been shattered.

'Well, here I am, Margaret, so you can stop worrying about me now. And look at you; what is that you're wearing?'

Margaret looked rueful as she ran her hands down the sides of her jacket. 'I am not saying that I agree with war, Jack. In fact, at heart I am a rampant conscientious objector, but after you left, I felt that I should do my bit. I couldn't see myself knitting socks or sewing uniforms, but the Explosives Factory Maribyrnong seemed to be a worthwhile project. Who knows, perhaps one of the bullets that I make might save some young man's life.'

Jack restrained himself from replying that bullets usually ended the lives of young men. Margaret knew that, firsthand.

She continued, 'Not that I'd mind firing a bullet or two into any Nazi that cares to come my way. I hate thinking about all the fellows that we send to the other side of the world to fight battles that...'

She never finished her rant, for the formidable charge sister appeared.

'Miss, it is time for you to leave. Now!' The sister's tone was absolute, quelling even Margaret's objections.

'Right-o. Bye for now, Jack. I will be back as soon as I can.' She quickly hugged him one more time before scurrying from the ward under the charge nurse's reproving gaze.

❧

Over the following weeks, the highlight of the long days on the ward was the routine of watery scrambled eggs, cold toast, tepid cups of tea and overcooked roasts and lemon sago pudding, of which Jack loved every mouthful. After years of roughing it in the army barracks, and then on the war fronts, and then on the island, he couldn't deny that it was pleasant to revel in the comfort and safety of home. Nonetheless, it did not stop Jack from joining in the other men's favourite sport: complaining loudly, teasing each other and chatting with the nurses, whose pleasant laughter and witty banter brightened their days.

His shoulder was dressed three times a day, its gash horribly deep, slow healing and repeatedly dogged by infection despite the nurse's best efforts to keep it clean. The nurses and doctors were in constant discussion about how it should be managed and various treatments were tried, with varying degrees of success. Jack had no doubts that had the wound been lower on his arm, the limb would have been removed without hesitation, and he would be left with a neat, clean stump for his left appendage. He wasn't sure that he would have minded, given the pain that he suffered each time the nursing sisters rattled their stainless steel dressing trolley towards him—continuously battling the wonky rear wheel that refused to align with its three counterparts—in readiness to cleanse his shoulder and replace the purulent dressings.

'Got your licence for that beast?' could be heard through the ward a dozen times a day, along with disparaging comments about women drivers. It was a credit to the patience of the nurses that they listened to the tired old jokes with such humour.

Before they even had to ask, Jack got into the habit of rolling over, baring his shoulder and gritting his teeth before swabs doused in saline and peroxide scoured the hole in his flesh. Gauze soaked in Acriflavine packed the cavity, with a layer of padding applied over that to provide protection; and then the whole affair was bandaged and strapped into a sling. Jack's ability to move was hindered by the immobility of his left arm—but that was all—and he knew that he was luckier than most of the men here. He was able to sit, stand and walk, and he passed the hours sitting beside those unable to leave their beds, fetching a urinal or extra blanket, and passing cups of tea to those with lost limbs, shattered nerves or any number of other equally debilitating injuries.

Alternatively, he'd go outside, joining the men who sat in the sunshine, smoking, playing cards and sharing stories of their time overseas.

Many of the men had been in the hospital for months, and although they were ready for discharge, they were reluctant to leave—anxious about what their futures held in the civilian world. Jack understood their fear of living amongst people to whom the loss of a leg, a cringe at imagined bullets ricocheting through a fragile mind, or a patch on an empty eye socket invited questions that were impossible to answer. And, for all of the grumbles about 'getting out of this prison,' when the nurses were bossing them, it was easy to see that many of the men were thrilled when one ailment or another held the time for their discharge at bay.

A cocktail of morphine mixture, taken morning and night, kept Jack pain-free, though nothing helped to quell the discomfort induced by the regime of penicillin injections administered daily. The wonder drug was going to kill his shoulder's lingering infection and thus save his arm, so he was told.

The injections were absolute agony—a thick, creamy concoction that was plunged deep into his gluteal muscle via needles as thick as a straw, attached to glass syringes that squeaked their resistance to being plunged. They might have been sharp once, but endless stabbings, cleanings and autoclave treatments had left them blunt—and daily the nurses cursed before stabbing his exposed rear, apologising in advance for the pain they were inflicting.

Jack was not alone in his dread of the penicillin injections. The sight of nurses approaching with their kidney dishes always brought howls of complaint from across the ward. 'Whoa, has that got a barb in it? What are you trying to do, catch a flounder?' the men often cried, or 'Those German bayonets were nothing compared to these bloody needles!'

With grim humour, they laughed at each other's pain, and the recipients made unseemly gestures to their teasing ward-mates before setting their jaws in readiness to endure the torture. Jack always knew when the brisk footsteps were coming his way, as if the glass syringe rattling in the silver kidney dish had its own signal for him. Ignoring the jokes of those around him, he'd roll over and cast his mind to those around him with shocking injuries they'd received on the battlefield. The pain of these lifesaving injections was trifling compared to the agonising wounds that some of these boys would carry for the rest of their lives. A hole in his left shoulder, and possibly an arm with limited movement, was nothing compared to missing limbs and blinded eyes. He was one of the lucky ones, he knew.

# CHAPTER 33

*I*n early March, Jack was surprised by the sight of a man approaching his bed, who greeted him with the warm familiarity of an old friend. 'Captain Tomlinson, how are you?'

It was John Treloar, Jack realised, the man who worked for the army's Department of Information. The man he'd met in Alexandria two years earlier and who, with the stroke of a pen, had reassigned Jack's status from private to captain and reallocated his commission from soldier to war artist. Inwardly, Jack squirmed, feeling a little fraudulent. He wondered if he was about to be officially reprimanded for dereliction of duties. As his Cretan ordeal had unfolded, opportunities to draw soldiers on the battlefield had ceased and all he had to offer Treloar were village scenes.

'So, Jack, I am glad to see you back. Very glad! I'm supposed to look after my war artists, be responsible for your health and well-being. As you might imagine, I was a little concerned when you went missing on me for almost two years! It was a happy day when I heard that you were back in Australia, and I am sure that your family is pleased as well.'

'Yes, sir,' Jack responded, wondering what Treloar might be expecting from him now.

'That friend of yours—Margaret—she was like a dog with a bone.

She harassed me non-stop, week after week, wanting to know what had happened to you. I don't like to think what she might have done with me if you hadn't returned!'

Jack laughed, relaxed by Treloar's humour. 'Yes, she's been known to take quite a few men apart in her time. I am rather glad that she is on our side and not the enemy's.'

'So, it's just your shoulder? Your left shoulder? Everything else is okay?'

Jack nodded.

'I can see that your right hand is safe. Do you think that you will be right to paint again? I mean, not now, but when you are feeling better?'

'I expect so. There is nothing wrong with my right arm, although painting one-handed might prove a bit tricky. I'm happy to give it a try. Mr Martin—my surgeon—believes my left arm should come good, once the wound heals and I do some rehabilitation exercises. It will probably be a bit stiff for a while. Time will tell, sir.'

'Right-o, then. That's wonderful. Anyway, never mind painting for now. I really just popped in to see that you were okay. War is the darndest thing, but at least you are alive!'

'Thank you, sir. I appreciate your bothering to come and see me.'

'Not a problem. If you like, I'll fish out some of those sketches of yours. If you are at loose ends, you might like to sort through them.

True to his word, the following week, Treloar arrived, bearing a satchel filled with sketchbooks. Picking out one, Jack noted how a front sheet had been attached that included a description of the work on each page.

There were over eighty sketches that he'd put together from Alexandria to Bardia to Tobruk. Looking through the drawings, Jack felt it all coming back to him. Not just the places, but the sound of the men's voices—Shorty, Snowy and Macka. Turning the pages, he saw them jogging in single file towards Bardia and then, a few pages later, in similar scenes at Tobruk. He wondered how they were. He could smell the cordite and taste the dust. Looking at the first sketch he'd done at Bardia, took him straight back to those early hours of shivering in the cold, waiting for the battle to begin; the dreadful combination of thrill and fear as he'd stood watching as the flickering fingerlings of sunrays filtered across the desert. He inhaled deeply as he relived the anticipation for the call of 'fire', heralding a cacophony of whistling bombs and thudding twenty-five-pounders, amid flashing lights and choking gunpowder, into which the men of the 17th had made their advance.

Jack smiled at his sketch of enemy POWs held behind the barbed wire enclosure, remembering the 2/7th singing with the Italian prisoners. He recalled how elated they'd all been after defeating the Italians in both Bardia and Tobruk, and how desperately they'd waited for their chance to be let loose on the Germans.

Lifting a second bundle from the bag Treloar had brought in, Jack realised it was, in fact, the package that he'd left with Marita. She'd found a way to send them after all, despite his insistence that she not take the risk. To have been caught with these drawings, portraying scenes around Suva Bay prior to the German invasion, the Fallschirmjäger dropping from the sky and sketches of young Cretan children playing cricket with Leo and Danny in Astikas, could have been a death sentence for her. He hoped that she was safe.

Glancing through the images, he thought of George and Michael, and Marita's uncle, whose lamp in the window had warned them when the village was unsafe. What extraordinary people the Cretans were, resisting the invasion of their island and caring for the Allies who'd been left behind as though they were family.

Jack flicked between the pages and waves of emotion ran through him. The battles depicted here were no longer with the Italians, but rather the Germans. There were the half a dozen sketches he'd completed around Kalamata, following the disastrous confrontation with the Germans in Larissa and before boarding the *Costa Rica*.

Jack looked closely at the scenes he'd drawn on the beach at Suda and those of the Fallschirmjägers tumbling from the skies above the Retimo Airfield, lost in his memories of the madness of that day, when Treloar spoke.

'This would make a wonderful painting, Jack. We have some camera footage of it, but a painting… it would be extraordinary!'

Jack nodded. 'Yes, sir. I knew, even as I sketched these, how they should be painted. No ordinary painting could portray the insanity of that day. These parachutists—they looked so beautiful, drifting on the breeze like dandelions on an air current. And then, as soon as they reached our gun range, we picked them off as if they were no more than wild ducks. Bang, bang, bang. It was surreal, seeing them slump, knowing that they were dead, and that is how it must be painted.'

Treloar nodded and looked at him curiously.

'You are the artist, Jack. You do what you think. After all, you can paint the scene a dozen times if you wish, until you are happy with it.'

Treloar did not stay long; it was as though he knew that Jack's reunion with his memories was deeply personal, and Jack appreciated his thoughtfulness.

He flipped through the pages a second time, this time looking for a specific image. It didn't take long. It was the drawing of the young Italian soldier who had lain on the ground in Bardia, his blood spilling from his leg. Just looking at his drawing reminded Jack of the lad, his face calm and resolute; how he'd gratefully accepted the sip of water Jack had offered, and then, in the shelter of Jack's shadow, he'd taken his last breaths.

Breathing deeply, he turned the page, gently passing his hand over the words the boy had scrawled. Written in Italian, they were indecipherable to Jack, but he recalled the promise he'd given: that he would send this message to the boy's loved ones. The number that Jack had recorded was clear, taken from the boy's tag. Hopefully, it would allow him to trace the family. He'd ask Treloar. The man seemed compassionate, and Jack thought that he would understand the gesture. It wasn't the thing to consort with the enemy, but those minutes beside the dying lad had been Jack's first encounter with death, and the boy was just that—a boy, dying for his country in the same way that Australian lads died for theirs. Nothing to do with right or wrong, friend or foe. Just a young man whose family loved him, and who'd doubtless want to learn something of their son's last moments and be glad to know that he had not died alone.

~

Three weeks later, Marian was excited when Jack asked if she could bring his old easel into the hospital, and he knew that she saw it as a sign that he was getting well. Treloar, also gladdened to see Jack improving and keen to encourage him to create paintings for the War Memorial, had already purchased a supply of paints and a roll of canvas. Very quickly it became a combined goal, with the rehabilitation officer putting a couple of soldiers to work banging together timber to create frames and, following Jack's instructions, helping him to stretch and prepare the canvas in readiness for painting. His left hand was useful for holding things, but the weakness in his shoulder limited his ability to lift anything heavier than a feather.

As soon as the first canvas was ready, Jack began painting. He decided to work in chronological order, thinking it would help to reconnect with the various emotions he'd experienced, and in doing so, ensure his paintings would better depict the truth of the events.

Treloar visited weekly, not only to check on the progress of the paintings, but also showing a genuine interest in his recovery—which was slow—and Jack realised that Treloar took the responsibility of managing his war artists' welfare seriously.

Each time he visited, they chatted for half an hour or so. Jack found the man interesting and was fascinated to learn how an idea born two decades earlier had been realised; and now an Australian War Memorial had been built in Australia's capital city because of their determination and fundraising. The idea had come to Charles Bean when he and Treloar had worked in London during the Great War, and together they'd ensured the return to Australia of the artefacts they believed were the property of Australians.

'You wouldn't believe what we managed to bring out,' he said. 'Thousands... tens of thousands... letters, photos, film and more. A shipload! There was no way that I was going to leave it for the British to use in their Memorial—they had enough of their own material. It's all here in Melbourne. I'll show you one day. And now, with our War

Memorial finally opened, I am slowly transferring everything to Canberra. It's wonderful!'

It was obvious that Bean and Treloar had made a formidable partnership; Bean, it seemed, was a man with a big vision, while Treloar had the skills and patience to painstakingly identify, categorise and pack over 25,000 items. What Jack also realised was that, even greater than Treloar's passion for collecting items was his determination to uncover the stories behind each. He was dedicated to creating not only an accurate record of war history, but also a display that was interesting to military historians and the public alike.

It was through their chats that Jack discovered Treloar was no longer employed by the Department of Information—something he was very pleased about.

'Thank God I left all that behind. We were expected to distribute factual information to keep the public informed, and yet were being instructed by the politicians of the need to keep the public happy! Honestly, in wartime, the facts are hardly likely to keep anybody happy. And the very notion that the Department could report the facts of war alongside propaganda and censorship was ridiculous.' But that had been only half of Treloar's problem.

'The worst of it was that I was expected to spruik about how successful the government was in its handling of the war, and hence promote its political ideology. The whole situation was appalling, what with the various prime ministers complaining that they were being under-acknowledged, the Opposition questioning everything we released and the poor public quite rightly annoyed that they were being fed sunshine and fairy tales.'

'Yes, I remember my friends saying exactly that,' Jack replied, recalling Neil's and John's grumblings about the newspaper articles they'd read even before Jack had enlisted.

To Treloar's relief, his complaints about the work at the Department of Information had been accepted and he had been allocated the role of Director of War Records, which had been expanded to include Military History and Information; and Treloar now worked out of the Victorian Barracks, just near the city, where his collection was stored.

While he was reserved about his personal life, Jack learned of his love of cricket, his commitment to his Methodist faith and his fears for his son. Warrant Officer Ian Treloar was currently missing in action: presumed dead.

'I can't help but believe that he's okay, Jack,' Treloar confided. 'Look at you. We were sure that you were gone... and here you are. Anything's possible.'

Jack dearly hoped that Treloar was right, and that his son was safe.

It was in the spirit of this disclosure that when next Treloar arrived, Jack produced an envelope, and emptying it, he unfolded the letter he'd written to an Italian mother he'd never met, where he'd described the circumstances of her son's death. Jack also showed Treloar the message that the boy had written and a sketch that he'd made, where the young man looked peaceful and rested. He asked if Treloar might be able to locate the origins of the boy's village based on the official number Jack had recorded, and perhaps get the documents to the family.

'Sure Jack, I'll see what I can do. I agree, the family would undoubtedly be thankful to hear words of his final moments. I know that I would be.'

# CHAPTER 34

*J*ack was surprised when, in late August, Treloar arrived, accompanied by a lady. Tall and slender, with fairish hair and a wry expression, she looked decidedly uncomfortable in her pencil-thin skirt and army jacket. The stripes on her shoulder revealed that she shared the rank of captain with Jack, and he saluted her. She was the first female captain that Jack had ever met, and he was amused to see her blush even as she fumbled a salute in reply.

Treloar was formal with his introductions. 'Captain Tomlinson, I'd like you to meet Captain Heysen. She, too, is one of our war artists and, indeed, the first female to join our team. Captain Heysen will be painting the women's services—nurses, munitions workers and so on. Her work will be a very valuable addition to the War Memorial's collection, don't you agree?'

Jack nodded, surprised at the incongruity of women artists, who struggled to gain respect within the art world in Australia, being shown respect from the military.

Treloar continued. 'Nora... Captain Heysen is Hans Heysen's daughter. You might have heard of him—the landscape artist? Very good, he is. A Director of the South Australian Gallery. He paints some of Australia's best landscapes, so Captain Heysen certainly comes with a good pedigree. I thought that since you were here, you might show her your work. Give her a sense of what we are doing for the Memorial.'

Hans Heysen's daughter! Of course, Jack had heard of Hans Heysen. Like Streeton and McCubbin, Heysen was well-known for his watercolour paintings of the Australian bush, and his exhibitions had often been featured in the newspapers.

'Certainly. It would be a pleasure.' Jack led them to the small area where he'd set up his painting materials. To the delight of his rehabilitation officer, Jack was increasingly spending a few hours wielding a brush before the fatigue that continuously dogged him resurfaced and sent him back to his bed for a rest.

Captain Heysen's expression revealed little as she studied the painting resting on the easel, a scene from the battle of Tobruk.

'And this was started during the fighting?'

'No, not during the battle. But while it was happening, I did some sketches… dozens of them. The landscape and the buildings. The planes coming in and the Matildas and infantry all doing their jobs. It is only now that I'm putting it all together.'

Treloar spied Jack's drawing books containing the sketches he'd made in Egypt and Libya. 'Do you mind, Jack?' he asked, before selecting one and handing it to Captain Heysen.

Again, the captain's face was blank as she turned the pages, one by one.

'See, Nora, how Jack captures the grit and determination of the soldiers as they enter the battle?'

Captain Heysen's reply was curt. 'Yes, John. I guess if one were in the battlefield, "grit and determination" would be a feature, but the women whose portraits you have me painting, with their dull uniforms and expressions of desperation to get back to their work after half an hour with me, do not lend themselves to grit and determination. Unless, of course, it is their determination to see me banished from their presence.'

Jack was both shocked and amused at the woman's disrespectful tone. It was obvious that she did not share the same easy relationship with Treloar that he did. To the older man's credit, his reply was patient.

'Now, Captain, you know it would not be right for a young woman to be out on the war front. What do you say, Jack? You'd agree that the battlefield is no place for a lady?'

Jack's thoughts turned to those women he'd seen clubbing the German parachutists who'd fallen from the skies onto the airfields of Crete; of Marita, moving across the mountains in her disguise; collaborating as an equal with the men of Crete; of the way Evanthia had so quickly and coolly responded the crisis of two dead German soldiers on her doorstep. Women determined to thwart the stranglehold the Germans had on their home territory.

He thought of Sofia, trying to capture an elusive image of his wife working under the flimsy canvas of the temporary hospitals set up as close to the front lines as possible, in earshot of exploding bombs and enemy gunfire as she tended to bodies broken on the battlefield—dressing wounds where flesh was torn by bullets and saving the eyes of wounded soldiers. Jack had no doubts that she would undertake duties on the war front with the same diligence and courage of any man.

He felt the cool grey eyes of the captain upon him, awaiting his response.

'I am not so sure, sir. From my own experience, women can be every bit as tough and clear-sighted as the men on the battlefield. Yes, it is dangerous, of that there is no doubt. But, by golly, in Crete many a woman stared down the enemy, thought quickly and endured hardship with a stoicism equal to that of the men that I served with—and some, with a lot more.'

'Humph. Well, yes, we'll see.' Treloar changed the subject and Jack knew that he hadn't provided the answer that Treloar had hoped for.

Gesturing to a painting set against the wall that depicted a ragged group of soldiers making their way along a steep, mountainous track, Treloar pointed out the two soldiers at the rear: how between them, a third—a man whose leg had been seriously injured—was being supported.

'So, Captain, what we are looking to paint is the truth of war. The triumphs and the trials. Not a rose-coloured picture of glory, but rather the story of hardship and mateship, as men–men *and women*–serve their country under terrible circumstances.'

Listening to Treloar, Jack was taken aback. That word—truth—so often repeated in the world of art, was here again, and it disturbed him. What was the truth of war? he wondered. Did anyone really know? Certainly, he'd learned as well as any soldier that it was the pounding of bombs, of chaos and yelling. Screams of warning and pain. War was men leaping overboard, risking their lives to save their mates, and it was civilians being lined up and shot because they'd offered food and drink to fellow human beings. But if that was the truth of war, could it ever be captured in a painting? Could feelings of terror or the smell of blood or the plunging of a bayonet into flesh be depicted by paints and a brush? Jack thought not. A war painting might evoke emotions for those who'd been there—who had heard the screams of their mate writhing in agony, or the shriek of a bomb whistling through the sky before erupting with a deafening thud that shook the ground and destroyed everything in its wake, or who'd seen a mother sobbing as she held a dying child—but for everyone else, paintings surely represented but a shadow of the truth of war.

# CHAPTER 35

*J*ack was surprised when Captain Heysen returned the
following day, this time alone. She wanted to know more
about his experiences as a war artist, she told him; and he
felt fraudulent as he answered her questions, for in his mind he'd made
a poor job of the role over the last two years.

Notwithstanding, even in the mountains of Crete, his artist's eye
and lifetime practice of observing and sketching human experiences
had stayed with him; and it was those moments that he referred to as he
spoke, describing scenes of ordinariness amid the horrors of the
island's occupation by the Germans. Children playing cricket with
soldiers. Young men, lifeless, their bodies forever stilled, but warm;
their faces young, their futures robbed from them as they'd fought the
enemies of their nation and lost. The everyday lives of soldiers as they
sat around sharing cigarettes, talking and playing two-up. The moment
when a man received a letter from a loved one, or the grim silence of
those who had not. How some fellows joked around to hide their hurts
and fears, and you'd just wish that they'd break and get it all out.

Over an hour had passed when, glancing at her watch, the captain
rose to leave, late for an appointment—a sitting with the Head Nurse of
the Infectious Diseases Ward.

'Do you mind if I come back again, Captain?' she asked. 'I have at least a thousand more questions for you.'

'Not at all, as long as you stop calling me Captain,' he laughed. 'My name is Jack, and it's nice to be able to talk about painting with someone for a change.'

'Okay, and you must call me Nora! Much better.' She grinned as she saluted him, the gesture light-hearted, as though she felt obliged to adhere to the formality of army protocols but didn't want to appear to be taking things too seriously. Chuckling, he returned her salute.

∼

Jack was sitting outside, enjoying the afternoon sunshine, when Nora returned two days later, her arms full with a brown paper bag precariously balanced on top of a large folder. The bag emitted the enticing aroma of cinnamon, and on opening, it revealed two apple slices, freshly baked. The folder held a large sketchbook—Nora's artwork. Her greeting was somewhat shy, as though she wasn't sure if Jack would appreciate either of her offerings, which she placed on the table before leaving him in search of a pot of tea and some plates.

Afterward, sipping his tea, Jack determined that today he would do more listening than talking. He was interested to hear about Nora's life as the daughter of a famous artist and, to that end, asked about her life.

She told him about her family home in South Australia, a beautiful property called Cedars, and although he commented that it sounded idyllic, from Nora's nonchalant expression and shrug, Jack gleaned that her childhood had been less than perfect.

She changed the subject quickly, turning the conversation to painting, and as Jack leafed through her drawing book, dozens of marvellous sketches of still-lifes, flowers and portraits leapt out at him. To his mortification, he recognised that Nora was exceptionally gifted.

'Nora, these are wonderful! Wow! You certainly have a good eye,' he commented enthusiastically.

She smiled at Jack's praise, and he wondered if she'd brought her drawing book specifically to demonstrate that, although she may be a recently appointed war artist and the daughter of a famous painter, she was not the amateur that Treloar had positioned her to be.

Turning a page, Jack looked closely at a half a dozen small tonal sketches beside a larger drawing. The subject was familiar: a woman in a jacket. Beside it, a row of paint strokes foretold the richly coloured palette that Nora had planned for the painting. A jewel-like crimson, a deep blue, the palest of greys and a soft rose. And then it came to him —how had he not realised!

'Nora, this work is familiar to me. Are you... did you win the Archibald Prize a couple of years back? Before the war?' Even asking seemed foolish. Surely if Nora had won the Archibald, Treloar would have mentioned it!

The mischievous spark in her eyes was a sure indication that Jack was correct.

'Why, yes, I did, as a matter of fact. 1938. Lucky me,' she demurred.

'But that's wonderful! And here was I, prattling on about how you should approach your drawings! You! An Archibald winner! Why didn't you stop me?'

'Well, the thing is, Jack, don't you know that women can't really paint?' she teased. 'I probably only won it because I am Hans Heysen's daughter. At least, that's what a lot of people believe.'

Jack nodded, recalling the afternoon he'd stood at the National Gallery before Nora's painting five years earlier and overheard Max Meldrum say that very thing.

'But your portrait was amazing. You absolutely deserved to win. What a wonderful honour! Congratulations to you! Surely women everywhere were thrilled! My friend, Margaret—she raved about your win. She was over the moon!'

'Not everybody shared her joy, I am sorry to say. The men couldn't believe that they'd been ousted by a woman. A few of them even banded together to have the decision overturned, can you believe it? And then there were the women's responses! One began a campaign, publicly demanding that I return my prize money. Of course, it all got played out in the newspapers. Truly, it was one of the worst experiences in my life!'

'Oh, no, Nora. That is awful! People should have been thrilled for you, excited to see a woman recognised for her marvellous work! Imagine you being the first woman to win the prize! What an honour!'

Nora shook her head, her laughter ringing across the garden. It attracted the attention of a group of men sitting smoking nearby, who were pretending to be oblivious to the attractive female bearing the rank of captain in their midst.

'You should have seen the women's magazines, Jack! I think that is what really got to me. *The Women's Weekly* actually had a photograph of me at my kitchen sink, chopping carrots, of all things, with the headline, "Girl Painter Who Won Art Prize is Also a Good Cook."' As she giggled helplessly, tears of laughter filled Nora's eyes. Or were they of laughter? Jack wondered.

'Who is she?' he asked, returning his attention to Nora's sketch.

'The esteemed Madame Elink Schuurman, wife of the Consul General of the Netherlands. And, I must say, that is a whole other story! Truly, the sittings were dreadful. Madame's a socialite, without a brain in her head. I only chose her because I thought that she would be a nice hanger for that gorgeous Chinese jacket—mine, of course. I knew it would make a wonderful painting, but didn't Madame Schuurman turn out to be a nightmare to paint! She sat for me twice and then made every excuse under the sun to avoid me. Headaches, toothaches… I had to bully her mercilessly until she finally completed the sit, tears streaming down her face as though she were a five-year-old. Honestly! And then, of course, when I won the prize, she was ecstatic! You'd have thought we'd been partners in the project—that it had been her idea to commission me to paint her portrait.' Jack laughed, imagining the scenes Nora had described.

'Listen, Nora! You've won the most prestigious prize in Australian portraiture! Nobody can take that away from you, so take no notice of the small-minded people who opposed your win,' Jack said, deeply impressed by her achievement.

'The sad thing about the whole experience was that, with all the controversy about my winning, the judges won't be game to grant the prize to a woman ever again! Instead of opening the door to women artists, I think that I have ruined it for them forever.

Nonetheless, I did win near five hundred pounds, so that was a blessing!'

Jack laughed with Nora, admiring her spunk.

～

Over the next few weeks, Jack deflected comments about 'The Captain' from the men on the ward.

'Will we be seeing The Captain today?' became a daily question, which developed into more pointed teasing. 'We're happy to clear the room if you and your girlfriend would like a little privacy.'

Although he laughed at the comments, inwardly Jack felt twinges of guilt for being the target of banter about a woman. But it was the comment from one of the nurses—half-serious, half-joking—that really provoked him.

'Perhaps you might like to surprise The Captain by placing a diamond on her finger. I doubt that she'd say no!'

That night, lying in bed, Jack gazed at the well worn photographs that had accompanied him across the world and back again, and he agonised over Sofia for the thousandth time—wondering where she was, how might he find her? Surely the world wasn't that big! She had to be somewhere. How many nursing units could there be? Jack decided that he would write letters to London. Perhaps someone here at Heidelberg—the ward's charge nurse, for instance—might suggest a contact in the British Nursing Service who could provide some helpful information.

When he finally fell asleep, Jack dreamt that he was back at the finca, reclining under the orange trees with Sofia. He'd held her in his arms just like he used to during siesta, when he and Sofia had carried their blanket outside and spread it under the trees. Holding each other close, they'd discussed their plans to return to Paris, Andrés' illness that was getting worse, and the child that they both had longed for.

Then Scotty had made a rare appearance, his presence so real that when he woke, Jack felt shaken to his core. The truth was that their little boy had never been in Spain. But in his dream, Scotty had been full of lively mischief, determinedly clambering over their bodies as though he were conquering mountains, just as he once did when they'd lain together in their cosy bed at Montsalvat.

On waking, Jack's arms felt warm from having embraced the wife he hadn't touched in years, his nostrils filled with the fragrance of orange blossom blended with the sweet aroma of Scotty that he'd never inhale again. Suddenly, the barrenness of the hospital ward seemed unbearable. Groaning, Jack squeezed back the tears that welled up and rued his losses. Again, he closed his eyes, wanting to recapture his dream and for a few more minutes, be with the two people he loved more than anything else in this world.

Even after he arose from his bed an hour later, the dream lingered. Jack felt as if he was lost between two worlds as he spent the morning quietly penning a half a dozen letters, each saying the same thing.

*Dear Sir/Madam,*

*I am seeking the whereabouts of my wife, Mrs Sofia Tomlinson, who was attached to a medical unit stationed in Alexandria in June 1942. Sofia is of Spanish heritage, lived in Australia from 1934 to 1939 and then moved to London. If you know of her whereabouts, please could you let me know at the address below? I am also enclosing a letter addressed to Sofia. If it is within your power, could you please pass this on to her immediately?*

*Yours faithfully,*
*Jack Tomlinson*

His letter to Sofia was brief, and his heart broke, six times over, as he penned the words.

*Dearest Sofia, my love!*

*I hope that this letter finds you well and safe, despite this dreadful war. I did enlist and came across to Europe to find you, but alas, to no avail. Due to a small injury, I have returned to Melbourne.*

*Please, please come home to me. If, for reasons of your own, that is impossible, could you at least let me know that you are safe?*

*My heart longs for you.*

*Your ever-loving husband,*
*Jack*
*XXOOXX*

After lunch, Jack felt exhausted by the emotional turmoil of the morning. Pulling the curtains around his bed, he lay upon it. He considered the broken bodies of the soldiers surrounding him, in various stages of recovery. He knew that some of them bore scars beyond rehabilitation; emotional injuries caused by the horrific circumstances that they'd endured. Haunting memories that locked them into hours of grim silence, or invaded their sleep where they thrashed and yelled, or worse, howled and screamed their grief into the night. Even as he reminded himself that he had much to be thankful for, Jack wondered if the scars on his heart left by the loss of Scotty, and then Sofia, would ever truly be healed.

After ten months in hospital, Jack's arm was almost fully functional. The recurring infection that had hindered its healing had finally been defeated through numerous courses of penicillin and the application of infrared lamps and hot packs—although an ugly red indentation would forever grace his shoulder. After being advised that his capacity to abduct and rotate his left arm would be marginally limited, Jack was finally discharged to his parents' home. On that same day, paperwork for his formal discharge from the Second Australian Imperial Forces was finalised. Margaret collected him, and stepping into the sunshine dressed in a clean set of clothing, the slouch hat he'd worn for almost four years replaced by a civilian trilby, Jack was a free man.

Freedom was accompanied by apprehension, he discovered. Leaving the hospital and simultaneously the military service, he felt akin to a raft drifting at sea, with no mooring in sight. Although his time in the ward was a far cry from the battlefield, he'd felt connected to the military amongst the men. His fellow patients—fellow veterans —shared a common understanding of life at the front, the bonds of mateship and the trauma of battle. They understood each other's silences, and instinctively knew when to step up to provide encouragement to a mate in his moment of weakness and when to shut their mouths and avert their eyes. Now, travelling towards his parents' house on a lovely spring afternoon, Jack looked at the men and women on the streets and working in their gardens—fellow Australians getting on with life—and felt utterly disconnected from them.

# CHAPTER 36

*I*t felt strange to be living in his parents' home after years of being in the company of men, in the cave on Crete and in the controlled routines of the hospital. For over six months, beyond choosing between lamb or beef roast, bread-and-butter pudding or lemon sago for sweets, Jack had had very few decisions to make for himself.

The changes he found at Copelen Street were well beyond those within himself. Sitting in the sunshine with his mother, Jack heard the full details of his father's decline. She told Jack of the dreadful day when they'd received a letter from the military advising them that their son was Missing In Action. It didn't say 'presumed dead', the terrible words that so many families had received, nor did it offer hope. His father's stroke had appeared the following day. Its arrival had been a quiet affair: his mother waking and rising from the bed she shared with William one morning, and his father uncharacteristically remaining behind. Jack heard how William had lain still and barely responded when Marian had shaken his arm. From the downward turn of his mouth and his inability to give voice to the words he tried to frame, she had known immediately that he'd had a stroke and had called an ambulance. The stroke had affected the left side of William's brain, unfortunately affecting his speech and causing him to drag his right leg.

Jack offered to assist with William's care—to help with his morning shower or to take him outside for a walk, and although Marian had welcomed his offer, it quickly became clear to Jack that his mother had her and William's daily routines under control. Jack couldn't deny it; he was impressed with his mother's courage, seeing the quiet lifestyle she'd developed that worked so well for both of them. She did have one concern, though, for which she sought Jack's advice and assistance. The Copelen Street house was way too big for her, and she desperately wanted to move to a smaller home—one with a little garden. Preferably along the bay, she thought, where she and William could walk along the foreshore and enjoy the afternoon sun.

Glad of a task to keep himself busy, Jack promised that he would help her look until they found the perfect home for her and William.

In no time at all, Jack created a routine of painting early in the day, sharing morning tea with his parents, and then putting in a few hours in the garden before returning to his painting in the afternoon.

In the second week following his discharge, Jack spent days cleaning and polishing William's Model-T Ford, which had lain idle in the garage since his stroke. Guided by Williams obscure instructions and the assistance of the local mechanic who checked the battery and changed the oil, eventually the vehicle spluttered to life. When Jack felt confident in his ability to crank the engine and manage the gear changes, he packed two completed works into the luggage compartment and drove to the Victoria Barracks, curious to see the rooms where Treloar's collection was housed, and also to see the premises where he knew Nora had been allocated a small room for use as a studio to paint her portraits of the women's services.

The Victorian Barracks were march larger than Jack had expected—a formidable looking building, with guards standing at the front door, opposite the Royal Botanical Gardens on St Kilda Road. Jack carried the paintings past the guards who barely glanced at him.

Evidently, he mused, artists were not perceived to offer any threat to the army's security. At the front desk, Jack was advised that Treloar was absent, so he handed his paintings to a young man who promised that he'd see that the Department Secretary got them. Jack then asked if he knew where Captain Nora Heysen was working, and after providing directions that were as convoluted as they were confusing, the young man decided he'd escort Jack to her studio himself.

As they walked across the courtyard, Jack was amazed by the sheer size of the buildings and wondered that he'd never even noticed them before, even though he'd travelled past this section of St Kilda Road hundreds of times. They were a blend of old and new, and Jack felt he was walking through history. The young man, clearly with the blood of a historian coursing through his veins, pointed out various features.

'That, there, is almost eighty years old,' he said with pride, pointing to a large building whose aged bluestone blocks were covered with ivy. 'It used to house the Garrison Battalions—long before we were a nation. You know, before Federation. Back in the last century. Those soldiers were the ones who put an end to the Eureka Stockade, when the miners revolted on goldfields. Can't you just picture them, charging through those gates on horseback with their muskets at the ready to quell the rebels!'

Pointing to Jack's right, the tour guide continued. 'And then, see those windows up there? That's where the War Cabinet is. Prime Minister Menzies and all of his men, the military commanders and generals. I've said hello to the prime minister a couple of times— especially when he first arrived and he was constantly lost. No one can get into those buildings—they're heavily guarded. I imagine that is where all the war secrets are held.'

Jack nodded, respecting the young man's enthusiasm for his work. Finally, they arrived at a nondescript brick building, and the young man pointed to the left, indicating that was the Military History Section, where Treloar worked, and to the right, a stairwell, where they ascended and passed dozens of tiny rooms.

'Ah! Here she is... I found it first go. Good afternoon, Captain Heysen. You have a visitor. Right, sir. I'll leave you to it.'

'Thank you, Martin. Hello, Jack. Whatever brings you here?'

'I had some canvases for Treloar. He's not in, so I've left them at reception.'

'No, he's in Canberra. Rushed off unexpectedly to oversee a display of vehicles that were used in World War One. I would have thought that anyone could park a few jeeps and motorbikes in a row, but Treloar insisted that it had to be done right. Right being his way, of course!'

Jack laughed. He was used to Nora's complaints about Treloar, whom she viewed as dogmatic and controlling. He didn't share her opinion: he liked their boss, and what Nora interpreted as controlling, Jack saw as passion—a determination to bring history alive, not just for historians and military buffs, but for everyone for centuries to come.

The room held the familiar smell of oil and turpentine, a dozen canvases set out along the wall to dry, two large easels and a workbench.

Looking out the window, Jack could see all the way to the back of the railway station. Flinders Street?

'Wow, you've got a nice spot here,' he said.

'Yes, I suppose it is, but the ventilation is terrible. I'm forever battling headaches. I've just about had enough for today. Want to slip into the city for a coffee?'

'Sure, but first you'd better show me what you're doing here. It's not every day that I get to see an Archibald Prize winner at work.'

'Oh, alright.... Here are the girls. Look at them, with their drab uniforms and irritated expressions. They dislike sitting for me as much as I dislike painting them, so I guess you could say we have a lot in common.'

Jack laughed. 'They should appreciate your work. They are being immortalised by a seriously talented, *acclaimed* artist.'

'I suspect that they would prefer to be immortalised in a photograph. You know—tidy their hair, freshen their lippie and then click! They'd be much more confident of the finished product than they are with me frowning at them every time they move as I slap paint onto a board. Who knows what I might do to them?'

'Yes. I imagine that you could inflict some damage. Look at this poor woman's glare!'

'That's Sheila McClemens, and believe me, I toned down her glare. She's quite the Somebody: a highly qualified lawyer and the Director of the WRANS. That is, the Women's Royal Australian Naval Service, if you don't mind. As I painted her, all I could think of was how sorry I felt for the poor girls she has charge over! I suspect they get a tongue lashing every time they have a hair out of place. My hands were literally shaking when I started… She was intimidating, I don't mind admitting. Look at the way she was looking at me. She'll spook the poor public when she's hanging up at the War Memorial with that frown. Mind you, it's probably what she's hoping to do. I suspect she's spent hours perfecting that expression in front of the mirror.'

'Okay. Let's get you out of here… Where would you like to go?'

'How about we walk across the bridge into town? We can find a coffee shop there.'

After coffee and lamingtons at a pleasant café overlooking the Yarra, Jack walked Nora to her lodgings and was amazed to see the fancy hotel that Treloar had organised for her stay in Melbourne.

'Whew, Nora, the Menzies Hotel! This place is like a palace! See? Treloar does value you! From what I've heard, only the important people stay here!'

'Including, if you don't mind, General MacArthur,' Nora replied. 'I often see him in the foyer, dashing about, looking oh-so-important amid his entourage of US officials. They are all very handsome, I must say!'

'Yes, so I keep hearing,' Jack replied dryly, displaying the same scepticism that half of the Victorian population—the male half—held for the thousands of Yankee GIs now walking the streets of Melbourne. The Americans filled the bars and dance halls with their drawling tones; handsome and full of charm as they sweet-talked young women across Australia into being mindless creatures who were incapable of anything more than adoring looks and rapturous giggles, besotted by the neat uniforms, clipped hair and smooth talk. The nurses at Heidelberg had been full of tales of their encounters with the Yankee soldiers, delighting in teasing their bedbound AIF patients by sharing tales of their charming, handsome foreign counterparts. Nonetheless, Jack had heard that many a serious romance now blossomed between US soldiers and Australian women, and the rumour was that, when the war ended, a ship would be requisitioned to transport hundreds of Australian girls across the Pacific: war-brides ready to make a life in America. Judging by the stories in the newspapers, it was the ultimate dream of any girl to gain a place on that ship.

Margaret and Nora were regular visitors to Copelen Street, often joining Jack and his parents for meals, sometimes even arriving together. The women got along well—both passionate about art—and with Margaret so effusive in her praise for Nora's Archibald win, that she almost made up for the tepid response it had received from women throughout Australia five years earlier. Jack, as well as his parents, enjoyed their spontaneous visits, finding their friendly chatter, lively energy and the pastries they'd bring a refreshing change from the house's otherwise uneventful routines.

Nora, hundreds of miles from her own family in South Australia, particularly enjoyed visiting and delighted Marian by sharing her love for flowers. Each time she came by, the two women walked around the garden discussing the blooms. Jack often grumbled that, while they were wandering alongside the flowerbeds, perhaps they might like to pull a few weeds and save him and his father a job—a joke that made William chortle till tears rolled down his cheeks, for his days of pulling weeds had long passed.

Throughout October, Jack chauffeured his parents to look at every house for sale from Elwood to Frankston. On these trips they were often accompanied by Nora, who was usually at a loose end on the weekends, given that she had few friends in Victoria.

In early November, they discovered a beautiful double-brick cottage at Beaumaris, within walking distance of Ricketts Point, a popular picnic destination. The house boasted a sun-filled front room that looked out across the bay, manageable-sized yards and established garden beds. A bonus was the string of shops, also within walking distance, and a path along the beachfront, which Marian declared was perfect for her daily stroll with William. At seven thousand pounds, they agreed the house was "a steal". With it being vacant, they were able to settle on the purchase and take possession of the property within twenty-one days. Marian and William could be in their new home before Christmas.

Nora happily volunteered to help with the move. As they wrapped crockery into newspaper together, Marian rued the loss of her garden.

'Marian, how about you take a piece of your garden with you?' Nora offered.

'Oh, I have already taken a few cuttings, but the new house has already got gardens, so I am not sure what I'll do with them.'

'Yes, but let's pick some of your favourite flowers, and I'll see what *I* can do with them!'

Together, they walked around the flower beds, selecting blooms from some of Marian's prized plants, which Nora arranged in an enormous crystal vase. During the following days, she worked with oils, painting a large canvas with images of cyclamens, forget-me-knots, phlox, and marigolds, all surrounded by sprigs of leafy greenery. She showed it to Jack when it was completed, and he studied her work, marvelling at the brilliant colours she had used, her skillful attention to the reflection of light bouncing off the petals and her meticulous attention to detail.

'Your work is amazing, Nora. Truly astonishing. I swear I have never seen anyone paint flowers like you do!'

'They don't call me the flower painter for nothing, Jack. It is my forte, you know.'

Jack hadn't known that Nora was called any such thing, but he did recall that, amid the portrait folio she'd brought into the hospital for him to see, there had been numerous pencilled flower designs.

∽

On Christmas Day, both Margaret and Nora joined Jack and his parents for lunch at the new home. All hands were on deck as they prepared roast turkey, chopped vegetables and made gravy. Margaret arrived with a plum pudding and Nora brought flowers for the table. She then presented a large parcel which, on unwrapping, revealed the completed painting, signed and set in a beautiful gilt frame. Marian was thrilled.

'It looks like it belongs in a gallery! And that frame! So grand! It must have cost you a fortune, you naughty girl! I will treasure it, mark my words.'

Nora smiled with pleasure, clearly delighted with Marian's reaction.

'I am so pleased you like it. Be careful! The oil is still drying in some places–in fact, it will take months to fully dry. I have plenty more flower paintings in my apartment in Canberra, including a pair that would be perfect for your front room, violas and pansies in little crystal vases. How does that sound? Would you like them, Marian? I will send them to you as soon as I am back home.'

'How sweet of you. She's a wonder, isn't she, Jack?'

Jack nodded, and as he did, he felt Margaret's eyes upon him. Looking at her, he shrugged. *Don't start, Margaret*, he thought to himself. *Nora is just a friend.*

# CHAPTER 37

*J*ack considered searching for a place of his own to live in, but Marian insisted that, since he'd declined her offer to join her and William at Beaumaris, he should continue living in Copelen Street until it was sold. His presence would deter would-be thieves and keep the house and gardens looking fresh and lived in, she told him. Jack was relieved at her suggestion for, in truth, he wanted to stay at Copelen Street for the simple purpose of waiting for the postman. Surely by now, his letters to England would have arrived at their various destinations, and he was confident that he could reasonably expect a reply to arrive any day. The waiting was not without anxiety; and at night Jack was haunted by dreams of canvas mail-bags lost to heaving ocean swells after a dreadful storm, or falling to the fathomless depths of the seabed following a bomb attack by German Heinkels and Junkers. By day, he found himself listening for the postman's arrival, alerted to the shrill repetitive call of his whistle even when he was half a block away. Some days, Jack waited at the gate to receive mail directly from the postman's hand; at other times, he stood just inside the front door, trying not to look ridiculously keen. More often than not, the letters that arrived were electricity or telephone bills, or the mail-order catalogues that his mother subscribed to.

Weekly, Jack met Nora for afternoon tea, or lunch or dinner, and then they would take walks together. Like him, she preferred to be outdoors and she told him how the beautiful parks of Melbourne reminded her of her family home in South Australia—The Cedars—a place she rarely visited these days. She loved walking in the Royal Botanical Garden to admire their garden beds, and when they had lunch in the city, they'd walk northward, to Fitzroy Park. It was there that Jack showed Nora Captain Cook's Cottage, explaining how the quaint one-roomed building had been dismantled in Great Ayton, Yorkshire and every brick carefully numbered and packed before being transported to Australia, where it had been rebuilt. Even the very ivy that clung to the building's walls had grown from cuttings of the same ivy that had flourished in its original location. Nora was enchanted and insisted that she and Jack return the following weekend and set up their easels to paint the picturesque landmark.

He enjoyed her company, and conversation came easily between them. They had much in common as artists, and also as employees of the military. And, whilst Jack had no inclination to advise Nora in her role as an artist—she was far too skilled to need his advice—he frequently acted as a sounding board to her ongoing frustration with military protocols.

'This drab uniform, Jack! I feel like a walking pretzel,' she complained. 'It would have to be the ugliest, most ill-fitting thing that I have ever had the misfortune to wear. I am sure that they make them like this just to deter women from enlisting.'

'You look fine to me, although I'm not sure if you would taste as good as a pretzel,' Jack replied, and then ducked with embarrassment, for the innuendo that his comment held was unintentional. 'No. I mean....'

'It's okay, Jack. You were joking,' Nora's voice carried a self-conscious ring even as she downplayed his gaffe.

Saluting was another problem for her.

'Just stand up straight and place your hand to forehead.' Finding a quiet spot in the park, Jack demonstrated the manoeuvre repeatedly, and they'd be in stitches—laughing at Nora's incapacity to perform the military manoeuvre without adopting a wry expression following which she'd withdraw her hand as if apologising.

'No, no... that won't do. You are a captain. You need to walk, talk and salute like a person with authority!'

Jack enjoyed having fun with Nora, even as he knew that, should he have dared to act any differently amongst Shorty, Snowy and Macka after he'd been appointed Captain, he would have been met with merciless teasing. Those blokes rarely took authority seriously. Not until it really mattered, like when they'd stood waiting to be transferred off the *Costa Rica* as it was about to sink. Notwithstanding, Jack couldn't imagine any circumstances where the role of Captain: War Artist would generate any level of deference from the lads he'd enlisted with.

'Just stare at them, alert and respectful. Come on, it's not that hard.' He showed her, yet again.

But to Nora, it was impossible. Saluting to superiors made her feel inept, she lamented. Even worse was that the officers of inferior rank were expected to salute her, and yet she knew that the majority of them were far more experienced in matters of war than she was.

'I feel like a fraud,' she said. 'I'm sure that they are mocking me even as they salute me.'

'Nora! You are a professional painter. An Archibald Prize winner, for heaven's sake! You are one of the most prominent women artists in Australia, if not the most renowned! The army is lucky to have you. You need to remember that. Stand up tall, look them in the eye and salute.'

'Well, there is one thing I have to say—the army does pay well,' Nora admitted. 'Much easier to get a regular wage than it is to live from the sale of one painting to the next, even if one is an Archibald Prize winner! And I have to hand it to Treloar—for all of his faults, he insisted, right from the beginning, that I should be paid at the full rate of an official war artist. The army refused, of course. They agreed to the rank of Captain, but said it was against their policy to pay a woman the same wage as men. But Treloar insists that I am a professional artist and deserve to be paid as one, though I think that he makes up the difference in wages from his own funds, which I suppose is pretty decent of him. Fourteen pounds! It's unbelievable. Back when I was making sandwiches at the naval base canteen, all I got was three pounds. And even then, I got the sack!'

'You got the sack? From a naval base canteen? I didn't know that could happen. What were you doing? Stealing the jam drops for your supper?'

'No, of course I wasn't. It was because I didn't make the sandwiches the way that they wanted!'

'What, you're a woman and you can't even make sandwiches?' Jack teased.

'I would argue that it was they who could not make a sandwich. They insisted that I should skimp on everything—one slice of tomato, a sliver of ham so thin that it was invisible, three shreds of lettuce. It was obvious they'd never heard that an army marches on its stomach. If Michael and Stefan are expected to function on such paltry rations, they will surely die of starvation, not gunfire!'

In this way, Jack discovered that Nora's two brothers were both pilots for the Royal Australian Air Force; indeed, it had been their enlistment that had prompted Nora to contribute to the war effort herself.

'It's such a turnaround for our family, Jack. During the Great War, our father was treated so badly by everyone—just because he had German heritage. Heavens, his family had been in Australia for thirty years; Dad was only a seven-year-old when they came, and yet he was viewed as a spy. Even the art community turned against him. I was only a child, but I still remember how worried my parents were at the time.'

Jack shook his head, disgusted at how quickly Australians could turn upon foreigners, including those who'd lived in Australia for years. Daily, the newspapers had stories of long-term migrants— farmers and businessman of German and Italian descent—who'd been placed in internment camps, causing terrible hardship to their families. Some of them even had sons who were serving in Australia's armed forces. The whole situation was ludicrous: another example of the madness of war.

'In this war, my brothers and I are all serving with the AIF and—thank goodness—Dad has been left alone. My dad is the gentlest person in the world. And forgiving, I must say. He was never once angered by the way he was treated. "That's how it is in war time, Nora," he'd say to me. "You just have to be patient and honest, and everything soon works itself out."'

Bit by bit, Jack learned about Nora's life in South Australia. How, as a child, she'd spent hundreds of hours at an easel alongside her father who had taught her how to paint trees and skies. As she'd developed her skills, they'd often painted the same subjects and even worked on the same canvas. In time, their work became so similar that it was sometimes hard to tell their styles apart.

However, Jack was surprised when, accompanying him to Beaumaris for a roast with his parents one Sunday, Nora had asked if the suburb of Mentone was far away.

'Not at all; in fact, it's only a very short distance from here.' He waited for Nora to explain her interest, but she remained silent and thoughtful as she sat in the car beside him.

'Who lives in Mentone?' Jack's curiosity got the better of him, and he had to ask.

'It's not a matter of who *lives* in Mentone, but rather who *died* there,' Nora's voice was low as she continued. 'My sister—Josephine. She lived there just before the war broke out.'

Nora stopped speaking for a moment, dabbing at her eyes, and Jack was not sure if she planned on continuing her story. She did, though, and her voice revealed a bitterness that startled him.

'She was cast out, not only from her home, but from South Australia. By our own mother.'

'Your mother! Why on earth would she banish your sister from her home?'

'The age-old thing, Jack. The family image. The family's reputation. Putting on a good show for the benefit of others. Josephine always loved horses. Was mad about them, and her love of horses led to her love of Max Williams, a horse trainer. A highly unacceptable match, according to Mother. Heaven forbid if anyone knew that Hans Heysen's daughter was to marry a mere strapper!' Jack listened, aghast

347

at Nora's tale as she explained how, according to her mother, Hans would lose all of his commissions if the word of Josephine's 'fall' got out. All her life, Nora had heard about the significance of their family's social standing, as if it were the most important thing in the world.

'While our mother did everything she could to thwart Josephine's relationship with Max, she didn't do enough, for a pregnancy ensued, leading to a hasty wedding and then banishment. I went overseas soon after. What with living in London, Italy and Paris, I didn't maintain close contact with Josephine, which of course, I will eternally regret.'

'That's awful, Nora. How terrible for you to lose your sister like that! How did they end up living in Mentone?'

'Because of its racetrack. It was mother who found the house for them. I suppose she thought that by moving Josephine out of the state, people would be less likely to talk, and that with the racetrack at Mentone, Max would be able to find work. Typical of Mother to organise other people's lives.'

'And did Max find work?'

'I don't know what happened. I know that they struggled to make ends meet—were as poor as church mice, really—and then Josephine died giving birth. Mum and Dad raised the baby. She's also named Josephine, but they call her Jilly. Dad has never gotten over Josephine's death. He still mentions it in his letters from time to time, or brings it up when we are alone together. Her banishment and then her death nearly broke his heart, I reckon. He must have asked me a hundred times, "What would it have mattered if Josephine was pregnant?" Occasionally, he asks Mum why she sent Josephine away, but our mother is tough. It was for him, she tells him. For the sake of his career!

'It's Mum who manages his career, that's for sure. She's made a life's work of pouring tea and serving cake to the gentry, all the while encouraging them to purchase a Heysen painting. A *Hans Heysen* painting. Mum is not such a big fan of my work. I'm not sure whether she views me as a distraction to my father or whether she thinks I am "the competition". It's all very odd, really.'

Jack felt sorry for Nora, sensing her loneliness. How awful, to have been born into such a renowned artistic family and yet not to feel encouraged by them. No wonder Nora was so drawn to his own parents.

'Is that why you left South Australia and went to Sydney?' he asked.

'I guess so. Yes. Dad took me there when I was young; he still has many contacts there. Sydney was a wonderful place for a young artist! I used to live right near King's Cross with my friend Evie. I met her in London and we've been friends ever since. She's since married to a man called Henry, and they have a child. There were a few of us artists all living close together: me, Russell Drysdale, Will Dobell and William Friend. Have you heard of their work? They're marvellous painters. We'd meet often for sherry parties. It was just like living in Paris, all over again. I must say, I did love it. Melbourne's quite drab in comparison.'

'Hey! What would you know?' Jack chided. 'There are wonderful painters here—me, for instance! And if Sydney was so fabulous, why did you move to Canberra?'

'The air raids, Jack. There'd been half a dozen of them. It was getting frightening. Evie and Henry had already made the move, and Evie insisted that I should join them. Everybody in Sydney was sure it was only a matter of time before the Japanese attacked, and they were right. No sooner had I arrived in Canberra than at least four submarines got past the harbour nets and managed to hit a few targets. The other thing that I hoped—that by getting to Canberra I would have a chance at applying for a commission as a war artist with Treloar.'

'And that you did, Nora. No doubt about you!'

～

Jack found that he could share stories about his life in Paris with Nora without being overwhelmed by thoughts of Sofia, and he was interested to discover that she, too, had met Picasso during her own time there.

'His work was just so odd. I found his paintings awful, really.'

Jack laughed. 'To be honest, I did, too. I'm not sure if we are allowed to admit to that. Here in Melbourne, we have the conservatives

349

and the modernists, and they are constantly at war with each other. You know the arguments—the evils of modernism versus the staidness of traditionalism. I feel as though, for the last decade, I have thrown my hat in with the modernists, but really, I'm a traditionalist at heart. All of my best works are far closer to traditional styles than to the moderns. And, like you, my first impressions of Picasso were that his paintings were downright awful. I will say, though, after the war in Crete, I now understand *Guernica*. You know—Picasso's painting of the town destroyed during the Spanish Civil War. I am going to paint my own version soon. It will be called *The Battle of 42nd Street*.'

In discussing his time in Paris, Jack found himself able to speak to Nora about Sofia. About meeting her and Andrés, and about the wonderful time that they'd shared exploring the sights of Paris, before travelling to Spain where he and Sofia had married; and then how circumstances had brought them home to Australia. As he spoke about their life at Montsalvat. Nora listened quietly, and put her hand over his as he spoke of the fire where he and Sofia had lost their only child, and then how, in their grief, they'd lost each other.

'Jack, that is the saddest thing that I have ever heard. Are you sure that Sofia is in England?'

Jack nodded, explaining that, although little information had been forthcoming, a soldier in Crete had mentioned Sofia's presence at Alexandria.

'I'm positive that she is with the war nurses,' he said. 'That would be exactly the sort of thing that Sofia would do.'

Jack felt himself go still, his heart beating rapidly as he shared his deepest of pains.

'The thing is, Nora, while I don't have any contact details for Sofia, she has always known how to contact me. She has my parents' address, and of course, Montsalvat's. Through either of those sources, she could have sent me a message at any time. And yet… she hasn't. That is the truth of it. Soon after Scotty died, Sofia left, and I got word that she believed coming here to Australia—that marrying me—was all a mistake. And, since then, I have heard nothing. Nonetheless, I still feel that, with the war and all, I need to find her. To be sure that she is okay. She was utterly devastated when she left, naturally. Sofia had already lost so many people in her life; it was awful. It still hurts me just thinking about it.'

～

It was barely a month later that an event happened which altered the course of Jack and Nora's friendship. It had been a quiet morning. Jack had spent a couple of hours painting before going outside to mow the front lawn. Now in autumn, Copelen's streetscape, adorned with trees gloriously coated in leaves of yellow, red and gold, was a picture. The gracious home, only minutes from the city, in a suburb growing in popularity, was attracting numerous prospective buyers, and Jack took care to keep its yards tidy.

Mowing the last strip, he heard the distant shrill of the postman's whistle and suddenly he was overcome with the feeling, the absolute surety, that today was going to be the day he would hear from Sofia. The feeling was so strong that his heart pounded, and he could feel the throbbing pulse in his ears. With excitement, he saw the postman squeeze half a dozen letters into the mailbox, and he quickly retrieved them.

There was the usual mail for his mother, but even as he pulled it through the narrow opening, one letter caught his eye—large and yellow, a row of British stamps in the top right corner—and he knew that his feelings had been right. The letter for which he'd been waiting had arrived.

# CHAPTER 38

*J*ack's hands trembled as he walked indoors where he cast the usual mail aside with barely a glance, before leaning the envelope upright, supported by the salt and pepper shakers in the centre of the table. The handwriting, with its neat small printed letters, was unfamiliar. Not Sofia's—of that he was certain. Surprising himself by his restraint, Jack walked to the laundry and washed his hands, carefully drying them before returning to the kitchen. Next, he thought he might pour himself a glass of water.

*What am I doing, delaying the opening this letter I've waited upon for so long?* he wondered. *Savouring it? Deferring the unwelcome news it may contain?*

Finally, he reached for a butter knife, slit the envelope open and carefully withdrew the folded slip of paper from within.

Its message was brief.

*Dear Mr Tomlinson,*

*I have been advised that you are seeking the whereabouts of Sofia Tomlinson, who, to your knowledge, is serving as a nurse attached to one of the British Hospital Units.*

*I believe that it was her, whom you describe as being of Spanish descent, that I met with recently. The lady that I met was in Harrods cafeteria and, by the badge on her uniform, I recognised her as a war nurse who'd served on the front. Having been recently appointed to the service myself, and desperate to get overseas to join the war as soon as I could, I was very keen to speak with her and hear of her experiences, and so asked if I might join her, to which she agreed.*

*We chatted for about half an hour, and she shared many insights of the time she'd spent in Alexandria, France and South Africa. It would appear that the hospital units are forever on the move, so I can well understand the difficulty that you have had in tracing her.*

*We had a lovely chat; however, I cannot recall that she knew where her next posting would be, only that she had seven days' leave. In time, her little girl became fidgety and so she needed to go.*

*Such a good little thing the child was, and I couldn't blame her for wanting her mother's attention while she was home.*

*I wish that I could say, with absolute certainty, that the woman that I spoke with is the Sofia Tomlinson that you are seeking. She was distinctly of Southern European heritage and her name was Sofia. I felt compelled to share this information in the hope that it might be helpful in your search.*

*Yours faithfully,*
*Genevieve Winters*


Jack froze. The woman described was with a child. A little girl? Two thoughts sprang to his mind. This couldn't be Sofia. It had to be someone else. The second thought, worse than the first, was the implications of the message—that Sofia had fallen into the arms of another man. Was married, even? Surely she was still married to him! Had she initiated a divorce, unbeknownst to him? Or perhaps she was living with her new lover. It was wartime—anything was possible. Jack remembered the way that Sofia had left, how vulnerable she'd been, loathing him even! He pictured her on the long journey back to London, and wherever else she'd taken herself; and he imagined her in her travels, falling prey to the sympathetic approaches of another man.

He stood up, pacing the floor and seething with anger. How dare she! He'd been searching for her for almost six years. Waiting for her, worrying about her all of this time, while she had moved on. As though the life that they'd shared together was nothing; as if it had so little importance that he and Scotty could be erased from her memories. Jack couldn't believe that he'd been replaced so easily by another man. That Scotty had been replaced by another child!

It was in this state of turmoil that Nora found Jack half an hour later—after she'd let herself through the front door and walked into the kitchen—her arms filled with fresh bread rolls, a cut of corned beef, an apple pie from the bakery and a bottle of sherry.

'Jack, whatever's the matter?' she asked, dropping the groceries on the table and standing before him, frowning in concern.

'Nothing, Nora. It's nothing at all.'

'No, Jack. It is not nothing. Something has upset you terribly!'

Jack saw her eyes flicker across the table, glancing at the opened letter.

'You've had bad news. I am so sorry! Damn this war!'

Jack picked up the letter and thrust it into her hands before resuming his pacing.

She read it.

'Sofia. Your wife? This is marvellous, Jack. You have found her at last! Or at least you have news of her. It doesn't say exactly where she is though, does it? Do you have any ideas?'

'She's found someone else. Had another child. She's moved on.'

'Oh!' Nora read the letter once more, this time more slowly.

'Jack. I am so sorry," she said again. "Perhaps it is not hers. Perhaps she was minding the child for someone else?'

'That's not how I read it, Nora. It is quite clear, don't you think?'

She was still.

'Anyway,' he continued, 'I was told, six years ago, that she was leaving me, and I refused to accept it. I guess the truth hurts.'

Jack gazed at Nora, searching for answers, but all he found were eyes softened with sorrow for him, and his mind tumbled with emotions. She stepped towards him and he placed his arms on her shoulders and pulled her close. He buried his head into her hair, his heart torn, his mind numbed.

Sofia was in London! Had been for all this time, without so much as a brief message to him. She had somehow summoned the strength to overcome the grief of losing Scotty, without his support. Well, after all, he reminded himself, hadn't he only sought to know that she was well and safe? Apparently, she was!

It was odd. In a moment of time, his purpose—to find Sofia—had ended, to be replaced with a sense of abandonment. Hollowness infused the place where, for months, Jack had nurtured hopefulness. The estrangement from Sofia was total. She was not missing; rather, she'd made a whole new life for herself. She was no longer his.

The pain was acute. In the Middle East, and especially for those years that he'd lived in the wilderness of Crete, his memories of Sofia had dulled, but so too had anything else about the life he'd led before landing on the island.

However, since he had returned to Australia—and especially since he'd returned to this house, sat at his parents' dining table, slept in the bed that he and Sofia had once shared, waited expectantly for a reply to his letters—the fullness of his wife's laughter and joyful presence had returned, warming him and giving him purpose. He'd believed in and, even worse, imagined their reconciliation: where there would be sadness for their loss of Scotty and regret for their time apart, but sweetness for being together again. In his mind, Sofia's presence had become tangible, their love for each other strong and indomitable. Now Jack was faced with the painful knowledge that the pictures he'd drawn in his mind were nothing more than portraits of castles in the air. Wistful dreams that had no bearing on reality.

Jack felt Nora stir in his arms and loosened his grip, realising that she must be feeling smothered. Looking into her eyes, he saw rivers of compassion pouring towards him. Her hands were firm as she moved them over his shoulders and down his arms as if to transmit her strength to him. She leaned towards him, an invitation for him to take consolation from her lips, and he pressed his own against hers, relishing their softness. Gently, at first, and then searching and deep.

Her taste was sweet with a hint of peppermint, her mouth yielding, opening to accept the fullness of his need, and Jack kissed her hungrily, deeply, moving her back towards the table and bending over her. He reached forwards to push the letters resting on the table aside and they fell over the edge, one by one. The rustling sound of them dropping to the floor caused him to glance up, just in time to see his glass topple and its contents flow across the table's wooden surface. He watched the stream of water racing towards the loose page that had travelled ten thousand miles to break his heart.

Reaching out, Jack tried to rescue the letter, but it escaped his grasp and fluttered to the floor, just as Sofia had escaped him. It settled, thankfully out of reach of the pond now forming on the floor, a safe distance from the waterfall trickling over the table's edge. It was safe, just as Sofia evidently was.

Alerted to reality, Jack gasped. What was he doing? He released Nora from his arms and stepped back. No. Not now. This was too fast. Barely an hour ago, he'd been thinking of Sofia with longing, ecstatic to have received news of her. Now, he was preparing to carry Nora up the stairs, to the very bed that belonged to him and his wife.

Nora looked at him, uncertainty in her eyes. 'Jack?'

'Nora, I'm sorry. I can't... not now.'

'It's alright, Jack. Of course. You've had a shock. I will leave you in peace.'

She paused expectantly, but Jack didn't answer. Instead, he turned away from her and bent to retrieve the letter from the floor.

Wordlessly, Nora picked up her bag and slung it over her shoulder. He felt her eyes upon him again, before she retreated through the house. Listening to the quiet click of the front door closing, Jack felt stabs of guilt. He knew his reckless behaviour had hurt Nora deeply.

# CHAPTER 39

Over a week passed before Jack saw Nora again, and he felt the change in their friendship, as one feels an icy breeze at the turn of autumn to winter.

It was Friday afternoon. After a long week of feeling sorry for himself, Jack decided to call in to the barracks to see John and, hopefully, to see Nora, too. Perhaps she'd agree to have afternoon tea with him. He hated knowing that he'd upset her so badly and wanted a chance to explain.

When he arrived at Treloar's rooms, he discovered Nora there, speaking with him. They were arguing and Jack hovered in the background, preferring not to intrude. He was used to Nora's ongoing disputes with Treloar; and while he accepted that some of her issues were valid, he did not share her belief that Treloar was controlling. Indeed, Jack felt that Treloar offered both himself and Nora a fair degree of freedom in the work they produced within the scope of his needs for the Memorial, and he often told her so. Jack suspected that many of Nora's irritations were borne of her years of independence, her battle to be taken seriously in a man's world and her life experiences travelling the globe. To adopt the subservient stance of military respect for senior officers, was near impossible for her; but then, Jack was sure that if she were speaking to the King of England, Nora would assert herself in the same argumentative manner.

Notwithstanding, today she seemed to have a valid complaint.

'If forty-three male war artists can be sent to the front, then surely so can I,' he heard her cry. 'War isn't only about men, John! It is about women and children, too. Old people and young people. What right do you men have keeping us women away?'

'Well, Captain—' Treloar's words were cut off.

'And in keeping me away from it, you are destroying my career! Look at this!'

Nora waved the newspaper that she was holding in front of Treloar before slamming it onto the bench.

Moving closer, Jack looked at her questioningly, but she didn't appear to see him, nor did Treloar reach for the paper, so he picked it up himself.

'*War Artists Show Their Work*,' the headline read.

Scanning the contents, Jack saw that an exhibition of war art was opening at the National Gallery that week. While the article was not totally flattering of the paintings, what was overwhelmingly obvious was that the artists being exhibited were all men, and all had served overseas.

'How can my role as a war artist ever be taken seriously if you are going to shield me from the front, locking me in a studio here in Melbourne? I want to paint the action. The grit and determination of the troops that you said you wanted! That is what the critics are asking for, and if you don't let me step forward, I will forever be seen as the flower painter who was too delicate for war.'

'Okay, okay, I will see what I can do,' Treloar said, gruffly. 'Jack, what do you think? Will we send Nora to New Guinea?'

At his words, she emitted a deep growl of utter frustration, threw up her hands and stomped from the room.

'I really don't know what to make of her, Jack. She has no discipline at all. Speaking with her is like handling a wild kitten. I am sure that she'd have the soldiers running scared! Probably send the Japanese flurrying back across the ocean.'

'Nora is a strong, capable woman, John. In honesty, I understand her frustration. How can she be taken seriously as a war artist if she is stuck here, painting portraits? I have no doubts that Nora would cope with anything that the war throws at her, don't you worry. You are thinking you'll post her to New Guinea?'

'Yes, I think that I might,' said John. 'There is a nursing unit there. She can pitch in with them, and the mud and leeches and humidity. We'll see how happy that makes her! I'll have to get special permission, though. These things are not altogether straightforward.'

Jack hoped it would work out, pleased that Nora might finally get the opportunity she so desperately desired—a posting where she could finally be recognised as a real war artist.

When Jack found Nora waiting out in front of the barracks, pacing the foyer, he was surprised. The usual smile that she offered him was replaced by a glare, and he could see that she was still angry with him.

'Nora. I just want to say… about the other day….'

'Don't, Jack. Don't say anything. I couldn't bear it.'

They walked out onto the road and turned left, with no destination in mind.

'But Nora, I need to explain. I just didn't want to use you… It was the wrong moment…'

'Jack! Just be quiet.' She turned on him. 'But know this. I am no feminist, whatever you may think. I am no feminist,' she repeated the phrase again.

'Why, of course not. But why? Who cares if you are a feminist?'

'Lesbian, Jack. Lesbian. I have been getting it for years. Ever since I met Evie.'

By now, Nora's face was awash with tears.

'Evie?'

'You know. My flatmate. The one I met in London. Together we travelled through Europe and then we returned to Australia and eventually we shared the apartment in Sydney. Goddamn it, she is married. She has a child, even. As if that is not enough evidence.'

Jack stopped walking and put his hand out to Nora, holding her still.

'Nora, I have no idea what you are talking about. Where is this coming from? Never, for a second, did I think of you as a… lesbian, for heaven's sake.'

'Oh! When you rejected me the other day, I just thought…' Nora inhaled deeply and started again. 'It's my mother. She's been on about it for years. She's convinced that my friendship with Evie is "unnatural." Gosh, she even has my father believing it. You should see the rubbish that they write—letter after letter making wild accusations, and ascribing my mother's failing health to my friendship with Evie. It's ridiculous. And then, the other day, when you pushed me away, I didn't know what to think!'

'Nora, you are a beautiful, talented, intelligent woman. And sexy,' Jack added, boldly. 'Don't think for a second that I didn't feel desire for you. I could have thrown you over my shoulder and carried you up those stairs in a moment, if you'd like to know. But—it would have been wrong. My head is too mixed up. I have been… I *am*… so attached to Sofia—to the idea of my marriage—that to make love to anyone else feels like a betrayal to her. And the other day I was too angry. Too lost.'

Nora nodded, seeming to accept his explanation.

'Now, tell me again, what is this about your being a lesbian? I never knew that a lesbian would kiss a man with such sweetness.'

They laughed, their friendship once again restored, and Jack listened as Nora revealed the pain that she'd endured, caused by her mother's refusal to accept her friendship with Evie; and the relentless barrage of poisonous comments she'd received about the only person who truly understood her in the whole world.

True to his word, Treloar gained special permission for Nora to serve overseas as a commissioned officer, and then organised for her to go to New Guinea, where she would be stationed at Finschhafen, on the

Huon Peninsula. He'd had her assigned to work with the medical teams there, and Nora was ecstatic.

First, she needed to return to Canberra to sort out her belongings and tidy a few loose ends before embarking on her tour overseas. Jack was pleased to see her so excited about the opportunity she'd been given. Together they spent Nora's last evening walking along the Yarra before sharing a meal in the Mural Room at Grossi Florentino, a lovely Italian restaurant in Bourke Street. Afterwards, he took her arm and they wandered around the city streets, peering into the store windows. Eventually they returned to the Menzies, where they purchased sherries at the main bar just before it closed.

'Jack, do you think that it's possible that Sofia is in New Guinea, somewhere?'

'I don't know. I understand that US troops are there, alongside the AIF, but I haven't heard of any British troops there. The truth is, Sofia could be anywhere. And, secondly, she isn't worried about me. She would have written by now, if she'd wanted to: she knows where I live.'

'But you did say she'd been asking after you, in Alexandria?' Nora persisted.

'Yes. Because she thought that I was there. She must have seen one of my drawings or something.' It hurt Jack to think about Sofia. He was still shocked by the fact that she'd managed to move on. That she'd replaced him when, all of this time, he'd been so worried about her.

'In any case, I will keep my eye out for her. If I find her, I'll be telling her that she needs to contact you. That you've been worrying about her for years, and that she has a responsibility to let you know she is safe.'

Jack nodded. It was strange to be speaking of Sofia like this. Until he'd received the letter, she'd felt so close to him. A part of him. Now, it was like she was a total stranger, somebody that he could barely recognise.

'So, are you all packed?' He wanted to change the subject.

'Yes. Two suitcases filled with khaki.' Nora grimaced.

'How about I meet you back here in the morning and help you

across to the station?' he offered. It was the least he could do. He'd enjoyed his friendship with Nora these last few months and knew that he'd miss her. Could the companionable ease he felt when he was with her have grown to something more? Jack wasn't sure. Regardless of Sofia's circumstances, in his mind and heart, he was still a married man and the only woman for him was Sofia.

~

A week later, Jack drove across to the Victoria Barracks with his latest painting, a scene of the last barge that had carried evacuees off the beach at Sphakia, leaving thousands of soldiers behind to fend for themselves on Crete. Whilst painting the scene, the haunting melody of the Maori voices drifting across the waters came back to him, evoking the feelings of that terrible moment when he'd learned that the vessel was departing, its decks filled to capacity, and no more ships were expected. Again Jack ached at the thought of how close he'd come to finding Sofia.

Had he joined the men evacuated on that day, perhaps he would have caught up with her in Alexandria. She'd wanted to see him then. She'd been asking after him. *She'd asked everybody about an artist called Jack*, the young soldier with the scarred face had told him. How different his life might now be if he'd been one of the lucky ones evacuated that day!

When he arrived at Victorian Barracks, it felt strange to know that Nora was no longer here, working in her studio. Jack missed their companionable outings together. He made his way to the wing where Treloar worked, and the older man's greeting was effusive.

'Jack, good to see you. I've been waiting for you to pop in. I have a question for you.'

Jack wondered what was coming. Clearly, Treloar had something in mind. 'Nice to see you, John. What would you like to know?'

'I was wondering if you would consider working here with me. I could sure use a hand. As you can see, the job is enormous, and really, I should spend far more time in Canberra than I have been.'

The offer caught Jack by surprise, although he'd known how

stretched Treloar was, constantly travelling between Melbourne and Canberra, fulfilling his role as the Director of the War Memorial as well as maintaining the Military History Section here at the barracks.

'Well… I don't know… I've done nothing like that before. I'm not really a historian…'

'You'd be fine, Jack. Come, let me show you around, and then you can decide.'

Jack followed Treloar into the room, glancing around at the walls lined with overflowing shelves, the large map cabinet, the piles upon piles of boxes set in the side storerooms, and the benches groaning under the weight of with still more boxes of all shapes and sizes. Although he'd been here a few times before, he'd never taken much notice of the crowded interior. Usually, he'd just passed his paintings across to Treloar and they'd had a quick chat. Today, Treloar led Jack through the room and then into each of the three storerooms to show their contents.

Jack was astonished by the collection—wooden clubs, muskets and grenades; ribbons and medals as well as the associated media articles reporting on their formal presentations; soldiers' kits and clothing. Still more boxes of photographs, letters, film reels and war diaries. Despite the clutter of the room, each item was neatly labelled.

'The thing is, Jack, it's not a matter of just throwing all of this into the back of a van and driving it to Canberra. Then we'd have the same mess there as I have here!' Treloar laughed. 'At least, whilst this may look chaotic, I do have some sense of order. What I have been doing… what we need to do, is to examine each item and record the details of its origins, of its relevance in the whole scheme of the war. You know… tell the story. That is what's important. That is the thing the public wants to know about.'

Jack smiled at Treloar's words, wondering how many times he'd listened as Treloar insisted it was the stories about the war that were most important to the public.

Jack considered the space the Military History Section occupied; dimly lit, freezing cold and with poor ventilation. Simultaneously, he observed the passion in Treloar's voice, the light in the older man's eyes as he spoke of his collection. It was then Jack realised that for all of Treloar's experiences—Staff Sergeant at Gallipoli, Equipment Officer in France, serving in London's Department of Information; his successive rankings as Lieutenant, Captain and Major; and the honorary title he'd been given as a Member of the British Empire—foremost he was a historian, happiest when he was surrounded by his enormous collection of wartime memorabilia, and committed to realising the dream he and Charles Bean had concocted two decades earlier.

Treloar described the task he had in mind for Jack.

'What I need you to do is to focus on the unit diaries. There're hundreds of them. Many of them are incomplete, unfortunately. You know what some officers are like. We need them collated and categorised. It's a slow process, because first I like to peruse them, noting any events of interest. These I can often cross-reference to other records. You wouldn't believe the stories that unfold... the different versions of the same event, or the way critical orders can be misconstrued at the height of a battle.'

Jack could well imagine the mixed messages surrounding the events of war that might come to light in time. Perhaps the underlying stories of his own experiences—the lack of basic supplies sent to Crete, the failure of the promised air support, so desperately needed, in Greece—would be revealed.

Beyond the fact that the work would be interesting, Jack knew that leaving the house and coming here to the barracks a few times a week would be good for him. His spirits had taken a knock since he'd received the letter from London. And now, with Nora gone, it was as if his life had lost purpose beyond completing the list of paintings he was working through for Treloar, work he was finding increasingly tedious.

'Yes, John, I imagine that the work could be interesting. I can put in a few days if that would help.'

And so it was agreed that Jack would spend Thursdays and Fridays working alongside Treloar at the Military History Section at the Army Barracks. In addition, he would spend Mondays to Wednesdays working on his paintings for the Memorial, paid at the same rate that he'd received as a war artist.

As if Treloar knew that Jack needed inspiration, he led him through a doorway. 'Come in here, Jack. I have just dragged these from the back of the storeroom. I'm about to send them to Canberra. You'll like them.'

Leaning against the wall were two enormous paintings. The first was breathtaking in its beauty and its horror: a stunning depiction of Australian and New Zealander soldiers—thousands of them—scrambling up a steep cliff face, their weapons poised even as they advanced. The images of bloodied bodies strewn among the climbers revealed that the soldiers were under enemy attack.

'You've heard of the Gallipoli Landing, of course? Well, here it is. I was there, you know. With the administration unit, not with the gunners, but it was every bit as awful as you would have heard. George painted this. And he did an incredible job!'

Jack read the cardboard label that had been inserted into the frame. *Anzac, the landing 1915; George Lambert.*

'And this is another of George's, titled *Charge of the 3rd Light Horse Brigade at Nek.*'

Jack gazed, open-mouthed. Almost as large as the first, this painting was also astonishing. Its colour was vivid, the landscape expansive, the devastation of the battle unquestionable. Without doubt, Lambert had captured the truth of the battle—the ugly truth—in this work of panoramic proportions. Jack had never thought to create anything this large, and wondered if he could, even if he wanted to.

'Astonishing, isn't it?' Treloar said, proudly. 'Not like those ancient paintings that make battles appear glorious, with soldiers in fabulous uniforms, seated upright and steady, their horses rearing in advance of the charge, flags held high. It was as if they believed that war was the culmination of human achievement—the most glorious state of man. In this, Lambert certainly strips away all notions of glory! He's captured the magnitude of the slaughter, the struggle of the men, perfectly.'

'Yes, John. He has,' Jack marvelled, as his own recollections of the battlefield were enlivened. The chaotic advances with panicked voices screeching orders that could barely be heard, the thunderous explosion of bombs landing just yards away, and the injured bodies that fell to the ground, sometimes with a surprised shout or cry; other times with a lifeless thud.

'Did you know Lambert, Jack?' Treloar asked.

Jack didn't.

'He died—oh, at least a dozen years ago. A real character, never so happy as when he was gadding about, surrounded by people, swigging wine and telling stories. And, I have to say, he drove me mad! Would deliver nothing on time—just made endless promises! The hours I spent cajoling him, trying to prompt him to finish a painting by offering further commissions, etcetera. It was pointless being annoyed with him; I wanted his paintings too much, and he knew it. And when he finally delivered a work... well, you can see the result for yourself. I waited eight years for this one. He must have shown it to me a dozen times, but it was never quite finished, he'd tell me. I just had to wait.'

'It's amazing! Well worth the wait!'

'You wouldn't know that he'd never been to Gallipoli.'

For all his earlier surprise at the panting, Jack found this utterly unbelievable. 'No! Really?'

'Yes, it's a fact. Never saw a battlefield. George painted these from photographs. They help when it comes to the little details, of course. However, its far better to have artists who have first-hand experience of the subjects they paint. That is why I commissioned you, Jack. When paintings are contrived from photographs and artefacts, they may be technically accurate, but very few can capture the essence of the battlefield. That's what made Lambert so special. He had a knack for getting it right.'

As Jack left the barracks, he decided to pay a visit that was long overdue. After driving over the bridge into the city, he pulled up outside the familiar office building on Collins Street. Sunday and John Reed had been on Jack's mind of late. It had been almost four years since he'd seen them, and despite his promises to write, he'd sent nothing beyond a postcard from Alexandria when he'd first arrived in the Middle East, followed by a hastily scribbled message on the back of one of his own sketches that he'd sent from Cairo one afternoon where he'd described the wonder of the pyramids. The Reeds had been very good to him, and he owed them a visit.

John's door was closed, and the room was quiet, but Jack could see the silhouette of a figure working at the desk through the frosted glass, and he took a chance on surprising him. He rapped on the door sharply, and without waiting for a reply, turned the handle and entered.

'Is this the office of Mr John Reed?' he asked, adopting a posh formal tone.

John looked up in surprise, then grinned and bounced out of his seat, vigorously shaking Jack's hand whilst simultaneously patting his shoulder.

'Jack! I don't believe it. Good to see you! Mind you, you've lost a bit of weight, don't you think? I barely recognised you!' John's enthusiastic greeting warmed Jack, and it felt good to be in his company again. 'Sunday will be thrilled to know you're here. You must come out. We have so much to catch up on. Damn this war. Who would have thought it would last so long? Are you painting?'

John's questions tumbled over each other, and Jack laughed.

'How is Sunday, John? I would love to see her.'

'You must. She'd love to see you, too, mark my words. I can't tell you how many times Sunday has said, "I wonder where Jack has got to," since you left! Wait until I tell her that you walked into my office today, large as life. She'll be amazed. Come tomorrow? Scones! Make it early! How about for afternoon tea and then stay on for dinner? We've got so much to catch up on.'

'I'd love to, John. It will be wonderful to see Heide again!'

# CHAPTER 40

*H*eide was even more beautiful than when Jack had seen it last, with the trees he'd helped John plant five years earlier now tall and sturdy and the garden beds a vivid display of blues, mauves and violets.

The house was full of visitors, just as it had been on most weekends before the war. Joy Hester and Albert Tucker were there, and they greeted Jack affectionately, sharing their news confirming that which was patently obvious—Joy was in an advanced state of pregnancy. She and Tucker had married two years earlier, and the baby had been a surprise to them. Jack was amazed on both counts. He remembered how they'd argued against the notion of marriage, believing it to be an outdated institution. And Joy had always claimed that she deplored children and insisted that she'd never have any. He supposed that war changed a lot about people.

Notwithstanding her pregnancy, it was as if the same hormones that were nurturing the baby in Joy's womb had simultaneously nurtured her artistic output, and she enthusiastically showed him a series of her latest paintings. The works were bold line drawings—full-figured nudes—and Jack wondered if Joy's foray into the curvaceous female figures stemmed from her own pregnant state.

Three paintings framed and hanging on the wall caught Jack's attention, and he could see that the Ned Kelly theme that Sidney and Sunday had toyed with prior to his enlistment had been developed.

'They are wonderful, aren't they, Jack? Not finished yet. Sid and I have got a few more ideas for them. The army has him, unfortunately, though thankfully he's stationed here in Victoria—out west in Dimboola, guarding government stores or something. It's not too bad. At least he's out of harm's way and he can still paint.'

'Is he working as a war artist?' It surprised Jack to think that, like himself, Sidney might work for Treloar.

'No, unfortunately. Or perhaps fortunately! Depends on how you look at it, I suppose.'

Jack was not sure what Sunday meant, and she explained, 'When Sidney applied for a commission as a war artist, he was told his work was too modern! However, given that most of the war artists were sent to the front lines, we are really quite thankful that Sidney's tucked away in the wheat fields. He's got a studio and everything, so—all things considered—it's not so bad. John and I miss him terribly though, don't we, John?'

'And Elizabeth… how is she taking it?' Jack asked.

John looked down at the floor as Sunday replied. Her answer saddened Jack.

'Oh, that didn't last. She and Sid married, but Elizabeth couldn't cope with an artist husband. You know, the financial difficulties, the uncertainty of it all. Her parents put a lot of pressure on Sid, to get "a real job", especially after the baby was born. In the end, he and Elizabeth called it quits. That was when Sidney moved in here. It was for the best, really.'

'A baby? They had a child?'

'Yes… Amelda. A sweet little thing. Sid sees her from time to time. It's a shame that Elizabeth was so clingy and demanding. They might have made a go of it had she been more understanding.'

Sunday's response, her focus on Elizabeth's shortcomings rather than acknowledging the obsessive relationship that had developed between herself and Nolan, reminded Jack of Sunday's inclination to see the world in simple terms that conformed to her own perspective of reality.

'That's a shame,' he said. 'I really liked Elizabeth. I hoped that things would have worked out better for her and Sidney.'

'How's Margaret?... I haven't seen her in months. Sometimes she pops into the office with Cynthia. They get along quite well, those two. I think that Margaret is good for Cynthia. Terrible news about Virginia, wasn't it?'

'Dreadful. You just don't expect these things to happen.'

Jack pondered the story Margaret had shared with him, only a few weeks ago. Old news, that had occurred when he'd been somewhere between Tobruk and Greece, and so although the papers had been full of it, Jack had been otherwise occupied. Her cousin, Virginia had died the previous March, she'd told him. Shockingly, by suicide– Virginia had filled her pockets with stones and walked into the river behind the house that she and Leonard lived in. Margaret had been sad, although with a year to reflect on Virginia's actions, she'd concluded that perhaps it wasn't so surprising after all. Margaret explained that Ginnie always had demons, and she'd suffered a number of breakdowns since she was a young teenager.

For all of Margaret's acceptance of the tragedy, Jack had been shocked, as memories of the fragile woman with flickering eyes and a haunted expression that he'd met at the Bell's home, Charleston, returned to him. He was overcome with the thought that some people seemed to live their whole lives at war with an enemy within, from whom they could never escape, and sometimes that enemy defeated them.

There was a new member of the Heide Circle, Jack noted. A young man from South Australia called Max, barely twenty, who shared the Reeds' love for poetry as well as their passion for modernism. Jack listened to him rant about the rising influence of a South Australian movement of anti-modernists, the Jindyworobaks, and how he'd created his own magazine in order to oppose them. Titled *Angry Penguins,* Max's magazine focused on modern poetry, literature and art, and had proved popular in South Australia. Encouraged by its success, Max had since expanded the magazine to Melbourne where the Reeds had been excited to offer their support, and John had agreed to accept the role of co-editor. Jack could see that the Reeds were ecstatic with this new project, confident that Australia's modern art movement had turned a corner and was finally gaining recognition. He mused there was no doubt about John and Sunday: they really poured their hearts and souls into the causes they believed in!

Later, Max cornered Jack and set about berating the Jindyworobaks for promoting their narrow nationalistic view of art and literature. Whilst there were aspects of Max's views that were interesting, Jack wished that both the traditionalists and modernists would learn to live with each other. What did it matter whether literature or art was traditional or modern; realistic or surreal; abstract or expressionist? Increasingly, he believed there were elements of genius and mediocrity in both. He knew there were paintings that people might love, and others that they'd hate. Some people chose a painting for its looks and colours, some for the memories that a scene evoked. Others liked a painting for the story it told, or for the truth it revealed, or how it moved them. But truly, he found the endless arguments wearisome. He'd lost a wife and child, and he'd stood by men as they'd taken their last breaths fighting for tenuous ideals on battlegrounds far from their homes. Could all of this concern about the words people wrote or what was painted on canvas, really be so important?

Jack enjoyed the afternoon spent at Heide, and the dinner meal was the best that he'd eaten in a long time. After drinking more wine than he had in years, Jack happily accepted Sunday's offer to stay the night, sleeping on their couch.

The following morning, he woke early to the aroma of bacon sizzling in the pan and the music of laughter ringing from the kitchen. Jack joined John, Albert and Max and accepted a cup of coffee and a plate of bacon and toast.

'Bacon, John! Really?' Jack laughed.

'It's Sunday morning, Jack. My one day of indulgence. Isn't it heavenly?'

The men chatted over breakfast, and Jack was surprised to learn that Albert too had worked for Treloar for a period, and furthermore

371

he'd been based at Heidelberg—the very same military hospital in which Jack had been a patient—and that Albert had finished his commission just weeks before Jack had been admitted.

'To think, Jack, I missed the opportunity to paint a masterpiece of you all bandaged up and a heartbeat away from death's door,' Albert laughed. 'It was awful there, though. Not just the physical wounds, terrible as they were. It was the emotional trauma that got to me. I don't think half enough is being done for some of those poor fellows.'

After they finished the washing up, Jack accompanied John on a walk through the garden and down along the river. Later, Sunday called them to the table under the magnolia tree, where they sat chatting and drinking the coffee she'd prepared. It surprised Jack when Sunday suggested that he might like to return to Heide, live there and continue his painting for the war memorial. He could help in the garden, just as he had before he'd enlisted.

Jack declined. Heide was lovely, but for him, it was part of a past life. He'd forever be thankful to John and Sunday for letting him live there, for the care that they'd provided through the worst year of his life following the death of Scotty and then the loss of Sofia, but it was time to move on.

Nora had been gone only two weeks when Jack stepped onto the front porch to find a parcel from her. He must have been concentrating so hard on his painting that morning that he hadn't heard the delivery man. He carried it inside, carefully cut the string and unwrapped the brown paper, revealing a large box.

On opening it, he found two small parcels wrapped in tissue paper. They were the pair of paintings that Nora had promised for his mother for the dining room wall in her new home. She was right, they would be wonderful there, Jack thought, looking at them. One was a small vase of violas; the other, pansies, just as Nora had described. Their colour was marvellous, the detail incredible.

Jack had never painted flowers, a subject he'd dismissed as the domain of female painters. He chuckled as he recalled letting this thought slip one afternoon as he and Nora had strolled through the Fitzroy Gardens. Her sardonic response had been immediate. *' I have two words for you, Jack! No, make it three. Van Gogh... Sunflowers!'* Jack had been suitably chastised, for the whole world knew of the extraordinary series of works painted by the Dutch artist. And if that hadn't been enough, Nora had added, *'And then, of course, there is Monet, with his* Water Lilies; *not to mention Klimt with his* Flower Garden! *Trust me, Jack, there is no shortage of male artists who are famous for their flowers. Soon, you, too, will turn your hand to them, mark my words!'*

Studying the paintings, Jack suspected that she may well be better than the lot of them, and he was sure that he could never paint flowers with the mastery that she managed so beautifully.

Besides the paintings, Nora had included a large brown envelope and a letter.

*Dear Jack,*

*I hope that all is going well for you and that Treloar has not bored you to death since I left.*

*Please give these paintings to your mother, along with my best wishes. I hope that she likes them!*

*I have also included prints for you, two of them, which I consider the very best of my portraits. Mother-and-child images that I painted before the war. Lastly, I have sent a small watercolour that my father painted for an exhibition back in 1940. He really is very good, don't you think?*

*Today is the big day of departure! Later this morning I will fly to Brisbane, and then I will go on to New Guinea to start my adventure. I must go now, but will write again as soon as I have settled and have something newsworthy to share.*

*Thank you again for your friendship. My time in Melbourne would have been very dull without our chats, walks in the beautiful gardens and the company of your delightful parents.*

*Yours affectionately,*

*Nora*

Jack looked at the prints that Nora had included. As she'd said, they were portraits of mothers with their children, beautiful in their simplicity. One was a very natural portrayal of a mother sitting on the edge of a field, her naked infant resting on her lap, and simply titled *Motherhood*. The other shared a similar setting and was titled *Dedication*. Both portrayed working-class women with their babies in everyday settings. They were the sort of thing he had sketched a hundred times as he'd sat in his cabin watching Sofia nursing their tiny baby, or when he'd captured Scotty leaning against her, sucking his thumb, absorbed in a story she was reading or listening to his night-time lullaby. More than once, Jack had made preliminary sketches that he'd planned to develop into a serious oil painting, but none had been taken to the point of completion. Their little cabin was too small, their lives too busy with the demands of Montsalvat, and there had always been the expectation of time. A "one day" that had never arrived and was now lost to him forever.

Distracting himself from wallowing in unhelpful thoughts, Jack turned to the Hans Heysen painting that Nora had included. It was a watercolour titled *White Gums*, with the most astonishing blue sky providing a perfect backdrop to a stand of gleaming white smooth-trunked trees. Ghost gums, he suspected. Uniquely Australian, the painting was surely a combination of realism and modernism, with its modern colours and classic subject, Jack thought. And utterly beautiful.

In the first week of July, a headline in Saturday's morning newspaper caught Jack's attention: '*Poets Use Nonsensical Verse for Great Literary Leg-Pull.*' The article attracted him, not because he enjoyed poetry, despite Sunday's best efforts to develop his interest when he was living at Heide, but rather because the word 'hoax' in the first sentence jumped out at him, intriguing enough for him to start reading. And when the first paragraph had a direct reference to *Angry Penguins*, the magazine that John and Max Harris were publishing, Jack was even more curious.

As he read, Jack felt concerned for John, for the article was damning in its criticism of the magazine he co-edited. Beyond simply regurgitating the tired old battle between conservatives and traditionalists, this was a scathing personal attack on both John and Max's professionalism, ridiculing their judgement because they'd succumbed to a hoax whereby they'd not only published nonsensical poetry that was deemed to be lewd and distasteful, but that they'd lauded the poems as the work of a genius.

The story did not go away and, day after day, the newspapers provided various angles on the hoax that made for captivating reading; and some reports extended into the lives of the Reeds themselves, questioning their decision to support *Angry Penguins* as well as their continued patronage for modern artists.

While Jack didn't have any opinion on the merits of the critics' views or of the value of *Angry Penguins*, he worried for the Reeds, knowing they'd find the media's attack deeply hurtful. He decided to visit them again the following Saturday. Not surprisingly, he found both very upset. The reputation of *Angry Penguins* had been destroyed, and John had taken it very personally.

'How on earth could this happen?' Jack asked.

'Oh, two rascals from Adelaide—university students—James McAuley and Harold Stewart. A pair of traditionalists who fear progress and therefore insist on attacking any steps towards modernism.'

'Yes, but how can their opinion matter?'

'It's not their opinion that's the issue. Everyone's entitled to an opinion. What these scoundrels did was create a bunch of poems and, using the name Ethel, submitted them to us, claiming they'd been written by her deceased brother "Ernest Malley". We thought they were interesting. Quite surreal. Very unusual, if not a little racy. Anyway, we did the right thing and gave them a good write-up in the spring edition of *Angry Penguins*, praising Malley's work for its originality and sharing a couple of verses with the public. Certainly, nobody could claim that they weren't original, could they? The poems were actually very well received! However, McCauley and Stewart have since come out, claiming themselves to be the true authors and declaring the poems to be a lot of rubbish that they'd written in an afternoon. They've made total fools of us. It's in all the papers, as you know, and now Max, because he's the publisher, has been charged for publishing obscene content!'

'Why do these people do this, Jack?' Sunday lamented. 'What is wrong with them?'

Jack had no answers, and later over dinner with Margaret, he discussed the story.

'It's typical, Jack,' she said. 'Just another example of Australia's dinosaur attitude towards the arts. For centuries, Europe has embraced the modernists, but here we criticise anything that is new, tear it down without a thought. Honestly, it's as though Australians are clinging to some British, elitist, high-brow version of art that was valued a century ago, but even the British have moved on. Mind you, I must say, some poetry that I hear these days does go way over my head.'

Over the next two weeks, articles about the hoax receded, and Jack returned to Heide, hoping to find John and Sunday's spirits lifted. However, he discovered that a new drama had entered their lives in the shape of Sidney Nolan, who, along with Joy and Albert, was sitting at the Reeds' dining table, looking totally unfamiliar with his neatly cut hair and the khaki uniform of a private.

'They want him to go to New Guinea.' John told Jack soberly. 'Really. You wonder at their judgement! Sid's no soldier.'

'He can't go, can he, Jack?' Sunday insisted, appealing to his judgement, based on his own service—the wavering in her voice revealing that tears were imminent.

'The problem is that if you don't go, Sid, you'll be jailed,' Jack offered, as unhelpful as the advice seemed.

'No! Going to jail is not an option either,' Sunday cried, and this time her tears spilled over.

'It's ridiculous!' Albert said. 'This war has killed thousands of our men, tens of thousands even, and yet they keep wanting to send more!

Where is it all going to end? After they've killed off every last one of us?'

'I'll be okay,' said Nolan, but his tone lacked conviction. 'What do you say, Jack? It must be all but over now. Just a bit of tidying up to do?'

Jack didn't know how to answer. Having been to the fronts of North Africa, Greece and Crete, where he'd observed battles at close range, followed by experiencing the military might of the German forces, and then on returning seen the broken minds and bodies of the young soldiers in Heidelberg Military Hospital, he felt conflicted. Certainly, in New Guinea, the battle would not be against the Germans but rather the Japanese. Yet recent stories of the atrocities that accompanied Japan's military successes in the Pacific meant Jack already held fears for Nora, sorry for encouraging Treloar to give in to her hankering for an overseas posting. He would not forgive himself if anything should happen to her and only consoled himself with the knowledge that Treloar's arrangements kept her well clear from the battlefields.

As for Nolan, his posting to New Guinea would not save him from the frontline, and Jack instinctively knew that the lad, with his penchant for art and poetry, did not belong on the front; worse, he would surely be a liability to those around him. However, such thoughts were not what Sidney needed to hear at this moment.

'Yeah, mate. The Americans have brought in their submarines, so that should slow the Japanese down.' Jack tried not to think about the *Centaur*, the hospital ship that had taken a hit from the Japanese the previous year, killing almost three hundred, or the stories that were coming out of the prisoner-of-war camps in Changi and Wake Island. Instead, he said, 'The Allies are pushing back now. We've nearly got them. It'll all be over soon.'

'Sidney.' Sunday had taken control of her wayward emotions, and now she showed the calculating demeanour of a strategist at the table of a council of war. 'What we must do is hide you!'

John sighed loudly, and his response was cutting. 'Sunday, that is bloody ridiculous. How on earth are we ever going to hide Sidney? Everybody knows that he lives here! If he goes missing, this is the first place they'll come looking for him. He's just going to have to man up and last the war out.'

'No, John. He can't.' The decisiveness that Sunday had mustered seconds earlier was abandoned, and she sobbed as she spoke. 'I don't mean that we hide Sidney here. I am thinking that he goes to one of the regional towns. Takes on a new identity. At least we can think about it.'

'Actually, a friend of mine, Doug, has offered me a place to hide out, if I want it,' Nolan said quietly.

Jack listened, fascinated, as pictures came to his mind of Sidney bearing a fake moustache and glasses, lurking around the towns of country Victoria. Perhaps he could adopt a limp, hinting at a past injury. Make people think he'd already served his time and hope they'd leave him alone. Jack knew the public could be savage towards those who had not played their part for the war effort. The newspapers were full of stories about men—whose applications to join the services were declined for health reasons—being subjected to the most appalling of insults, even having white feathers thrust into their hands, branding them as shirkers–cowards–who refused to step up and do their bit for the nation. Jack occasionally felt the sting of judgement from strangers who did not know his service history and was very thankful that these days he wasn't dependent on public transport, where derogatory confrontations abounded.

John continued, 'For heaven's sake, Sunday, they could lock Sidney up for years if he goes into hiding. The army takes a very serious view of soldiers who go absent without leave. There's got to be another way!' He was every bit as upset as his wife over the predicament that Nolan found himself in, and Jack could see that the closeness the three shared had only deepened.

Over the next few hours, the discussion evolved, assisted by the opinions of Joy and Albert, and a plan was formulated. Sidney would adopt a false name, 'Robin Murray.' Jack knew that Robin had always been Sunday's nickname for Nolan but guessed none of them could ever have imagined the name would be used in this way.

They agreed that after his leave, Nolan should catch the train as usual, as though returning to his post, but instead he would go to his friend Doug's house. That way, if army officials arrived at Heide, John and Sunday could honestly insist that Nolan had caught the morning train to the barracks, and they hadn't heard from him since. They would insinuate that foul play must have beset the young artist.

Returning to Copelen Street later that day, Jack felt guilty for his role in encouraging Nolan to shirk his duty. He marvelled how Heide was like Montsalvat, each its own little universe, where it was easy to ignore the rules that everyone else followed. Had he done the right thing in supporting the plan for Nolan to escape his posting to New Guinea? Yes. He was sure he had—both for Nolan's sake and also for the poor buggers over there who would have had him at their sides as they fought the Japanese. With a bit of luck, the war would be over soon; Nora and the soldiers in the Pacific and his old mates Snowy, Macka, Leo and Danny would be home again. And Nolan could happily continue to do what he was born to do: paint.

~

Jack enjoyed the days he spent at the barracks, sorting through hundreds of service unit diaries—more than he'd expected. As requested, he spent hours skimming through their contents, on the alert for interesting facts that could be cross-referenced to the other resources, helping Treloar in his bid to glean the fullness of the stories that they told.

Letters from Nora arrived regularly, reassuring Jack that she was indeed safe from imminent danger, though it did not stop him from writing back encouraging her to make her overseas service brief, a suggestion that she utterly ignored. Instead, she regaled him with stories of a lifestyle at total odds with the luxury of the Menzies, yet which she clearly loved.

Stationed at the army hospital in Finschhafen, she'd been delegated her own little tent and straw mattress, which she'd set up amid mud and creepy crawlies at a distance from the hut the nurses shared. She'd explained how, on arriving with her spotless uniform that had never seen so much as a scratch, and her captain pips and inflated wages, the nurses hadn't accepted her; but thankfully, she'd found the surgeons more cooperative. They actually called her in when they had interesting operations for her to paint and invited her to join them when they were off duty, creating opportunities for her to sketch Medical Corps members relaxing.

Painting in the tropics was proving challenging, she'd added, and she had a constant battle with mildew forming on her canvases overnight because of the humidity. To Nora's credit, she seemed to find humour in it all, and not for the first time, Jack admired her pluck. By her third letter, though, he could see that distance had not improved her relationship with Treloar, and she still itched to get closer to the frontline action.

～

'That woman,' Treloar said, shaking his head. 'Look at these paintings, Jack. Tea parties and a dance! What does that tell anyone about the war? I want to see the nurses at work! The ambulance drivers! Captain Heysen's impossible. Anything I suggest to her, she misinterprets, and accuses me of controlling her! And look at these!' John unrolled two canvases. 'Men! I send her to paint women at work, and she paints men. And not satisfied that I have sent her overseas, now she's demanding that I get her closer to the front—so she can access the men's quarters and the battlefields. It's unthinkable! How can I send a woman into men's camps, with their open-air showers and male-only facilities? The AIF would have my head! It won't be happening!'

Jack agreed with Treloar, not because he was worried about the notion of a woman in the man's world of an army camp, but because he wanted her to be as far away from the Japanese soldiers as possible.

Nora's letters to Jack expanded on the conflicts from her point of view.

*Who the hell does Treloar think he is, telling me what I should paint?* she demanded, before adding, *You won't believe it, but he's told me off for giving away my work! How on earth does he know these things? Is someone here spying on me? Wouldn't surprise me! I am sure that Treloar is hoping that I'll slip up in some way, so he can bring me home! He wrote and told me that anything that I draw, no*

*matter how slight, is the property of the Commonwealth. Truly, I detest
the man! I don't know how you can work with him!*

Jack couldn't help but feel sorry for Nora, and remembering the
dozens of sketches that he'd so happily given away to his friends on
Crete while he was being employed by the army, he also felt guilty. It
was hard to be an artist and yet be told what you could and couldn't
paint, and even worse, be told that your paintings were no longer
yours.

~

In late January, Jack received a phone call from the real estate agent.
An offer had been made for his parents' home which met their asking
price. On behalf of his mother, Jack agreed that the offer should be
accepted immediately. Hanging up the phone, he looked around the
kitchen. He had eight weeks to empty the house of his belongings, tidy
the shed and give everything a final clean in readiness for the new
owners.

Suddenly, Jack's life was busy with his work at the barracks,
cleaning the house and searching for accommodation for himself. He
considered buying a house. He had four years of wages from the army
which he'd barely touched, and in addition, his mother wanted him to
accept two thousand pounds from the sale of Copelen Street.

The real estate officer who'd managed the sale enthusiastically
took Jack on a tour of available properties. However, each, with its
floral wallpaper, family living rooms and children's bedrooms, proved
a poignant reminder of a life lost, and Jack's desire to buy a house
quickly waned.

Instead, thinking that it would be good to remain near to his
parents, he accepted a lease on a nondescript apartment with two large
bedrooms, barely fifteen minutes' drive from them, on Acland Street in
St Kilda.

A thought that constantly nagged Jack was that, once he left
Copelen Street, Sofia would have no way of finding him again should
she ever return to Australia. He knew he was being irrational, given the
news he'd received from Genevieve Winters. Nonetheless, Jack had

381

never shaken the hope that a second letter would arrive—a letter in Sofia's own handwriting. A letter telling him that she'd never forgotten him and that leaving him had been a terrible mistake. Jack chided himself for such foolishness; it had been almost seven years since Sofia left, heaven forbid! Still, he decided he'd discuss the problem with the postmaster.

Explaining that his parents' house had been sold, he asked, 'What do I do about forwarding mail from Copelen Street to my new address?'

'No worries, sir. Happens all the time. To which address are we redirecting your mail?'

'Unit 6, 57 Acland Street, St Kilda.'

'And how long would you like to have your mail redirected?'

'Forever.'

'No, no… We do three months, six months or a year.'

'For as long as mail might be sent to Copelen Street for me, I want to ensure that I receive it, promptly.' Jack could hear the growl in his voice as he spoke.

'Well, how about we get you a post office box? Would that work?'

'No, it won't work. I don't want to be driving here every day to check a post office box for the rest of my life, do I now?'

'Okay, okay. Don't get upset. I will see what I can do.'

A few minutes later, the clerk returned with a new suggestion, and Jack agreed that he would take a one-year subscription. In twelve months, the post office would send out a letter notifying him that the arrangement would expire. It was Jack's responsibility to return there, complete a new annual redirect and pay the fee. It appeared to be the best solution available.

By late March, the house William and Marian had owned for almost three decades was all but empty. Over a four-week period, Jack had moved his bedroom furniture and belongings, taking up residence in his new apartment. Since then, in every spare minute he'd returned to Copelen Street to clean out the shed and wash the windows. When the real estate agent suggested he employ the services of a professional cleaner, a lady called Shirley whom they'd often used and who worked marvels to put the final polish on bathrooms, kitchens and floors for just a few pounds, Jack was quick to accept.

While cleaning the shed, he had selected a few tools that he thought worth keeping: an old axe for firewood, a hoe and mattock for the garden that he might create one day, and an ancient toolbox that his father once used. He transported these items to his parents' shed in Beaumaris late one Sunday afternoon.

'Jack, do you remember if you checked under the stairs at Copelen Street? I meant to have a look last time I was there, but forgot. I don't think there would be much, but can you just have a look anyway?' Marian asked.

Jack hadn't even thought to look at the small space under the stairs. He agreed to make a last visit to the house that very afternoon, before slipping the keys into the real estate office's letterbox in readiness for the official settlement on Tuesday, where Copelen St would be transferred to its new owners.

Two hours later, Jack opened the door, removed his shoes and tiptoed across the carpet. The aroma of eucalyptus filled the air, different from the delicate odour of lemon and lavender cleaning products his mother had used Jack's entire life. It felt strange, as if already the house belonged to someone else, and he was trespassing.

Opening the small door under the stairs, Jack immediately saw his mother's vacuum cleaner. Of course! He recalled how she'd left it for his use while he was living here, electing to purchase a newer, lighter model for her new home. Whilst Jack had regularly swept the kitchen and laundry floors, he had never once felt the need to vacuum the carpets of rooms that he barely entered.

Behind the vacuum cleaner, there was a large cardboard box labelled 'curtains'. Jack dragged it out and opened it. It held the original curtains from the room he and Sofia had occupied. The ones that had been hanging for years until his mother redecorated the room with the blue floral print ready for his and Sofia's return from Spain. The best place for these was the opportunity shop, perhaps even the garbage, Jack decided.

A last glance into the shadowy recesses of the stair cavity caused him to gasp with surprise. A rectangular box remained, which Jack immediately recognised. Sofia's chest! Sofia's Spain, as he'd always called it. He hadn't seen or thought of it for years. In fact, the last time Jack had seen this chest was on the Skippers' porch, the day he'd returned to Montsalvat—before he'd moved to Heide, long before the war. On that occasion, the very sight of the chest had been like having a knife plunge into his heart, causing a pain so acute, Jack had all but collapsed. He remembered how he'd gasped in shock before turning and running away from it.

Today, he simply stared at it in disbelief, stunned both at its presence under the stairwell and by the thought that it had been left behind. Resolutely controlling his emotions, Jack dragged the chest into the hallway, hefted it into his arms and carried it to the car. He returned to gather the unwieldy vacuum cleaner, followed by the box of curtains.

Still shaken by the fact that the chest had not only reappeared, but had been so close to being overlooked, he took one last walk through the house, wondering if anything else of significance had been missed. From what he could see, nothing had been, and the sense of finality at shutting the door to the house felt strange. Another chapter of his life over, Jack thought as, driving home via the real estate agency, he dropped the key into the after-hours letterbox.

# CHAPTER 41

*W*hen he arrived at his apartment, Jack placed the vacuum cleaner and box of curtains in his garage, and then he carried the chest upstairs, where he set it in the centre of his living room.

This chest had been part of his life for over a decade and held memories that were not only Sofia's. He recalled their last days in Malaga, when together they'd packed up the finca, ready for its sale; and Sofia had been brutally efficient in reducing all that she treasured into the chest. He remembered how they'd sealed it, first with tiny tacks, then with tape, securing it to ensure that it would endure the long sea journey to Australia safely. On arriving, the chest had been stored under the stairs at Copelen Street, where occasionally Sofia had sorted through its contents.

Jack's thoughts turned to the afternoon when, after moving from their caravan at Montsalvat into the larger student's cabin, he, Mervyn and Matcham had driven across the city in Mervyn's van, collected the chest and returned it to an ecstatic Sofia. It had been in the weeks preceding Scotty's birth, and Sofia had joyfully searched through its contents, reliving the bittersweet memories that they aroused.

And he remembered, of course, that final, awful day when his relief at rescuing this chest from the fire had been shattered by the knowledge that Scotty had been trapped in the burning building, asleep in the next room. He could never forget Sofia's horror at seeing the chest, her howls of grief as she'd pummelled its sides, rejecting the precious items he'd been so relieved to have saved for her, and instead found that he'd failed to save her greatest treasure, their son.

The memories were disturbing, but time had blunted the acute, stabbing heartache that Jack had experienced when the sight of the chest on the Skippers' veranda had been unbearable.

~

Twilight encroached, darkening the room, and Jack lit a lamp and poured himself a glass of sherry. Again, he looked at the chest. This time he knew, with certainty, that he wanted to open it.

He loosened the top hinge and over the next hour carefully laid out its contents, piece by piece, until he could barely move in his living room. It amazed him that the box could contain so much.

There were silver candlesticks and a large pottery dish. The lace squares that had been Sofia's mother's and the feather-light black mantilla Sofia had worn on their wedding day. Jack opened a small box and discovered a few pieces of jewellery, including the coral necklace he'd bought for Sofia all of those years ago, in Paris. Unpacking a parcel wrapped in white cotton, he was surprised to find the wedding shirts Sofia had sewn for him and Andrés, the colours of their delicate embroidery as bright as they had been on the day they'd been worn.

Breathing deeply, Jack set them aside and lifted a leather-bound book—an old Bible. Inserted within the parchment pages were half a dozen certificates for birth, marriage and baptism, all but one bearing the signature of Father Sebastian. And, of course, there were the paintings. Hundreds of them. Dozens stored in flat boxes, others separated by tissue paper and carefully rolled in the same cardboard cylinders that Sofia had once offered to clients of Galleria Toulouse so they could mail their purchases across the world.

Jack refilled his sherry glass. Taking his time, he looked at every single item, surprised at how calm he felt, pleased that he could control his emotions as he viewed the items.

The Picassos and Matisses were just as Jack remembered them, and he calculated that they'd be worth a small fortune now, for both artists had maintained their popularity in the modern art world. Now their work was highly coveted, their value far beyond the reach of all but the most serious collectors. He gazed at the Solleros, which had always been his favourites, and laid them on his table, using silver cutlery to hold their edges flat.

Gently Jack passed his hands over a painting, his fingertips brushing the uneven surface that had been created by Andrés' palette knife, and his heart felt heavy as he remembered his brother-in-law. Sofia had agonised as she'd selected from her brother's works, for each held memories for her. This one, a scene of Castillo Gibralfaro, was done in an experimental cubist style, and Jack remembered standing beside Andrés as he'd finished it.

Later, studying a painting depicting two smiling children playing in the orange orchard, Jack raised his glass to Ramón Fernandez, the man he'd never met, whose love of art had created such a legacy. Yet he suspected that, like himself, the twins' father would trade the life of an artist for that of the most menial labourer in a moment—if it meant that his wife and children would be granted long, happy lives.

For two days, Jack left the contents of the chest around his new living room, surprised by the comfort he felt amid Sofia's belongings.

Repeatedly, he returned to the paintings, and particularly the Sorollas—they were truly wonderful. Jack had always intended to paint portraits of his own family like these. Paintings that captured an ethereal translucence, a breathtaking, timeless beauty, yet at the same time were grounded in the reality of everyday lives. Returning to gaze upon the image of Sorolla's wife and children walking along the beach, Jack made up his mind: Sofia may be lost to him, but that did not have to stop him from painting her the way he'd always intended to.

Looking around at the contents of the chest, Jack selected a few items. A filigree hair comb and the cobweb-fine mantilla. He searched among the jewellery for the gold locket that he'd bought Sofia before their wedding, but it wasn't there. He did find the tiny diamond and sapphire earrings that he'd bought her in Paris. He walked to his bedroom and collected the photograph he had of Scotty—the one that had travelled from Australia to the Middle East and back again, and which now remained at his bedside alongside Jack and Sofia's wedding photo. All of these would combine to tell the story of the woman he loved. This painting would be the master portrait he'd never created, one worthy of withstanding time and history.

Since he'd moved into the apartment, Jack had used the spare bedroom as a studio to work on his paintings for the War Memorial. For this painting, though, he decided to work amid Sofia's possessions. First, he moved the strewn contents of the box to the perimeter of the room: the paintings and the jewellery, her mother's lace and the wedding shirts—all the bits and pieces that represented Sofia's life. Only when he was happy with the feel of the room, when it felt joyful rather than melancholic, did he drag his easel into its centre and measure it to determine the largest size of painting it would hold.

Next, returning to his studio, Jack spent half a day building a frame, cutting and tacking the canvas carefully in position and hoping that it would be adequately stretched despite his weakened left arm. He then searched though the jars of turpentine and oils till he found an old jar of rabbit skin glue, which he applied to the surface, and the following morning, he added a coating of white lead which he knew would give his finished work luminosity and texture. As he worked, it seemed as though Monsieur Simon was there beside him, reminding him that '...for a painting to endure for centuries, its surface must be perfectly prepared before the pigments are applied.'

With twenty-four hours required to allow the surface to dry, Jack turned to his sketchbook, where he used charcoal and pencil to create dozens of loosely arranged drawings, each an improvement on the last, until he was finally satisfied with the layout of his design.

Two days later, rather than commence the painting he'd planned for that week—the dreadful bombing that had been followed by the pamphlet drop across Crete—Jack began painting Sofia.

For this piece, he'd already determined he would use the methods of Johannes Vermeer, the wonderful Danish artist, who like most of the masters, created an underpainting in a single colour—a monochromatic version of the planned work. This would add volume and depth to the finished portrait, and additionally, Jack hoped it would highlight the glow of Sofia's skin, further enhancing illumination as if a light were shining from within the canvas.

Jack blended umber brown with a touch of blue and used broad strokes to transfer the drawing he'd made onto the canvas. He paid particular attention to light and shadow, deepening and lightening the tones as he moved from one feature to the next.

The work was quick and easy, and from a blank canvas the figure of a woman took shape. Despite the shadowy brown tones, Jack could see her emerging before him.

The following morning, he woke early. His sleep had been consumed by dreams of Sofia, but he felt rested. The dreams had been good. When he stepped into his living room, the sun's low rays fell onto the canvas and Jack was pleased with what he saw. 'My sweetheart,' he murmured as, without bothering to change from his pyjamas, he picked up his palette and applied paint.

As his brush moved across the canvas, Jack barely thought about Sofia's liquid dark eyes or the smooth arc of her forehead. Nor did he focus on the soft curve of her nose or the angle of her cheek. Rather, he felt Sofia's humour soften her brow, and saw the sparkle of joy that lit her eyes and radiated to where the corners of her mouth crinkled into her cheeks when she laughed. He gave her jaw a touch of firmness, a hint of her resolute spirit, and then deepened the shadows to the left of her face and lightened her forehead to accentuate the tilt of her head, which enhanced her teasing expression. He added detail to her hands, which he'd once thought of as dainty and fine, but had learned were equally firm and strong; purposed for tending gardens, slicing onions and beans, stroking the forehead of a child who was ill and for roaming across Jack's own shoulders and down his back. Jack groaned with the ache of missing her. He moved his brush over Sofia's throat, defining the delicacy of her collarbones, then added depth to her shoulders and arms, squaring her stance and conveying her bearing as a proud Spanish woman. He remembered how she'd stomped, as she'd danced the fandango on a night so many years ago.

As Jack painted, he recalled the advice Picasso had given to him a decade earlier. *'Don't paint what you see... paint what you feel. Paint your emotions. Paint the truth.'*

Which truth? The truth was... complex. Two lives that had become three, and then two again. Lives lived joyously, abundant with hopes and dreams that had been crushed in a moment by tragedy. But there was also the enduring truth of his love for Sofia.

That would be the story of this painting. Yes, it was a painting of Sofia, but really, was it not as much a portrait of Jack himself? For with every sweep of his brush, it seemed to him that he was laying bare his heart on the canvas, his love, for all the world to see.

At first Jack had considered positioning Sofia in her kitchen, a place that she loved, but decided that had been Andrés' vision—the subject of the painting that won the Prado's Portraiture Prize fourteen years earlier, providing the funds that had allowed the twins to go to Paris. Instead, he depicted Sofia standing beside a large window, her hand resting on its ledge, her body half turned toward him. To her left he added shelves where the photo of Scotty sat amid the folds of lace, the silver candlesticks and her mother's earthenware bowl. Outside the window he painted a garden, which he filled with geraniums and bougainvillea, and then he added a single tree: an orange tree bearing both blossom and fruit.

The garden fell away to a small dam, and he added a smattering of colour that formed the illusion of lilies floating on its surface. The scene beyond the window was utterly fanciful—a hybrid that was half Malaga, half Montsalvat, each of which had been sources of joy to Sofia.

After changing his mind repeatedly, in the end Jack painted her looking directly at him, her eyes peering deeply into his, with a hint of laughter combined with her quizzical expression. It had been his favourite expression, the look that she used to give him when he'd advance towards her, teasingly drawing her to him with loving on his mind.

'Where are you, my love?' Jack whispered as he gazed back into her eyes. 'Please be happy. Please be safe. Scotty and I, we love you. Don't ever forget that.'

~

For five days Jack painted, starting early each morning and working until late into the night. He gave little thought to meals, but filled up on cheese, bread, biscuits and fruit. He barely heard the knock on his door, so engrossed was he in his work, deeply immersed in a world where only he and Sofia existed.

However, when the knock turned into a pounding, it broke through his concentration. Opening the door, he found Margaret standing on his front step.

'Oh, wonderful, Jack! I was hoping that you would be home. So much has happened. Are you okay? You look different.'

'Of course I'm okay. Come on in. Mind the mess.'

He led her down the hallway into the living area and moved the box holding Andrés' and his father's paintings off a chair for her; but rather than sitting she stood, gazing at his easel.

'Oh my, Jack. This is amazing! Truly! What's going on? What is all of this?' She cast her arm out, embracing the mess in the room, the paintings and artefacts that filled every surface. 'Is Sofia here? Where is she?'

Margaret moved as if she intended to search the apartment, excited by the thought of seeing Sofia at last.

'No, Margaret. Sofia's not here. But I found this—' Jack gestured towards the chest. 'I thought … well… I suppose I shouldn't have opened it, really. It is Sofia's, after all!' He felt a wave of guilt as he looked around the apartment, strewn with Sofia's possessions.

'Jack, no! It's alright. You're Sofia's husband. She left it here with you. She wouldn't mind at all. So, you decided to paint her?'

Jack nodded.

'This painting! Wow… it is truly exquisite! Wonderful! I am stunned! You need to enter it into the Archibald.'

'The Archibald?'

'Yes, Jack, the Archibald. Entries are being accepted now. That painting is superb. I can't take my eyes off it! It's Sofia, but it is more than that. She's … sublime…. If the mad Mullah can win the Archibald, then with that painting, you'll win easily.'

Jack laughed. He'd heard that Max Meldrum had won the Archibald not once, but twice in recent years, and he'd been impressed by the old man's efforts. 'I don't know about that—but thank you. I am glad that you like it. It's rather big, isn't it? I've never painted anything this size before.'

Gazing at the painting again, Jack saw it as he imagined Margaret was viewing it. It was beautiful, he knew. Possibly—no, easily—the best painting he'd ever done. It was still not finished, of course. There was much more detail to be added, weeks of work to get it right, but it was unquestionably very good.

'So, what's your news?' he asked, hoping to divert Margaret's intensity. For all the beauty of the painting, Jack had never planned it to be for an audience beyond himself.

'Well, you are not going to believe this, but I have been seeing someone ...'

'I guessed that.' He hadn't, actually, but in hindsight, it explained the long absences between their encounters and Margaret's rushed visits when they had seen each other lately.

'Yes, but what you didn't guess, I bet, is that he's an American!'

'No! Not you, too, Margaret. I thought that you would have had a bit more sense than all the silly girls who've lost their heads to the GIs swanning around Melbourne.'

'Greg's not a GI, Jack, and he doesn't swan around. He's really nice. He works for the Guggenheim family. They have mining interests all across the world.'

'Aren't they into art?' The name was unusual and Jack recalled

Sunday and John speaking of the Guggenheims years earlier—something about an art fellowship that they were offering. At the time, he'd gleaned that the Guggenheims were like an American version of the Reeds—albeit a ridiculously wealthy version—who were determined to see the advancement of modern art in their own country.

'Yes, they are, but first and foremost, the Guggenheims made their money in mining. They are almost out of it now, but I guess mining is in the family's blood, and they are interested in Australia's resources. Greg's an accountant, and he's here with one of Guggenhiem's engineers, Lawrence, to meet with the Consolidated Zinc Corporation who, would you believe, has connections to the Bailleaus, Sunday's family. In the next month they plan to tour some of our mines. But, as you said, the Guggenheim family also has a serious interest in art, and whilst Greg and Lawrence are here, they plan to follow up on some of Australia's modern art.'

'And I suppose then you'll be sailing off to America to marry a millionaire?'

'No, sadly, I won't be. Gregory is not a millionaire, nor are we talking about getting married. But he is very good company. I met him and Lawrence at the Young and Jackson, and we got chatting. Of course, with *Chloe* there—you know, the nude—we got on to art, and from there, our shared interest emerged. They've nominated me as their tour guide, and I've already taken them to the National Gallery and a few of the smaller places. They've asked me to go to Sydney with them! I've got a few contacts already. Apparently, the Sydney art scene is fabulous!'

'So I've been told,' said Jack, further irritated. 'Nora was full of it—the excitement of living around King's Cross surrounded by artists. How boring we all are in Melbourne!'

Margaret laughed. 'One thing I do know, there are some fabulous women artists in Sydney. Grace Cossington Smith and Margaret Preston, to name a couple. And there's Dorrit Black, who has her own Modern Art Centre there and is pushing for women artists to be recognised. Greg and Lawrence can't wait to meet her.'

Margaret was clearly excited, and Jack felt guilty. Here she was, after all these years, finally seeing someone. Hopefully she'd overcome the loss of her childhood sweetheart—the boy whose lofty ideals about serving his country had been blasted out of him by enemy fire twenty-five years earlier, along with his lifeblood and final breath. To Jack's knowledge, Margaret had never even gotten close to a romance since then. He resolved to be a little more pleased for her.

'Sounds wonderful, Margaret. I am happy for you!'

Apparently, his words didn't have the desired effect.

'Don't worry, Jack, I won't forget about you! And if you keep painting like that, you'll knock the Sydney artists out of the water. Now, sorry to rush, but I have a dinner date.' She raised her eyebrows at him, suggesting the date held the promise of something more.

He laughed. 'Okay, then. You go and have some fun. You deserve it.'

'Don't forget the Archibald. You've got a couple of weeks to get this finished, dried and packed! It'll have to go by courier, I imagine. Drop by the National Gallery, you'll find an entry form there with all the necessary details.'

Jack shook his head as he returned to the living room. The Archibald! Honestly, there was no end to Margaret's aspirations for him.

Over the next few days, a peace descended upon Jack. He'd packed up most of the contents of the chest, but still a few objects remained scattered about. He decided *Sofia* needed a frame, but rather than wrestle the large painting to a framer, he purchased the materials ready-cut and framed her himself. Daily, he found himself gazing at the painting and adding touches of detail. It was as though by dabbing a brush stroke here, a highlight there, he was gently caressing her. Sofia was with him again, and Jack no longer felt alone. Perhaps a day would come when he would finally let go of the other Sofia. The one who'd made a new life for herself, across the world, far from him.

It was a Wednesday afternoon, two weeks later, that Jack opened his door in answer to a knock and found Margaret standing there, flushed with excitement. Behind her stood a tall man with an easy smile, whom she introduced as Gregory.

'We're heading off to Sydney in two days, Jack, you know, on the trip that I told you about. I wanted Gregory to meet you before we left.'

The man was quick to shake his hand, and Jack sensed his warmth immediately.

'Hi there, Jack. Nice to meet you. Margaret has told me so much about you.'

'I am sorry that I can't say the same about you, because it seems that Margaret is far too busy to see the likes of me these days!' Jack laughed, hoping that Gregory hadn't noticed the trace of petulance that seemed to have crept into his voice. Even after all these years, Margaret had a way of drawing from within him the behaviour of a teasing younger brother.

'Come on in. Is it coffee or sherry time?'

'Jack! *Sofia's* still here! You haven't even packed her! Why? She was due in last…. No… What day is it? Next Wednesday, Jack, we've got five days to get her to Sydney!'

'Margaret, slow down. I can't enter *Sofia* into the Archibald Prize. Haven't you read the terms of the competition? Famous people. A painting created from sittings.'

'Oh, rubbish, Jack! Who cares about that? Those rules are designed to keep the ordinary folk out. Which artists have access to Important People, you tell me? Just tell them that *Sofia* is a Spanish princess or something. They'll never know! In any case, I have attended the Melbourne exhibition of the Archibald every year for the past decade, and believe me, the rules seemed to have relaxed considerably. The exposure you'll get for showing *Sofia* will be wonderful, even if you don't win.'

'I'm not so sure. To be honest, I am quite attached to the painting. I like having *Sofia* here with me. What if something happens to her?'

Margaret looked at Jack as though suddenly remembering all that he'd lost; he saw the compassion in her eyes.

'I know, Jack. I understand. But you will get her back. She'll only be gone for a few months. Imagine the commissions you'll receive when everybody sees what a marvellous artist you are. You've never capitalised on your time in Paris. You know that, don't you? What with burying yourself with Jorgensen and his ridiculous ideas about exhibitions, and then taking yourself off to war!'

'I don't know, Margaret.'

'Of course you do! This portrait needs to be shared, and where better than at the Archibald?'

'See what Margaret's like, Gregory! I will get no peace unless I submit to her demands. She'll probably sneak in and whisk *Sofia* away in the middle of the night if I don't give in!'

'I think you may be right, Jack. That painting is wonderful, though, and deserves to be seen,' Gregory replied.

'Thank you, Greg!' Margaret exclaimed. 'Come on. If we are going to get her in, we better get organised! I don't trust that a courier would get *Sofia* to Sydney on time. Do you think that we could squeeze her in with us, Gregory? Take her to Sydney ourselves? It would mean that you, I and Lawrence would have to squash into the front seat for the drive, but the Archibald is Australia's most prestigious art prize. Fifty thousand pounds to the winner!'

'Sure, Maggie. No worries.'

Jack had no doubts that if Margaret had asked the tall man with bright blue eyes smiling down at her to reach out and pluck a star from the sky, she would have received the same answer.

With Margaret's powers of persuasion having their way, they sprang into action. While she grabbed a pen and worked on the application form Jack had left on the bench two weeks earlier, Greg helped him carry the painting into his studio. They used the wrapping materials intended for the paintings for the War Memorial to package *Sofia* and then carried her down to the enormous Mercedes Benz that Gregory and Lawrence had hired for the duration of their visit in Australia.

Afterward, in a celebratory mood, they agreed that a drink was called for. Squeezing into the front seat of the Mercedes, they drove into the city, and in no time at all they were ensconced in what

Margaret and Gregory referred to as 'their table' in The Latin. The casual statement revealed the amount of time that Margret and Greg had been spending together over the last few weeks. Laughing, they toasted Jack's entry into the Archibald and, of course, Margaret announced her conviction that he'd win.

Jack found Gregory to be a nice chap who was clearly besotted by Margaret. He smiled and nodded at everything she said, and leapt up and returned with one tray of drinks after another, followed by meals of steak and chips, and then more drinks. He refused Jack's offer to pay for anything with a wave of his hand. The Guggenheim expense account was unlimited, it seemed. Margaret's affection for Greg was equally obvious, and she was clearly looking forward to her trip with him and Lawrence—a trip Jack discovered had been extended—and now Margaret was accompanying the Americans as they explored the mines in the Northern Territory and Western Australia!

Margaret explained how she'd received a month's leave from her job at the munitions factory, gaining special permission to undertake what she'd described as the equally important duty of escorting the Americans to the mines to investigate potential business interests. Jack could only imagine that her supervisor had withheld any arguments opposing her plans, knowing that he wouldn't stand a chance of denying her request.

Leaving on Friday, they would drive to Sydney, stopping first at Canberra to explore the capital city, only decades old—and built to the design of the prize-winning entry of Gregory's distant relative, the American architect Walter Burley Griffin. In Sydney, they intended to peruse the art galleries for a few days before continuing their journey into the Australian Outback. A small plane had been chartered to hop, skip and jump them from Sydney to Ayers Rock and then all the way to Mulga Downs Station in the northwest—the home of Lang Hancock, owner of Australia's largest mining company.

Gregory explained that, although the Guggenheim family had relinquished most of their mining interests, they'd recently bought a copper mine in Chile and were curious about the iron reserves that had been discovered in Australia, hence his and Lawrence's visit down under.

Jack tried to picture Margaret flying in a light aircraft across Australia and suppressed images of the planes he'd seen at close hand—smoke and flames pouring out of their fuselages, the explosion of sound as they'd thundered into the ground—assuring himself that those planes had been under attack in very different circumstances. He thought he'd made a good show of looking excited for Margaret.

At six PM, a group of long-haired, casually attired men arrived: artists, accompanied by Justus Jorgensen. Of course, this was the old routine! Jack felt bad, for he had made no effort to contact anyone at Montsalvat since he'd returned to Australia. Occasionally, he'd thought that he should; certainly, he'd love to know how Helen and Sonia were faring and to catch up with Matcham, now a young man in his early twenties. However, part of Jack had held back, and he knew that he balked at the fear of arousing emotions by returning to the place that had cost him so dearly.

These days he was coping well. His work with the Military History Section at the barracks kept him busy, and more than ever he was enjoying painting again. Nonetheless, Jack knew that 'doing well' was a fragile state, and that given the right circumstances—an intrusive odour of eucalyptus, the call of a magpie in the early morning or the sight of a small, slim, dark-haired woman pushing a pram could plunge him into days of depression. He dared not think of the effects a visit to Montsalvat could have on him.

'What a surprise! How are you, Jack? So wonderful to see you. Dodged the bullets, I see. Good on you!' Justus clapped him on the back, and Jack was filled with affection for the man he'd once admired so much.

'I'm well, Justus. A bit of a bust-up to the shoulder, but all is good now. Still teaching at Queen Street?'

'Yes, yes. Some things never change. Are you painting, Jack? Perhaps you'd like to come along and have a look at what we are doing? Or better still, come out to Montsalvat! We'd love to see you there, though I fear your van has been taken over by some of these rascals.'

Jack smiled at the half-dozen faces turned towards him with

interest. He could imagine them besotted by Justus' big dreams and joining in the building projects in Eltham.

'No worries,' he said. 'If people don't use the van, the possums will move in! I've been painting for the Australian War Memorial for the last few months, painting up my experiences. You know the army gave me a commission as a war artist, would you believe?'

'Jack's just submitted a portrait to the Archibald, Justus.' Margaret spoke from behind his left shoulder. She couldn't help herself, Jack thought. She knew of Justus' aversion to exhibitions and his disdain of artists who sought public approval. She was just trying to rile the old man!

'Good for you, Jack.' Justus was generous in his pleasure. 'I'll make sure that I keep an ear to the ground. I'd be thrilled to hear if you're following in Meldrum's footsteps and adding to the annals of Australia's illustrious portrait artists.'

Jack grinned self-consciously. While he didn't share Justus' disdain for exhibitions, it did feel awkward admitting that he was promoting his artwork in none other than the Archibald, yet Justus' enthusiasm for his entry seemed genuine. Perhaps he'd softened his opinions as he'd aged, Jack thought.

'Please don't be a stranger. Lil, Helen, all of us, would love to see you at Montsalvat.'

'Thanks, Justus. It's wonderful to see you. Give my love to everyone,' Jack replied, without committing to visiting. Somehow, his life at Montsalvat seemed best left to the past.

Four months passed, in which Jack's routine of painting, work at the barracks and visiting his parents filled his days. Letters from Nora arrived intermittently, and he laughed as he read of her tales of life on the front: her meetings with soldiers like Bulldozer Bluey, the Queenslander who defied the fire of the Japanese to forge through the forest, making roads for army tanks on the bulldozer he'd named 'Dearest'; and the astonishing skills of the surgeons as they performed work that was as wonderful as it was terrible. What Jack could not ignore were the repeated references to a Dr Robert Black, a specialist whom she said was making enormous gains in the treatment of malaria. Jack suspected that a romance had developed between Nora and the doctor, and he was pleased for her.

~

During September, Jack finally focussed on his painting of the parachute landing, that event so bizarre that the disturbing emotions it aroused had never left him.

He drew on his memories, determined to portray the irony, the distortions, of that fateful day. As he'd always intended, he adopted the methods of surrealism, a style that he'd once deplored, but which so well suited this event. When he was finished, he took the painting to Treloar.

'Tell me about it, Jack,' the Treloar asked, his face expressionless. This was Treloar's genius, Jack knew. He never passed judgement on anything. Every item that he collected for the museum, whether from soldiers, enemies or civilians, offered perspectives and experiences that Treloar valued.

Jack pointed to the blue sky and sunshine that dominated the upper corners, depicting the perfection of the fine summer day. Next, he'd painted the planes—but they weren't planes, they were large dragon-like creations, a dark menacing mass that was swarming directly towards the viewer.

'You had to be there to see it, John. There were thousands of them. The sky was black, the roaring thunderous.'

Treloar nodded.

The largest of the creatures Jack had painted hovered directly overhead, and from its open hatch, an assortment of incongruous items spilled out.

Balloons—puffy and round—drifted downward. Pretty, like those that would be found at a child's birthday party. The ones closest to the ground revealed that, attached to the balloons, were chains. And captured in the chains were grotesque shapes. Some were like the concentric circles of a dartboard. Others were like spacemen wearing strange uniforms and helmets. And others were like birds. More objects also fell from the sky, distortions of body parts with dripping splashes of red. On the ground, Jack had painted trees, but rather than branches, he'd drawn menacing-looking claws, and within the claws were naked, wide-eyed babies.

Helpless and innocent? Was that how Jack viewed the young German soldiers? Was that the truth of all the young men packed off to war with a gun and a hat the world over?

'The thing is, John, when those fellows were dangling from their chutes, high in the sky, we didn't see them as human. They were targets, and it was as though we were duck shooting. That's why I've drawn the birds. They were like ducks. The chains symbolise how they didn't have a chance, you know. They were utterly trapped and could not surrender, even if they'd wanted to. The minute that those lads left the plane, they were dead. It was only as they drifted close to us, or we saw them swinging from a tree or lying on the ground, that we really comprehended the reality of the battle.'

Where grass might well have been seen waving in the foreground, Jack had drawn hundreds of gun barrels. Old relics. A mix of handguns and machine guns, all pointed skyward. He'd also added women and children, wandering the landscape, clubs and nooses in hand ready to finish off that which the Allies had started. The civilians of Crete fighting to defend what was theirs.

John nodded, accepting Jack's interpretation. Certainly, the finished product was every bit the bizarre contradictions of beauty and horror that Jack had described.

In December, Jack received a letter from the Art Gallery of New South Wales advising him that *Sofia* had been shortlisted for the Archibald Prize, and he could not deny his feelings of pride for her.

He lunched with his parents, and they discussed the award. He wondered whether to make the long trip to Sydney or not. The exhibition would open on the first week of January, and the prize winner would be announced.

'Jack, of course you must go! It will be wonderful,' Marian insisted. 'In fact, we'll all go. What do you think, William?'

'Mum, it's a two-day drive! That's too far for you and Dad.'

But Marian's mind was made up. 'How about we make it a holiday? Fly to Sydney and stay in one of those lovely little cottages in Manly for a couple of weeks. I'd love to travel in an airplane. And how wonderful it would be to see the Harbour Bridge! What do you think, William, love? We'll go to Sydney and see Jack's painting?'

'Yes. Yes.' William nodded eagerly, his eyes bright and tearing up with pleasure for Jack's achievement.

'Okay, Mum. I will look into it,' Jack agreed, amazed and pleased that his parents were so keen to attend the opening of the Archibald Prize with him.

Jack could barely wait to see the expression on Margaret's face when he told her that he was an Archibald finalist. He tried phoning her at work, but she'd left early. When he answered the knock on his door the following Wednesday evening, he felt sure it would be her.

Instead, a burly young man with a reddish tinge to his beard filled the doorway, his eyes familiar, his grin broad. Within seconds, Jack found himself hauled into strong arms.

'Jack!'

'Matcham!'

The pleasure of seeing each other was mutual, and Jack laughed joyfully.

'Where has that wild lad who raced around annoying everybody gone?' he asked.

'Oh, don't you worry, he's still here. Just give me time.' Matcham laughed with the same loud guffawing that Jack remembered so well.

He led Matcham into the lounge and poured two sherries, and they caught up on each other's news. Jack asked about Helen and Sonia, and was pleased to learn that they and their babies were doing well. Helen now had a second child, a little boy called Sigmund, while Sonia had moved into a small cottage on the grounds with Arthur. His parents were the same as ever—doting grandparents—and Lena acting as a sort of secretary to the daily running of Montsalvat, whilst Mervyn still wrote articles for *The Bulletin* and now also dabbled in writing stories for children.

They spoke of the Jorgensens, and Matcham described how Lil's health had continued to decline, although—as always—she and Justus treated her condition as psychosomatic, thereby giving it very little attention. Matcham seemed aggrieved by this. He'd known Lil almost his whole life and now, as an adult, he realised the lack of treatment sought for her illness was questionable. Seeing her confined to bed for days without the intervention of medical advice troubled him.

'That reminds me, Jack. I have a message from Lil. When she heard that I was coming here, she said to tell you that she has some news from London that you might be interested in. You remember Justus' friend, Colin Colahan?'

Of course, Jack did. Colahan was the charming artist who'd been linked to that murder case, way back in 1930 when his girlfriend, Molly, had been found dead in a laneway in St Kilda. A chill ran through him as he wondered if Colahan had met up with Sofia in London. Was he the man that she'd fallen in love with? He'd certainly known how to attract women. Back in the days when he used to visit them at Montsalvat, he always had one female or another on his arm.

'I've already heard,' he said. 'Sofia's living in London, too. She's remarried. Had another baby.'

'Oh, so that's it, then. Lil didn't go into details, just said for me to ask you to call over. That's bad news. I am so sorry, mate!'

'What about you?' Jack asked, changing the subject. 'Has any woman managed to tame your wild and reckless heart?'

'Oh, there's been one or two that had me going for a bit,' Matcham laughed.

Their conversation turned to art and jewellery making. Arguing that he was a conscientious objector, Matcham had avoided overseas service and instead been appointed to a munitions factory. There, he'd developed an interest in metalwork, which had inspired a fascination for the craft of silversmithing. Presently, he was making women's brooches and necklaces in his spare time, and quite enjoyed it.

In turn, Jack told Matcham of his appointment as a war artist, and then of painting *Sofia* and how the work had made the cut as a finalist for the Archibald Prize.

'Incredible, Jack. I'd love to see it! Congratulations! Justus did mention that you'd submitted an entry to the Archibald. They'll all be thrilled to know that you're a finalist. All the best to you, mate! I hope you win!'

'We'll see,' said Jack.

It was after eleven when Matcham rose from his seat, and while Jack was almost staggering from consuming sherry followed by two bottles of red, he looked as alert as when he'd arrived. Jack watched fondly as Matchum walked across the room and picked up the photo of Scotty that had remained resting on a cabinet from when Jack had painted his portrait of Sofia. He gazed at it, then looked at Jack in silence for a few seconds before returning his eyes to the photo.

'Love you, little man. Miss you!' he said softly, and then held the photo to his chest, as though hugging him. Jack appreciated the gesture. Besides himself, Sofia, Marian and William, no one had loved Scotty more than Matcham.

'Mate, where is the Archibald being held? I'd normally avoid those fancy dos, but I reckon a drive to Sydney would be fun, and I can think of no better reason to go than to see you win the Archie.'

'Good on you, Match! Love to see you there!' Jack was sure that Matcham would have forgotten his enthusiastic offer by the time he woke the next morning.

Farewelling each other at the door, they promised to catch up soon, and Jack was glad to feel the warmth of the brotherly affection that he'd always shared with Matcham rekindled.

# CHAPTER 42

*A*s she'd done for the past few years, Margaret joined Jack, Marian and William for Christmas lunch. Gregory and Lawrence had returned to America two weeks earlier, and with no family in Australia, it was an expectation that she'd spend Christmas Day with the Tomlinsons.

Weeks earlier, she'd been thrilled when Jack had told her that he'd made the finalists for the Archibald, and she remained adamant that he'd win the fifty thousand pounds prize money. She described the painting to Marian, explaining how truly amazing it was, and when Marian told her of their intentions to fly to Sydney and stay in the small apartment by the harbour that Jack had booked, Margaret asked if she might join them.

'Why, yes! That would be wonderful, wouldn't it, Jack? William, did you hear that? Margaret's going to come up to Sydney with us! Won't that be lovely!'

'Really? You'd come to Sydney with us, Margaret? That would be incredible! Thank you! Our place has two rooms, but you can have mine. I'll sleep in the lounge!' While Jack had looked forward to the week in Sydney, having Margaret along with them triggered a whole new level of enthusiasm for the trip.

'The thing is, I may not see you for a while after that, because in

405

February, I'm going to America. Greg has been talking to Peggy Guggenheim. She's the one in the family who is the serious art collector, and she is full of plans. Wants to open up a museum, apparently.'

'So, you are getting married then!' Jack exclaimed, fighting the disappointment of knowing that, should Margaret marry Gregory, she'd live in America and be as good as gone from their lives forever.

'Now Jack! Don't get ahead of yourself. Greg and I will just see how things go.'

'Of course. And honestly, Marg, I hope that they go really well. You deserve to have a nice man in your life. And Greg is really very nice. All the best to you and all!'

The flight to Sydney was a thrilling experience for both Jack and his parents. Sitting in the plane's cabin, feeling it vibrate as its engines roared to life, they braced themselves for the ascent. Their apprehensions were diminished by the calm manner of the immaculately dressed stewardess—who guided them through the safety procedures that would be applied in the event of a mishap—and by Margaret's squeals of excitement as the airplane began moving along the runway. Since her journey through the Outback with Greg and Lawrence, she claimed to adore flying, and the anticipation of hurtling through the sky at hundreds of miles an hour had her quivering with the enthusiasm of a child.

As Margaret had promised, after the plane burst through the grey Melbourne sky, they entered a whole new fantasy world where sunlight bounced off snow-white puffs of cottony clouds with dazzling brightness. They drank the cups of tea accompanied by scones and jam offered by the air hostess; no sooner finishing them when the plane began a smooth descent, circling over the most beautiful harbour Jack could imagine. Hearing his mother's delighted cries and seeing the thrill of pleasure in his father's ever-moist eyes, he was glad that Marian had suggested this trip.

By the time they left the airport and taxied to their apartment—not the one in Manly that his mother had originally suggested, but instead a city apartment offering a more central location for sightseeing—it was after four PM. After unpacking their cases and seeing Marian and William settled on their bed for a rest, Jack and Margaret went in search of takeaway fish and chips to take back to the apartment for their dinner. Later that evening, the two of them wandered up and down the roads around the harbour, finally settling on a small pub by the water that offered spectacular views of the Harbour Bridge. There they drank beer and wine, and chatted about Margaret's recent trip via Alice Springs; and she tried to describe the complex line paintings that were being created by the Aboriginal people living there.

The following day, Jack, Margaret, Marian and William again returned to the harbour, where they caught a ferry across to Manly. They had pies for lunch and wandered around the seaside village before returning to their apartment for a rest. That evening was the opening of the Archibald. Each time he thought about it, a shiver of excitement ran through Jack. He already knew that some of his friends would be there. Sunday and John were coming, as was Nora, who had recently returned to Australia. Jack wondered if she would be accompanied by the doctor.

Since the newspapers had listed Jack's name amongst the finalists, he'd been contacted regarding commissions, with offers to pay prices exceeding anything that he'd ever earned for a painting. One man, who told Jack that he'd previewed the Archibald entries, asked him to name his price; he'd pay whatever Jack asked if he would just remain in Sydney for a few weeks, to paint his wife's portrait.

Knowing that he was a finalist for the Archibald was a great feeling; but in truth, Jack didn't care if he won the prize or not. In honesty, the thing that he most looked forward to tonight was seeing his painting, seeing *Sofia* again. He'd missed her presence in his apartment more than he'd ever admit!

~

The National Gallery of New South Wales was impressive—a beautiful building with massive stone columns leading into an extraordinary lobby. The ornate arches that connected the high-ceilinged exhibition rooms and complex parquetry floors reminded Jack of the galleries that he'd visited in Paris.

They made their way through the crowded lobby, Jack's footsteps aligned to his father's slow pace, his mother's arm resting on his, while Margaret cleared the way before them to allow William a path through. More than one person seemed to know who Jack was; and every few steps people stopped to congratulate him, expressing their admiration for his painting. For his own part, Jack preferred not to meet with anyone until he had laid eyes on *Sofia*, and had reassured himself that she'd survived the trip to Sydney without mishap.

The exhibition room was full, of course. Jack wasn't sure if he imagined it, but the artists seemed easy to pick out. Men with slightly longer hair, or a more flamboyant style of dress even within the constraints of their suits, with moustaches and beards groomed and shaped for the auspicious occasion. Women that wore their elegant evening wear a little more loosely, with flowing sleeves and colourful headscarves; their dresses adorned with chunky bangles and beads.

The Reeds found him immediately, and Jack introduced them to his parents. Sunday looking beautiful—contented and glowing—and in her arms, she held a young child.

At Jack's puzzled expression, Sunday laughed. 'It's Sweeney,' she explained. 'Joy and Albert's little boy. They are about somewhere, although with this crowd, we might never find them again!'

Whilst Sunday looked quite thrilled at the idea of never seeing Joy and Tucker again—hence claiming the baby for herself—the child appeared less certain. He looked back at Jack with a solemn expression, and Jack tickled his cheek in the same manner that he had once done to Scotty, pleased to see that the gesture achieved the same toothy response. Again, Jack looked at Sunday, and behind his smile for her, he felt sad. For now, Sweeney was hers, and she looked as happy as any new mother might; but soon he would be returned to his own parents, and her arms would be empty. Jack knew that a baby, her own baby, would have meant the world to her.

Walking along, seeing the paintings mounted on the walls, he marvelled at the quality of the works on display. Certainly, the notion of 'portrait' was diverse. Some paintings, like Jack's, had sought realism, while in others the artists had adopted modern interpretations of their subjects. Others yet again had gone for minimalist effects, and one was almost a caricature of its sitter.

Suddenly, he found himself standing before his own *Sofia*, and he gasped, for the portrait was even better than he'd remembered. Hanging on the wall, with soft lighting enhancing the inner glow that she emitted, *Sofia* was displayed to her best. Tonight, she looked peaceful and serene, yet mischievous all at once. Although her stance was erect, almost that of a dancer, her shoulders were relaxed, and the arm that reached to the window sill was graceful. As he met her eyes, Jack almost felt that she was communicating with him. Had his *Sofia* come to life? He shook himself and looked closer, pleased to see that, even in this public space, and despite the hundreds of eyes now upon her, *Sofia* had retained her sense of intimacy; her gaze was for him alone.

'Jack, it's wonderful!' Marian spoke first. As she looked at the painting, she reached for the handkerchief that was always folded neatly in her handbag. She dabbed the lace-edged cloth to her eyes before clutching it and again gazing at the painting of her lost daughter-in-law. Her eyes moved around the edges, and Jack knew that she noticed his rendition of the photo of Scotty that William had taken many years earlier.

'So proud of you, Jack,' his father said, and his mother's eyes were again filled with tears. He squeezed her arm.

'It's okay, Mum. I'm okay!'

'She is lovely, Jack. So beautiful!'

Jack found himself surrounded by well-wishers: some he knew, most he didn't. Margaret nodded at him, indicating that she would remain with William and Marian and see that they were okay, allowing him to mingle and chat.

'It's a wonderful portrait, Mr Tomlinson,' offered a man with the notepad of a reporter, keen to ask a few questions.

'Who is she? She is beautiful!' came a voice from the side.

'Well done!'

Overwhelmed with pride and the pleasure of the moment, Jack tried to answer the questions as quickly as they came at him.

After about twenty minutes, a stirring from the front of the room rippled through to the back, and quiet descended. It was eight PM, time for the official announcements to begin. Jack was surrounded by a gathering of well-wishers, all sure that *Sofia* would be named as the winning entry, including the Reeds, and Nora who'd squeezed through the crowd to hug him. Hearing the tap on the microphone from a man in a gaudy blue suit who was attempting to call everyone to attention, Jack cast his eyes around, looking for his parents and Margaret. With so many people around, he couldn't see them.

The man with the microphone cleared his throat, in readiness to speak when the quietness was interrupted by a jostling from the back of the room. A group of late arrivals made a noisy entrance and proceeded to weave through the crowded room to the front.

As they came closer, Jack laughed. It was the Montsalvat crew, looking as eccentric as ever! Justus was out front, with Lil on one side and Helen on the other. Jack saw Lena and Mervyn close behind, clinging to three young children. The Skipper babies had grown! Along with them were faces Jack had never seen, but then that was Montsalvat! An ever- changing crowd revolving around the central orbit of the Jorgensens and Skippers.

'Shh,' said a couple of bystanders, clearly irritated by the disruption to the evening's formalities, and Matcham's voice rang out as, waving his left hand in the air, he pointed to his watch.

'Excuse me! The catalogue says that formalities begin at eight PM. It's only seven fifty-five! We're not late! You are early!'

As Matcham finished speaking, he sighted Jack, and with a loud 'Hoy, over here,' he steered the group towards him. Back-slapping and kisses for the ladies ensued with much laughter and praise for *Sofia,* who smiled upon them from the wall.

Jack greeted his old friends one by one, amazed to think that they'd travelled so far to be with him. He laughed as Sonia stepped forward with a chuckle, grinning broadly, tanned and healthy, her eyes sparkling with pleasure as she congratulated him. But it wasn't her that Jack's eyes settled upon.

Beside Sonia, a dark-haired woman stood, her hair fixed in a bun, her dark eyes liquid soft, but also nervous as they locked onto Jack's.

He gasped. She was here? Before him? He looked up to the wall at his *Sofia*, and then back to her, confused. Two Sofias!

Once again, a voice rang out, calling the attendees to attention, announcing that the speeches were about to begin and inviting the Honourable Reg Bartley, the Lord Mayor of Sydney, to come forward to open the twenty-fourth exhibition of the Archibald Prize.

Jack did not hear one word of the announcements as first the Lord Mayor spoke and then the President of the Gallery. Then someone else, who spoke at length about the value of the Archibald, the contribution of artists, the high quality of work that had been submitted, etcetera.

A buzz filled Jack's head as he absorbed the vision before him.

'Sofia,' he said, feeling foolish. Was this his imagination? Certainly it wouldn't be the first time. He shook his head, and then noticed that, beside the woman, there stood a girl. Her eyes were dark, like Sofia's, but her hair was fair and falling in soft curls around her face. The child looked up at Jack, her eyes wide. The child that had been referred to in Genevieve Winters' letter?

'Jack.' Sofia's voice, saying his name with her soft Spanish accent, was unmistakable. '¡Hola! I am so proud of you. You have made a wonderful painting!'

'Sofia? It's really you?'

'Yes, Jack. It's me. At least, I think that it is. I can barely believe that I am here myself!'

Jack reached out to touch her, running his hand along the side of her face, as one might touch a priceless sculpture, scared of leaving a mark upon it. Automatically, his hands then reached for hers, and he gripped them tightly, without removing his eyes from her face, lest she vanish.

'Jack!' she whispered, in a voice that was barely audible. 'I am sorry that I left you. So sorry! I was confused. It was all just, so awful!' Tears welled in her eyes as she spoke.

Jack shook his head. Yes, it was awful, of course. No, she should not be sorry. It was dreadful and confusing. He understood!

411

'I have missed you, so much,' he whispered in reply. 'Every single day, I have thought of you! Wondered where you were!'

Still barely believing what his eyes and ears were telling him, he glanced again at the little girl. The child cowered behind Sofia's legs, and Jack determined that, whatever her story was, whatever Sofia may have been through in her time away, he did not care. Sofia had come back to him, and that was enough.

Bending down on one knee, he looked into the little girl's eyes, and he felt sorry for her. What had she been through, to leave England and her home? He imagined how strange she must be feeling right now, thrust amongst hundreds of strangers in this crowded room in a foreign country.

'And what is your name?' he whispered, gently holding out his hand to her, inviting her to take it.

The child's reply was clear, her voice bearing a distinctly British accent. 'My name is Andreana,' she replied. 'Andreana Marian Tomlinson.'

'Andreana… Andreana Marian Tomlinson. Well, I am very pleased to meet you, Andreana.' He shook her hand solemnly, and then turned it over and kissed her fingers, as a gallant knight might kiss the hand of a fair maiden. She giggled.

Standing, Jack looked into Sofia's eyes, his confusion welling up.

'Sofia?' he asked as he tried to make sense of the child's answer. Andreana... for Andrés, perhaps? Ana, Sofia's mother? Marian after his own mother? Tomlinson?

'Jack, Andreana is our daughter. She is yours. I am so sorry.' Tears spilled from Sofia's eyes, and Jack shook his head, reaching out, his own eyes blurring as he pulled her to him. He held her tightly, determined that never again would he let her go.

As he did, Jack felt the little girl tugging against Sofia's dress, captured in their embrace. He pulled back and bent low, lifted Andreana into his arms and smiled at her before pulling Sofia to him again.

'My Sofia,' he whispered. 'I can hardly believe you are here. Please tell me that this isn't all a dream! I don't think I could bear it if this isn't really happening!'

But she was here. The familiarity of her sweet aroma, the softness of her breath, the warmth of her arms entwining his neck, her hands reaching out to stroke his face, her lips on his… It was all wonderfully, undeniably real.

Jack raised his head as clapping and cheering filled the room. Not for them. Not for Jack's painting. For, while it would always have the distinguished status of being counted amongst the finalists, *Sofia* was not the 1945 Archibald Prize's winning entry.

But that didn't matter to Jack. Nothing mattered to him other than that Sofia had returned. Sofia, with their child, with his own sweet little Andreana. Jack's heart was beating so hard, he felt it might explode with joy. Such happiness! Fulfilled. Completed. All he'd ever wanted, since he'd first laid eyes upon Sofia all those years ago in Paris, was to have her by his side and here she was—her eyes expressing the deep love he'd always known she had for him, as he had for her. Seven long years had passed since they'd lost Scotty, and in losing him, had been lost to each other. There was so much he wanted to know of Sofia's story. Her time away from him, how she'd coped alone, bearing a baby and then being caught up in the war in Europe. But there was plenty of time for that. Now it was enough that she was here with him, and Jack knew for certain that nothing would ever separate them again.

THE END

# WHY????

## Want to know more?

Why on earth did Sofia ever leave the man she loved and travel across the world, pregnant and alone? Overwhelmed with grief and sorrow, how did she cope?

To learn the answers to these questions you may like to read *Sofia's Story*, which will be released in late 2021.

If you want to get updates on Sofia's Story, or get news of its release date, send a quick message to me at PennyFieldsSchneider@gmail.com

**Have you enjoyed reading Searching for Sofia?**

If so, I would be very grateful if you would consider leaving a review on your favourite book sites!

# LET'S TALK ABOUT READING AND WRITING

I would love you to become a part of my writing journey. Subscribe to my monthly newsletter to learn more about the settings and characters in the Portraits in Blue series. Additionally, you will receive freebies including short stories and articles of interest and you will be the first to know when my books are available at discounted prices.

To join, drop me a message at
penny@pennyfields-author.com

## Acknowledgements

Thanks to the many people who have read and critiqued various drafts of the *Portraits in Blue* series. Cassie, Rosemary, Pauline and Jany - your collective feedback forced me to dig deeper to polish my manuscript.

Special thanks to Jacques-Noël Gouat for your unfaltering enthusiasm for The *Portraits in Blue* series. Your time spent reviewing drafts to assist me getting the French components of the story accurate is hugely appreciated. If any inaccuracies remain, they are my own!

Thanks to the wonderful Tarkenberg, who patiently bore the grunt work of editing *Portraits in Blue*. I am so appreciative of all that I have learned through your patient teaching as you've attempted to turn a very green, first-time writer into an author and a rough draft into a somewhat publishable manuscript. I am in awe of your attention to detail and frequently amused by your humour even as you recommended corrections to the manuscript, and revisions to my 75 word sentences!

To my husband and children, my enormous thanks for sharing in my all-consuming creative endeavours. Your support, encouragement and time spent reading drafts and listening patiently as I bounce the multitude of thoughts I have off your well-worn ears are much appreciated!

**PENNY FIELDS-SCHNEIDER** worked as a Registered Nurse before completing a Bachelor of Arts and Diploma of Education and henceforth, redesigning her life as a secondary teacher. An avid reader from a very young age, Penny has always aspired to be an author. In recent years, she became seduced by the world of art, dabbling with paint and brushes, attending art courses and visiting galleries. Penny aspires to create works of historical fiction that leave readers with a deeper understanding of the art world as well as taking them on emotional journeys into the joy and heartbreak that comes with family, friendship and love.

When Penny is not writing, she enjoys helping her husband on their cattle farm in northern NSW, loving every minute she can spend with their children, grandchildren, friends and family.

Penny would love to hear from her readers and you can join her newsletter or contact her through the following channels

**Email** PennyFieldsSchneider@gmail.com
**Website**
**http://www.pennyfields-author.com**

facebook.com/PennyFields-Schneider

instagram.com/pennyfieldsschneider